Pashmina

Nidhi Chanani

Pashmina

First Second

New York

For Nick,
Lil Moon
& Leela

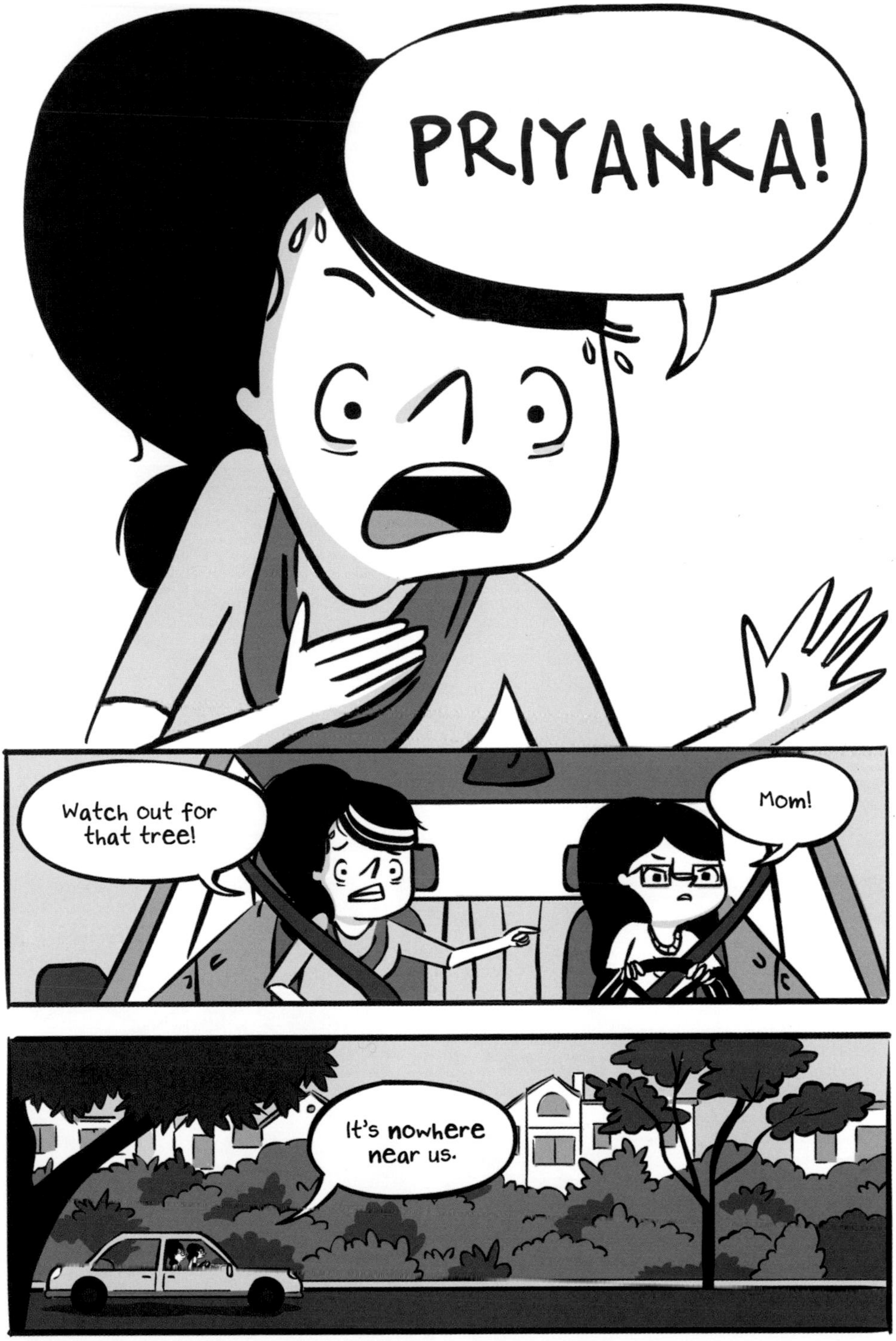
PRIYANKA!
Watch out for that tree!
Mom!
It's nowhere near us.

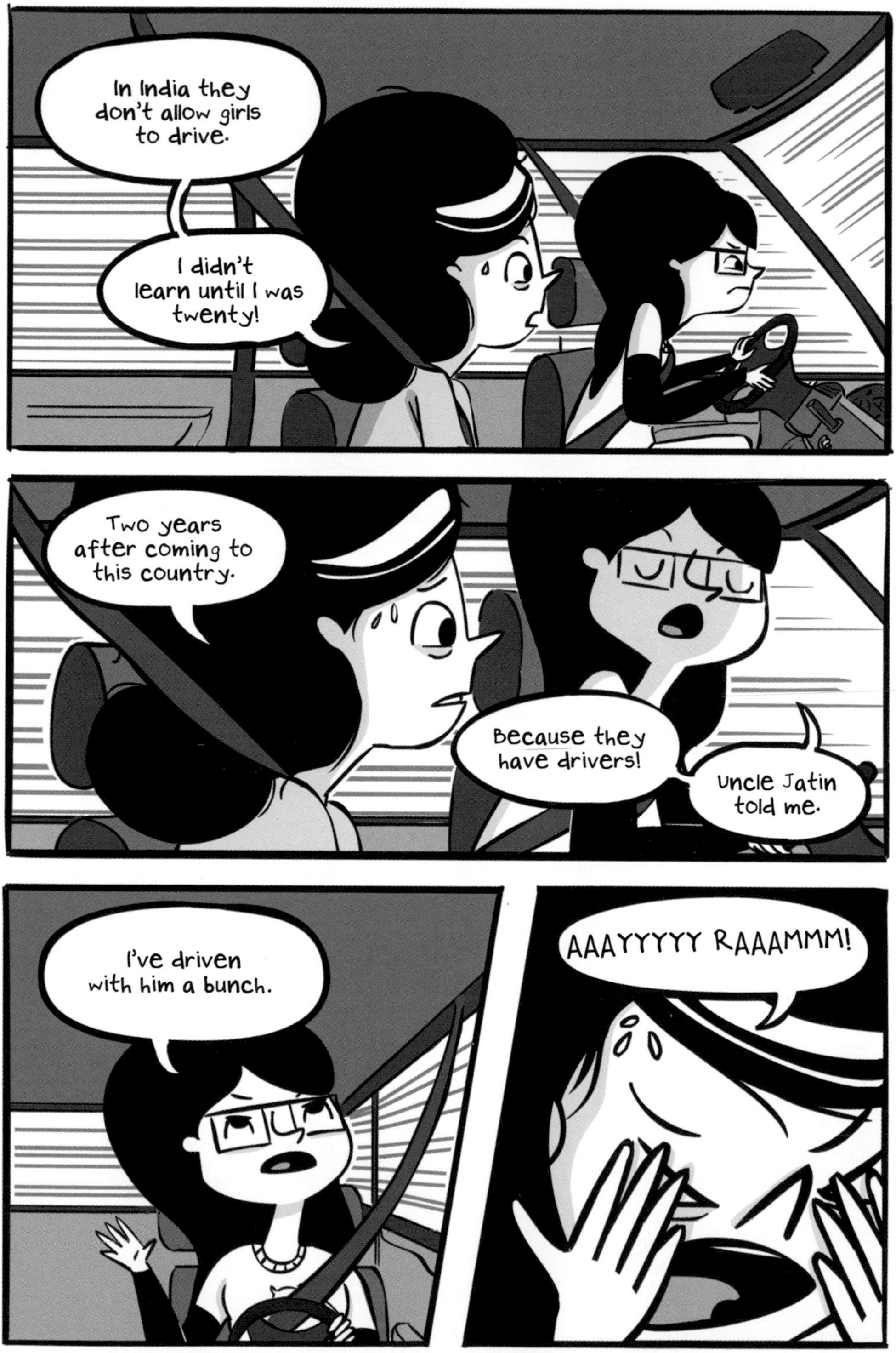
In India they don't allow girls to drive.
I didn't learn until I was twenty!
Two years after coming to this country.
Because they have drivers!
Uncle Jatin told me.
I've driven with him a bunch.
AAAYYYYY RAAAMMM!

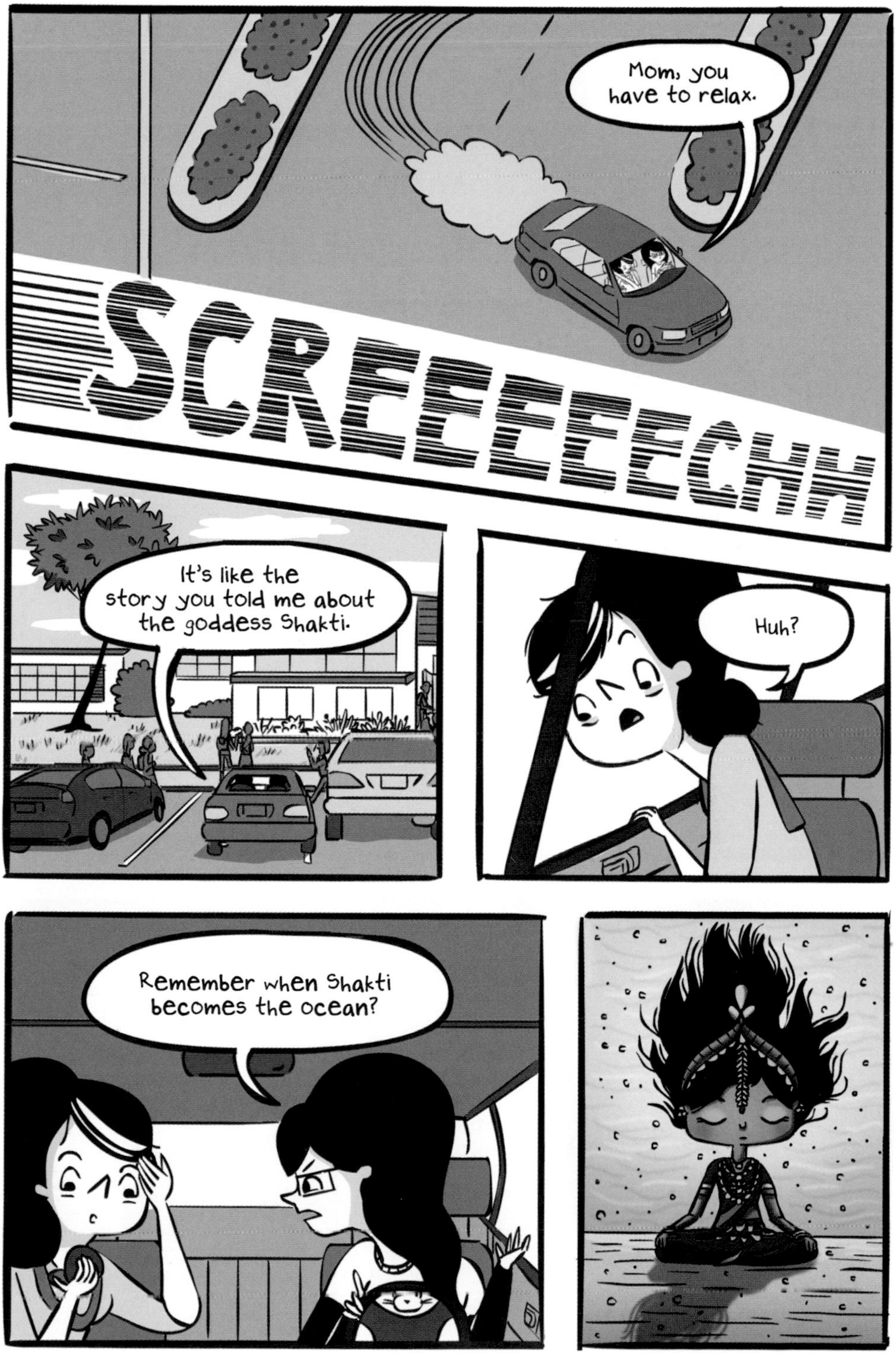
Mom, you have to relax.
SCREEEECHH
It's like the story you told me about the goddess Shakti.
Huh?
Remember when Shakti becomes the ocean?

You know, Shakti misses Shiva, so she asks the gods for advice.

They say either choose sadness or choose to meditate on the word om. Shakti chooses to meditate.

She repeats om over and over loudly. It begins to rain. She doesn't notice.

Eventually the rainwater makes an ocean. She's under it, but still she meditates.

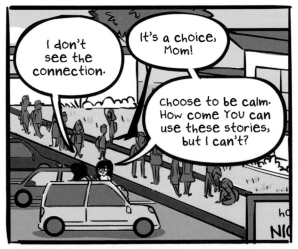

I don't see the connection.

It's a choice, Mom!

Choose to be calm. How come you can use these stories, but I can't?

Shakti didn't have to ride in the car with a teenager.

4

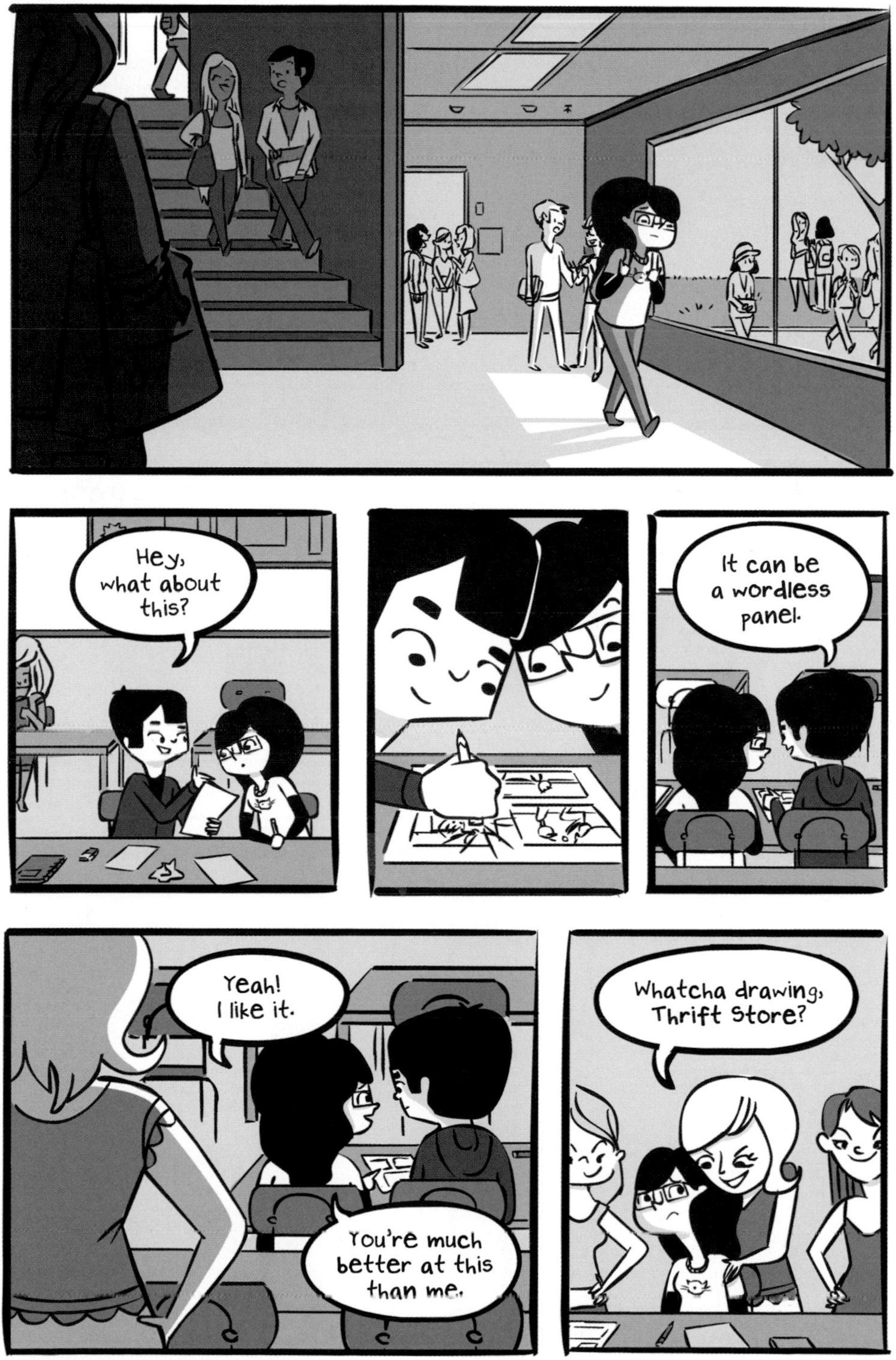
Hey, what about this?
It can be a wordless panel.
Yeah! I like it.
You're much better at this than me.
Whatcha drawing, Thrift Store?

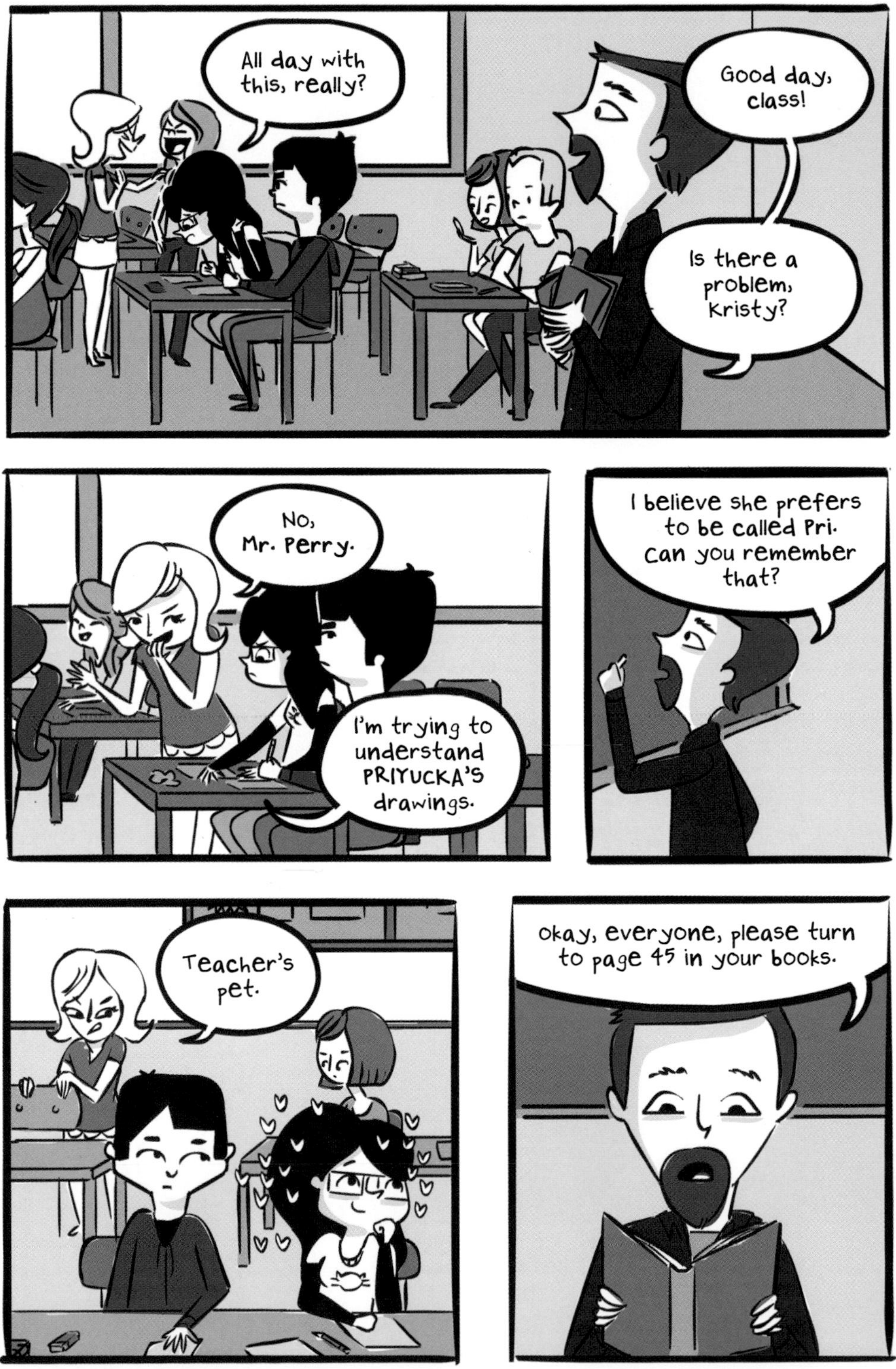
All day with this, really?
Good day, class!
Is there a problem, Kristy?
No, Mr. Perry.
I'm trying to understand PRIYUCKA'S drawings.
I believe she prefers to be called Pri. Can you remember that?
Teacher's pet.
Okay, everyone, please turn to page 45 in your books.

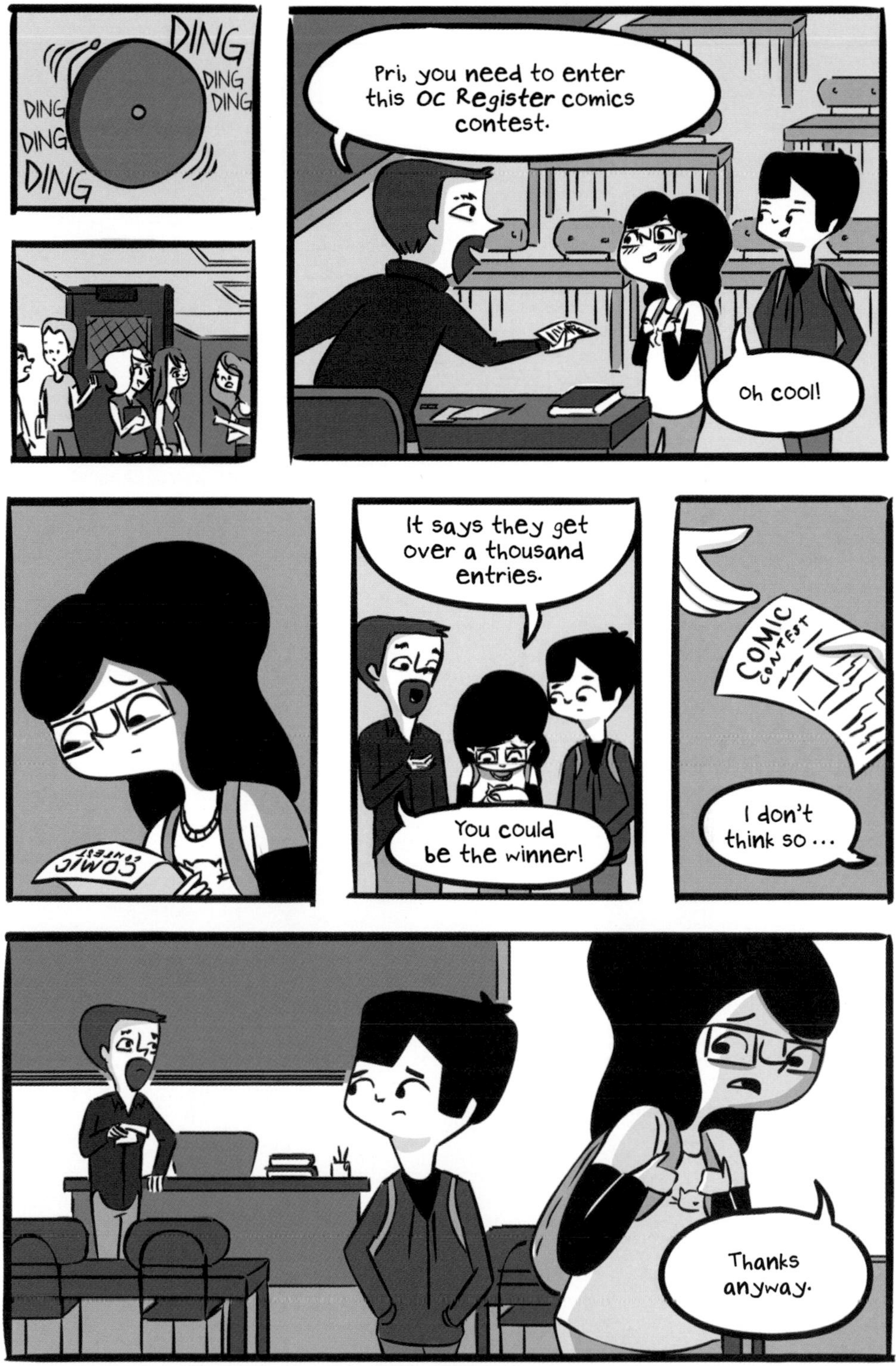
DING
DING
DING
DING
DING
DING
Pri, you need to enter this OC Register comics contest.
Oh cool!
It says they get over a thousand entries.
You could be the winner!
COMIC CONTEST
I don't think so...
Thanks anyway.

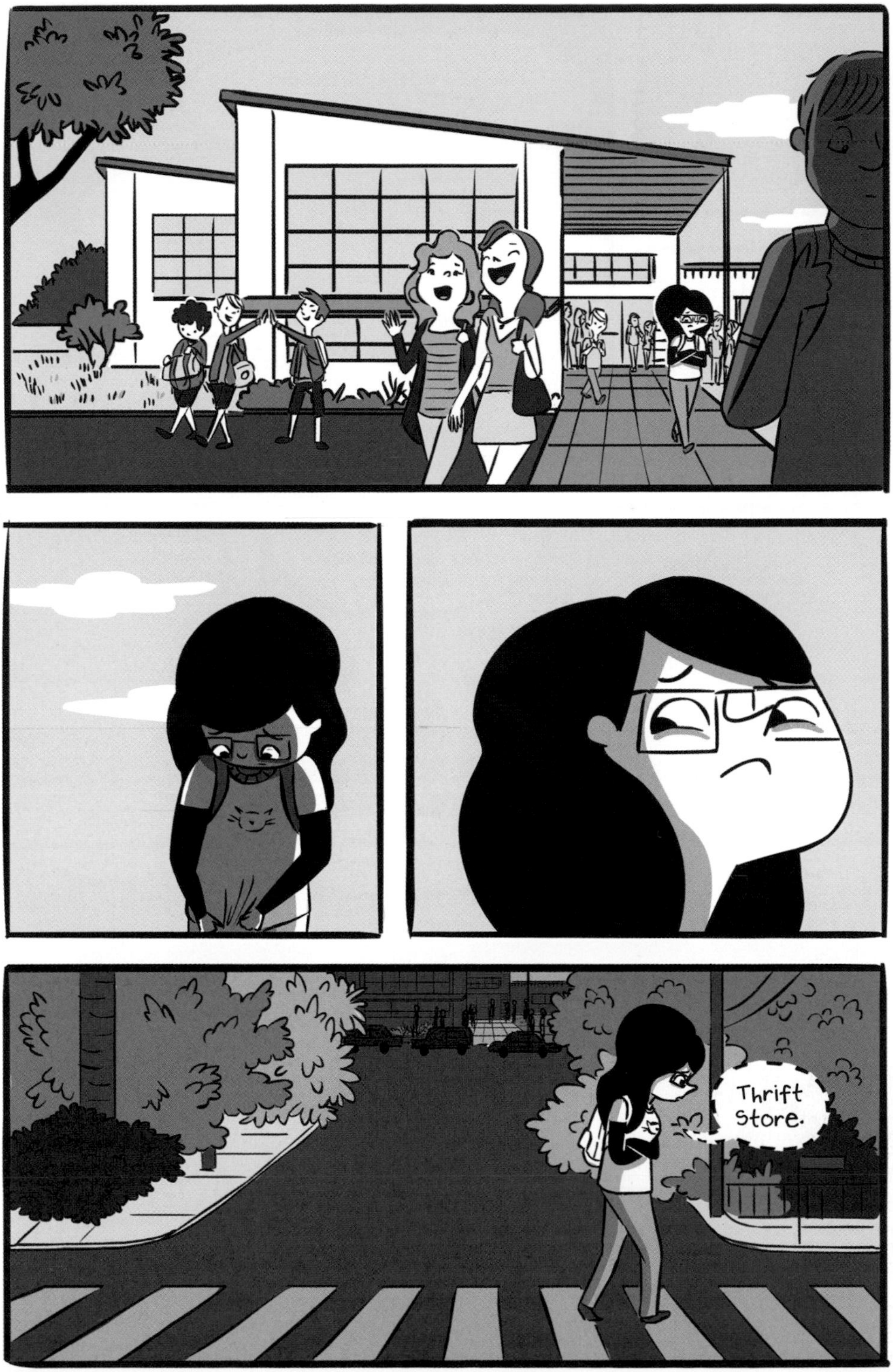
Thrift
Store.

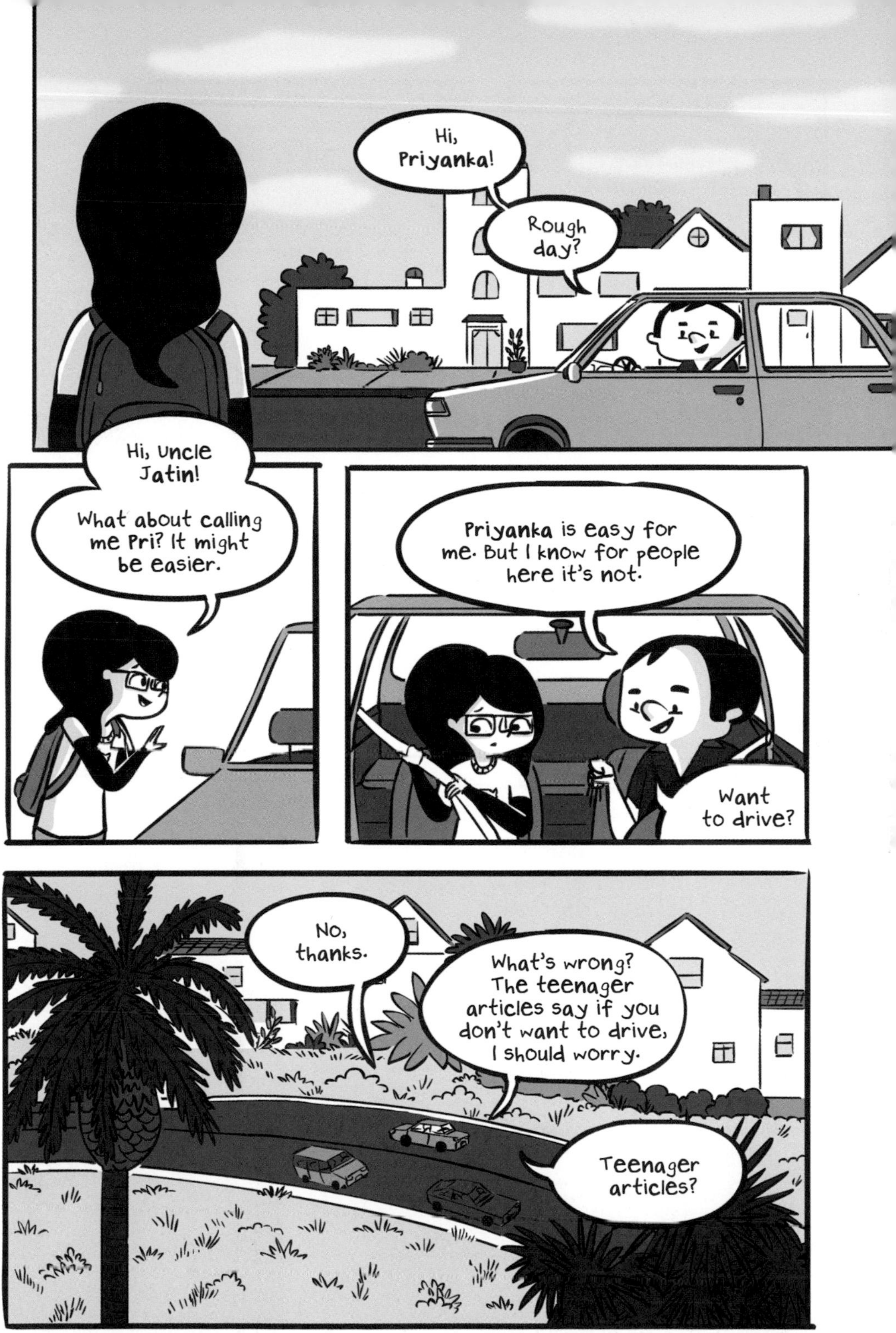
Hi, Priyanka!
Rough day?
Hi, Uncle Jatin!
What about calling me Pri? It might be easier.
Priyanka is easy for me. But I know for people here it's not.
Want to drive?
No, thanks.
What's wrong? The teenager articles say if you don't want to drive, I should worry.
Teenager articles?

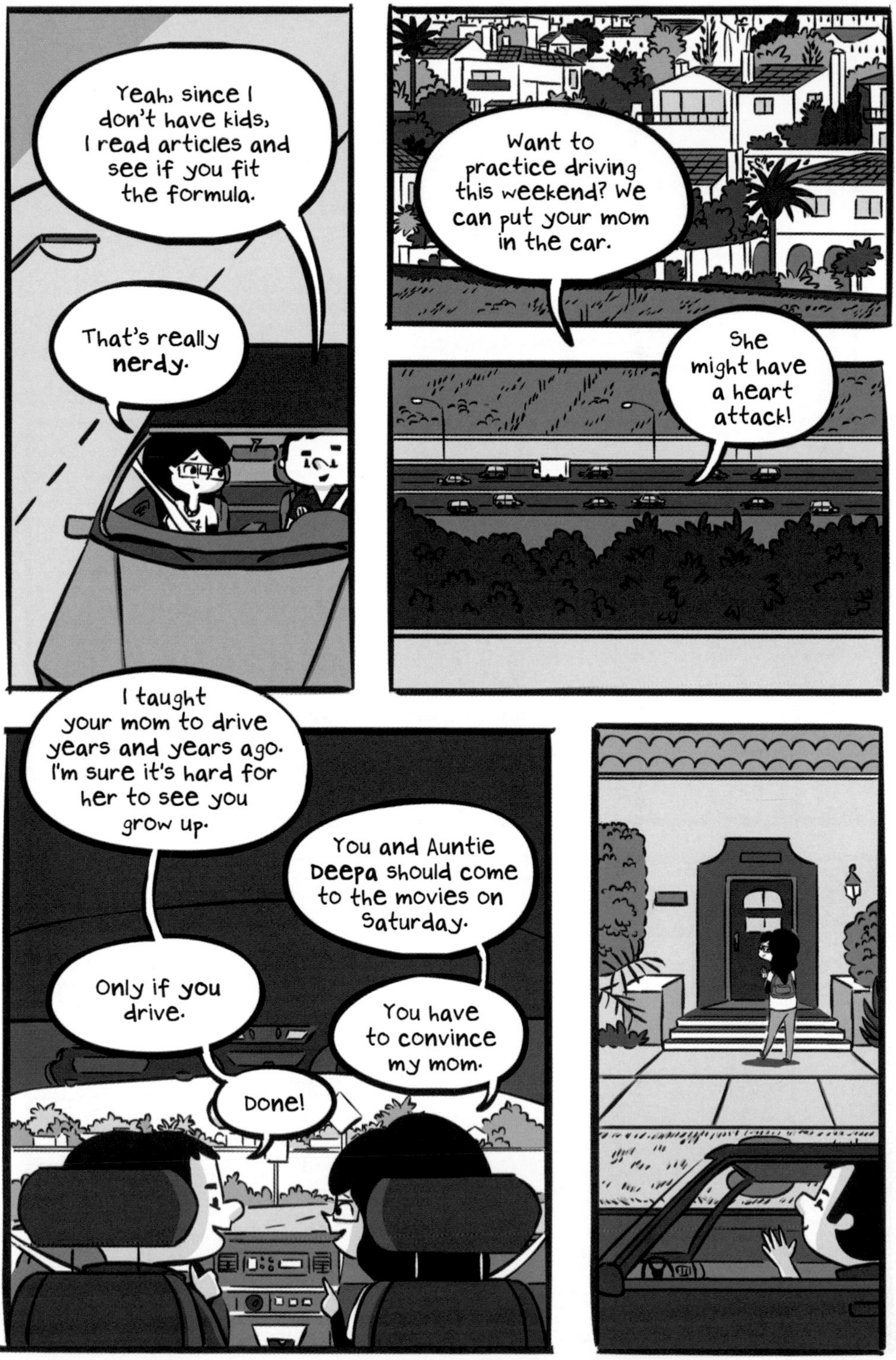
Yeah, since I don't have kids, I read articles and see if you fit the formula.
That's really **nerdy**.
Want to practice driving this weekend? We **can** put your mom in the car.
She might have a heart attack!
I taught your mom to drive years and years ago. I'm sure it's hard for her to see you grow up.
You and Auntie **Deepa** should come to the movies on Saturday.
Only if you drive.
You have to convince my mom.
Done!

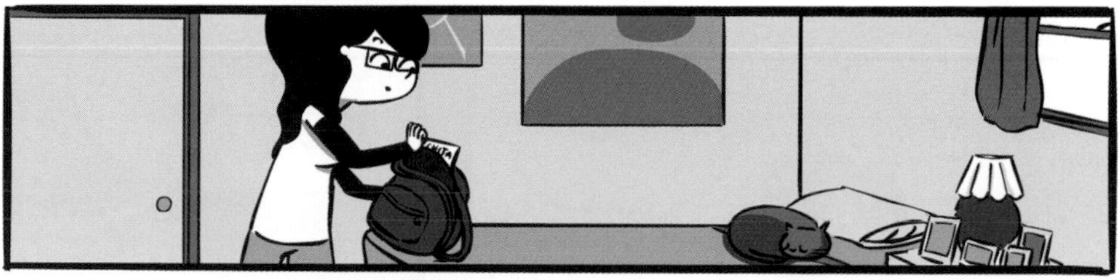

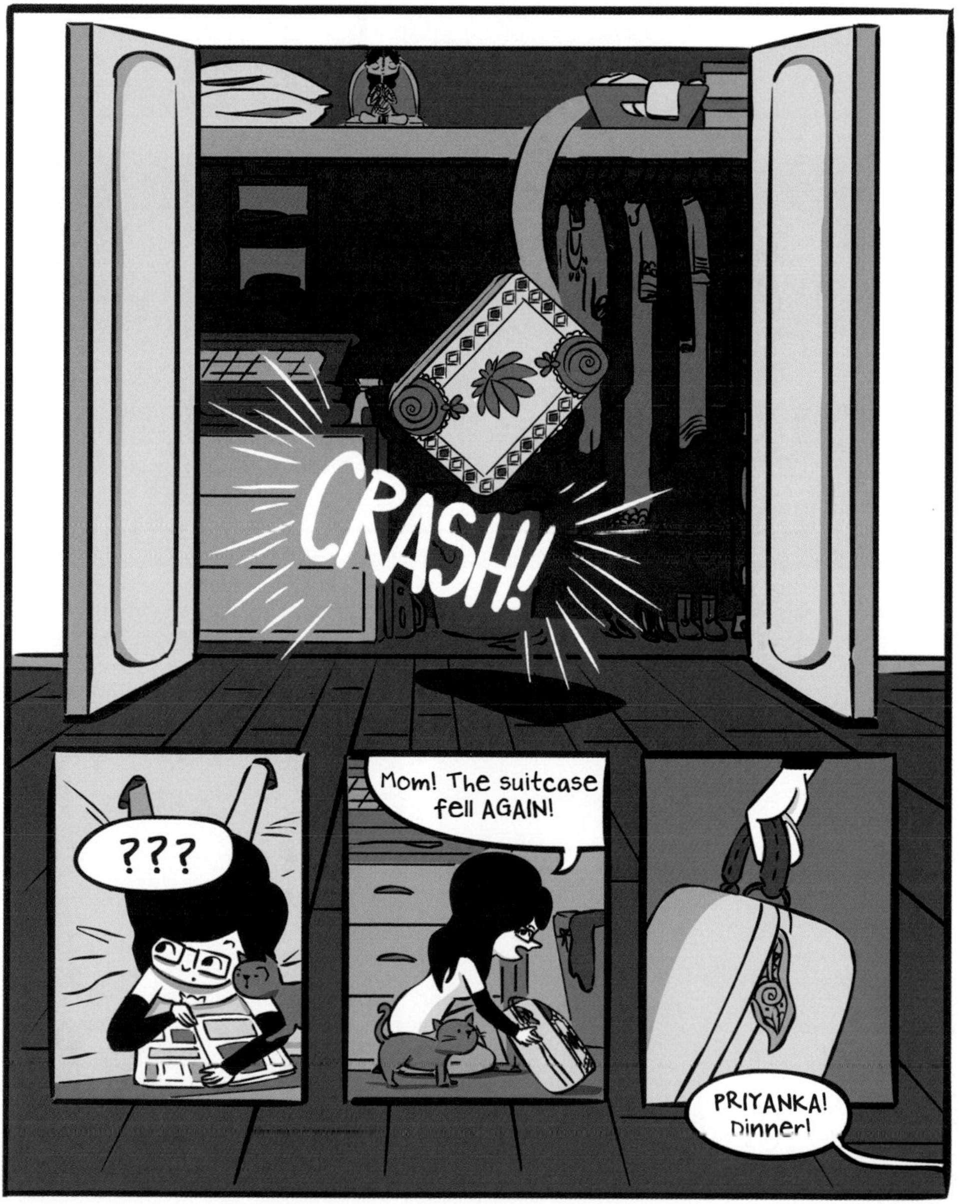
CRASH!
???
Mom! The suitcase fell AGAIN!
PRIYANKA! Dinner!

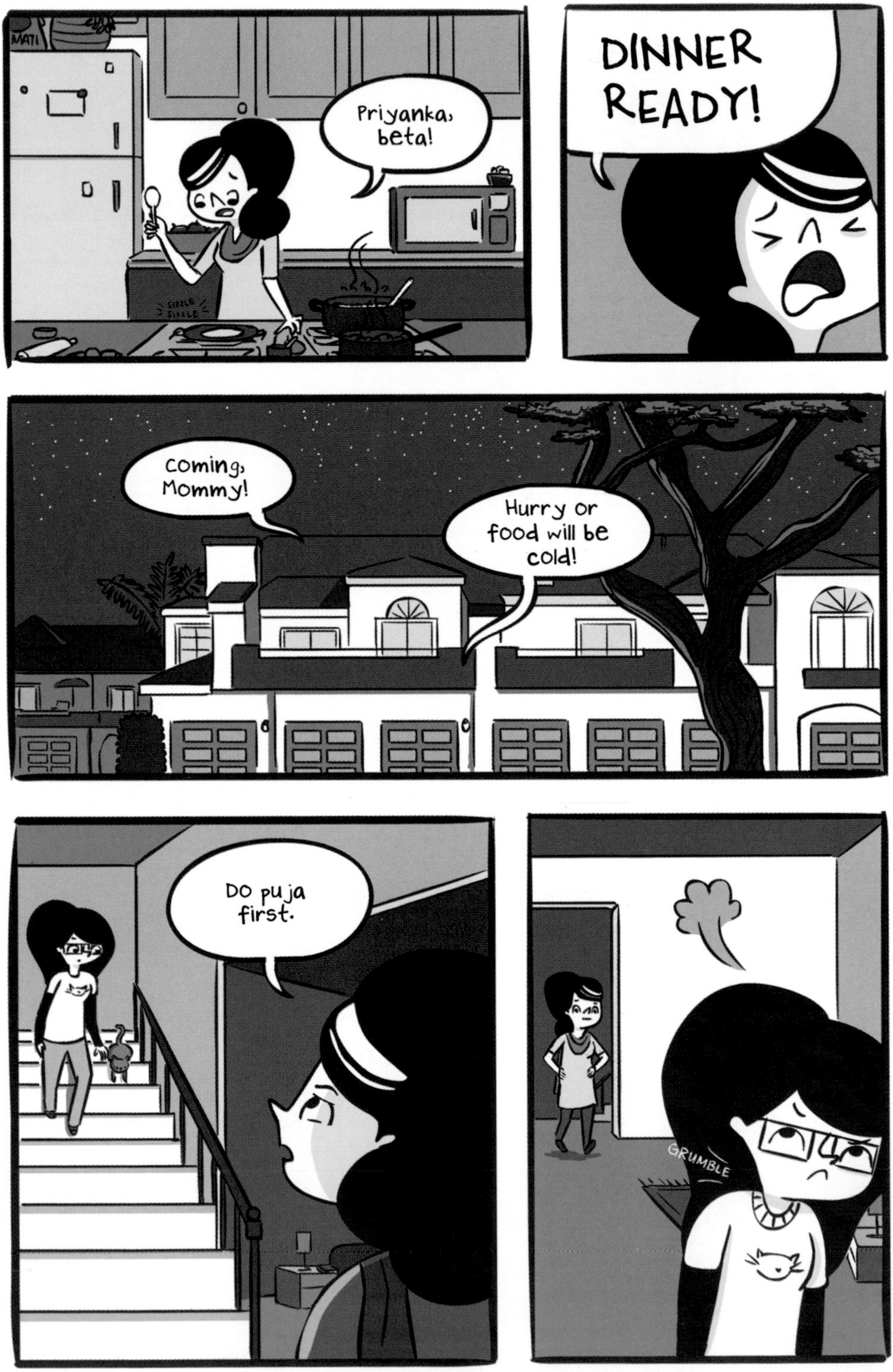
MATI
Priyanka, beta!
SIZZLE SIZZLE
DINNER READY!
Coming, Mommy!
Hurry or food will be cold!
Do puja first.
GRUMBLE

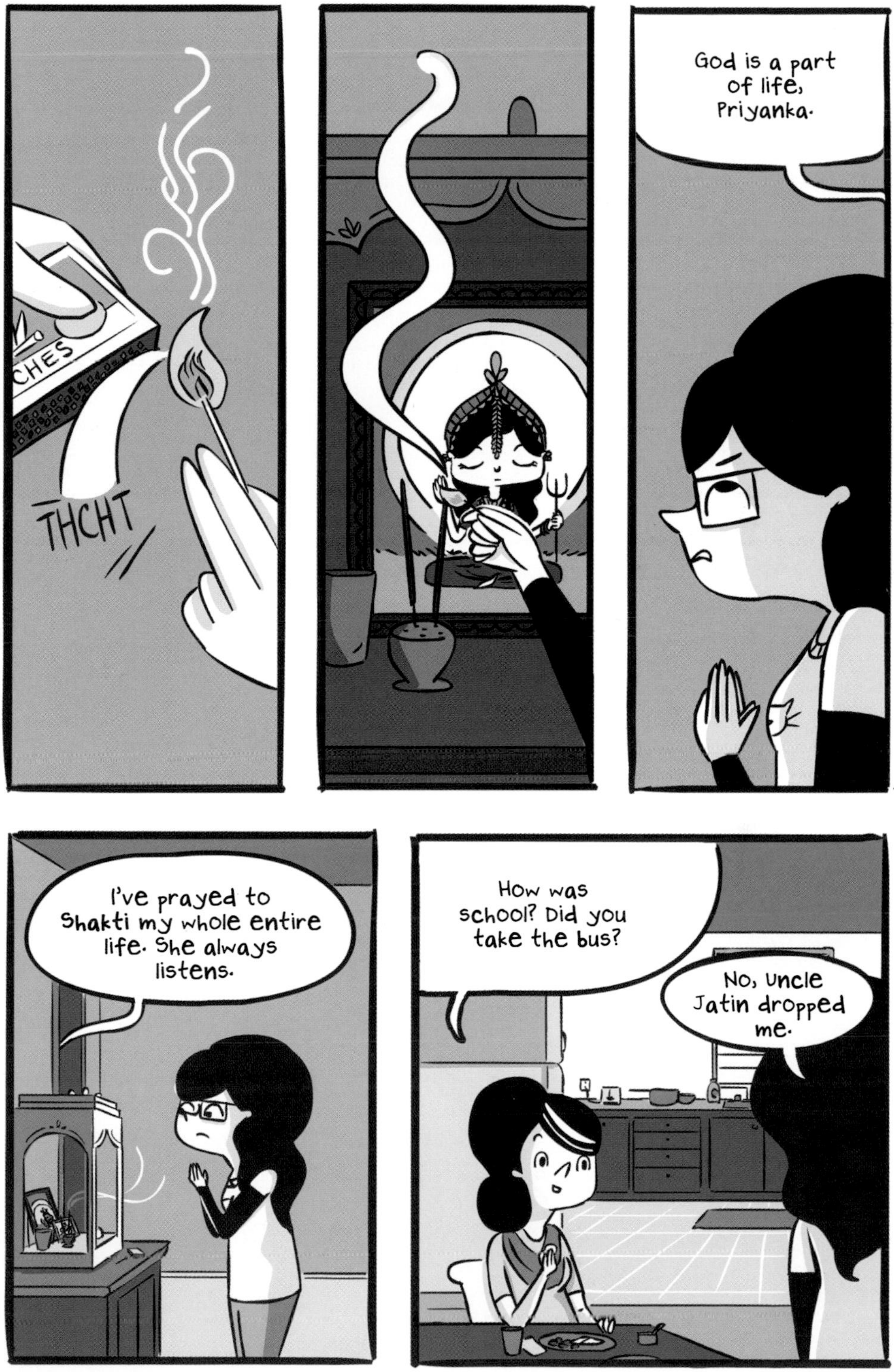
CHES
THCHT
God is a part of life, Priyanka.
I've prayed to Shakti my whole entire life. She always listens.
How was school? Did you take the bus?
No, uncle Jatin dropped me.

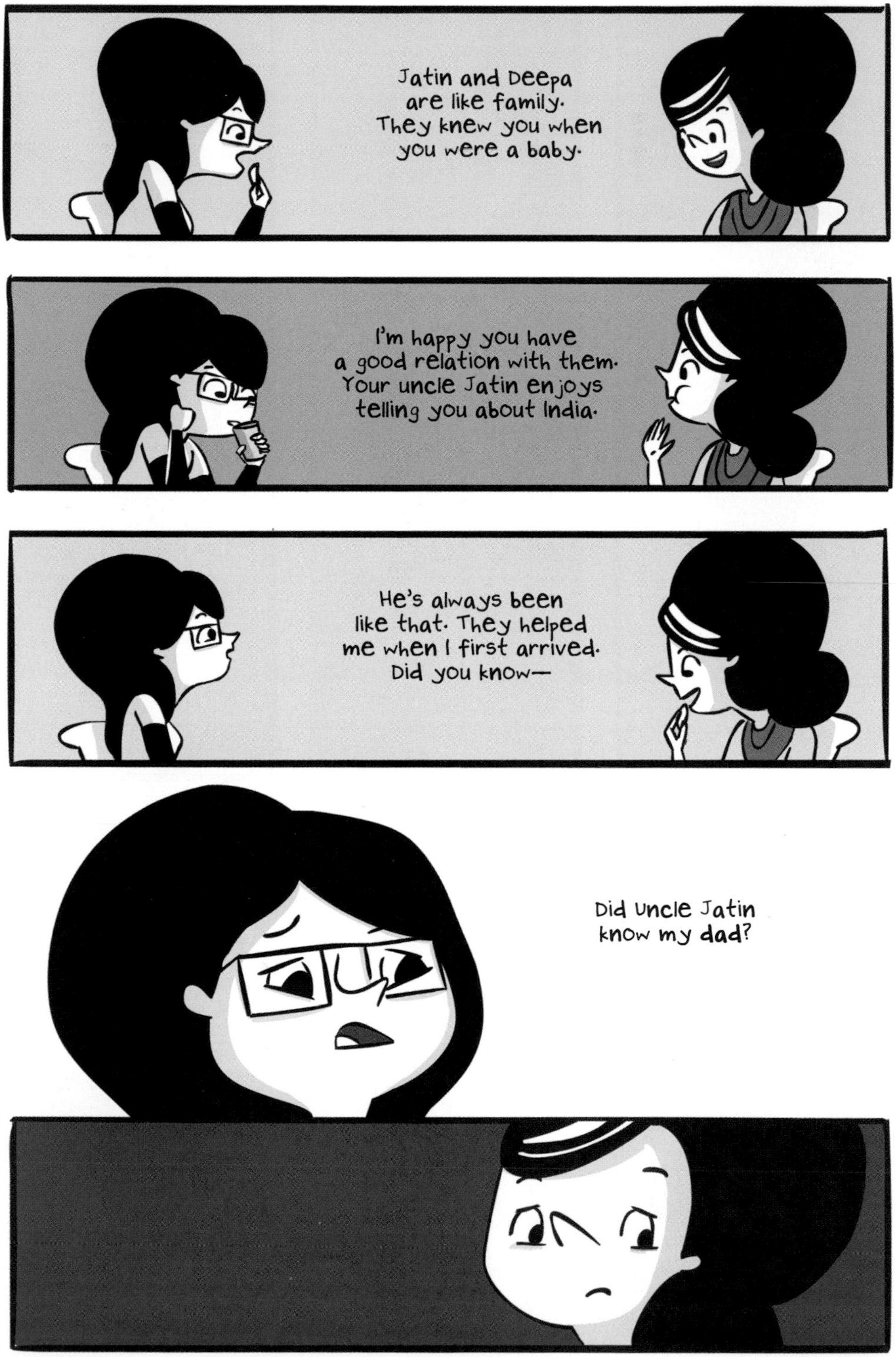
Jatin and Deepa are like family. They knew you when you were a baby.
I'm happy you have a good relation with them. Your uncle Jatin enjoys telling you about India.
He's always been like that. They helped me when I first arrived. Did you know—
Did uncle Jatin know my dad?

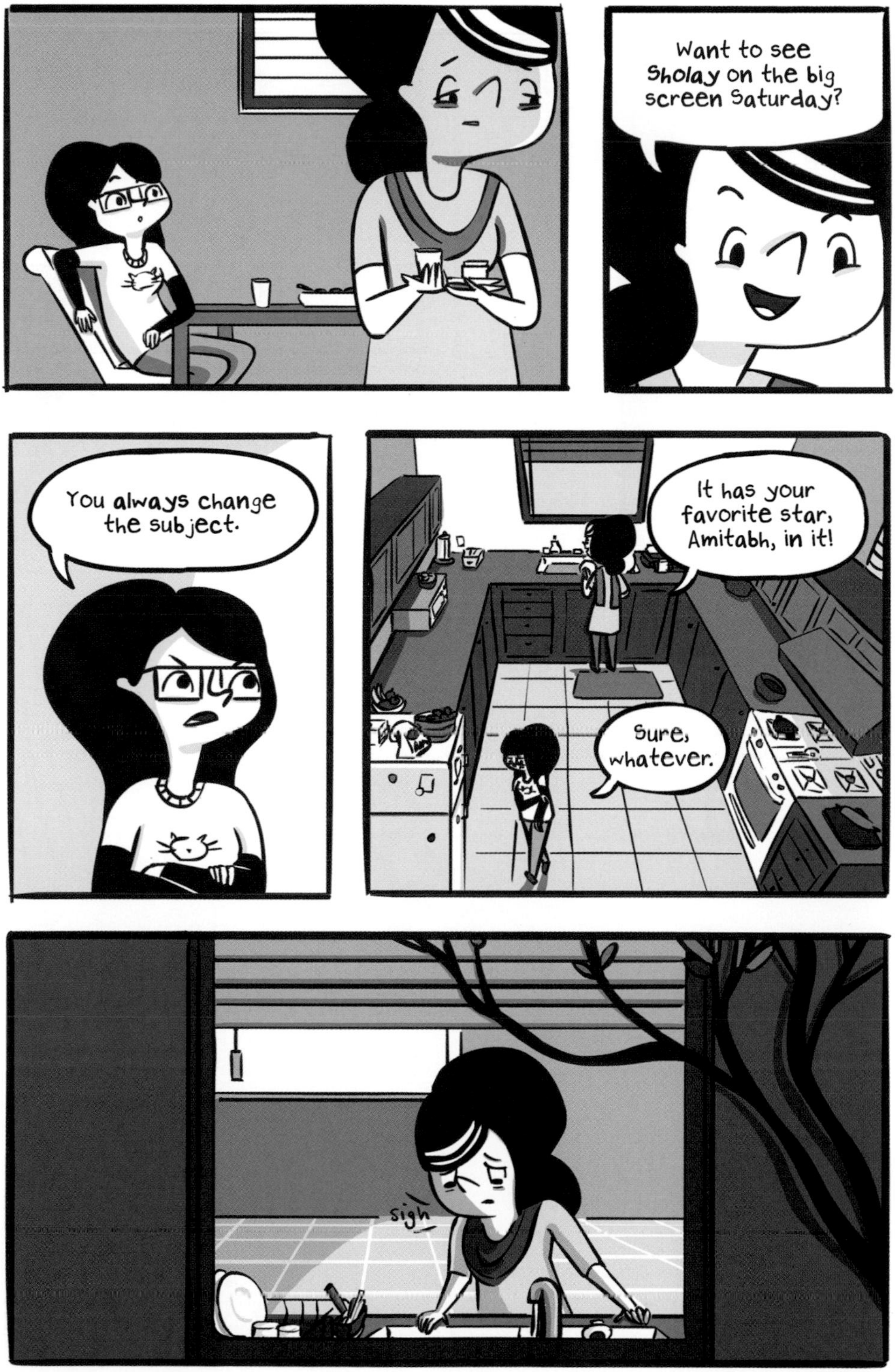
Want to see Sholay on the big screen Saturday?
You always change the subject.
It has your favorite star, Amitabh, in it!
Sure, whatever.
sigh

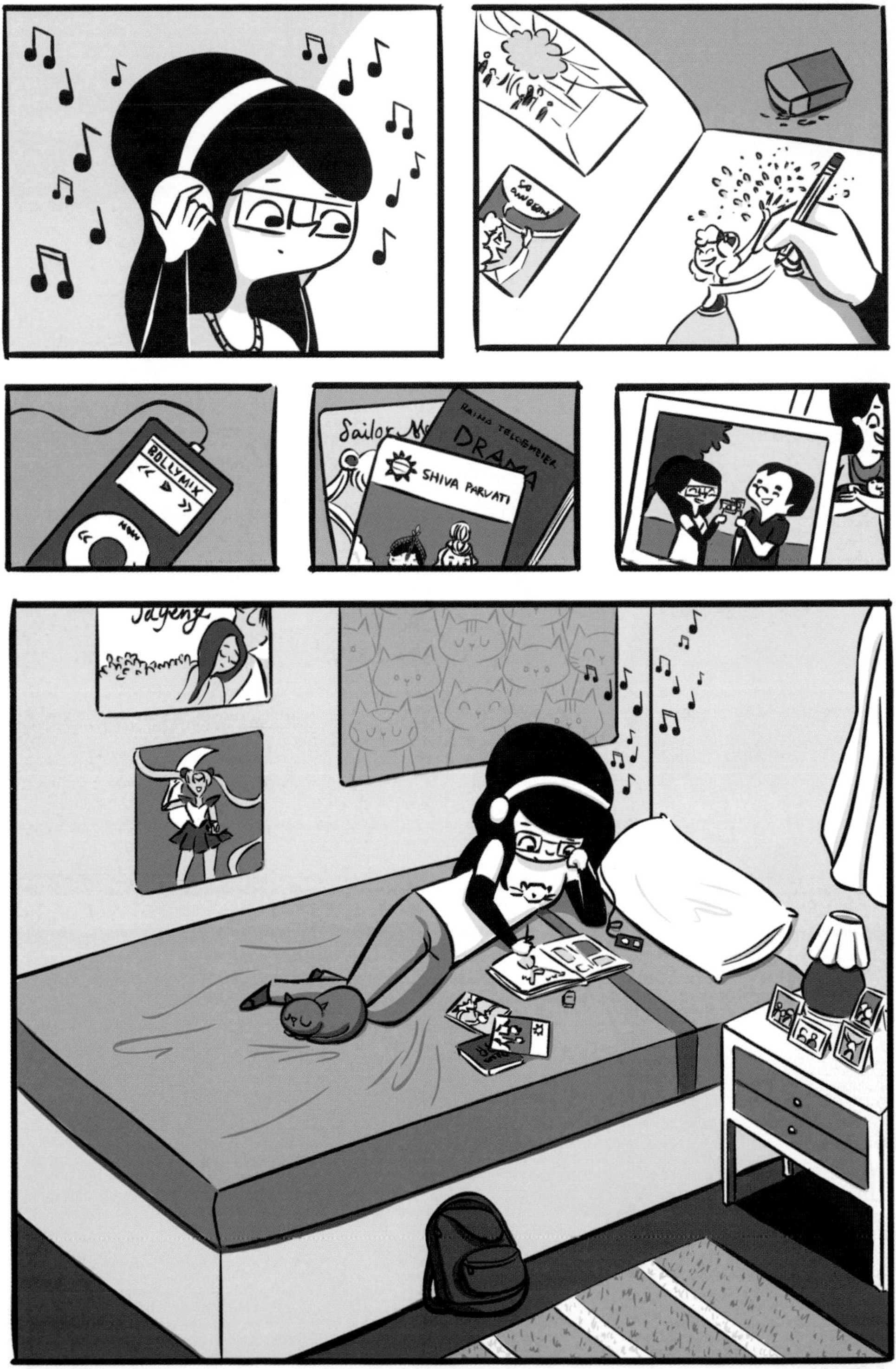
BOLLYMIX
RAINA TELGEMEIER
DRAMA
SHIVA PARVATI

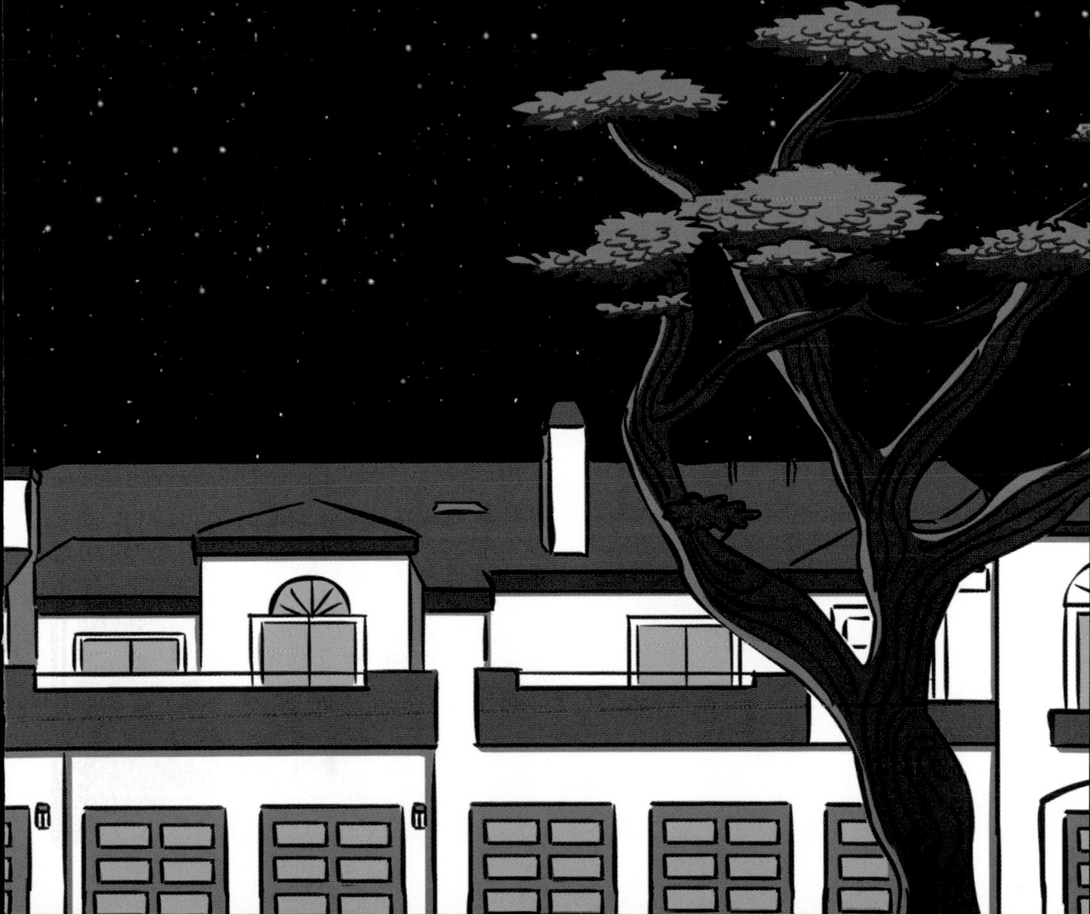

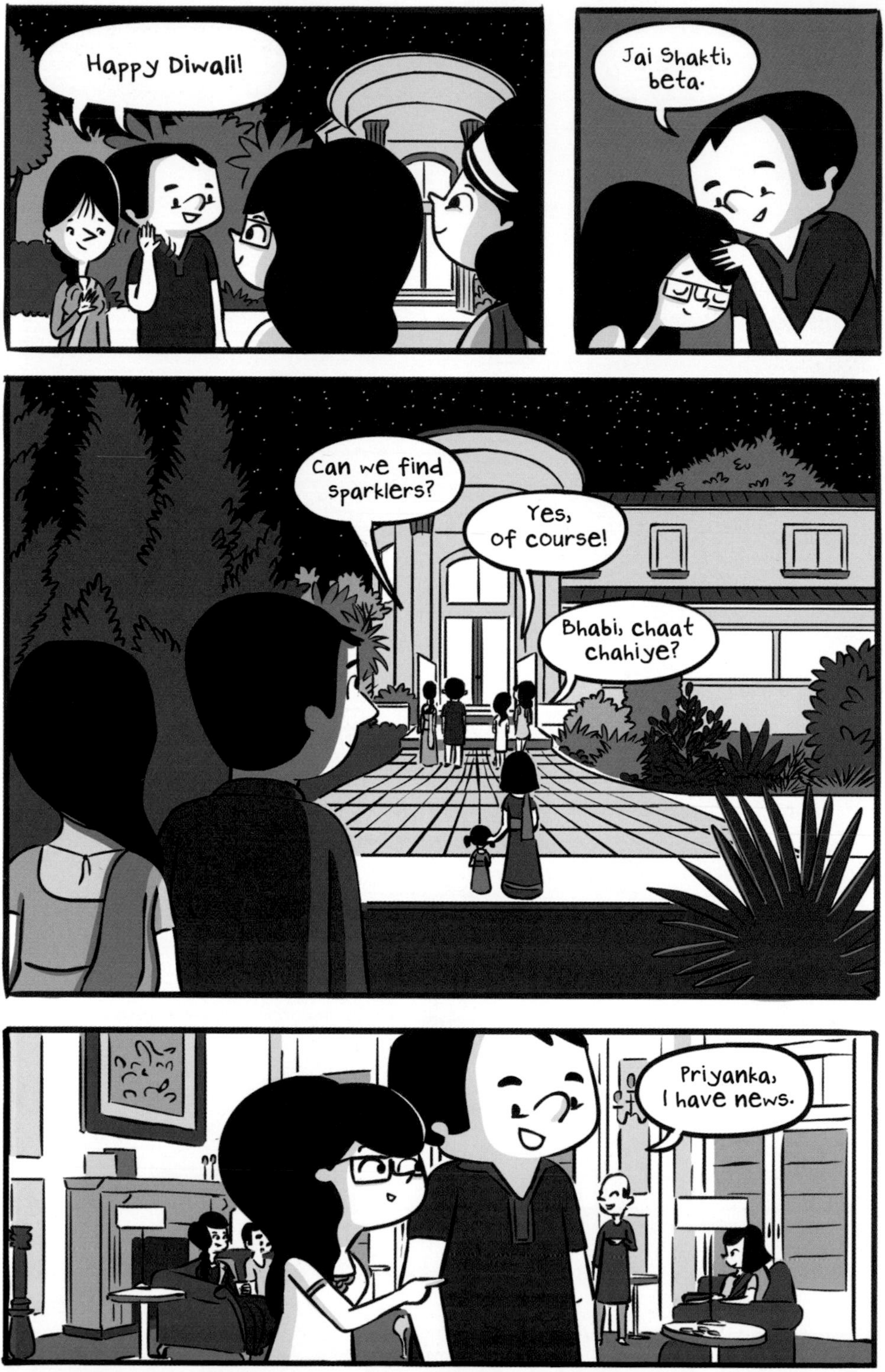
Happy Diwali!
Jai Shakti, beta.
Can we find sparklers?
Yes, of course!
Bhabi, chaat chahiye?
Priyanka, I have news.

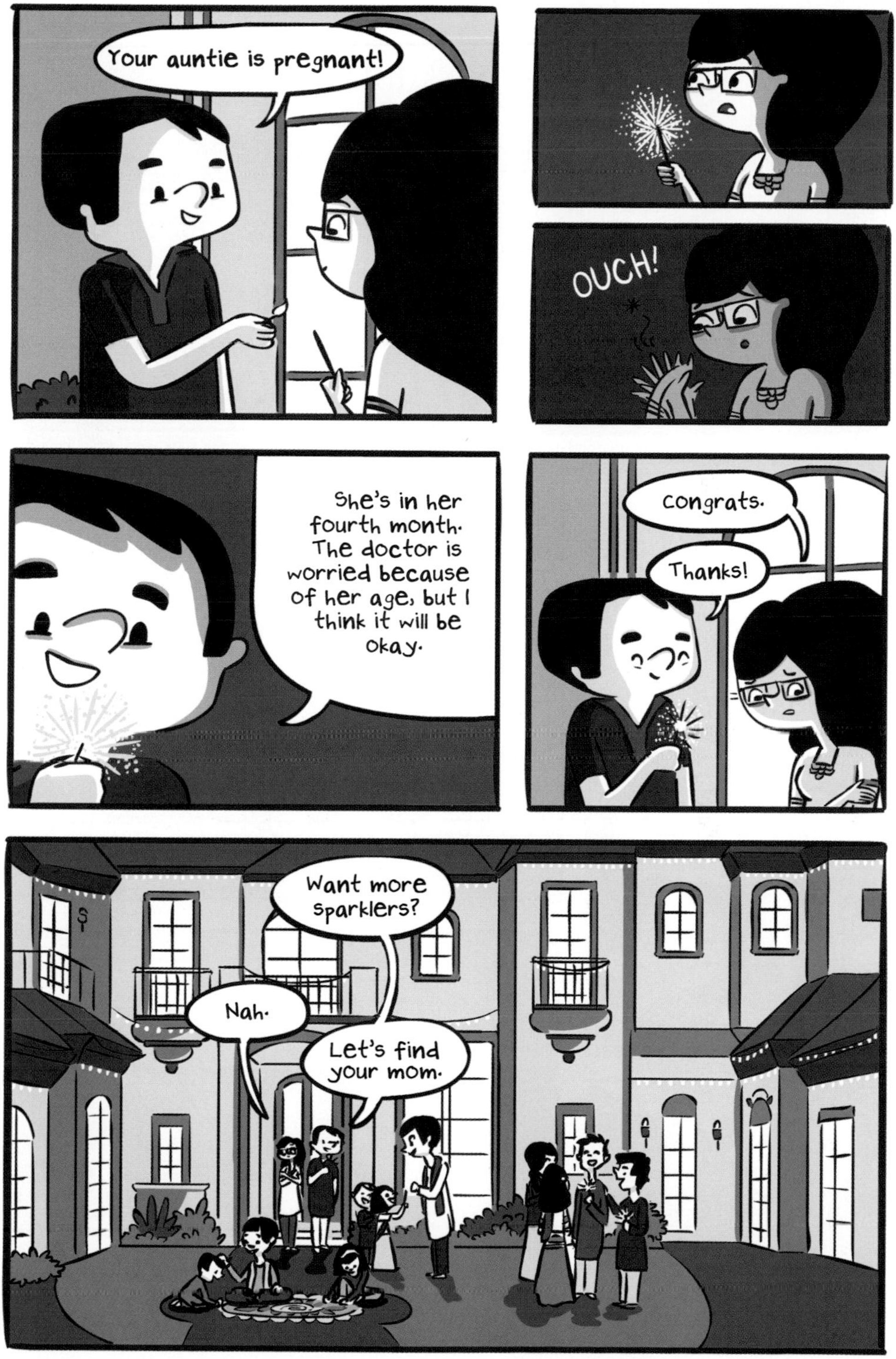
Your auntie is pregnant!
OUCH!
She's in her fourth month. The doctor is worried because of her age, but I think it will be okay.
Congrats.
Thanks!
Want more sparklers?
Nah.
Let's find your mom.

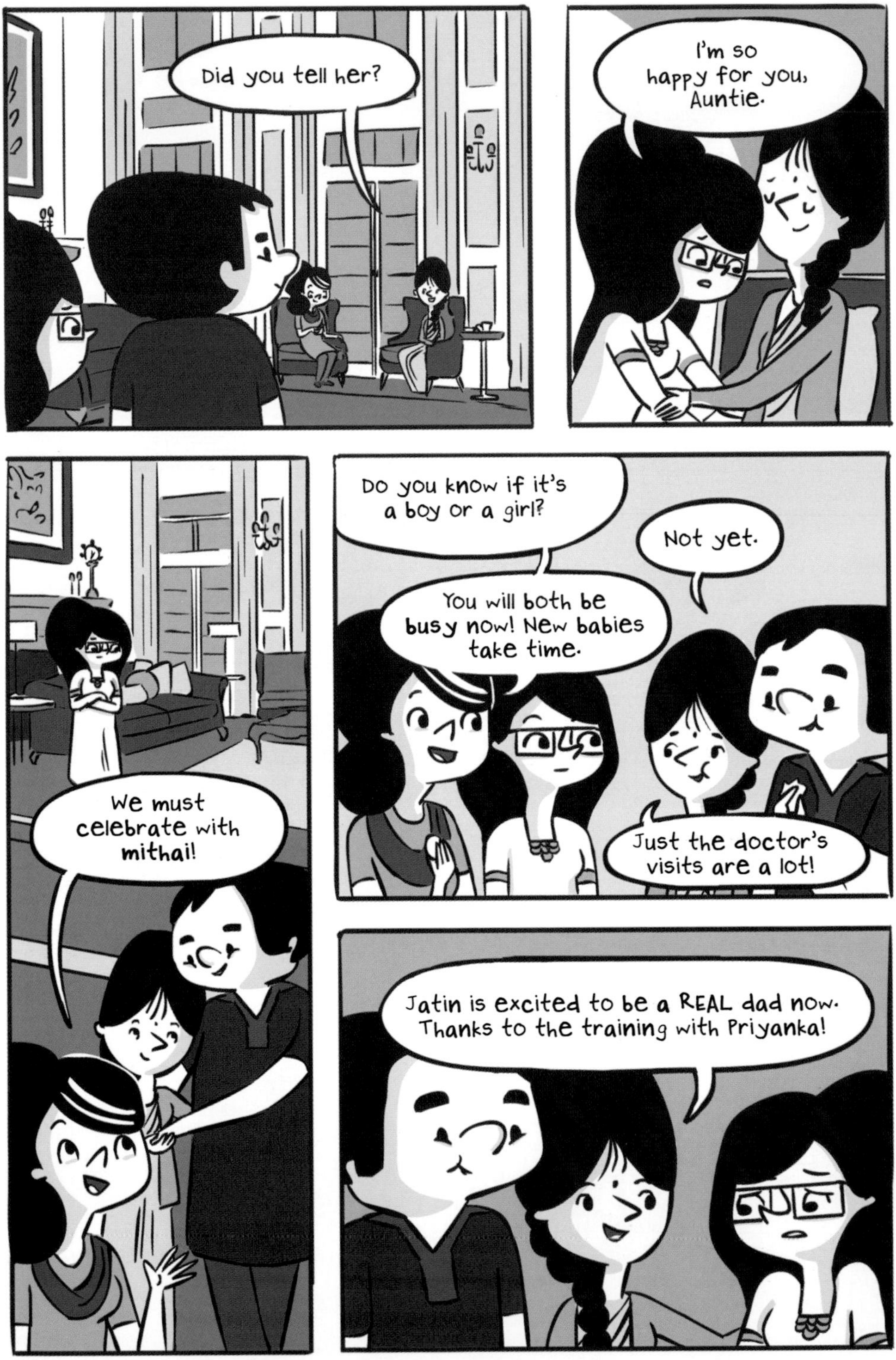
Did you tell her?
I'm so happy for you, Auntie.
We must celebrate with mithai!
Do you know if it's a boy or a girl?
Not yet.
You will both be busy now! New babies take time.
Just the doctor's visits are a lot!
Jatin is excited to be a REAL dad now. Thanks to the training with Priyanka!

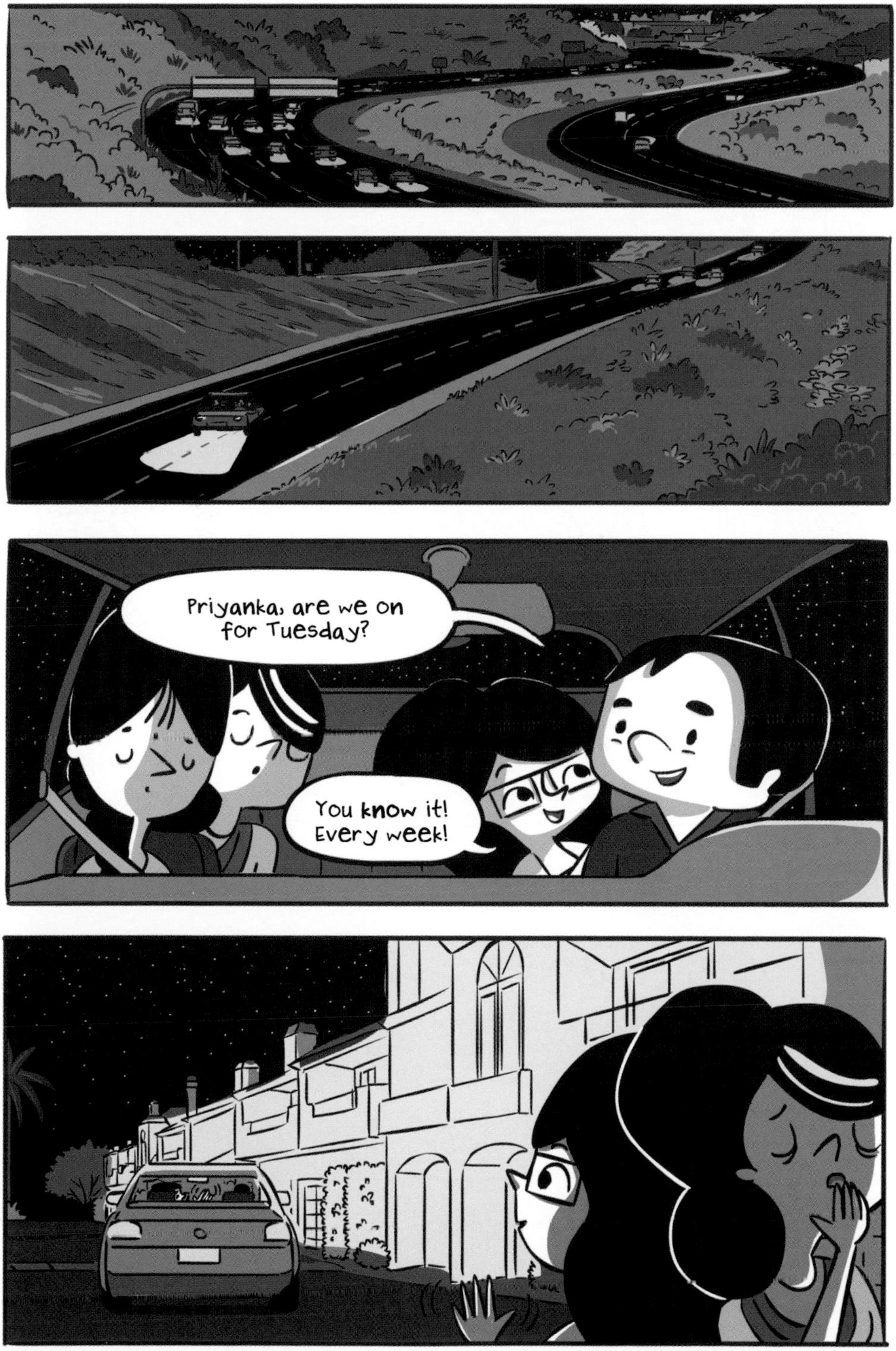
Priyanka, are we on for Tuesday?
You know it! Every week!

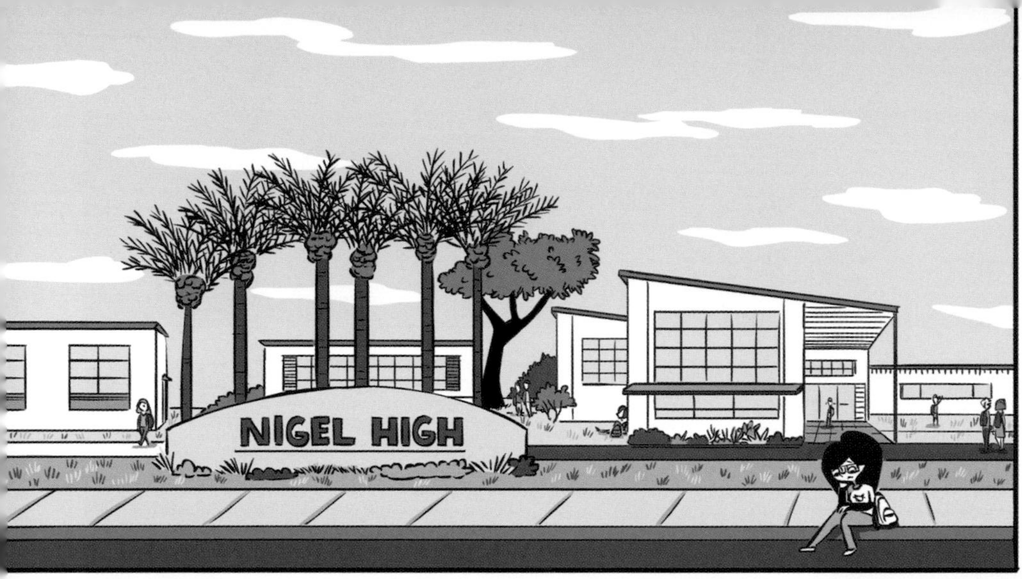
NIGEL HIGH

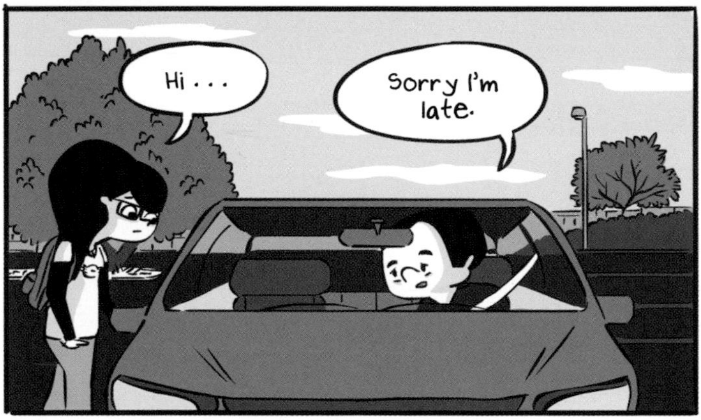
Hi . . .
Sorry I'm late.

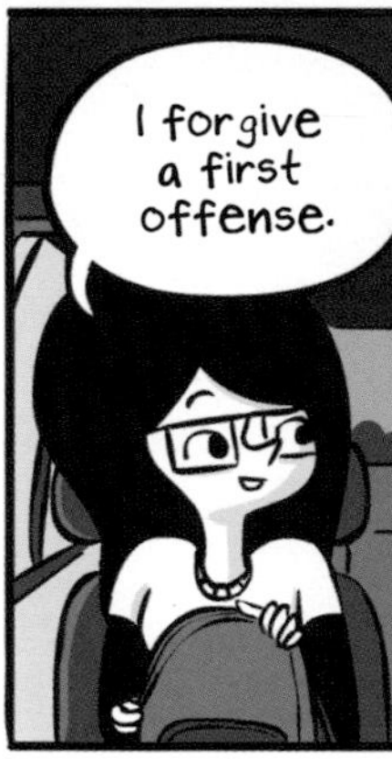
I forgive a first offense.

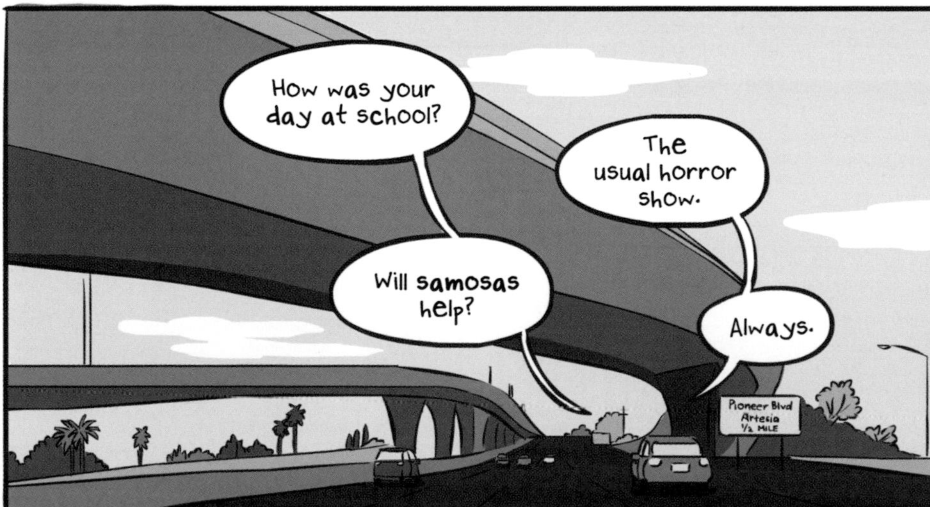
How was your day at school?
The usual horror show.
Will samosas help?
Always.
Pioneer Blvd
Artesia
1/2 MILE

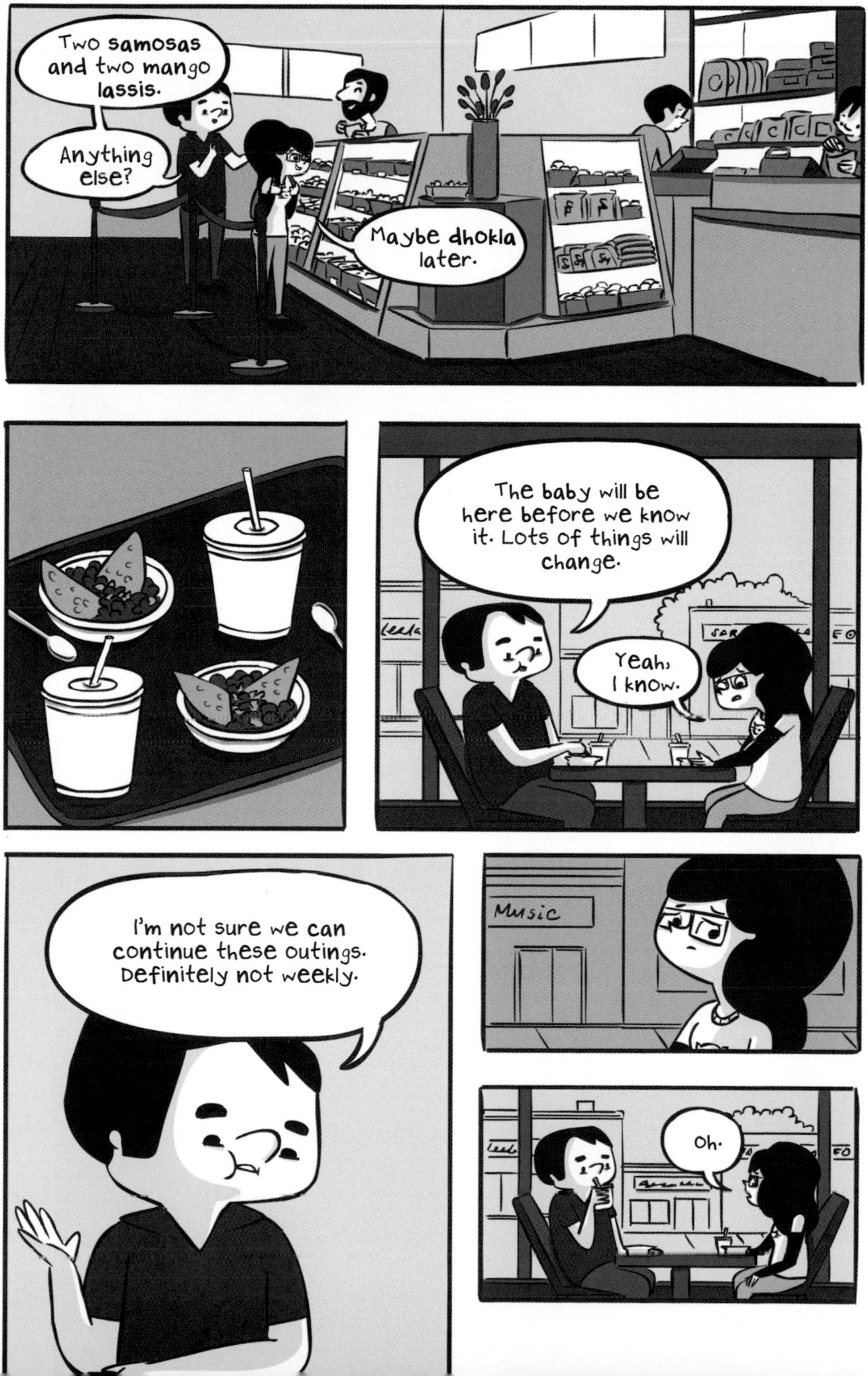
Two samosas and two mango lassis.
Anything else?
Maybe dhokla later.
The baby will be here before we know it. Lots of things will change.
Yeah, I know.
I'm not sure we can continue these outings. Definitely not weekly.
Music
Oh.

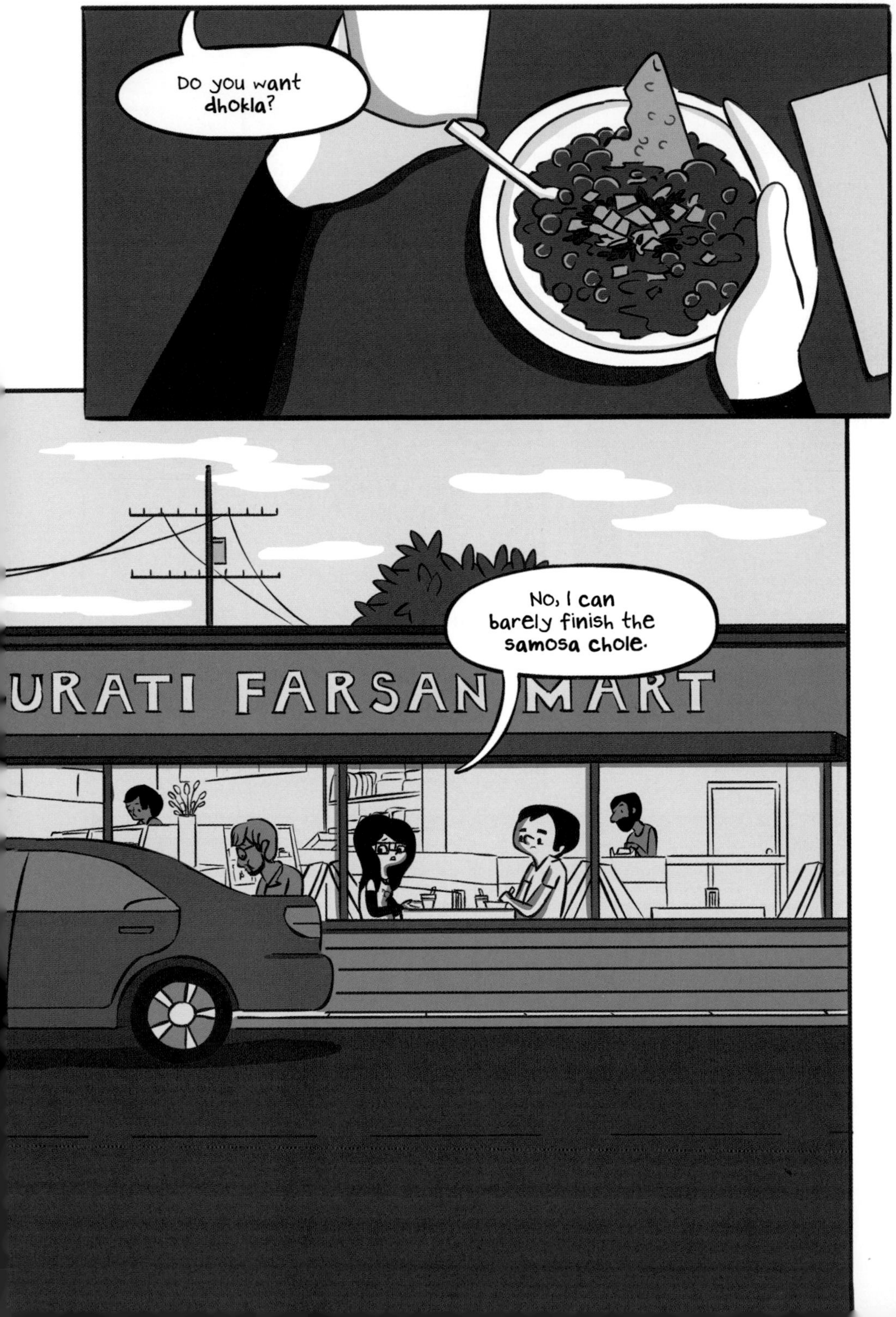

Do you want dhokla?
URATI FARSAN MART
No, I can barely finish the samosa chole.

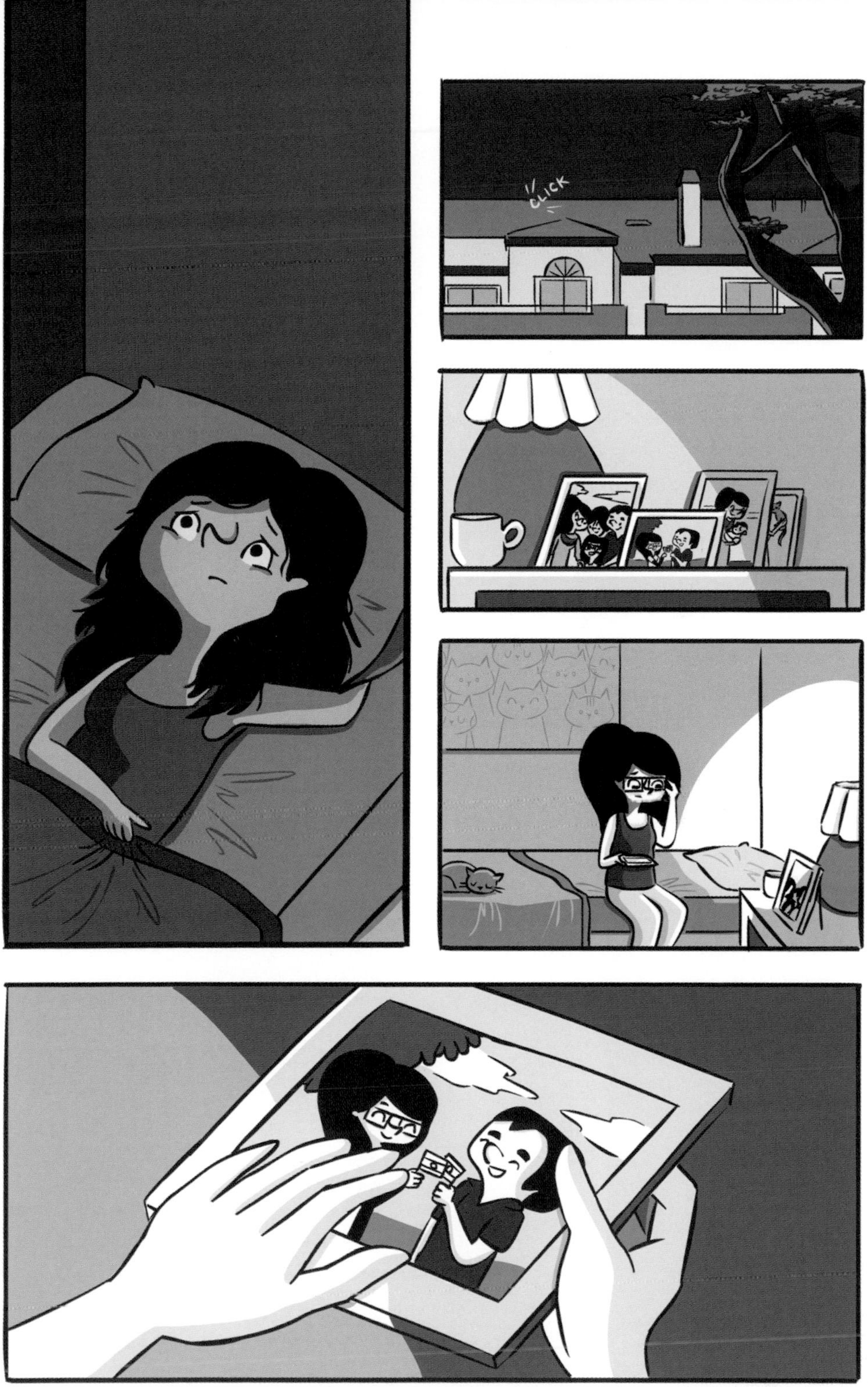
CLICK

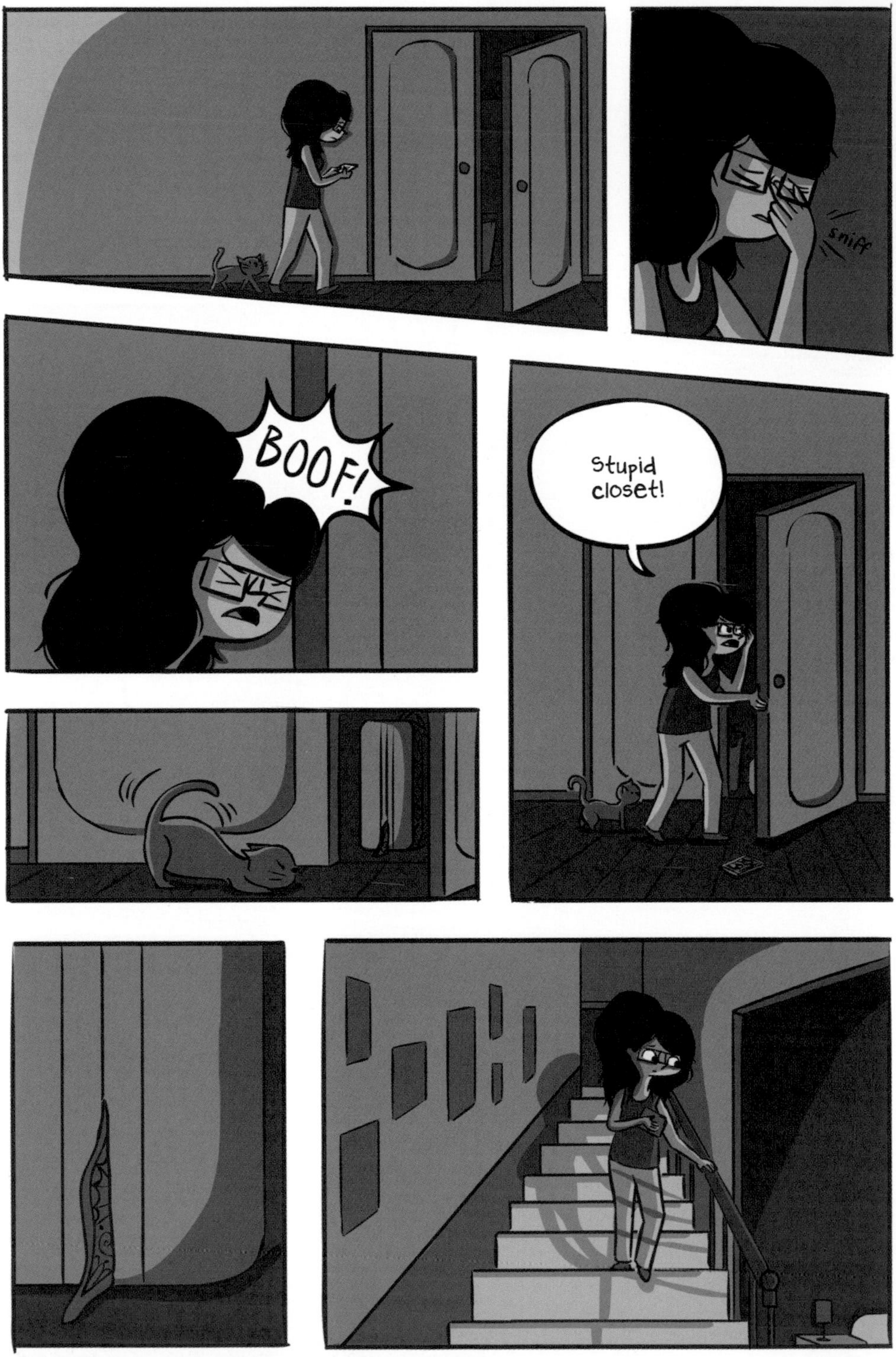
sniff
BOOF!
Stupid closet!

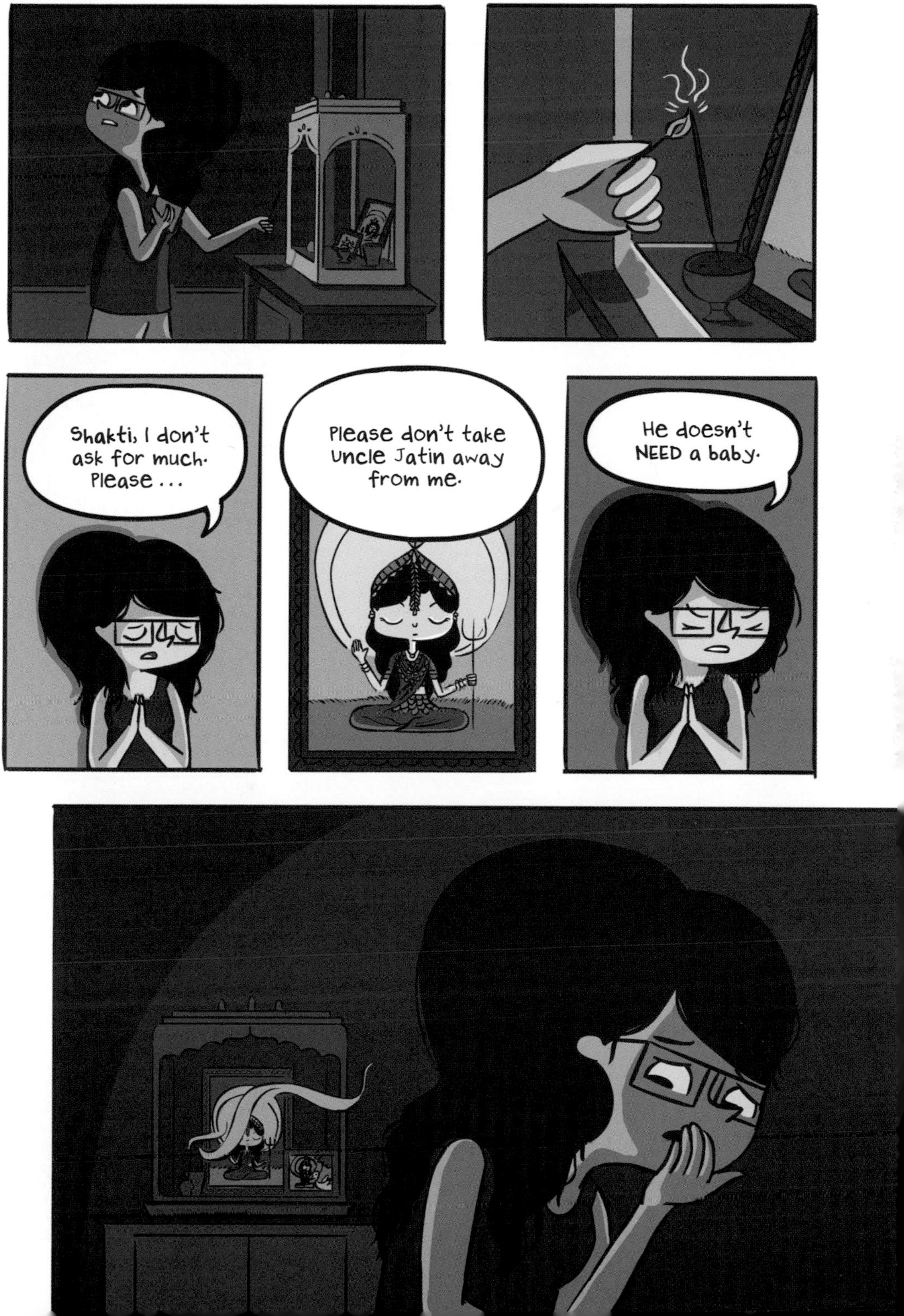
Shakti, I don't ask for much. Please . . .
Please don't take Uncle Jatin away from me.
He doesn't NEED a baby.

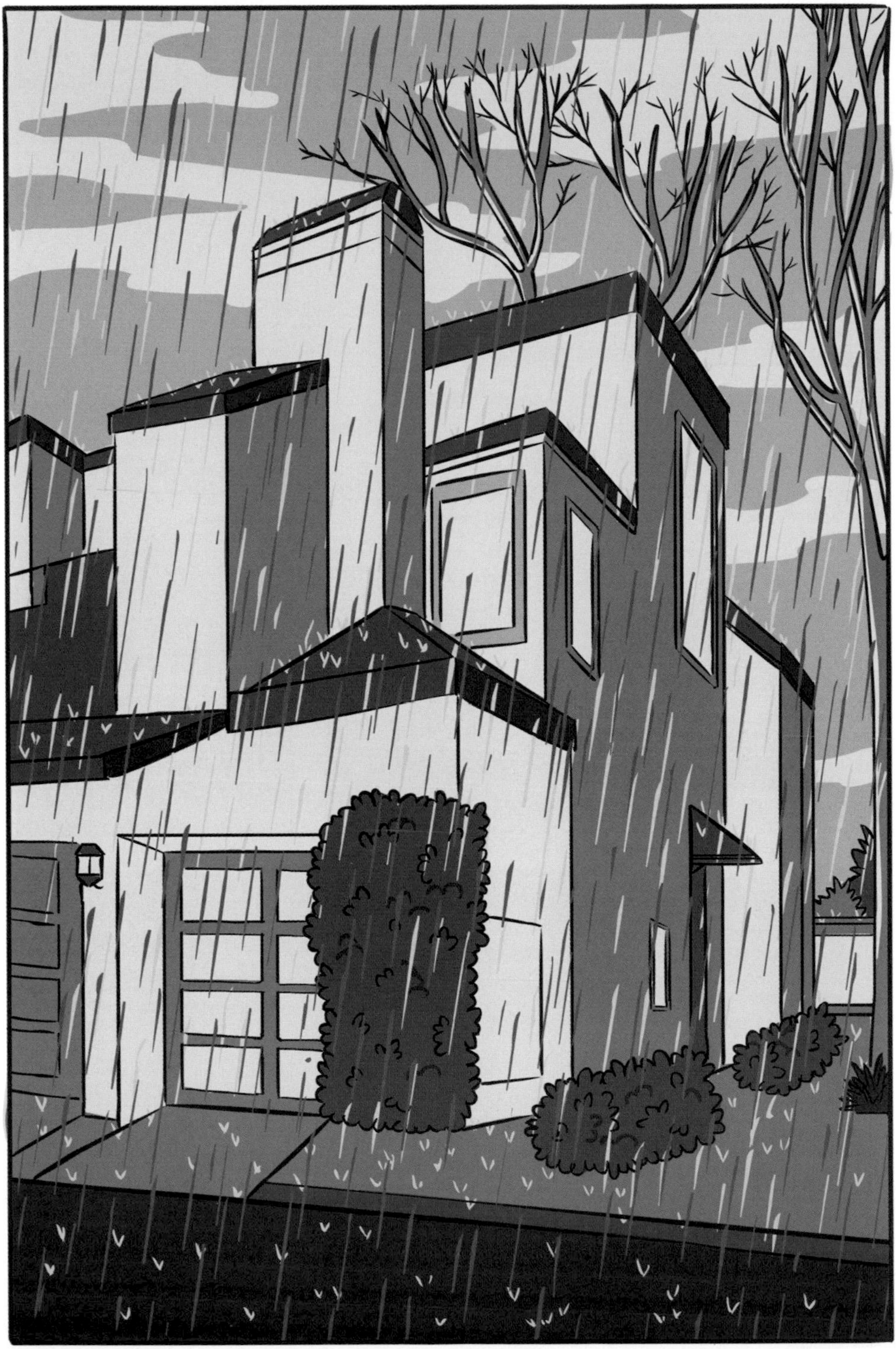

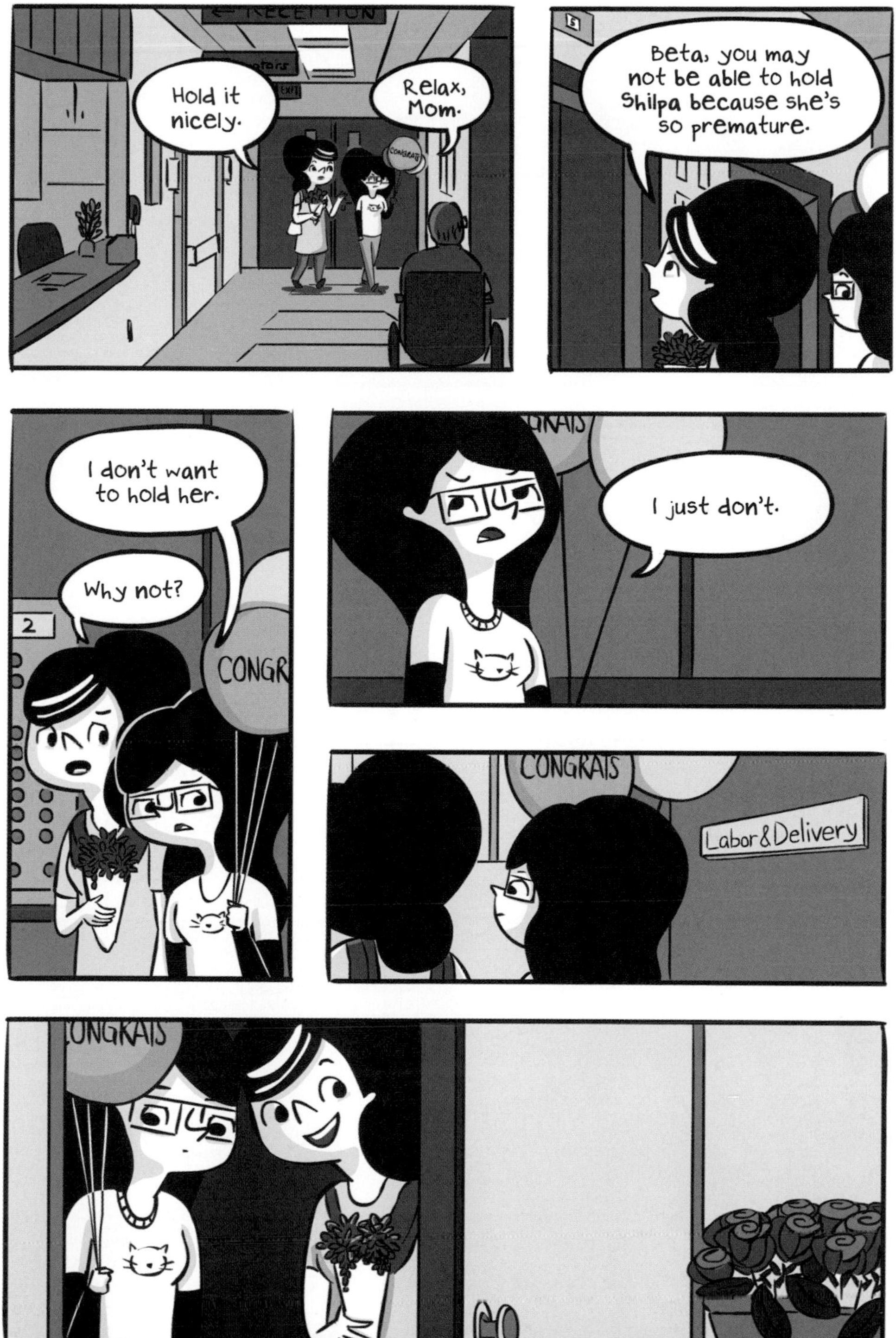
RECEPTION
Hold it nicely.
Relax, Mom.
Beta, you may not be able to hold Shilpa because she's so premature.
I don't want to hold her.
Why not?
CONGR
I just don't.
CONGRATS
Labor&Delivery

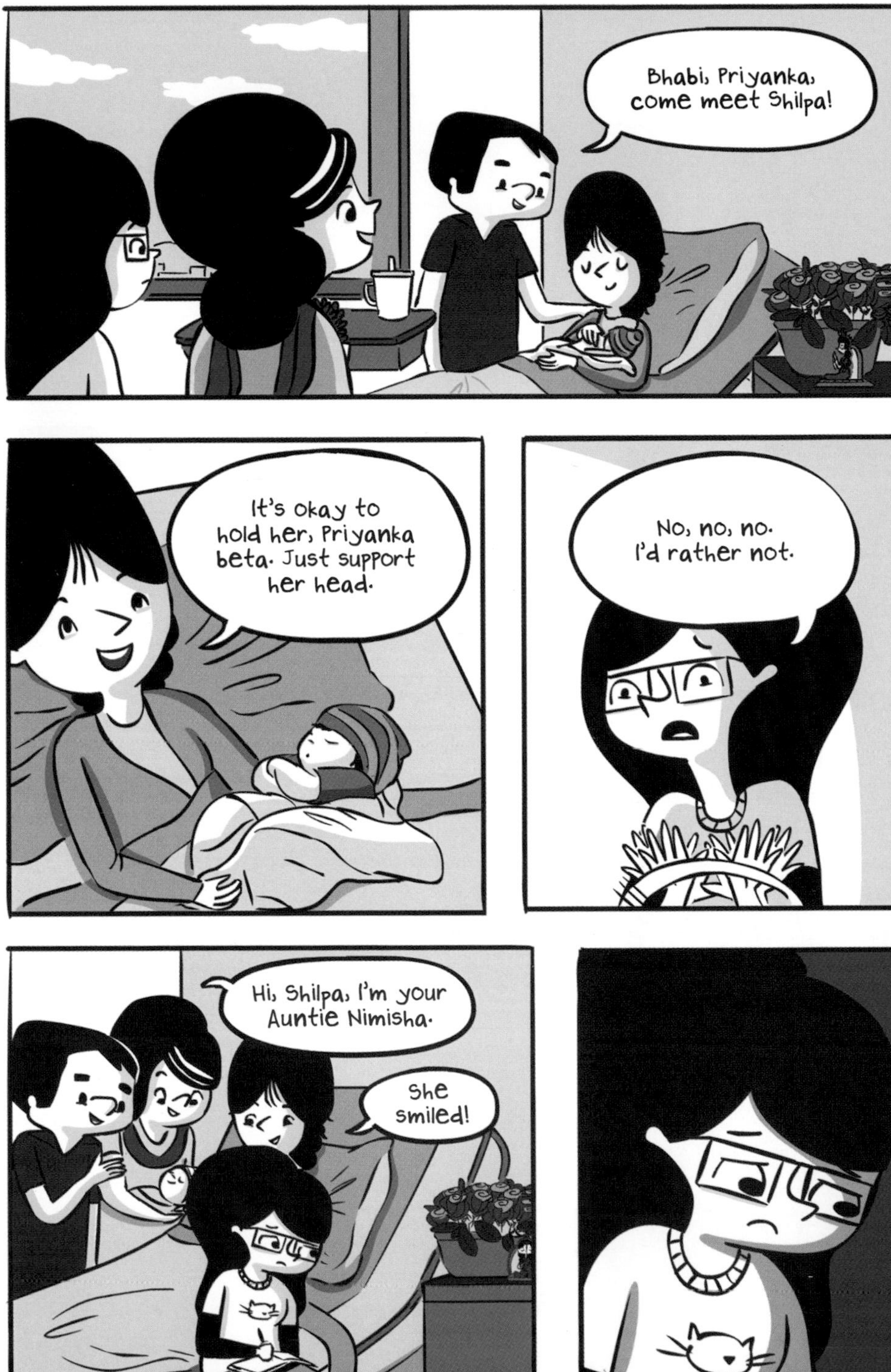
Bhabi, Priyanka, come meet Shilpa!
It's okay to hold her, Priyanka beta. Just support her head.
No, no, no. I'd rather not.
Hi, Shilpa, I'm your Auntie Nimisha.
She smiled!

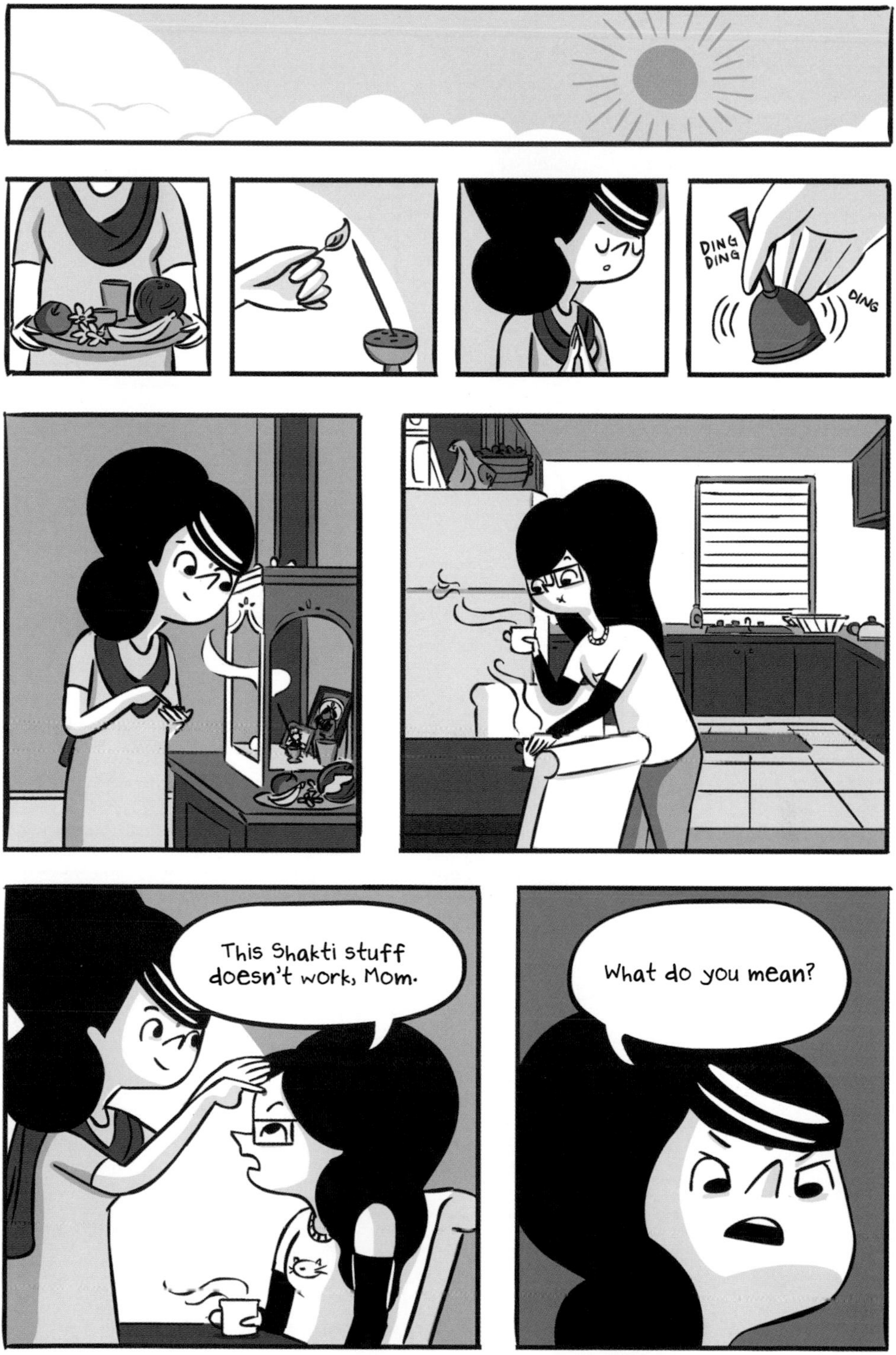
DING
DING
DING
This Shakti stuff doesn't work, Mom.
What do you mean?

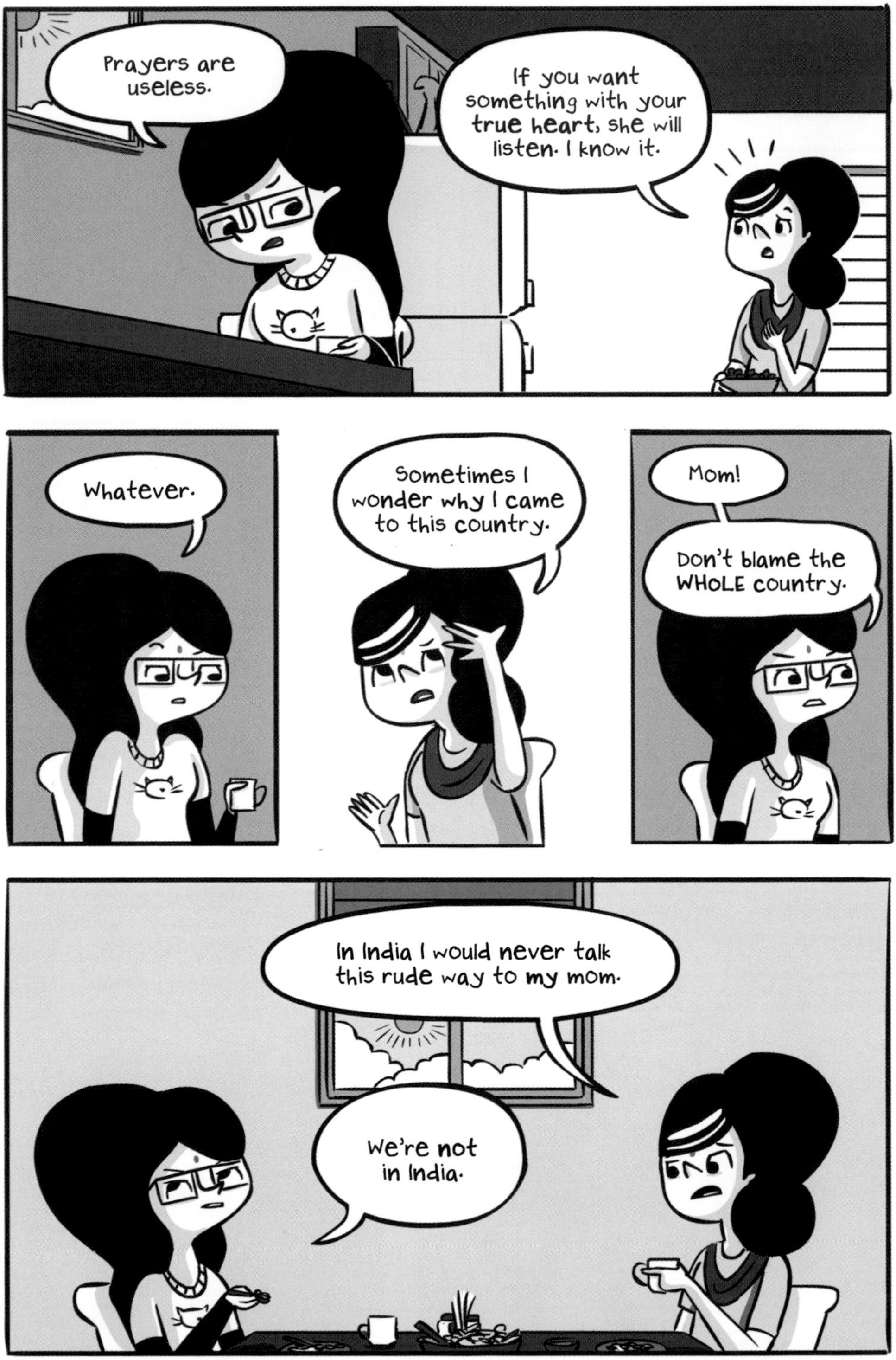
Prayers are useless.
If you want something with your true heart, she will listen. I know it.
Whatever.
Sometimes I wonder why I came to this country.
Mom!
Don't blame the WHOLE country.
In India I would never talk this rude way to my mom.
We're not in India.

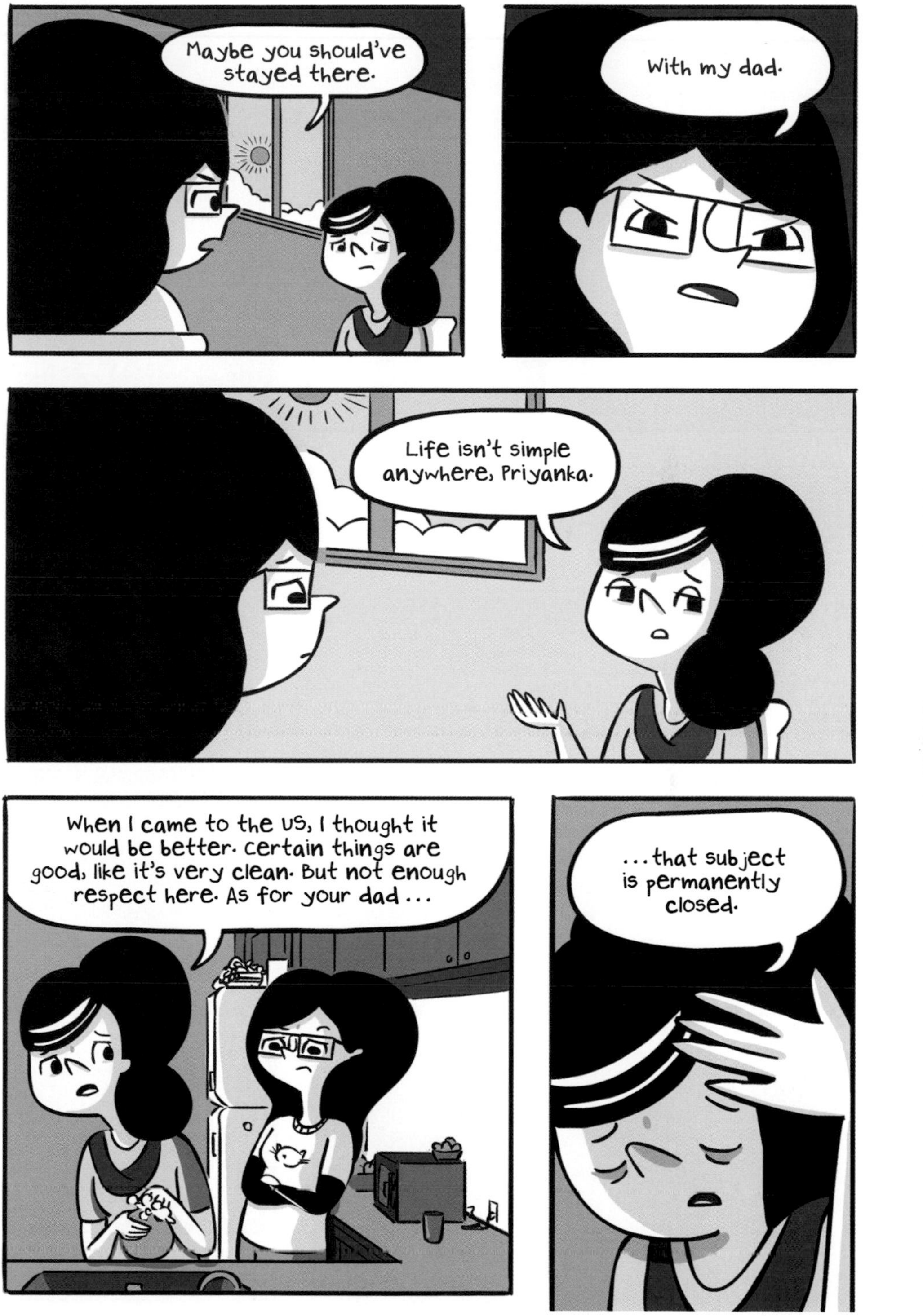
Maybe you should've stayed there.
With my dad.
Life isn't simple anywhere, Priyanka.
When I came to the US, I thought it would be better. Certain things are good, like it's very clean. But not enough respect here. As for your dad . . .
. . . that subject is permanently closed.

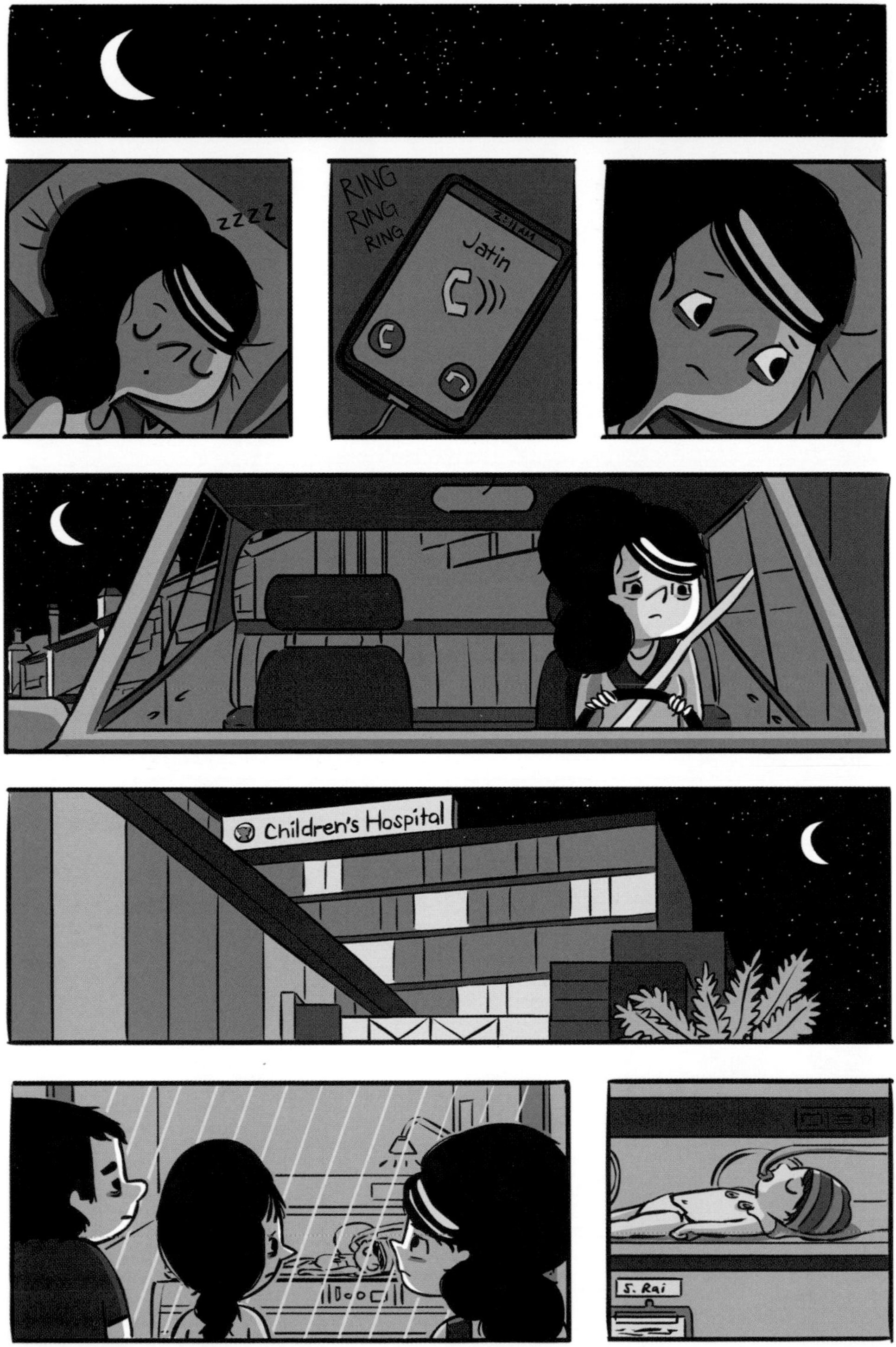
zzzz
RING
RING
RING
Jatin
Children's Hospital
S. Rai

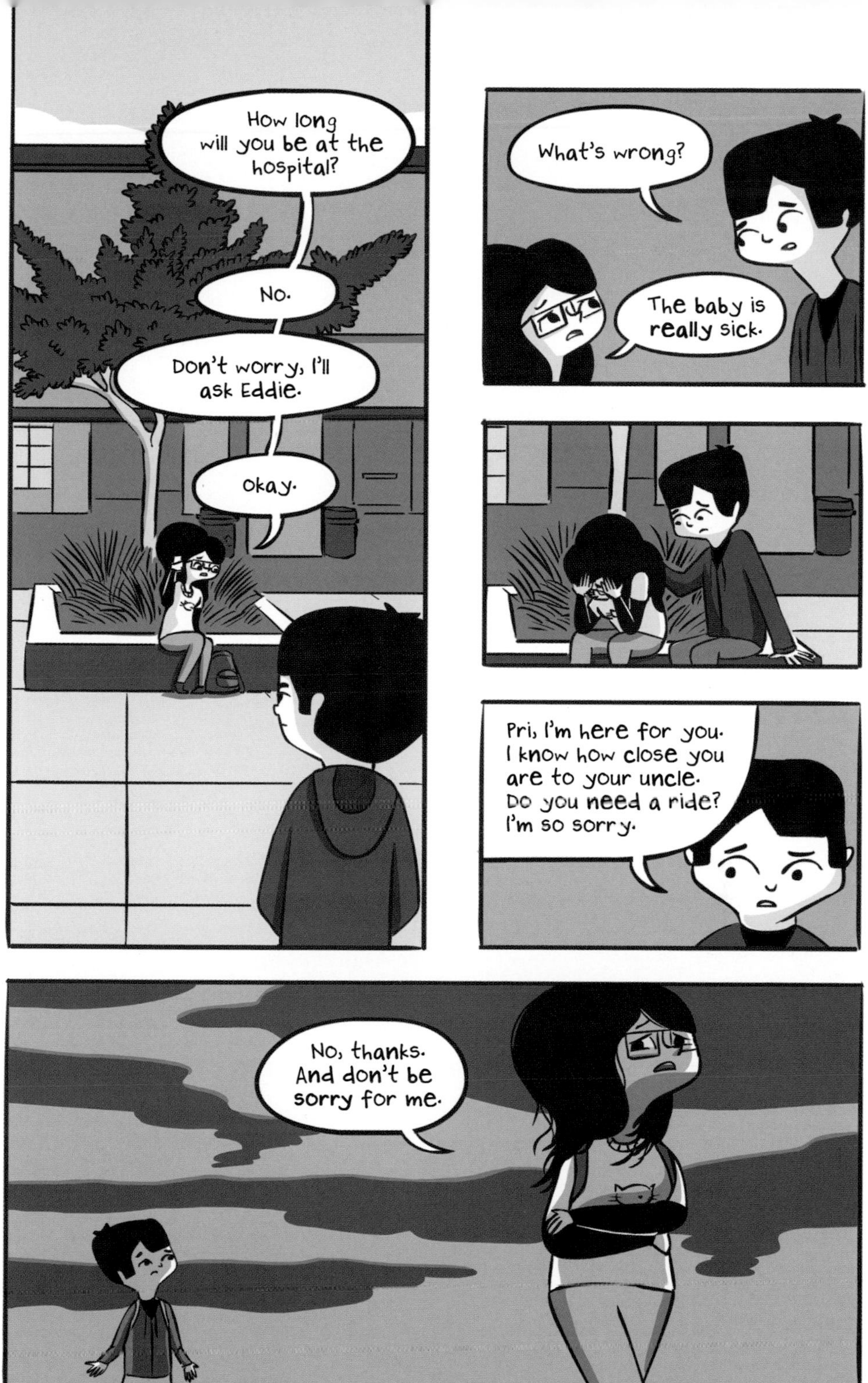
How long will you be at the hospital?
No.
Don't worry, I'll ask Eddie.
Okay.
What's wrong?
The baby is really sick.
Pri, I'm here for you. I know how close you are to your uncle. Do you need a ride? I'm so sorry.
No, thanks. And don't be sorry for me.

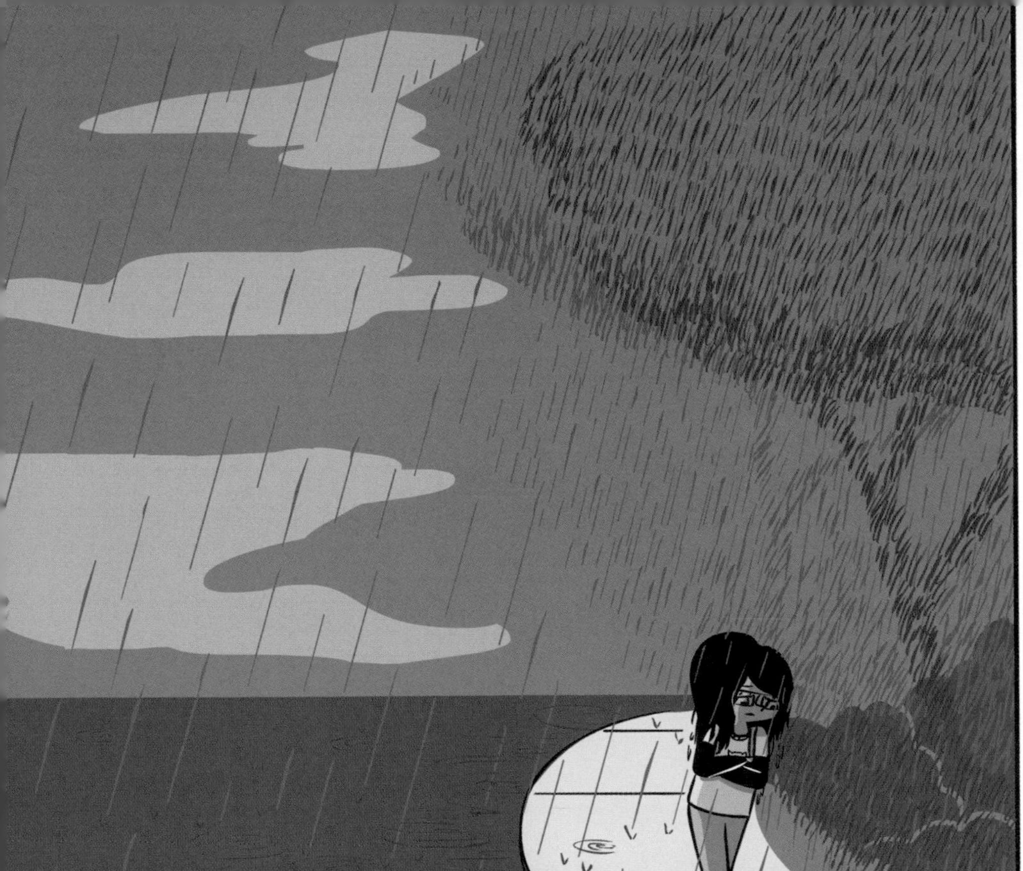

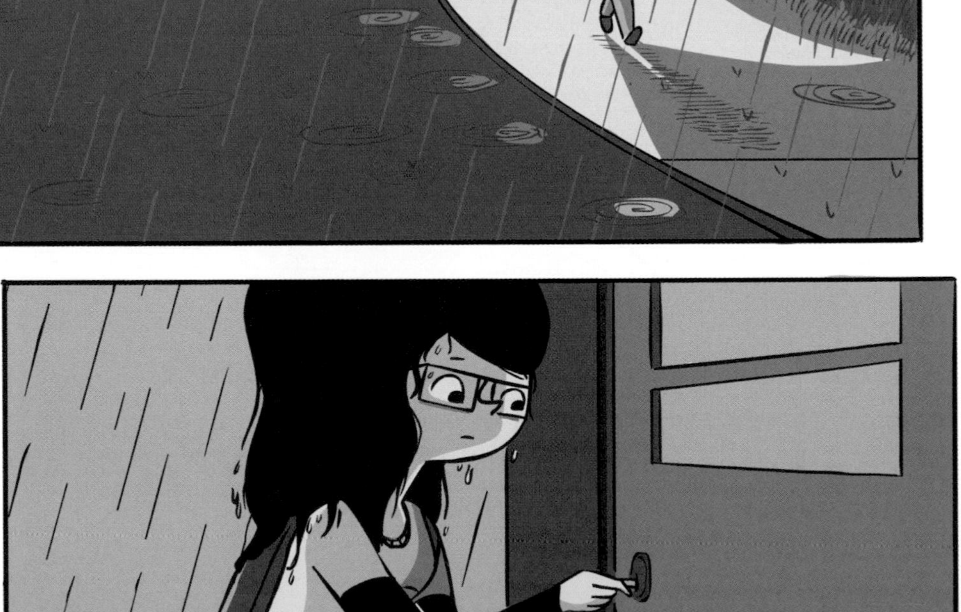

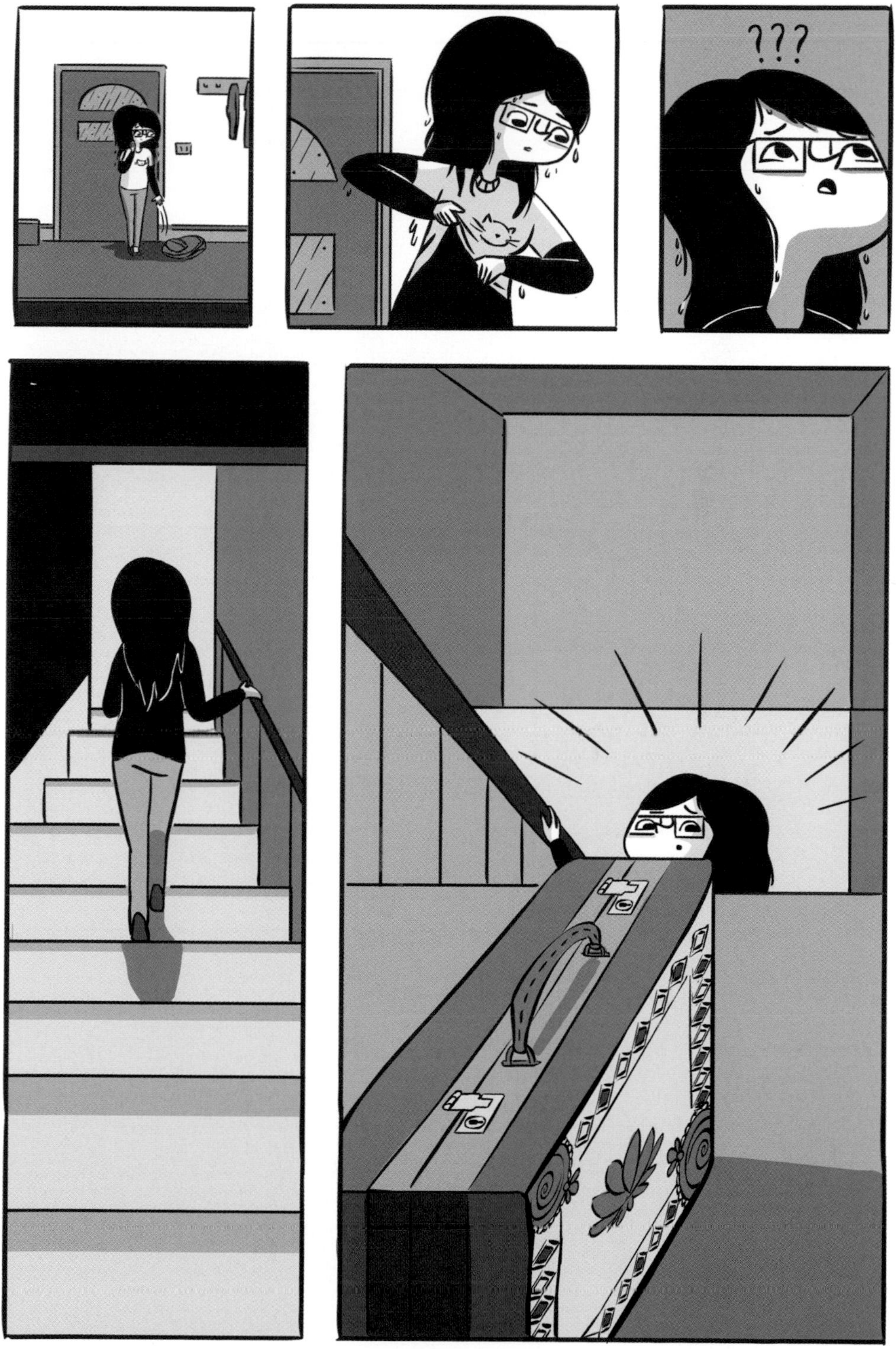
???

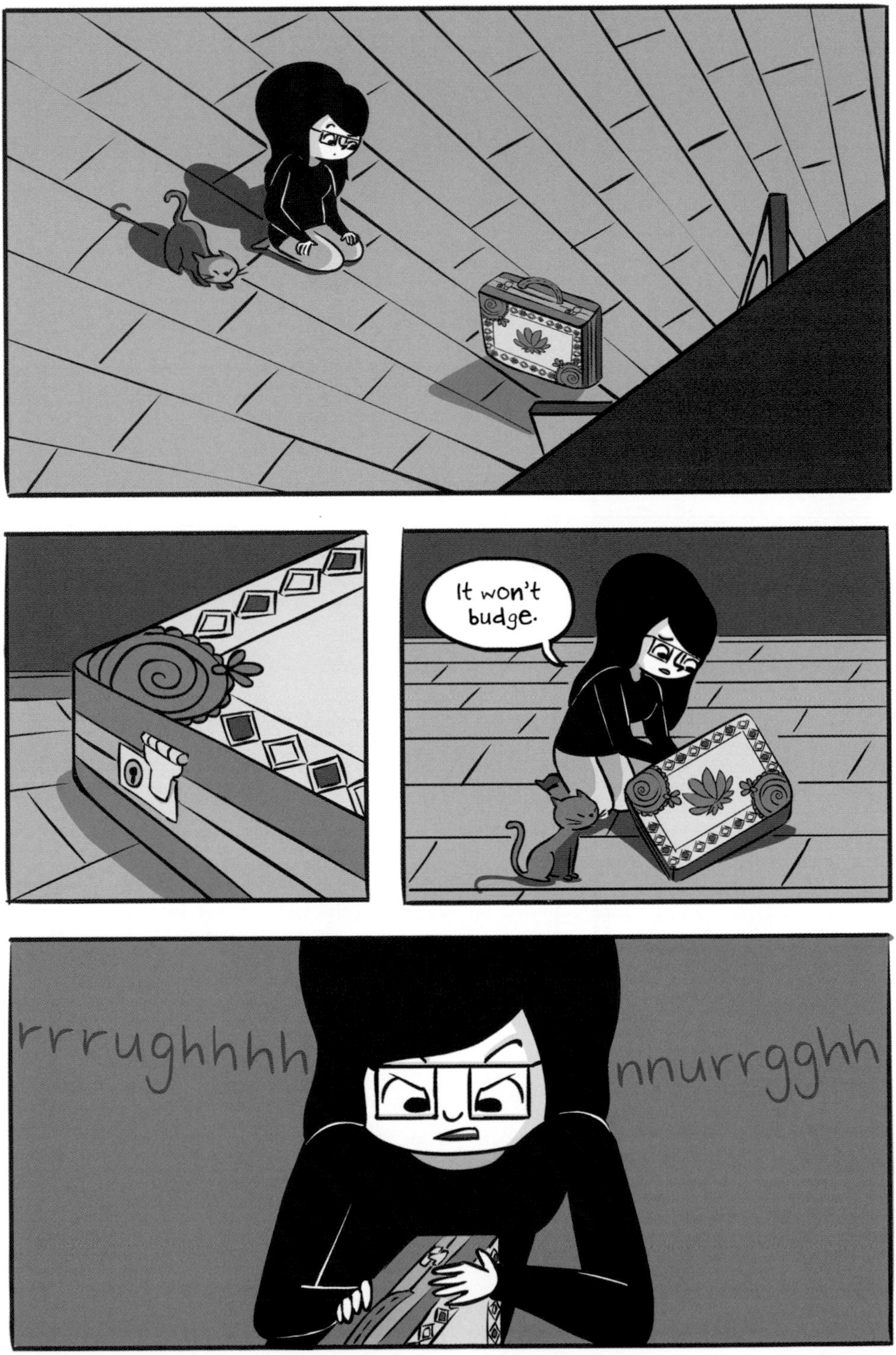
It won't budge.
rrrughhhh
nnurrgghh

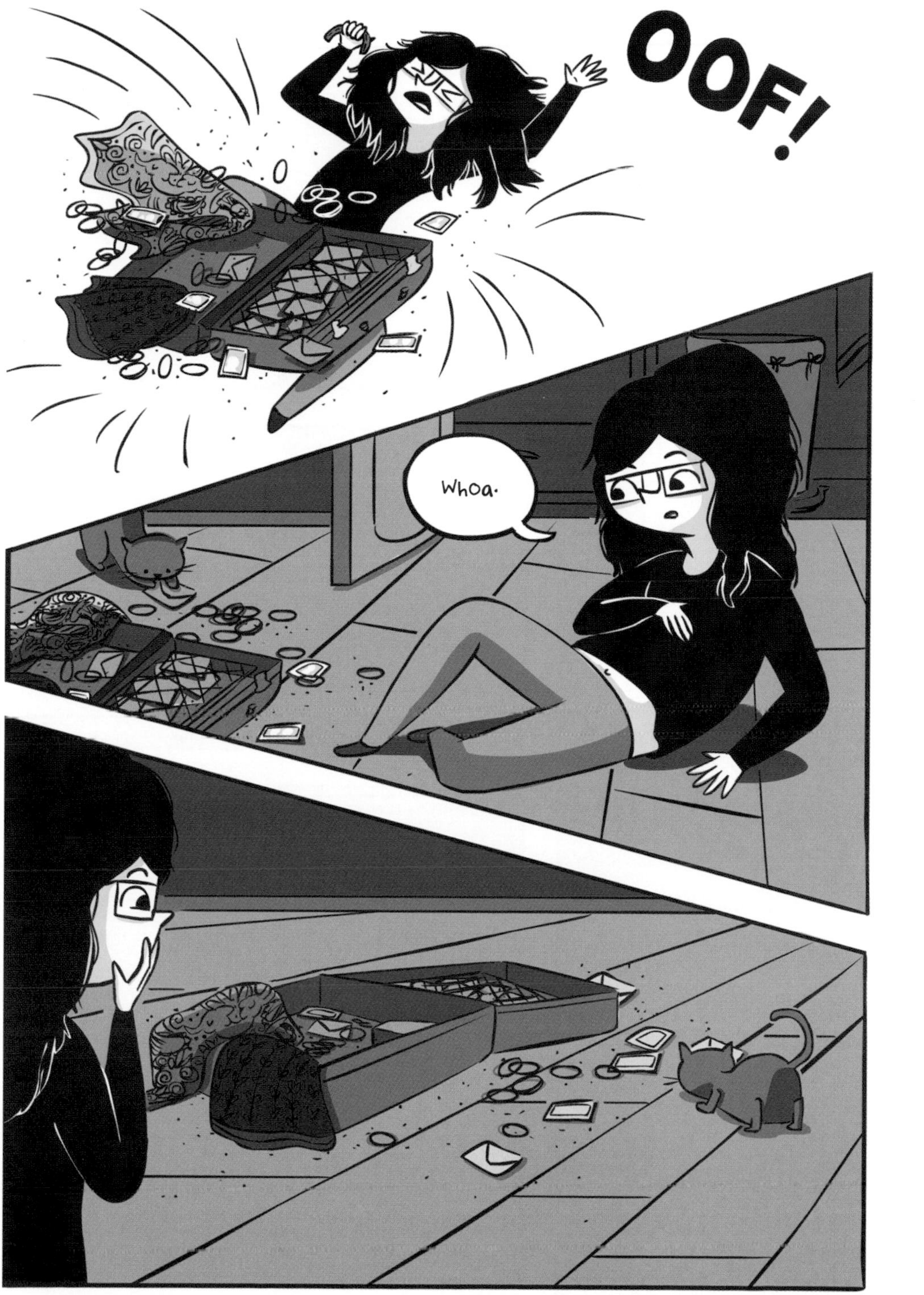
OOF!
Whoa.

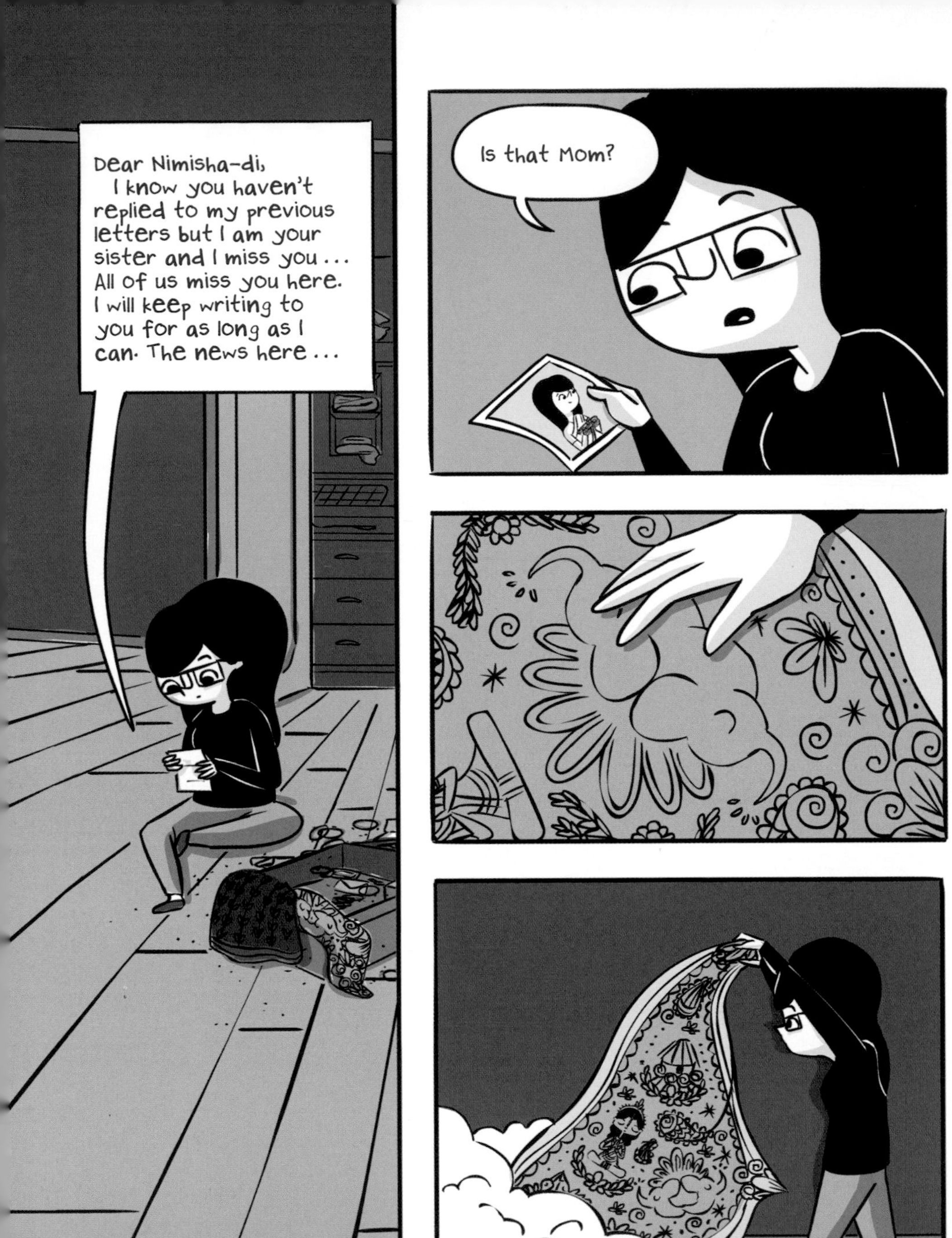
Dear Nimisha-di,
I know you haven't replied to my previous letters but I am your sister and I miss you . . . All of us miss you here. I will keep writing to you for as long as I can. The news here . . .
Is that Mom?

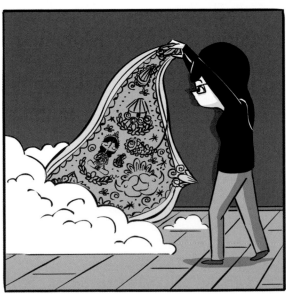

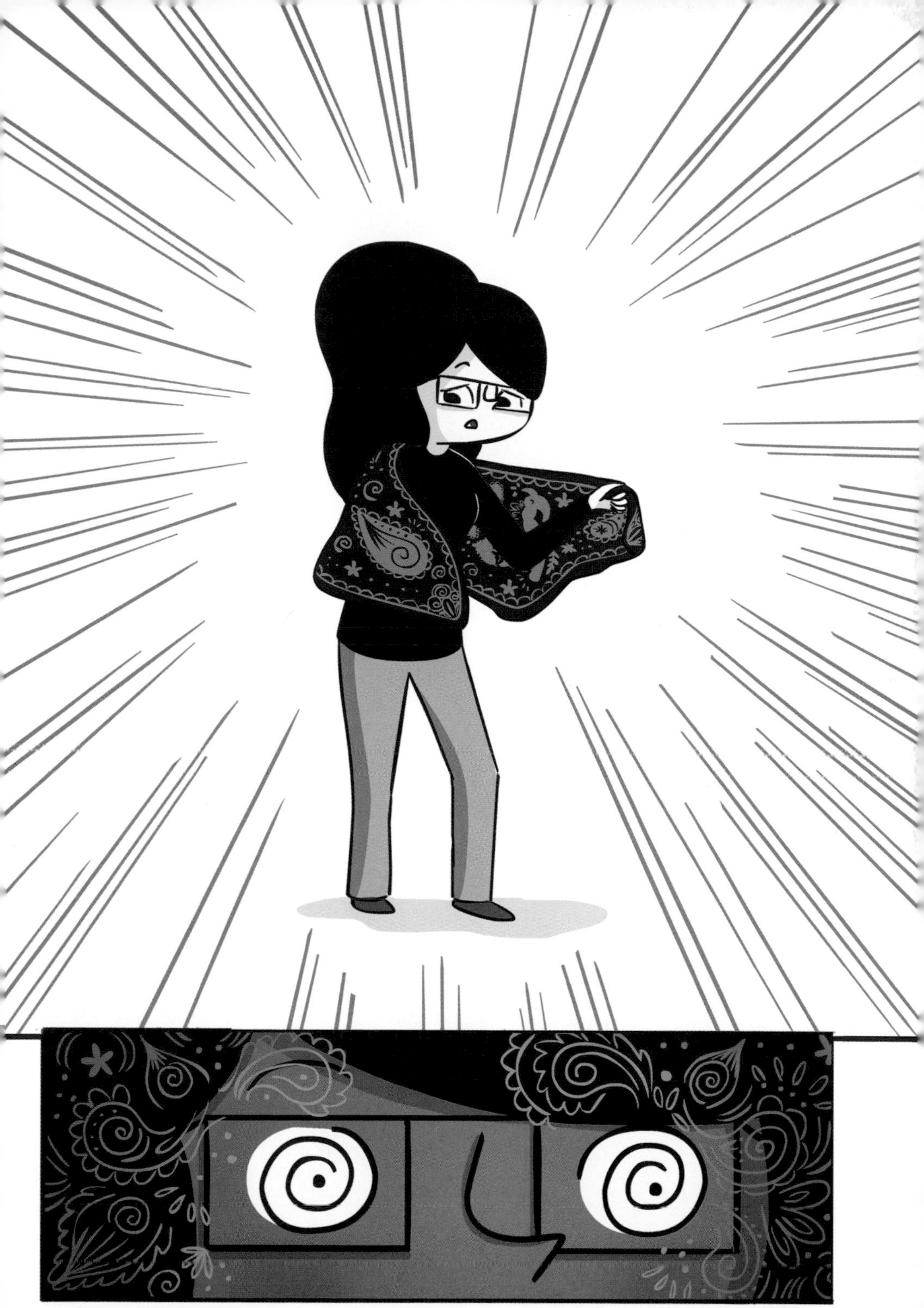

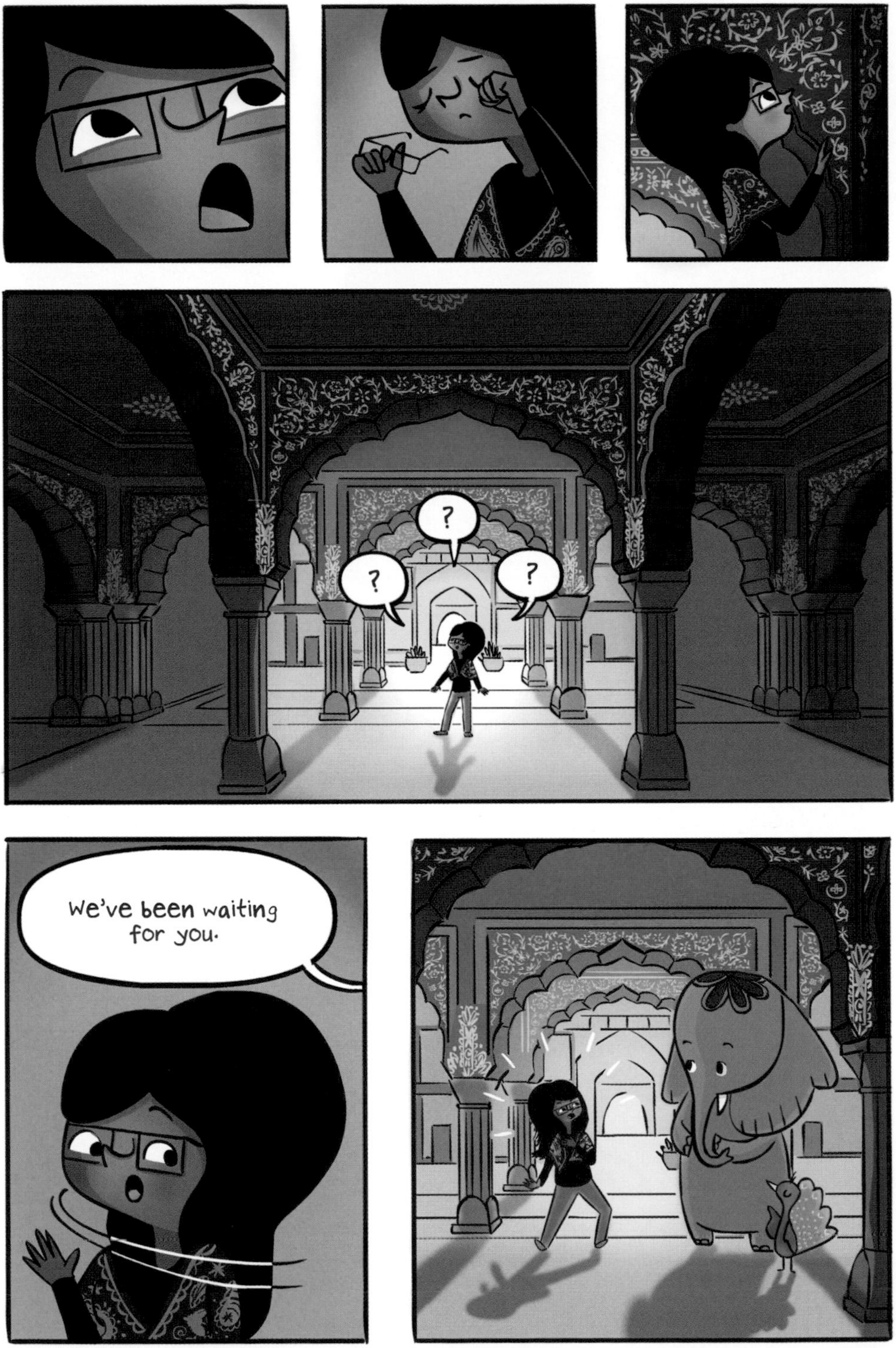
?
?
?
We've been waiting for you.

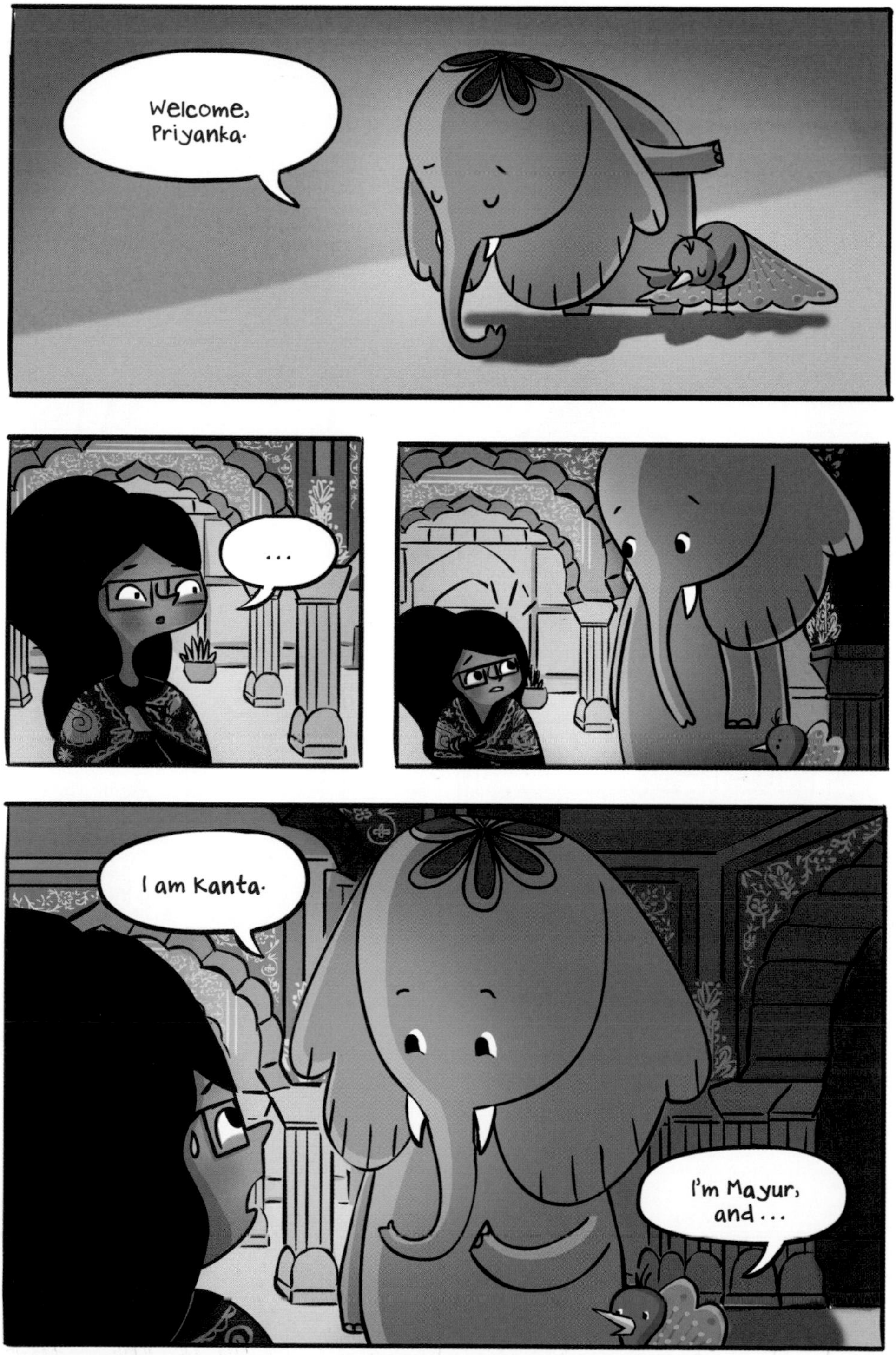
Welcome, Priyanka.
...
I am Kanta.
I'm Mayur, and ...

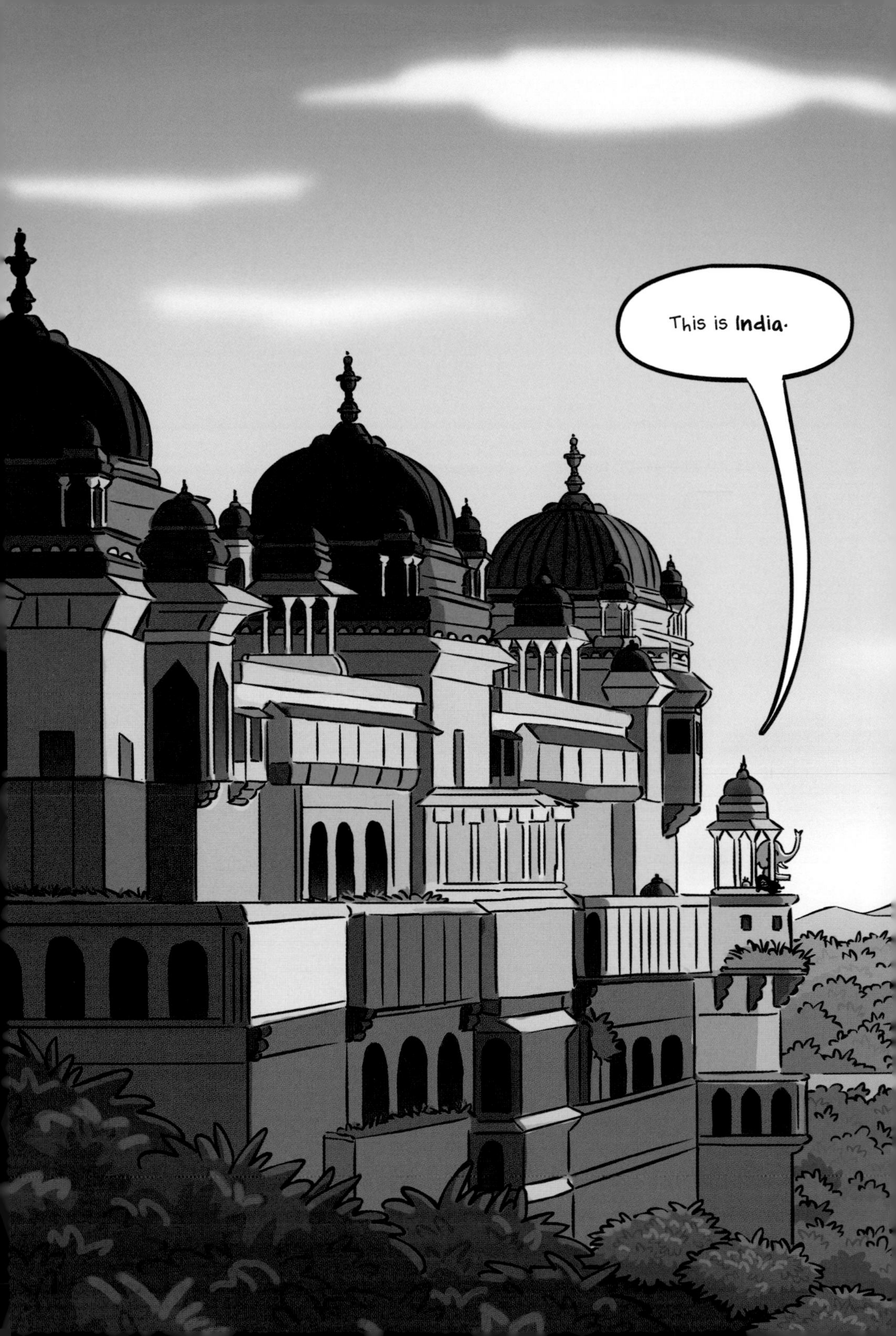
This is India.

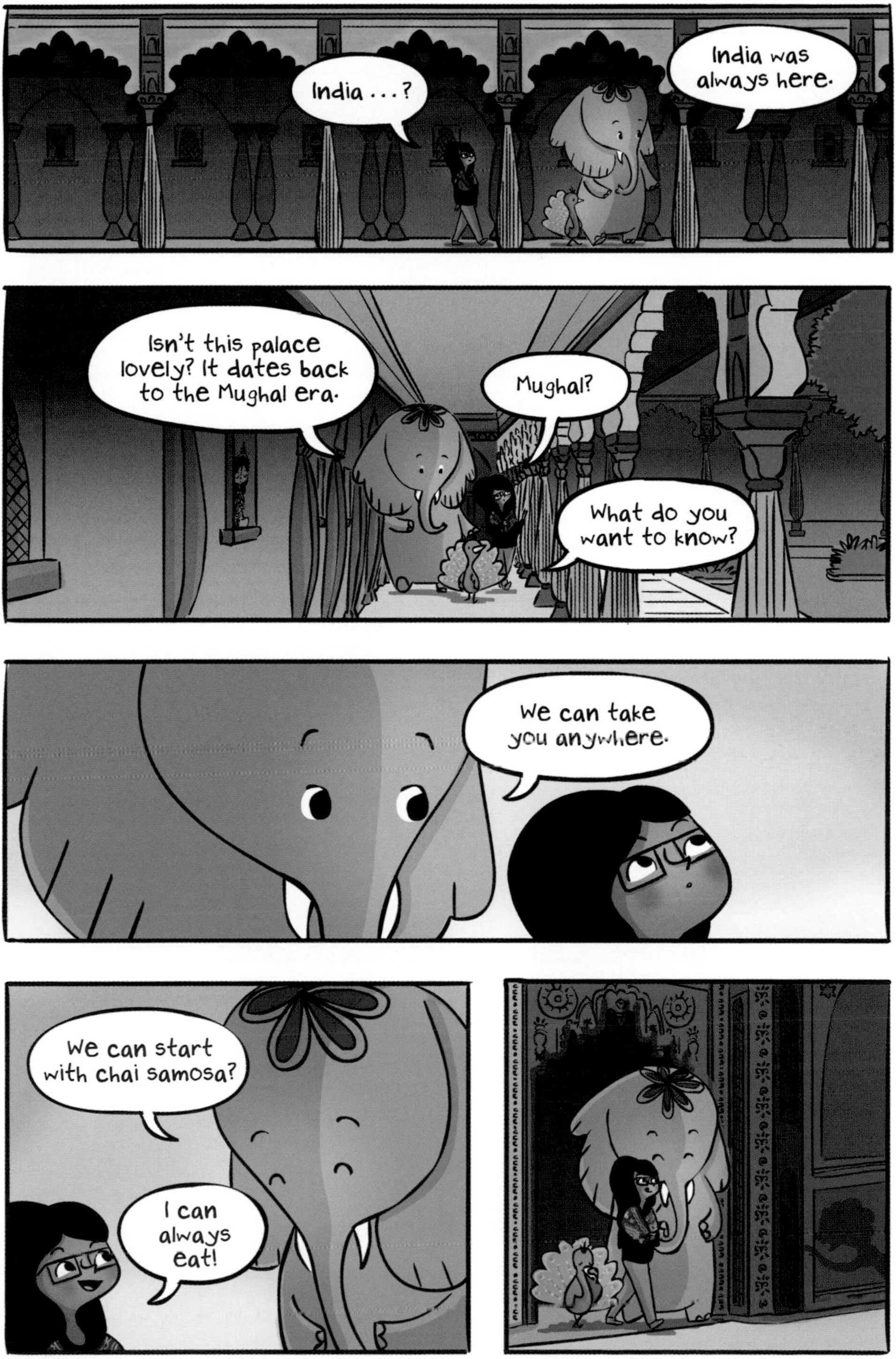
India . . . ?
India was always here.
Isn't this palace lovely? It dates back to the Mughal era.
Mughal?
What do you want to know?
We can take you anywhere.
We can start with chai samosa?
I can always eat!

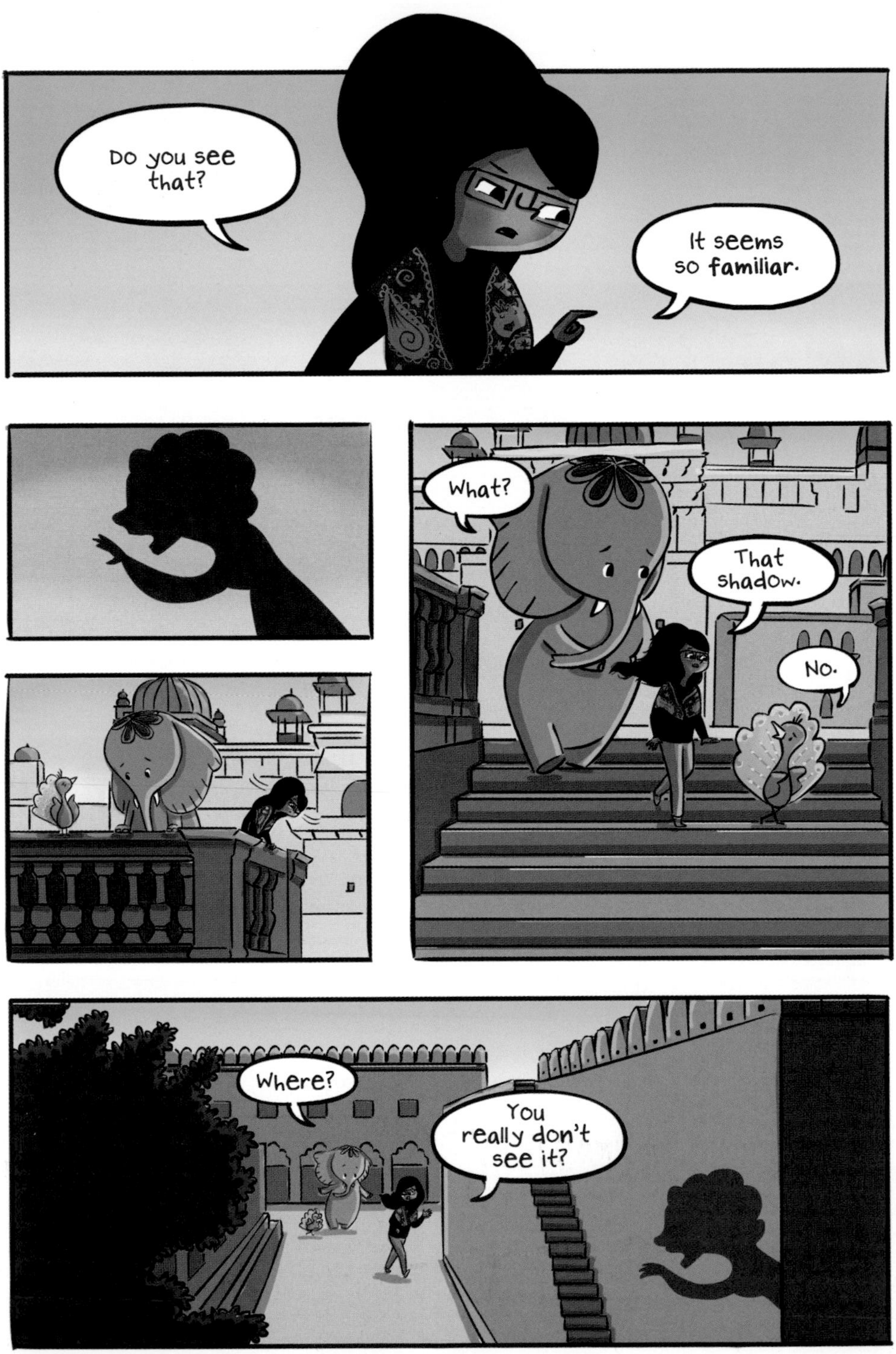
Do you see that?
It seems so familiar.
What?
That shadow.
No.
Where?
You really don't see it?

I wonder what it's doing here.

Trust us, it's not important.

Are you sure?

Of course!

It's samosa time!

WHOOSH

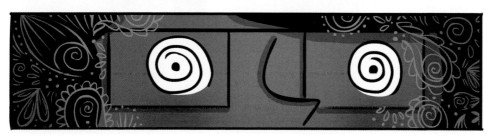

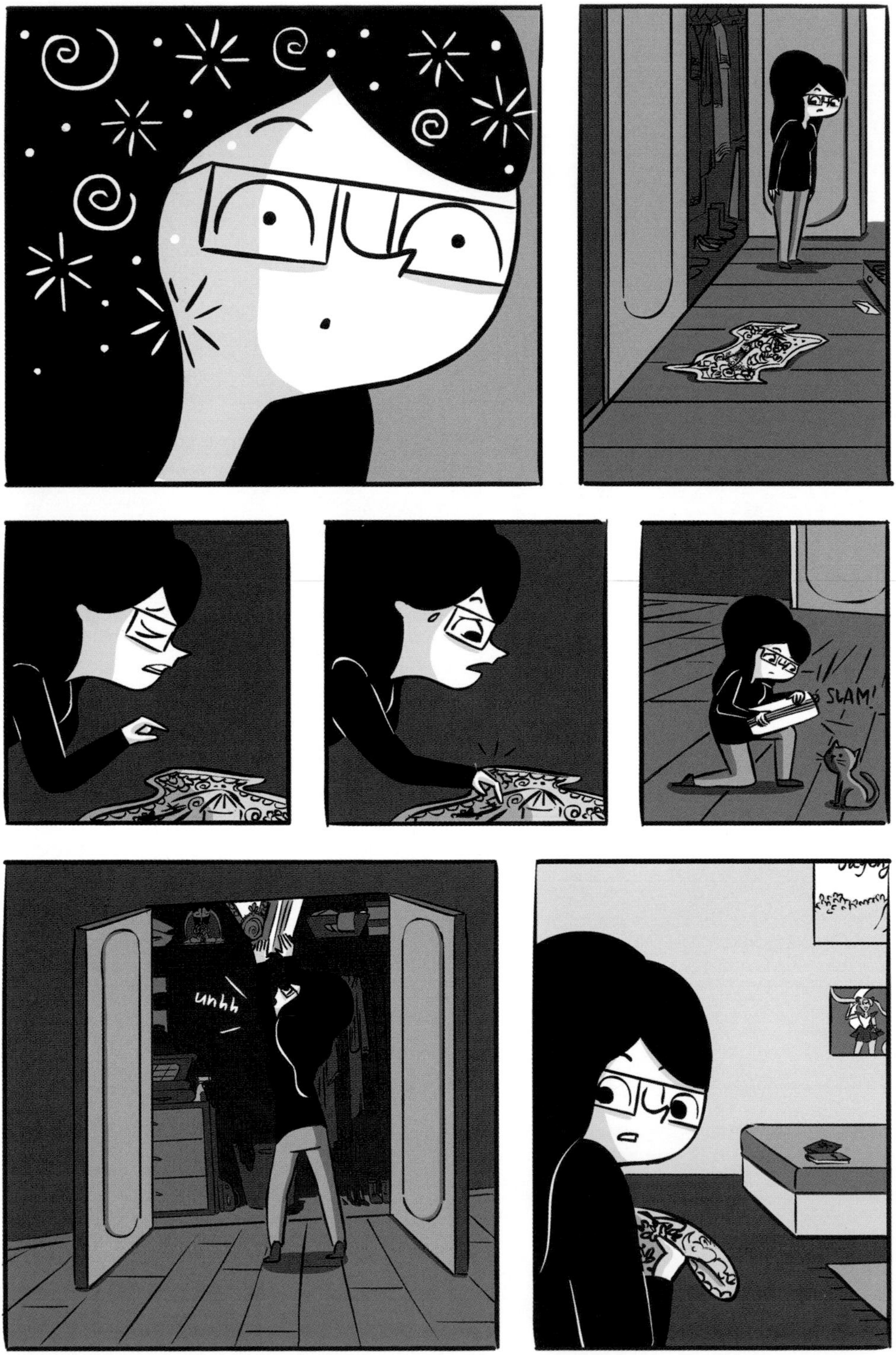
SLAM!
unhh

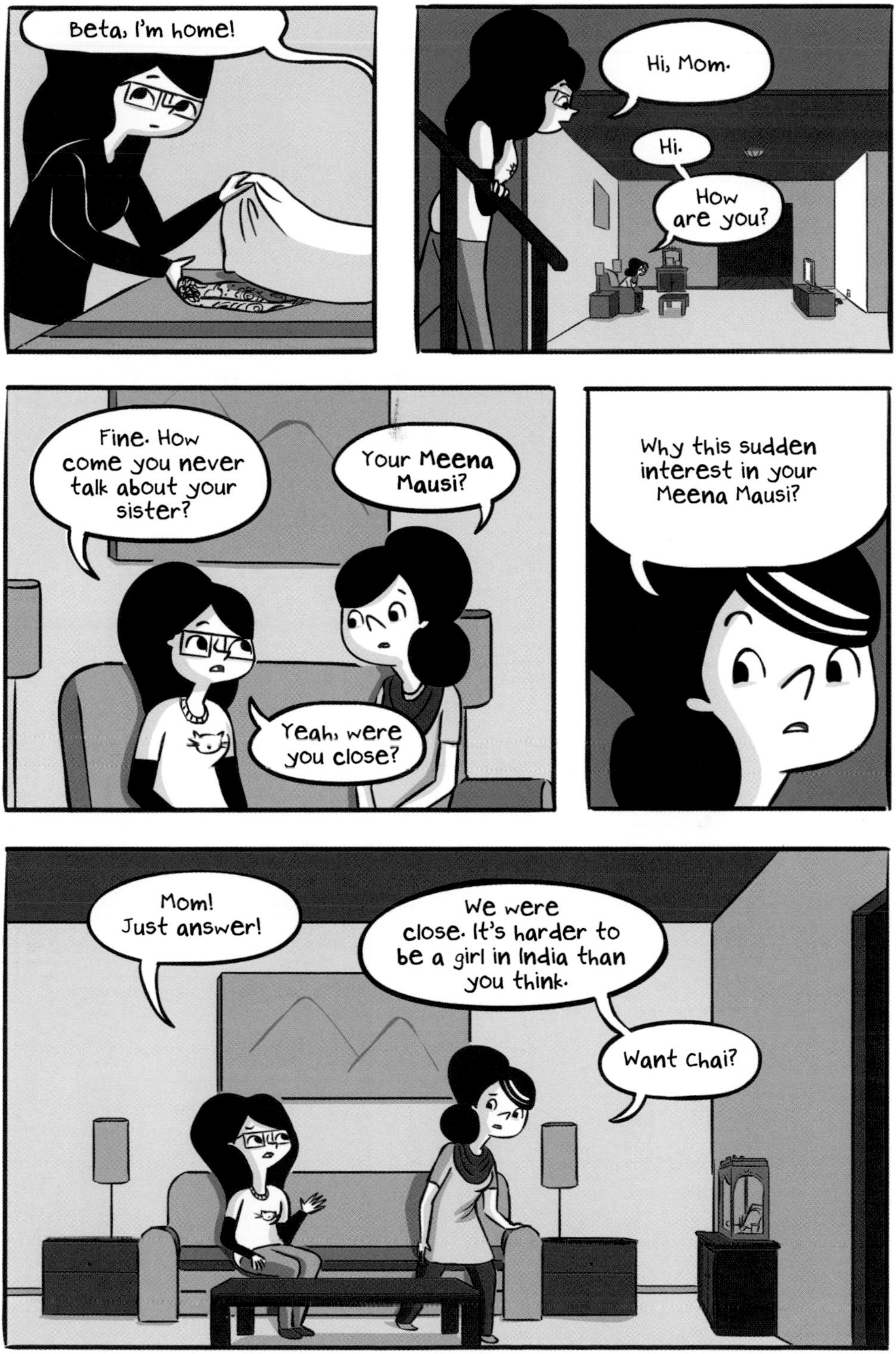
Beta, I'm home!
Hi, Mom.
Hi.
How are you?
Fine. How come you never talk about your sister?
Your Meena Mausi?
Yeah, were you close?
Why this sudden interest in your Meena Mausi?
Mom! Just answer!
We were close. It's harder to be a girl in India than you think.
Want chai?

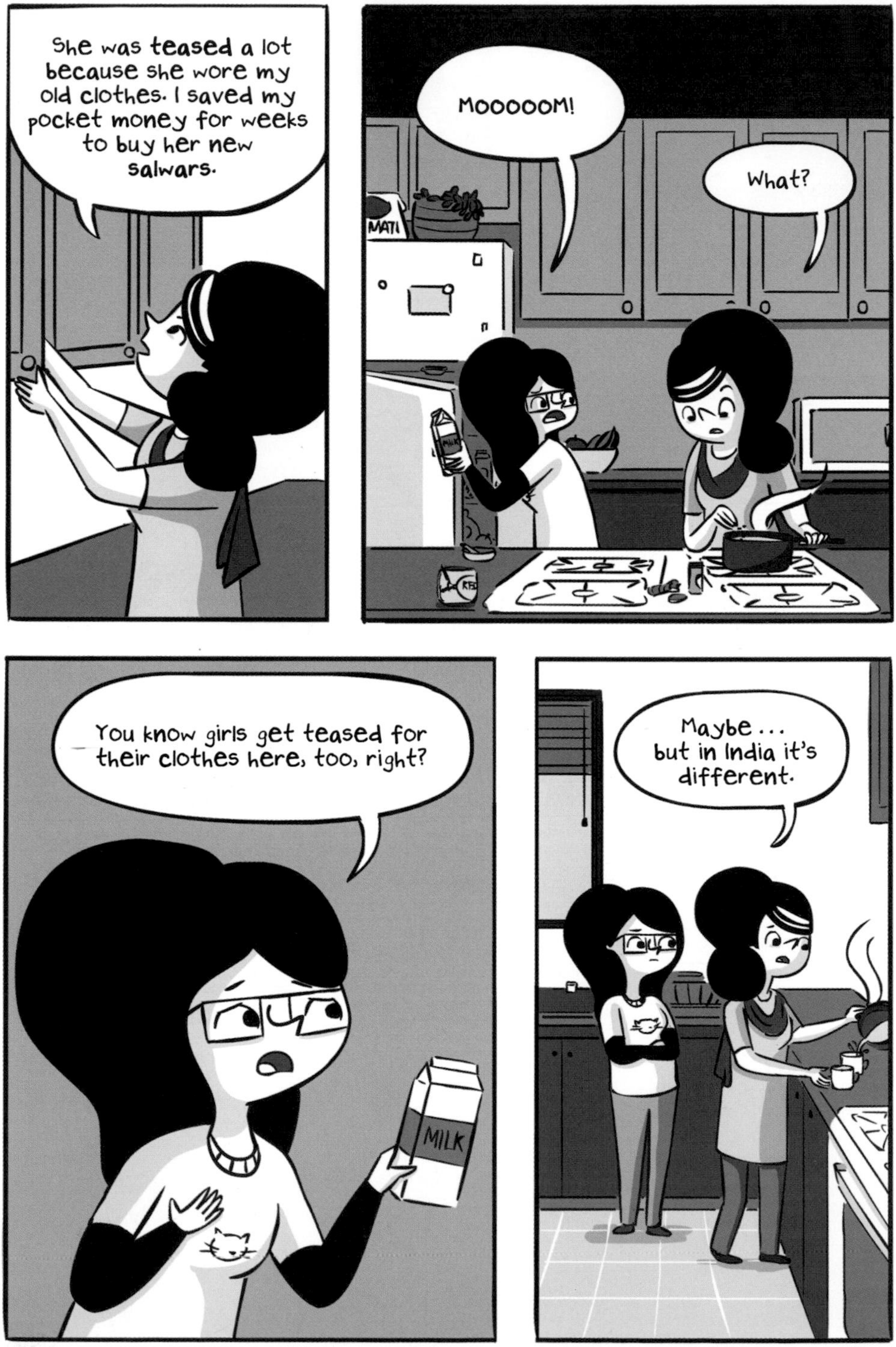
She was teased a lot because she wore my old clothes. I saved my pocket money for weeks to buy her new salwars.
MOOOOOM!
What?
MATI
MILK
You know girls get teased for their clothes here, too, right?
MILK
Maybe... but in India it's different.

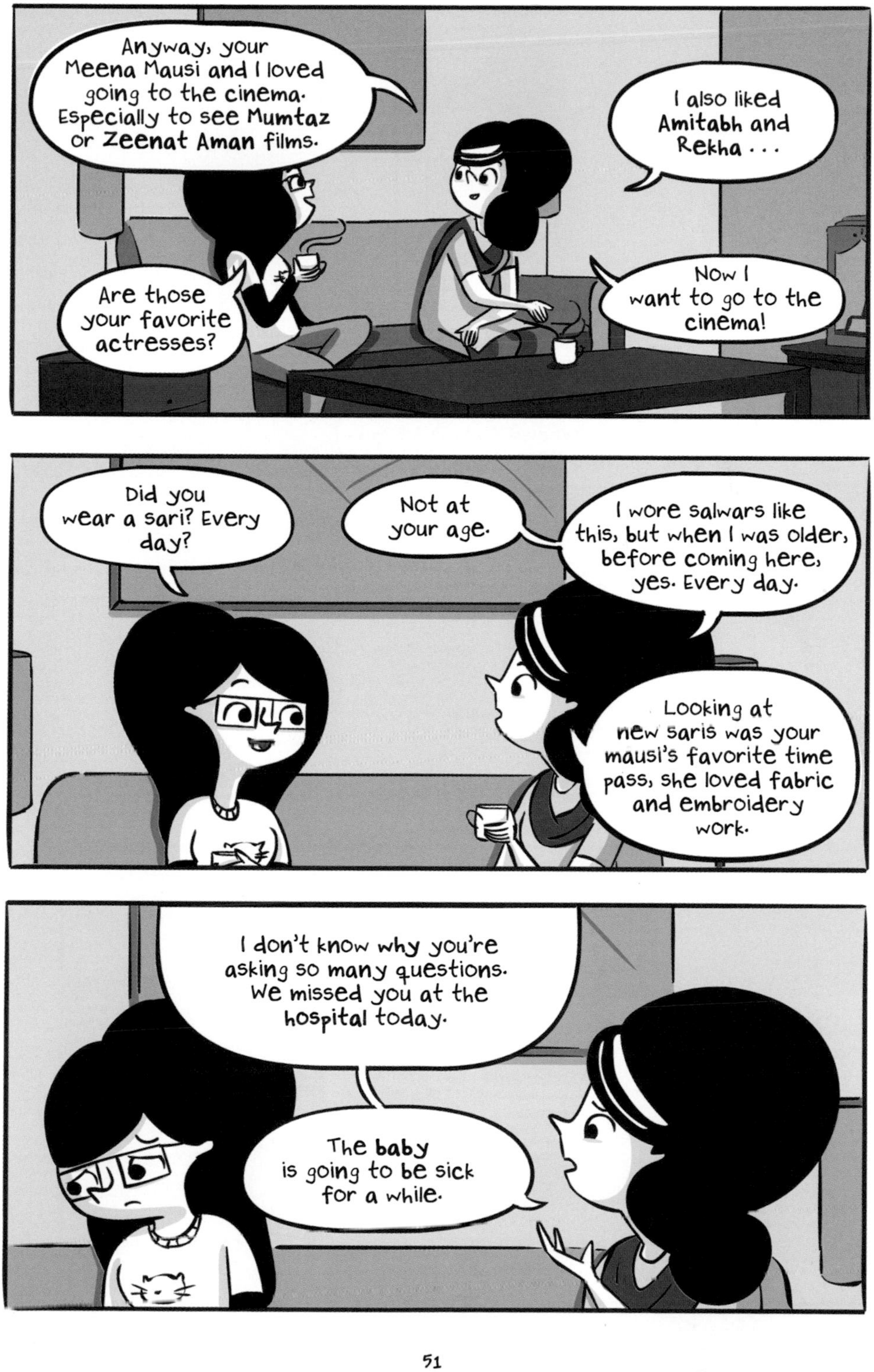
Anyway, your Meena Mausi and I loved going to the cinema. Especially to see Mumtaz or Zeenat Aman films.
I also liked Amitabh and Rekha . . .
Are those your favorite actresses?
Now I want to go to the cinema!
Did you wear a sari? Every day?
Not at your age.
I wore salwars like this, but when I was older, before coming here, yes. Every day.
Looking at new saris was your mausi's favorite time pass, she loved fabric and embroidery work.
I don't know why you're asking so many questions. We missed you at the hospital today.
The baby is going to be sick for a while.

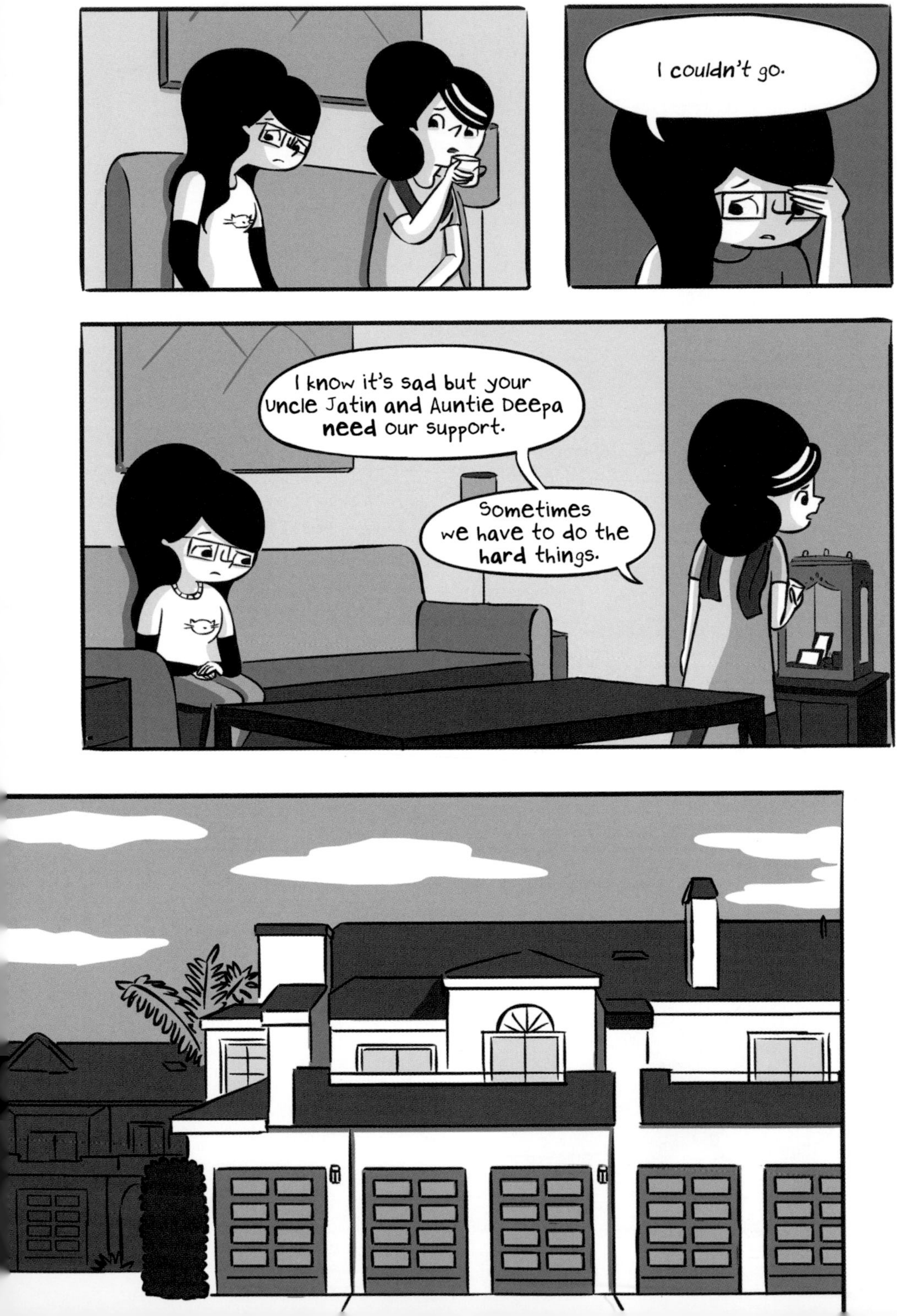
I couldn't go.
I know it's sad but your Uncle Jatin and Auntie Deepa **need** our support.
Sometimes we have to do the **hard** things.

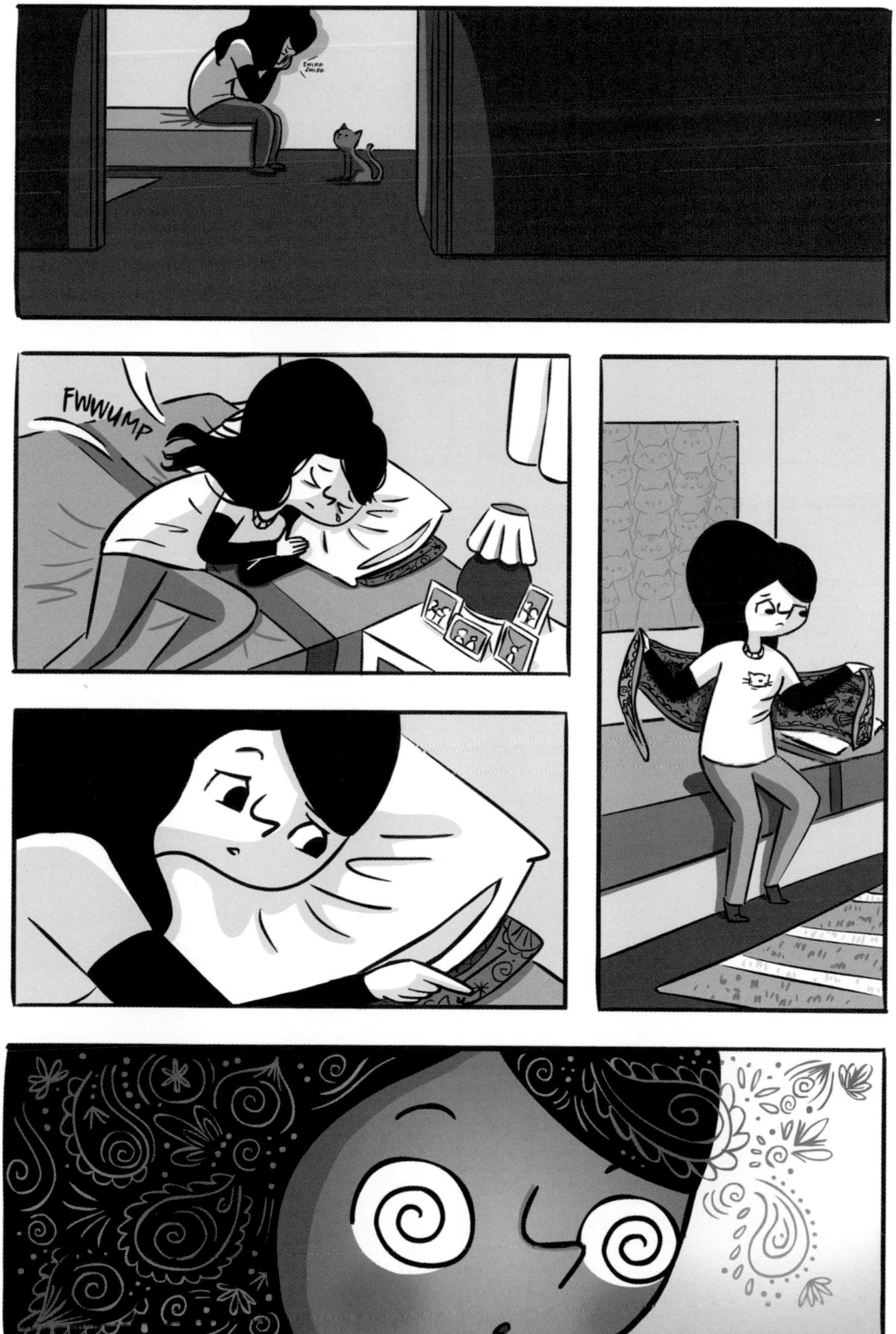
SNIFF
SNIFF
FWWUMP

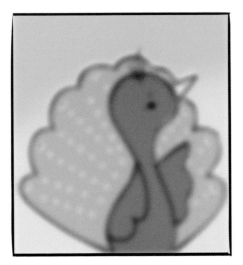

What happened?

I can't see!

Say good-bye to those date killers, Priyanka Das!

It's Pri. Whoa, how strange.

Oh my gulab jamun, you're in for a treat!

Huh?

Follow me.

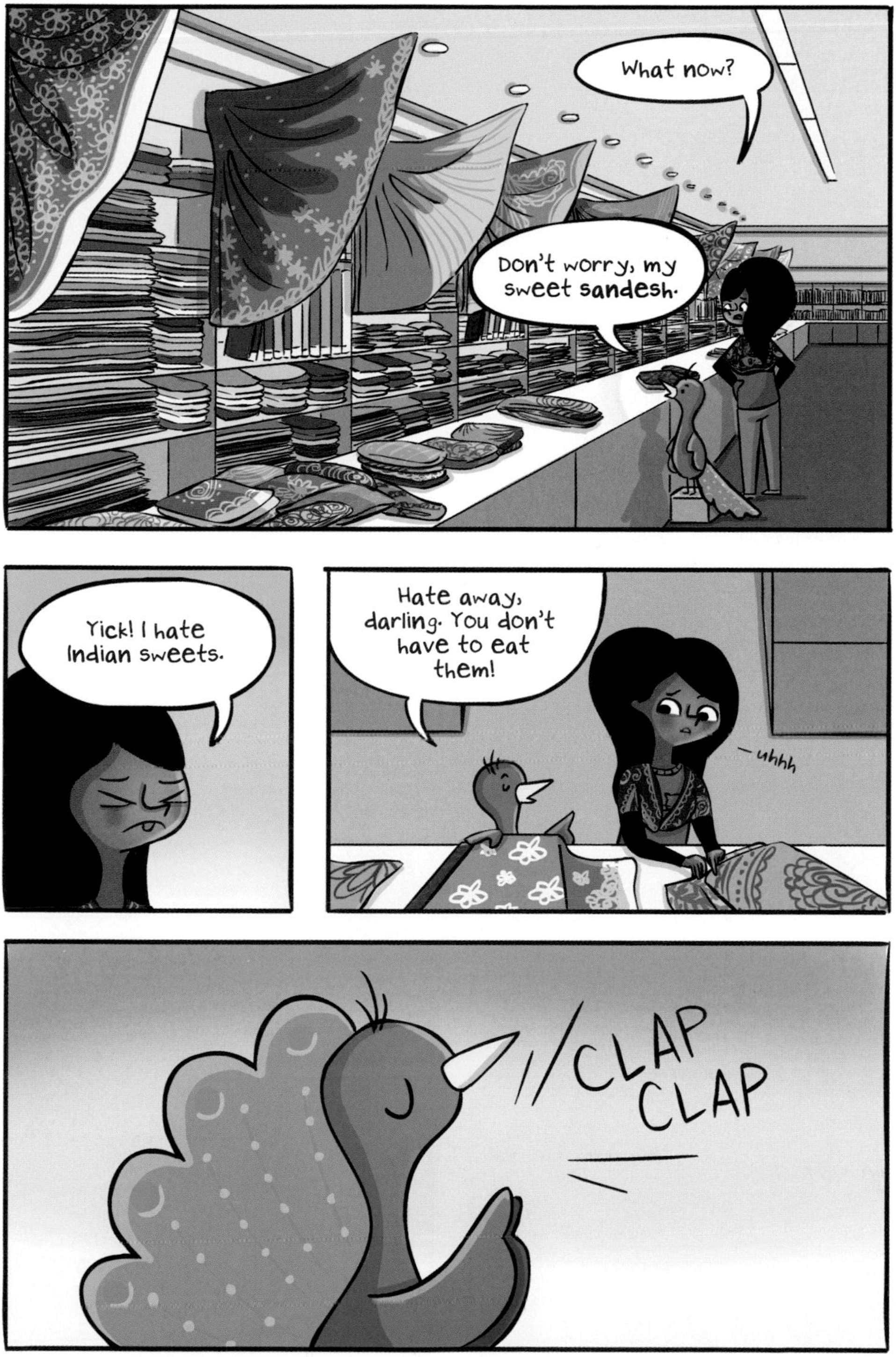
What now?
Don't worry, my sweet sandesh.
Yick! I hate Indian sweets.
Hate away, darling. You don't have to eat them!
uhhh
CLAP CLAP

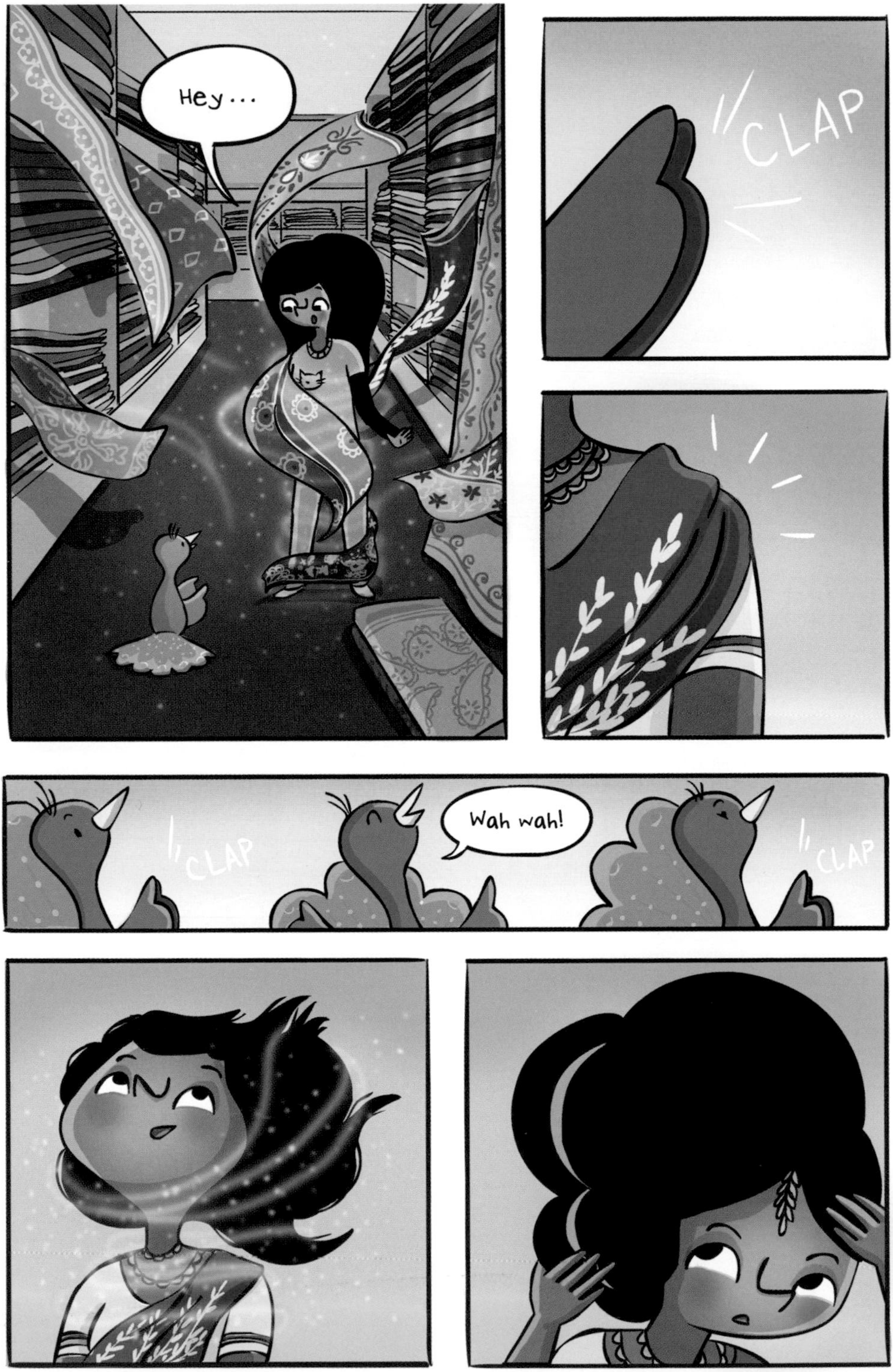
Hey...
CLAP
Wah wah!
CLAP
CLAP

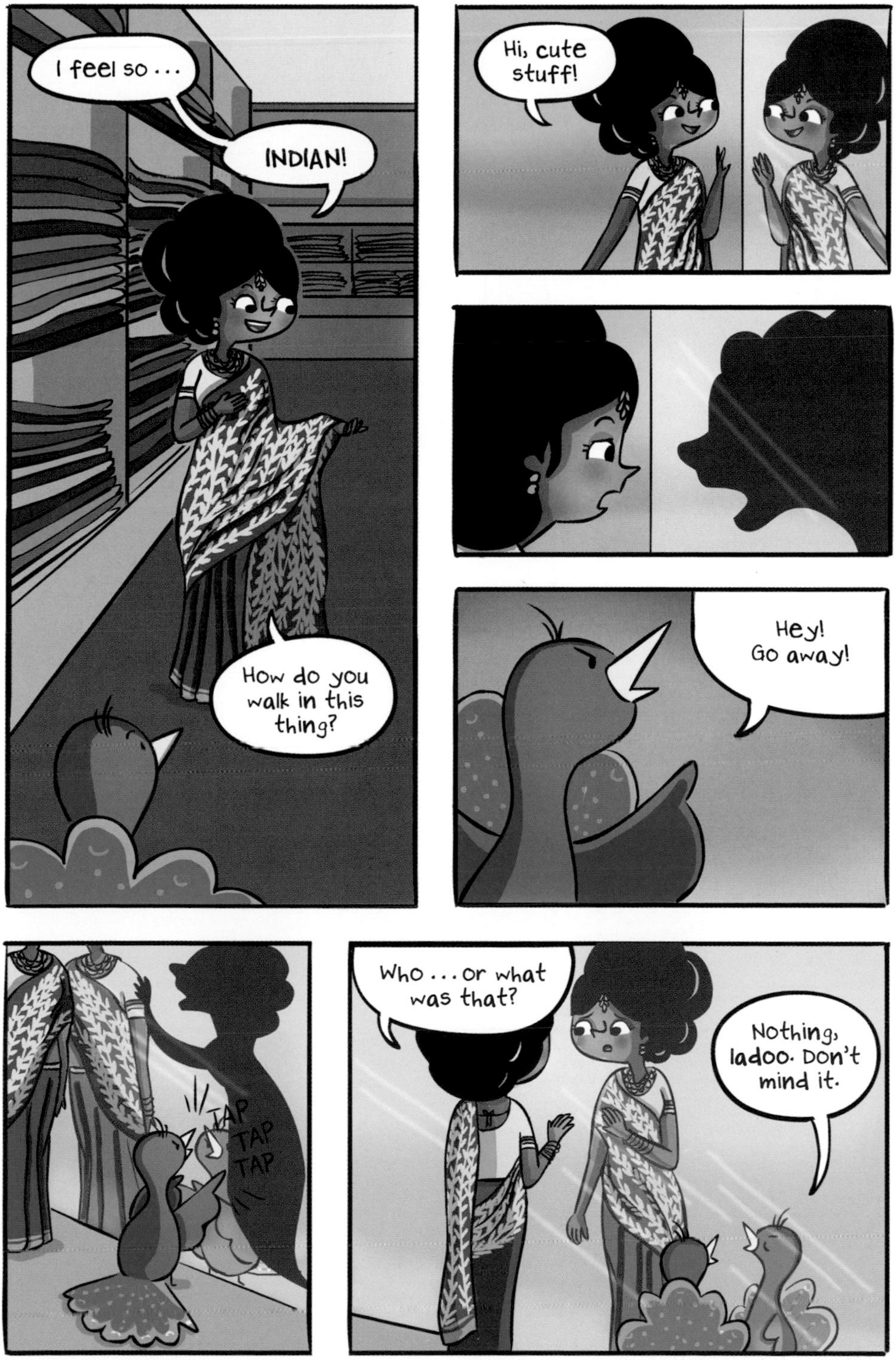
I feel so . . .
INDIAN!
How do you walk in this thing?
Hi, cute stuff!
Hey! Go away!
TAP TAP TAP
Who . . . or what was that?
Nothing, ladoo. Don't mind it.

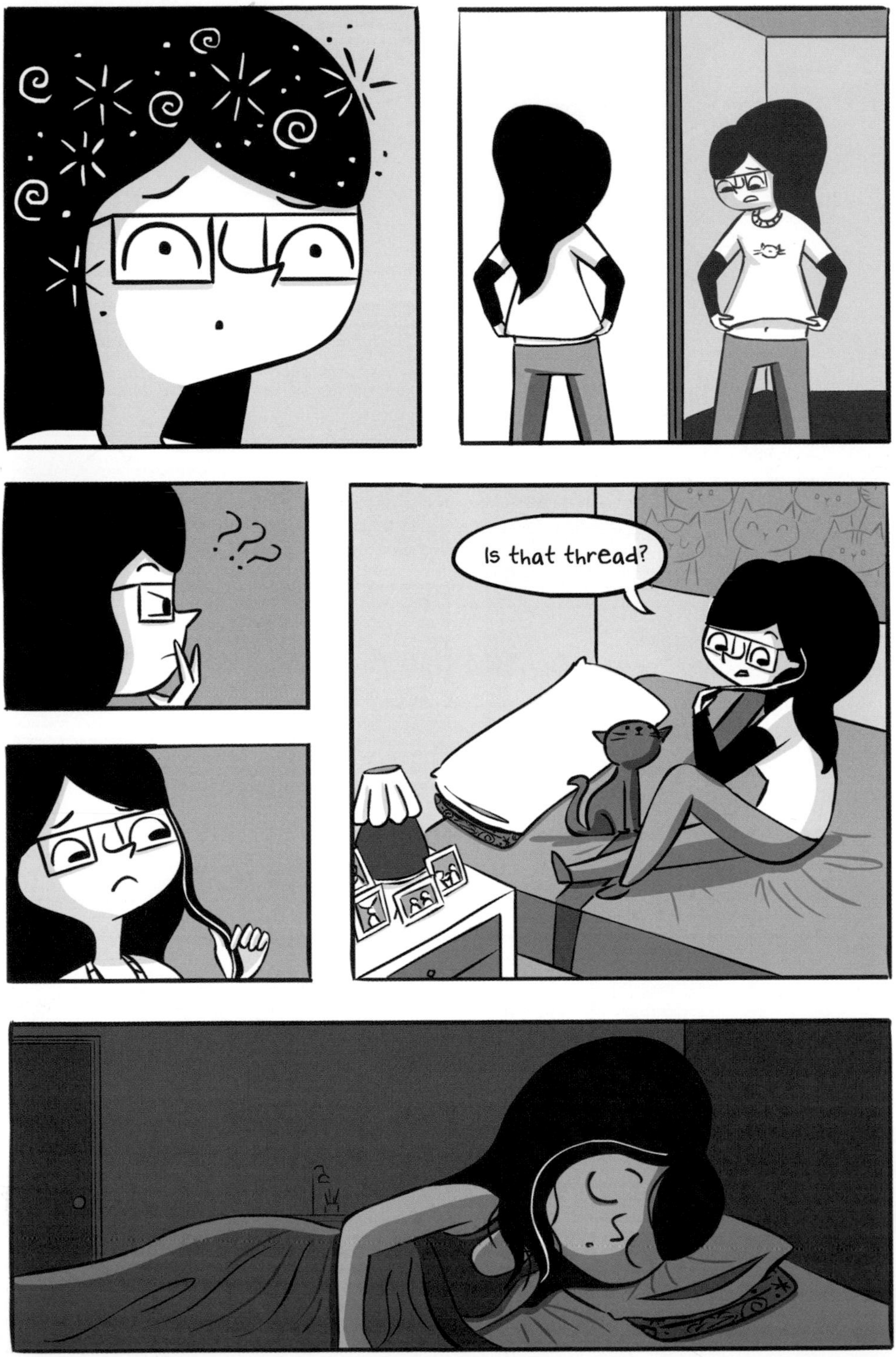
Is that thread?

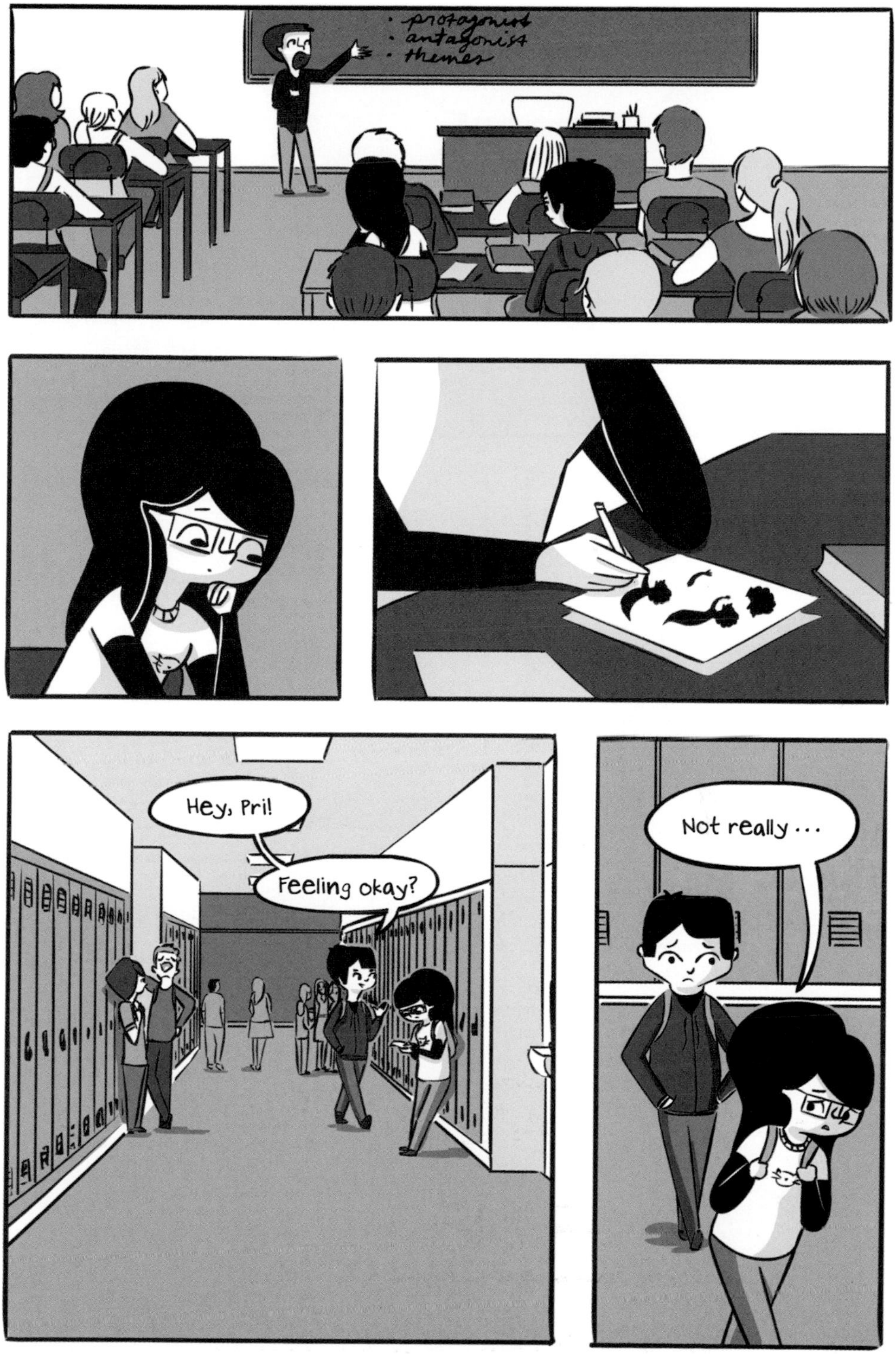

protagonist
antagonist
themes
Hey, Pri!
Feeling okay?
Not really . . .

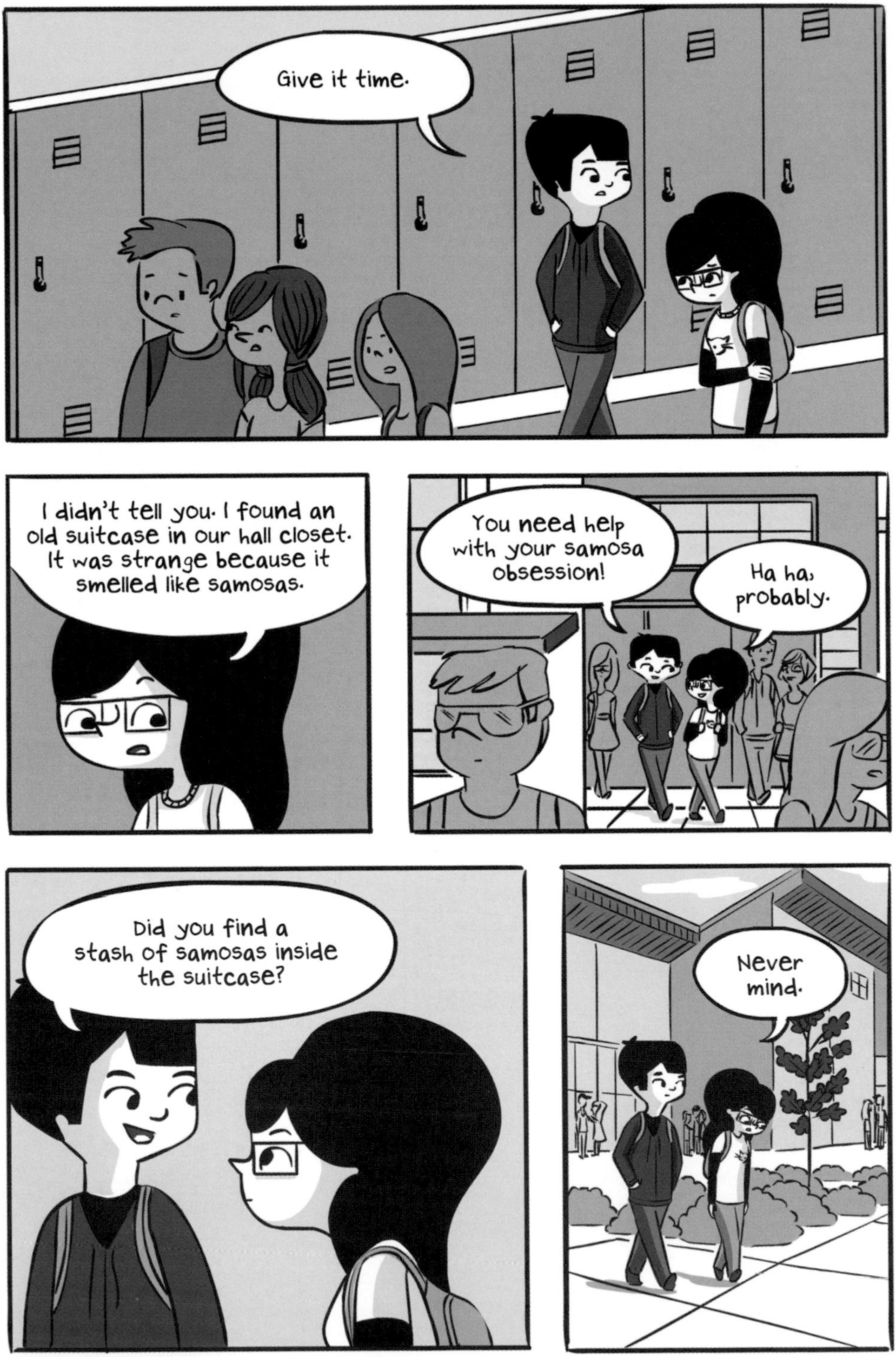
Give it time.
I didn't tell you. I found an old suitcase in our hall closet. It was strange because it smelled like samosas.
You need help with your samosa obsession!
Ha ha, probably.
Did you find a stash of samosas inside the suitcase?
Never mind.

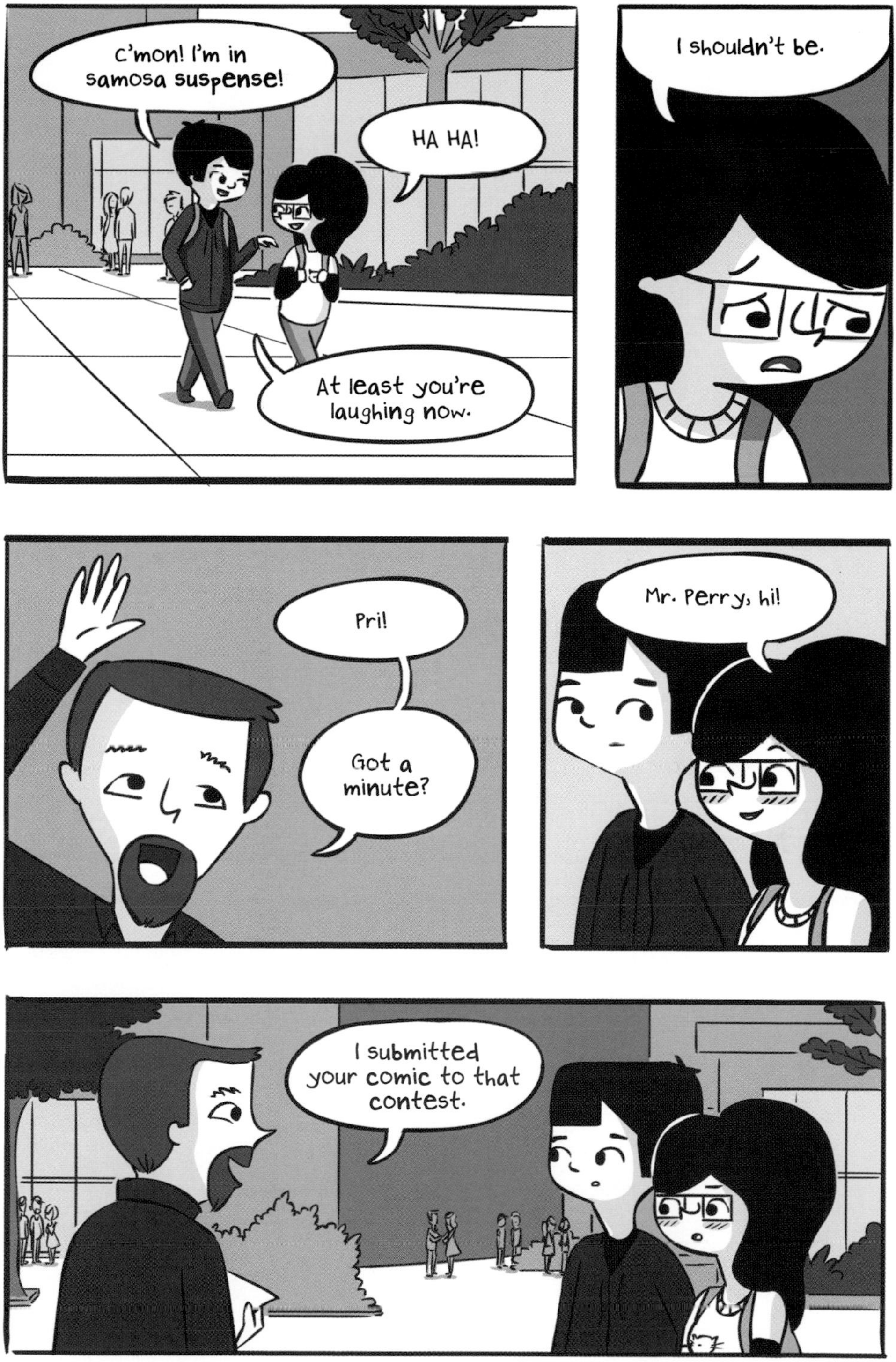
C'mon! I'm in samosa suspense!
HA HA!
At least you're laughing now.
I shouldn't be.
Pri!
Got a minute?
Mr. Perry, hi!
I submitted your comic to that contest.

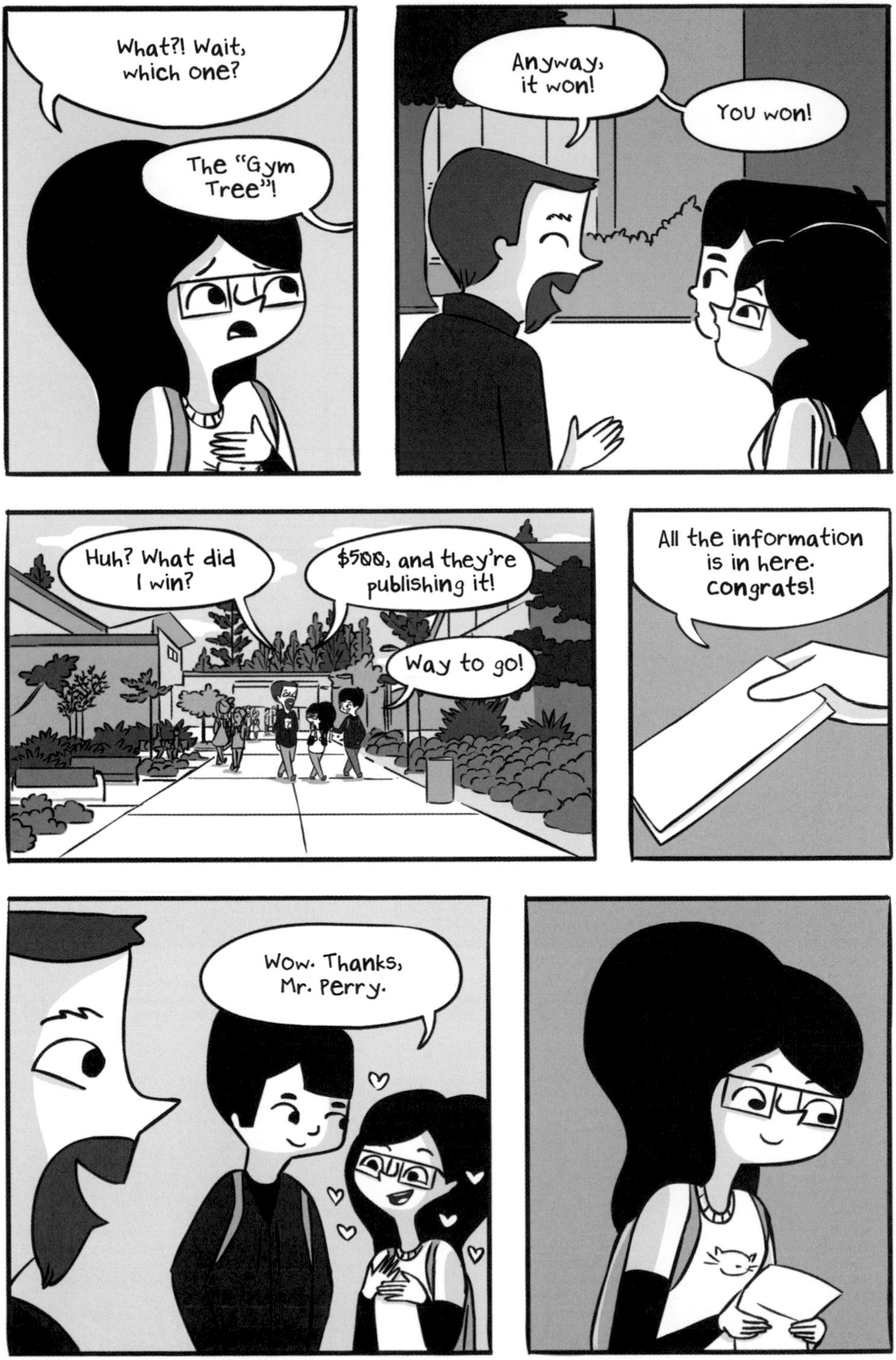
What?! Wait, which one?
The "Gym Tree"!
Anyway, it won!
YOU won!
Huh? What did I win?
$500, and they're publishing it!
Way to go!
All the information is in here. congrats!
Wow. Thanks, Mr. Perry.

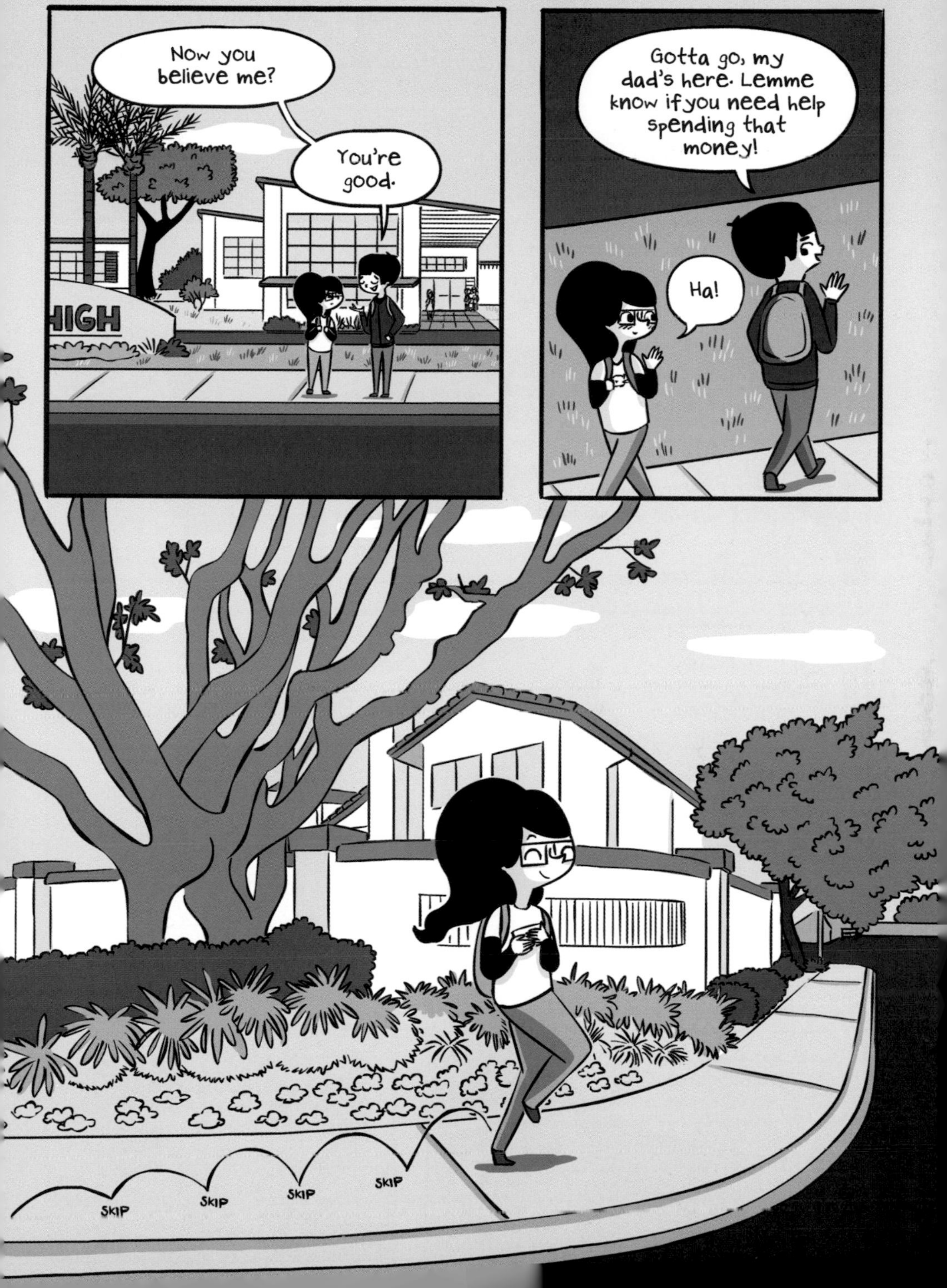
Now you believe me?
You're good.
HIGH
Gotta go, my dad's here. Lemme know if you need help spending that money!
Ha!
SKIP
SKIP
SKIP
SKIP

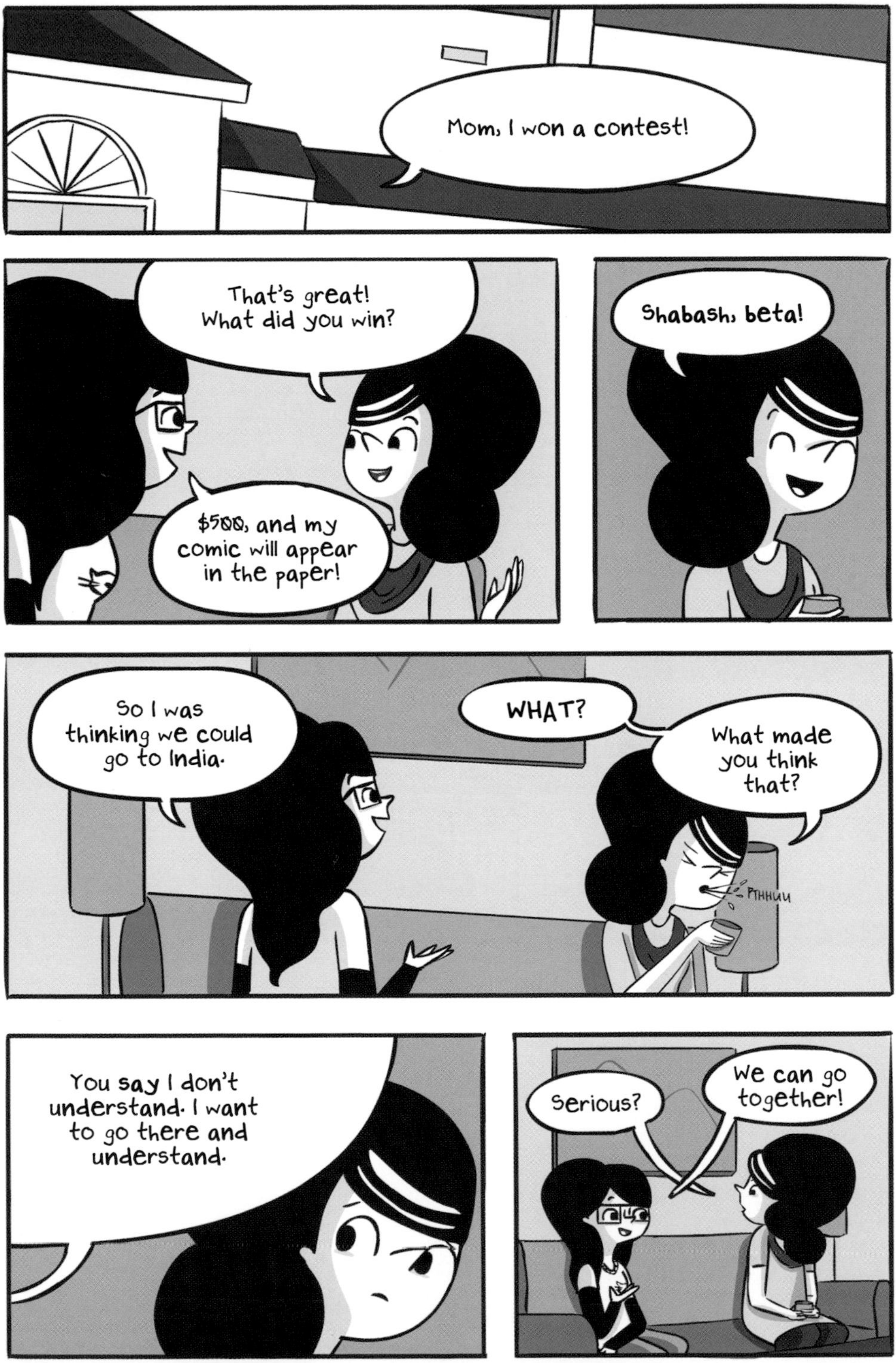
Mom, I won a contest!
That's great! What did you win?
$500, and my comic will appear in the paper!
Shabash, beta!
So I was thinking we could go to India.
WHAT?
What made you think that?
PTHHUU
You say I don't understand. I want to go there and understand.
Serious?
We can go together!

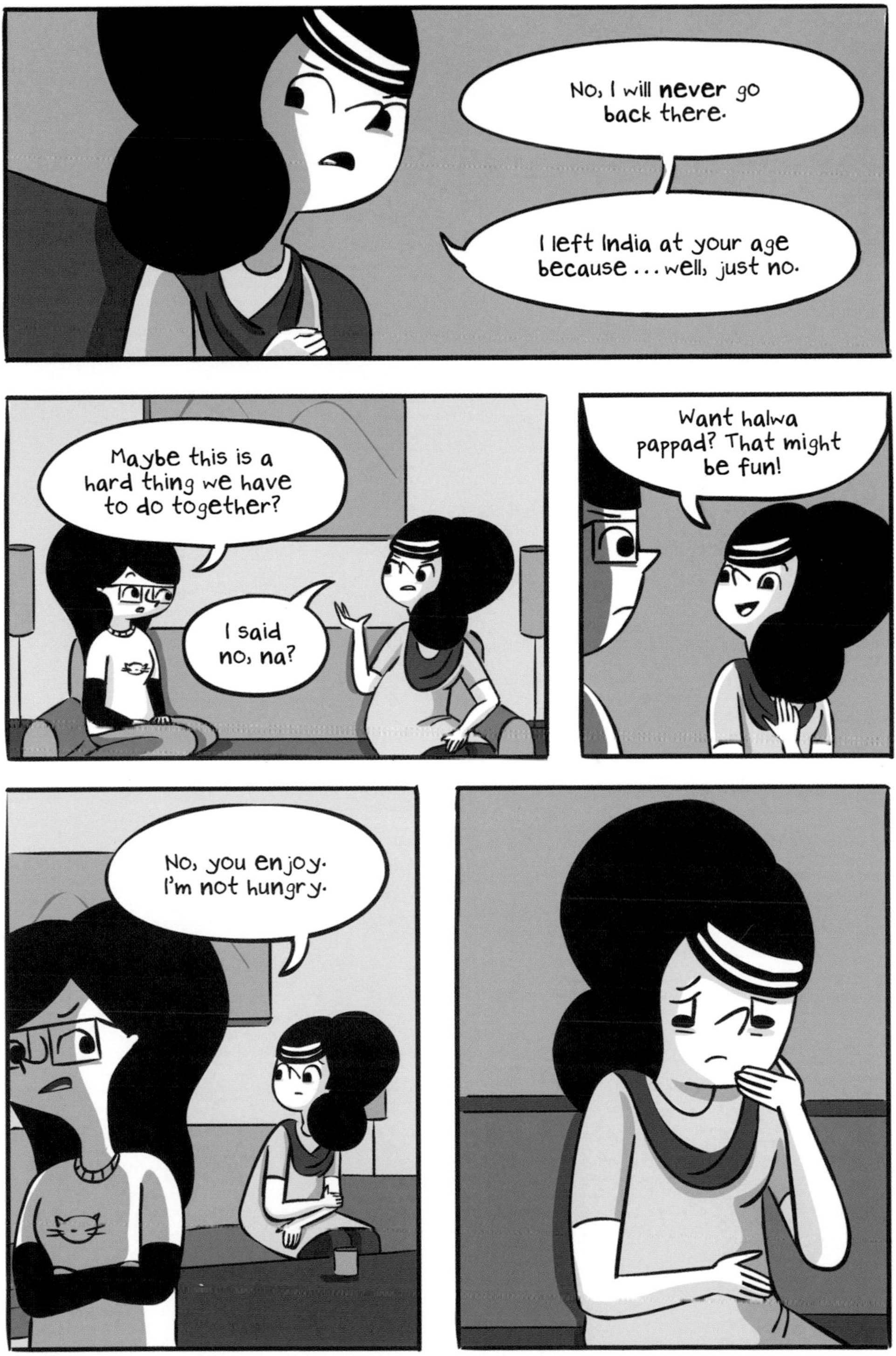

No, I will **never** go back there.
I left India at your age because . . . well, just no.
Maybe this is a hard thing we have to do together?
I said no, na?
Want halwa pappad? That might be fun!
No, you enjoy. I'm not hungry.

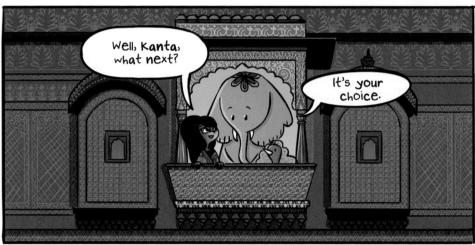

Well, Kanta, what next?

It's your choice.

What do you want to see?

I guess I want to see more.

Done!

1/ CLAP CLAP

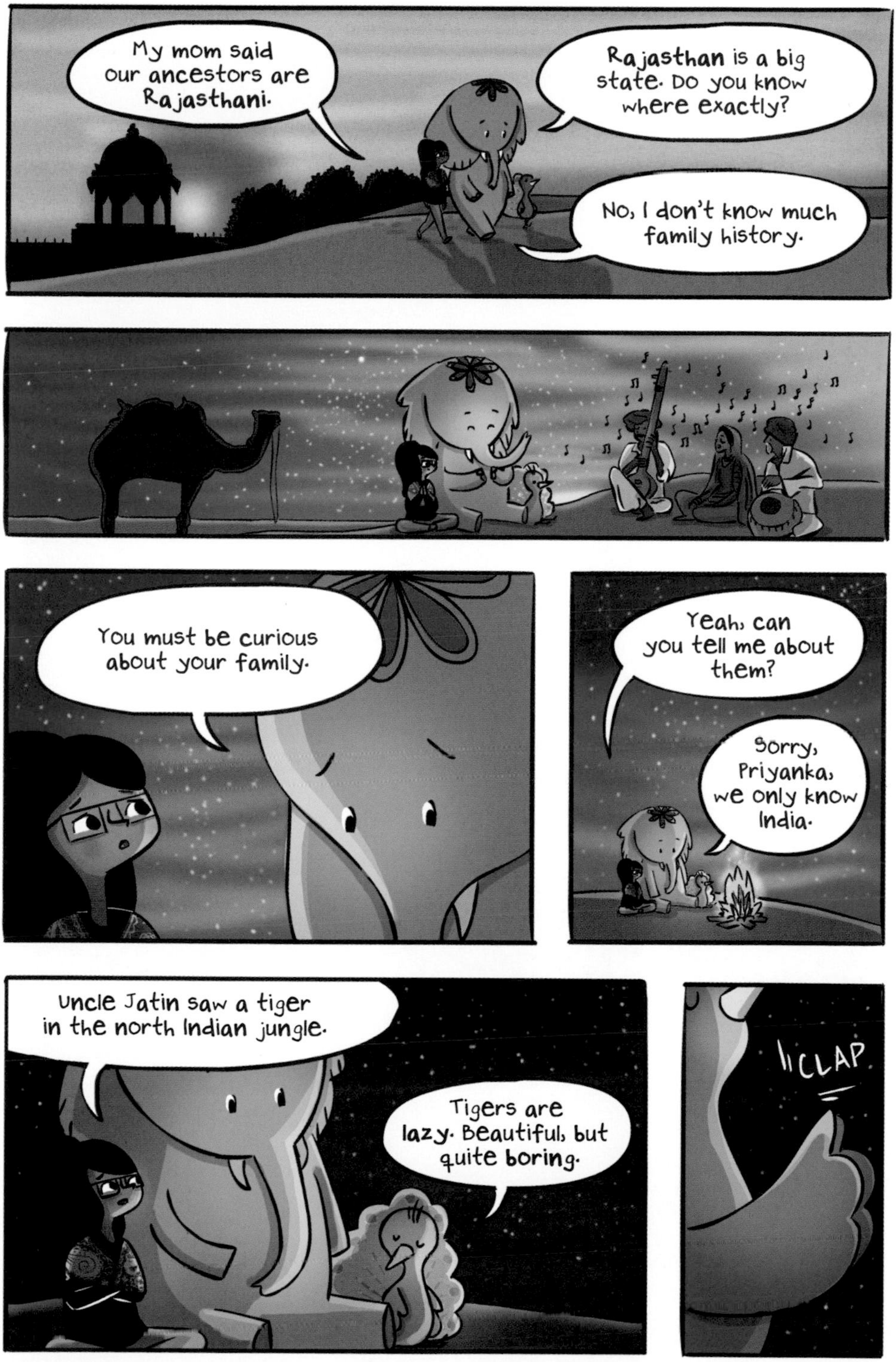
My mom said our ancestors are Rajasthani.
Rajasthan is a big state. Do you know where exactly?
No, I don't know much family history.
You must be curious about your family.
Yeah, can you tell me about them?
Sorry, Priyanka, we only know India.
Uncle Jatin saw a tiger in the north Indian jungle.
Tigers are lazy. Beautiful, but quite boring.
CLAP

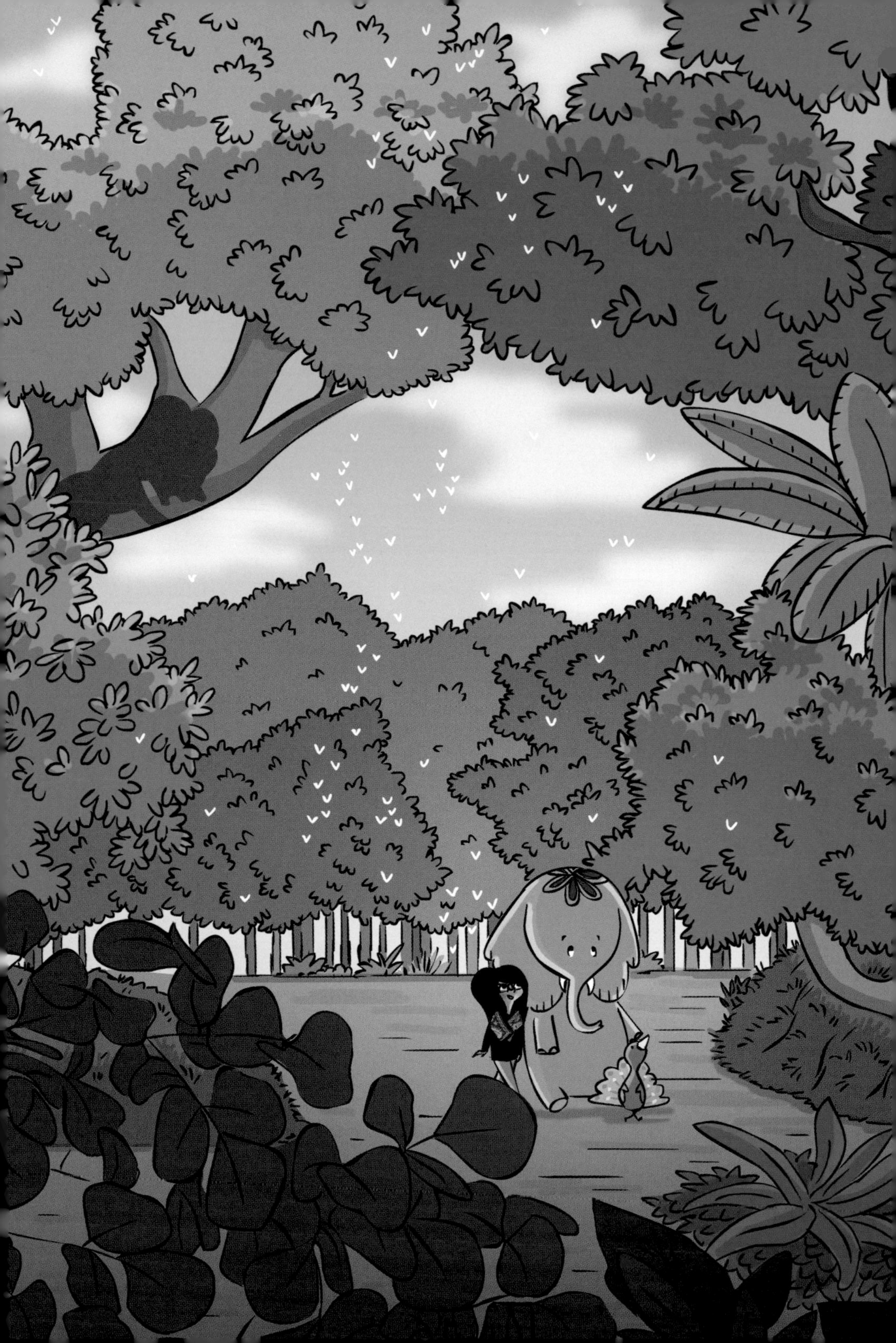

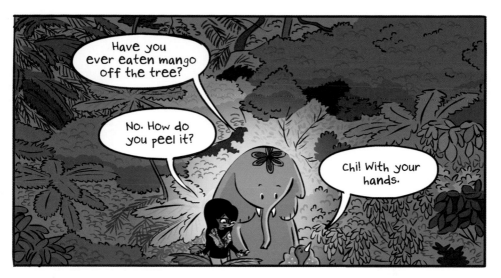

Have you ever eaten mango off the tree?

No. How do you peel it?

Chi! With your hands.

Here, Mayur. I peeled one for you.

oh!

hi!

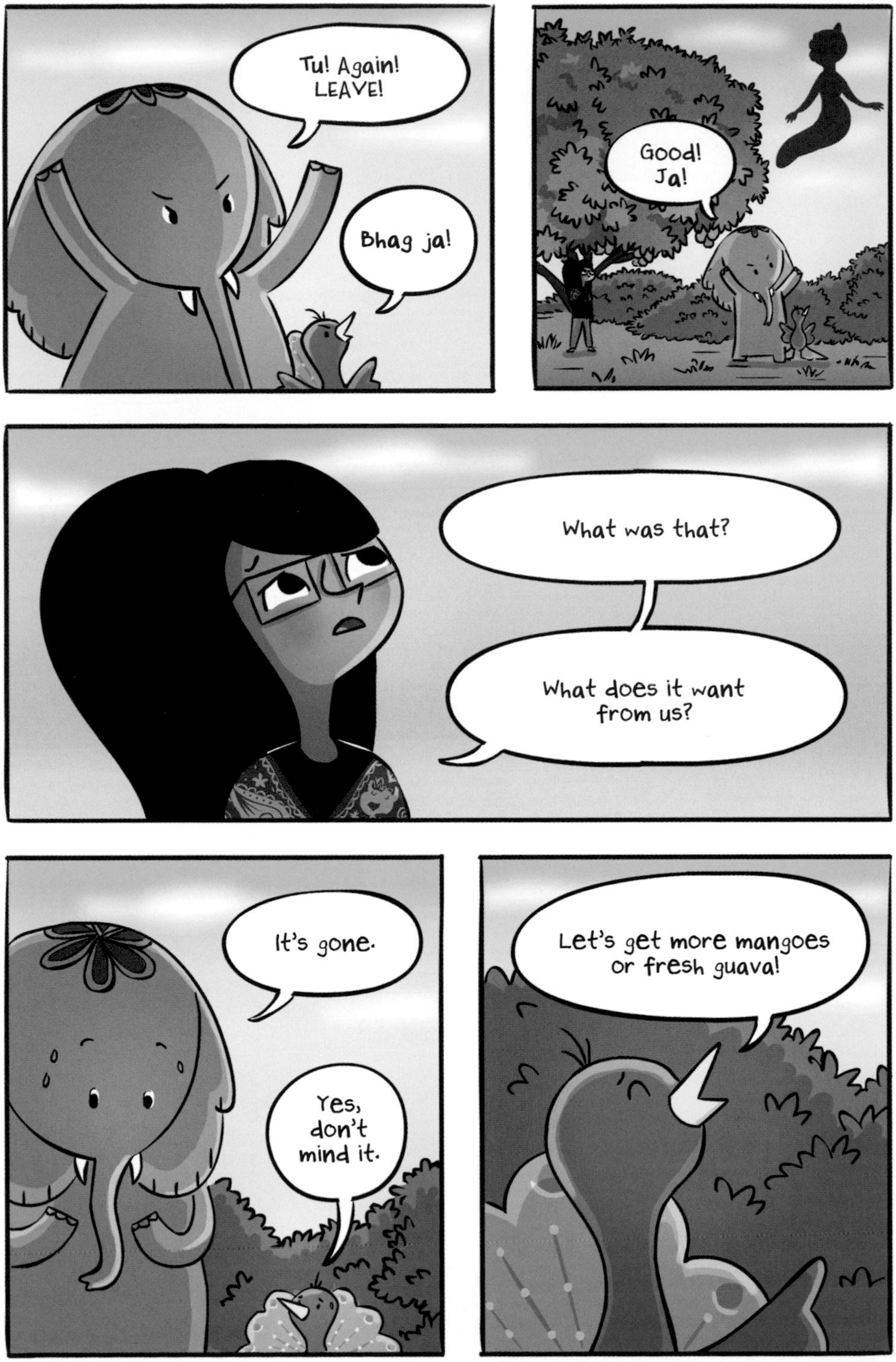
Tu! Again!
LEAVE!
Bhag ja!
Good!
Ja!
What was that?
What does it want
from us?
It's gone.
Yes,
don't
mind it.
Let's get more mangoes
or fresh guava!

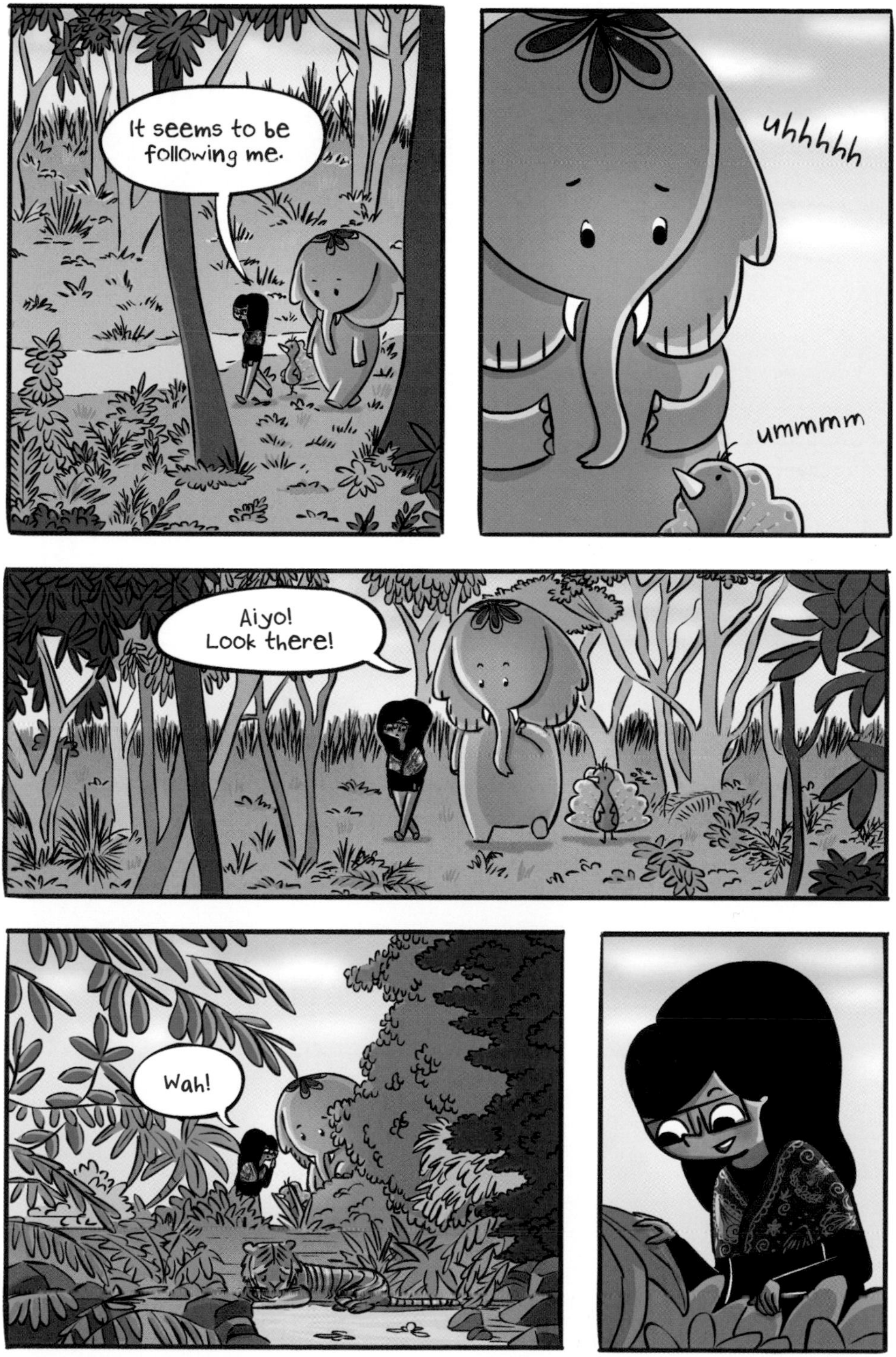
It seems to be following me.
uhhhhh
ummmm
Aiyo! Look there!
Wah!

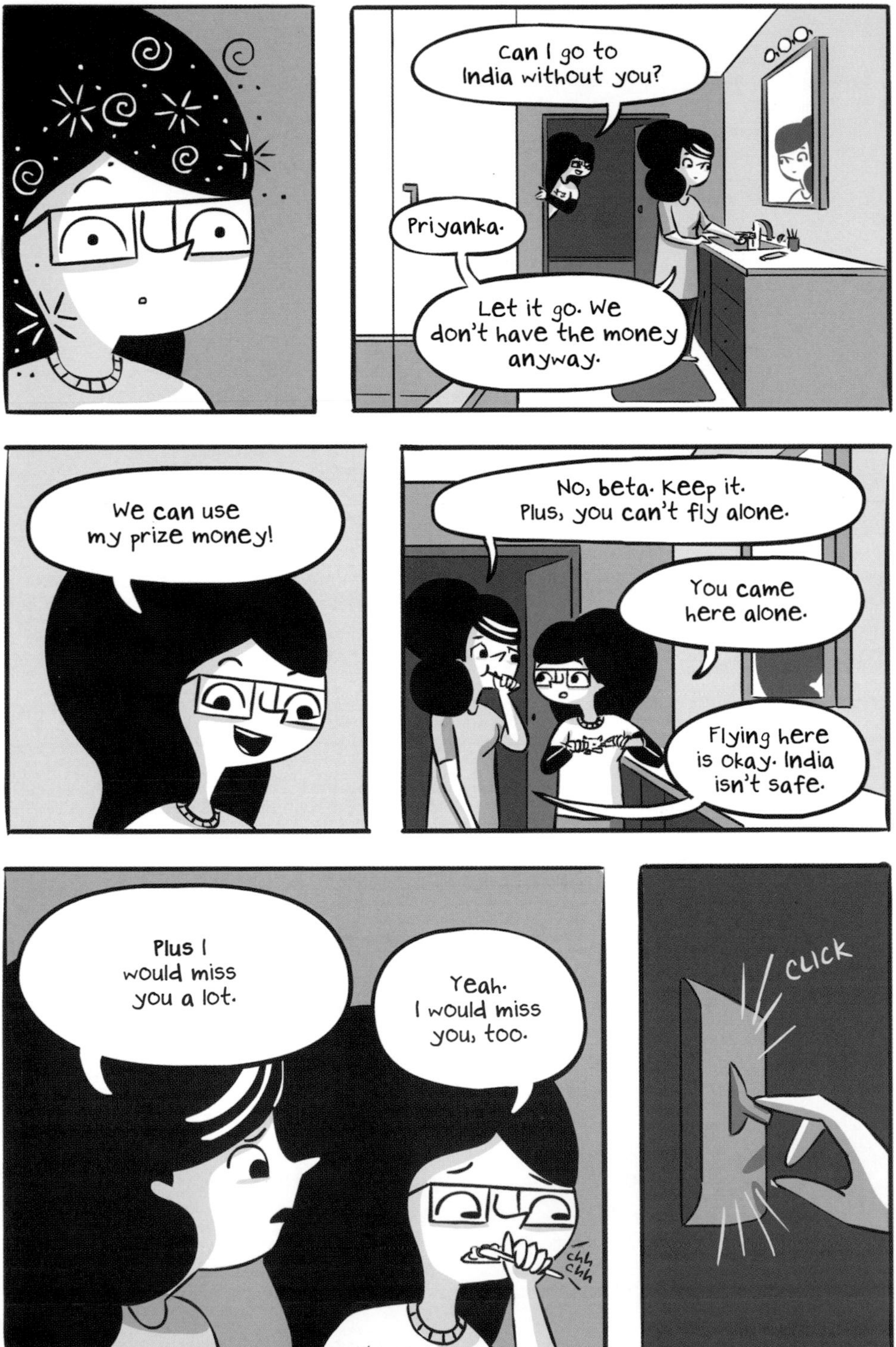
Can I go to India without you?
Priyanka.
Let it go. We don't have the money anyway.
We can use my prize money!
No, beta. Keep it. Plus, you can't fly alone.
You came here alone.
Flying here is okay. India isn't safe.
Plus I would miss you a lot.
Yeah. I would miss you, too.
chh chh chh
CLICK

How's my award-winning cartoonist?

Uhh, okay.

Working on the next great American comic?

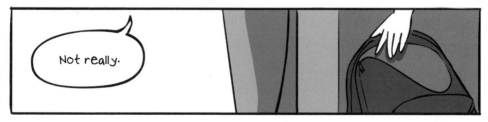

Not really.

Gotta go.

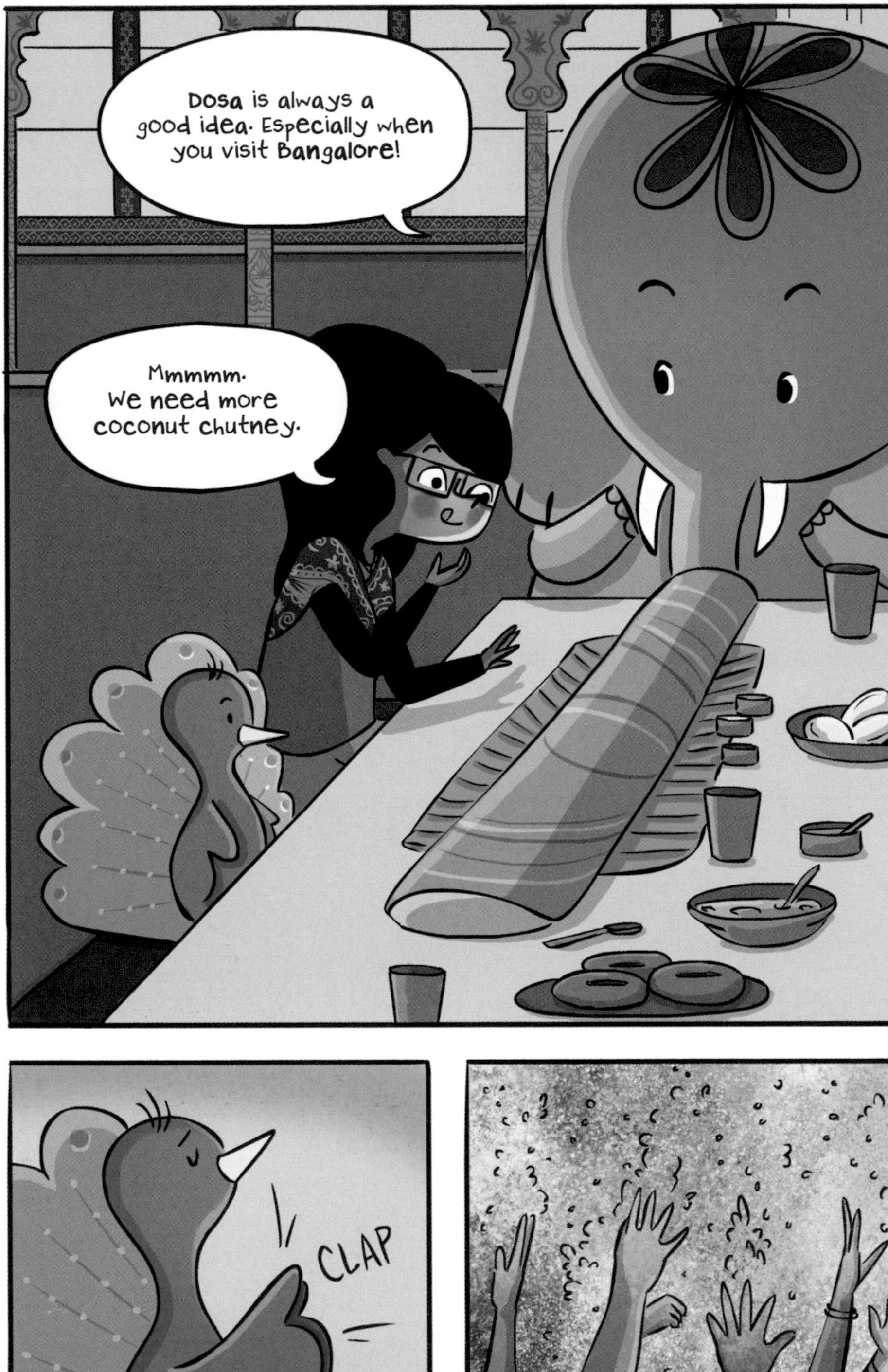
Dosa is always a good idea. Especially when you visit Bangalore!
Mmmmm. We need more coconut chutney.
CLAP

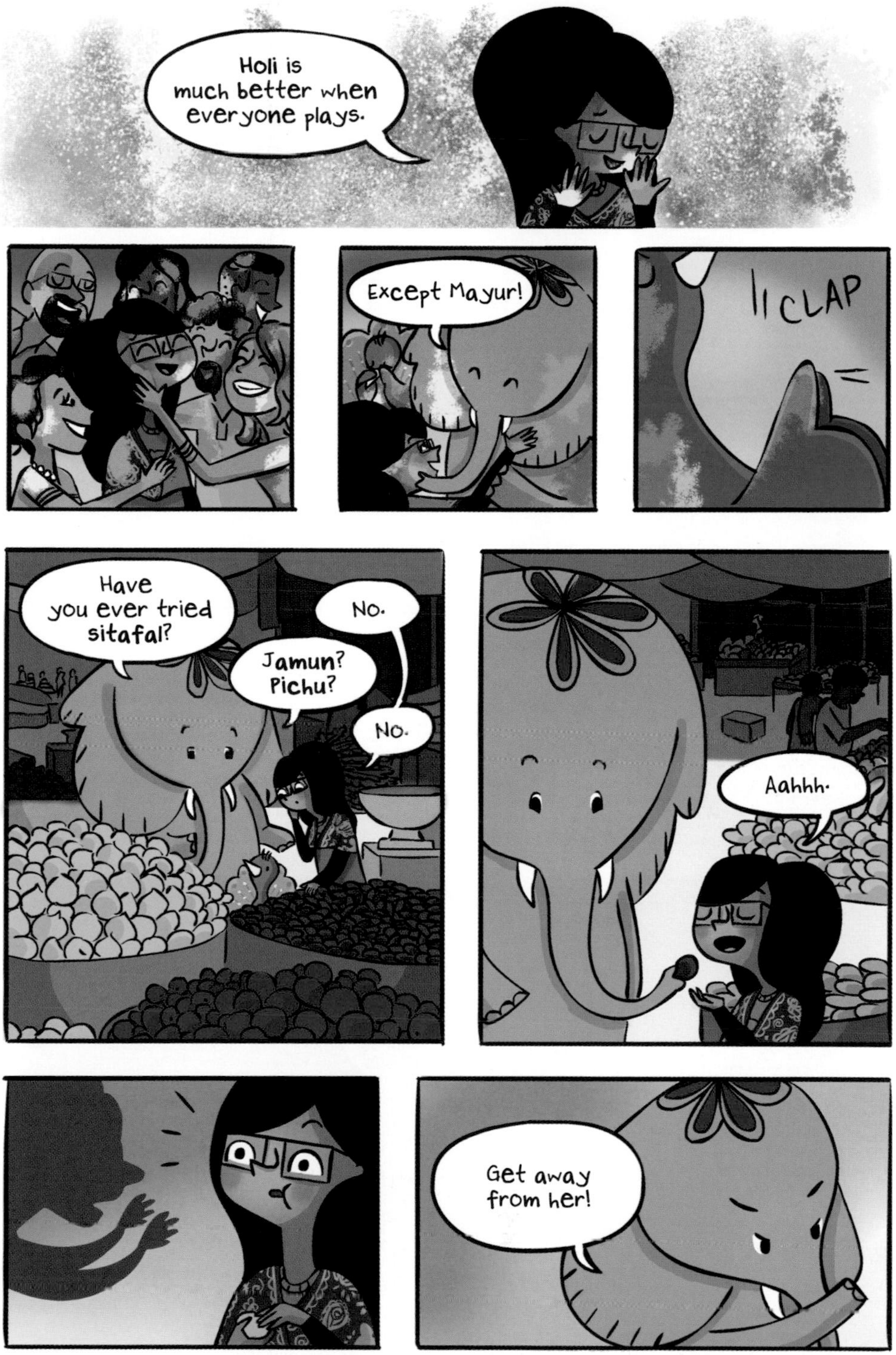
Holi is much better when everyone plays.
Except Mayur!
CLAP
Have you ever tried sitafal?
No.
Jamun? Pichu?
No.
Aahhh.
Get away from her!

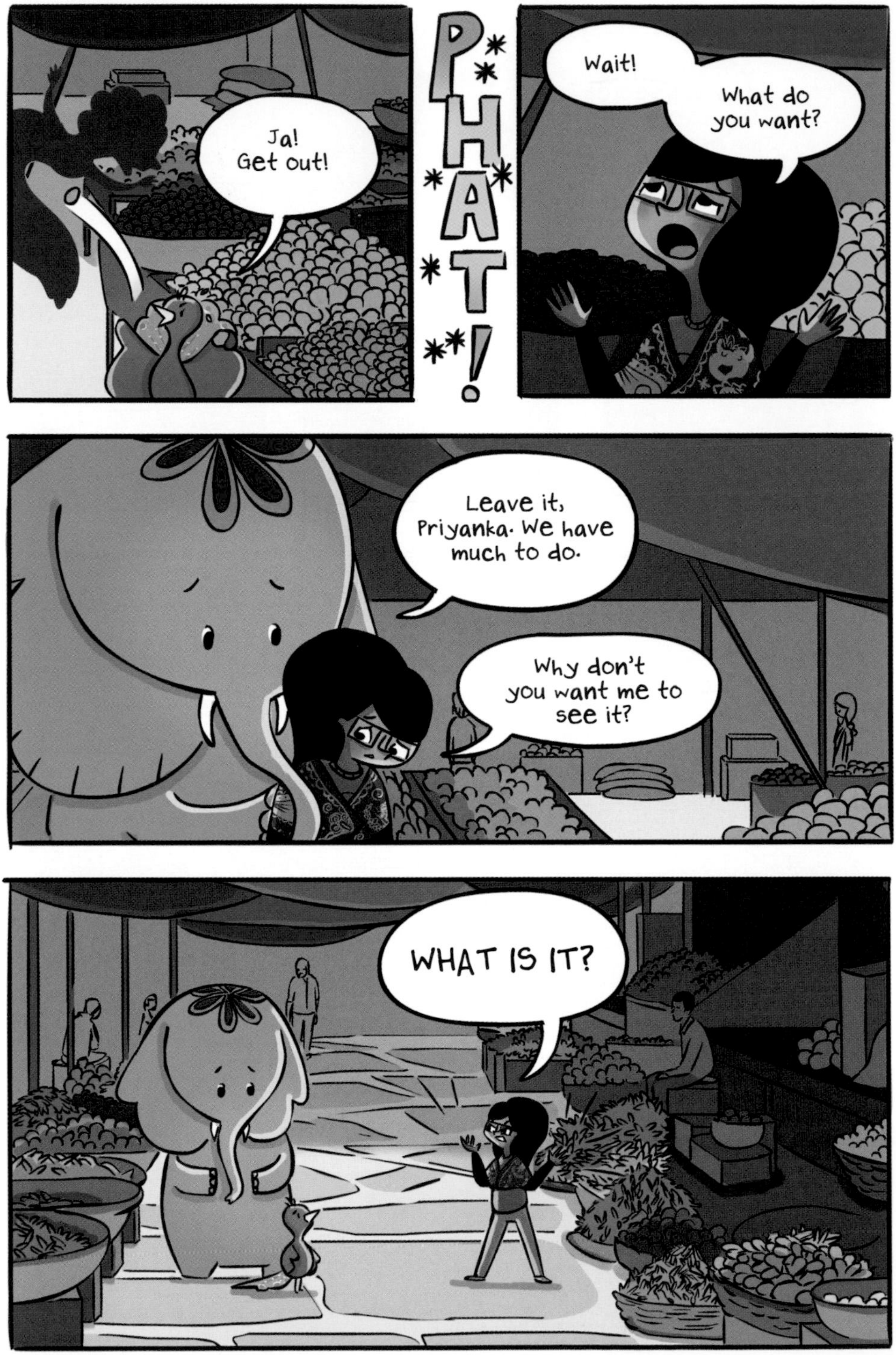
Ja! Get out!
PHAT!
Wait!
What do you want?
Leave it, Priyanka. We have much to do.
Why don't you want me to see it?
WHAT IS IT?

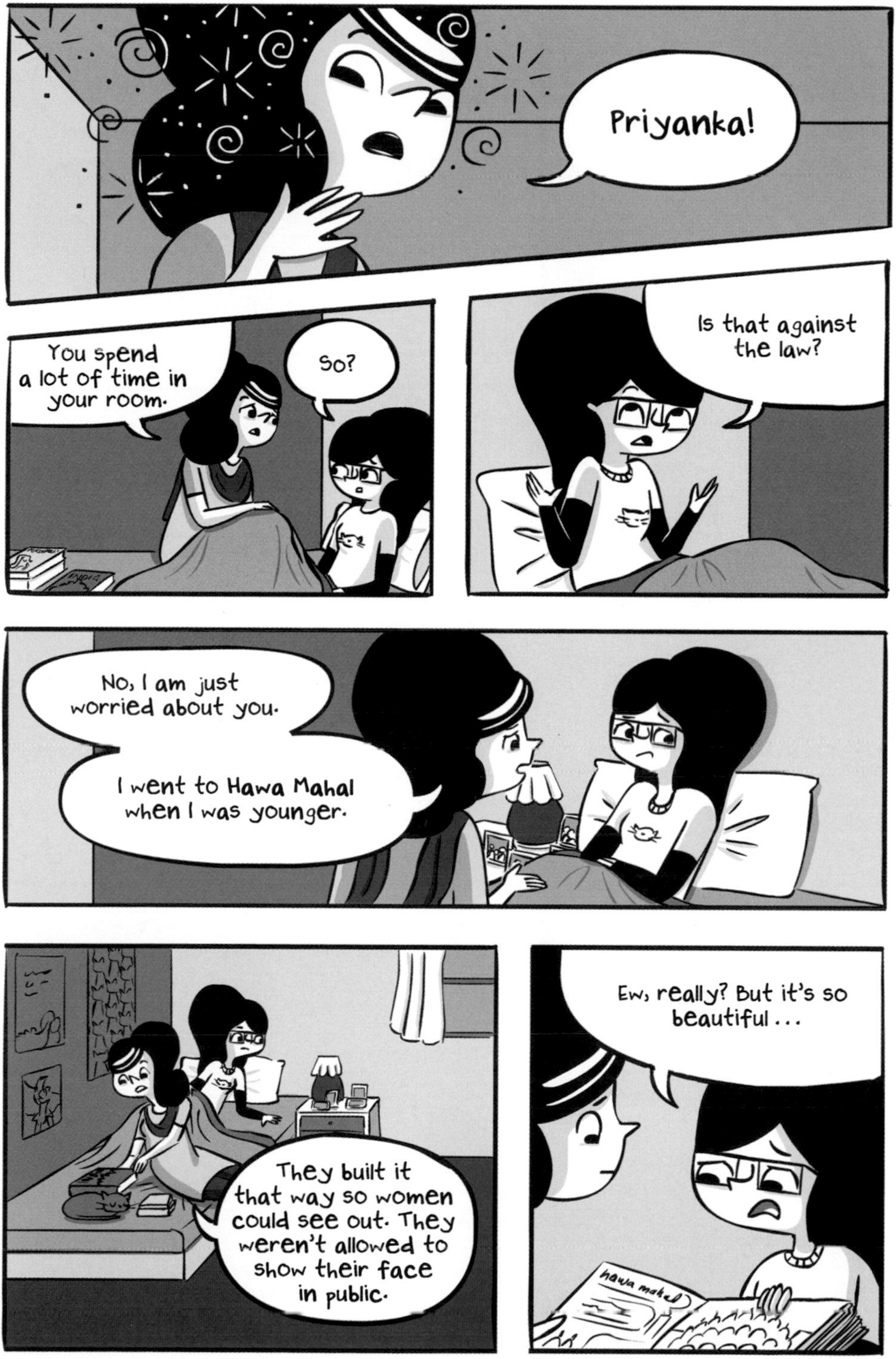
Priyanka!
You spend a lot of time in your room.
So?
Is that against the law?
No, I am just worried about you.
I went to Hawa Mahal when I was younger.
They built it that way so women could see out. They weren't allowed to show their face in public.
Ew, really? But it's so beautiful . . .
hawa mahal

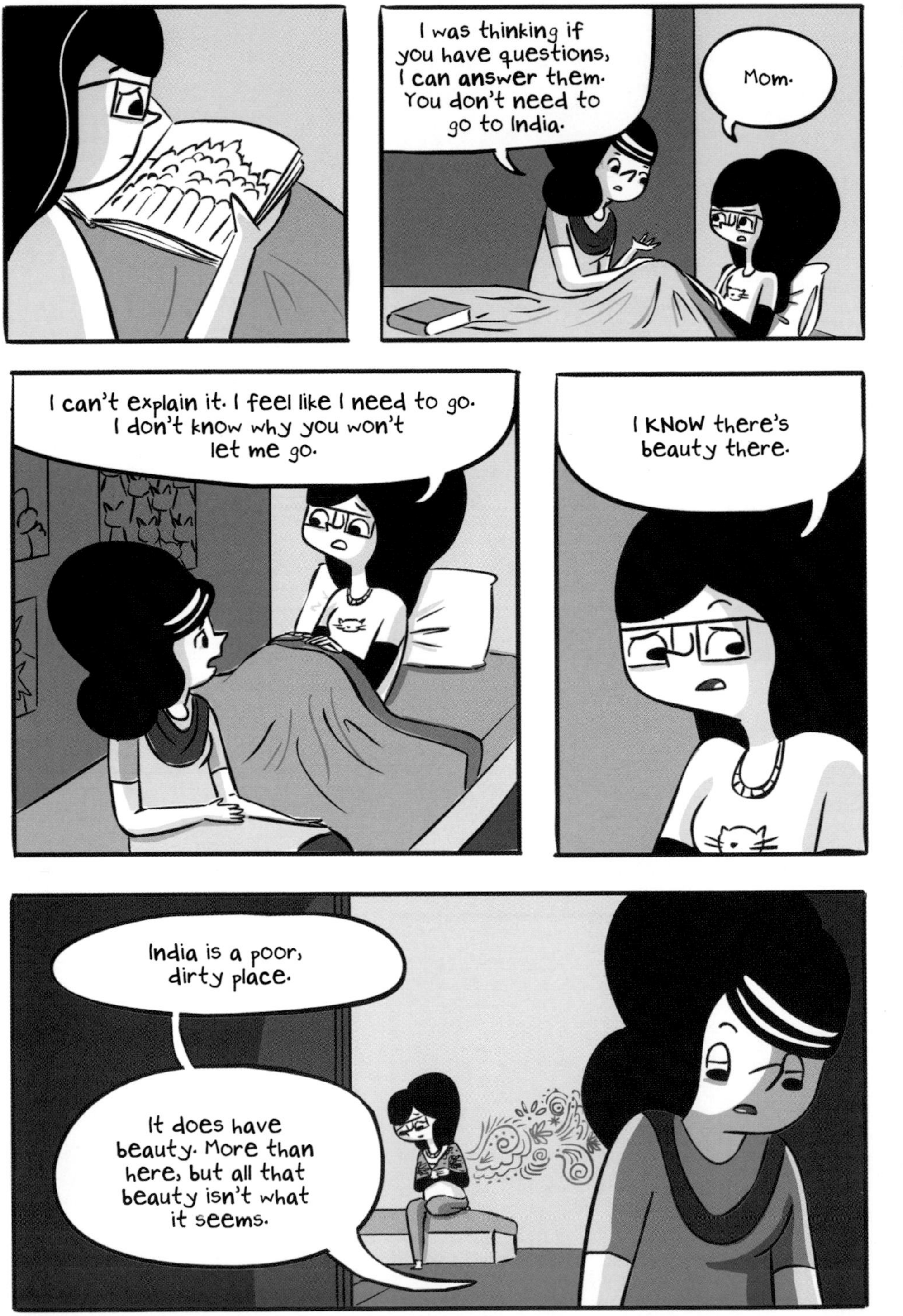
I was thinking if you have questions, I can answer them. You don't need to go to India.
Mom.
I can't explain it. I feel like I need to go. I don't know why you won't let me go.
I KNOW there's beauty there.
India is a poor, dirty place.
It does have beauty. More than here, but all that beauty isn't what it seems.

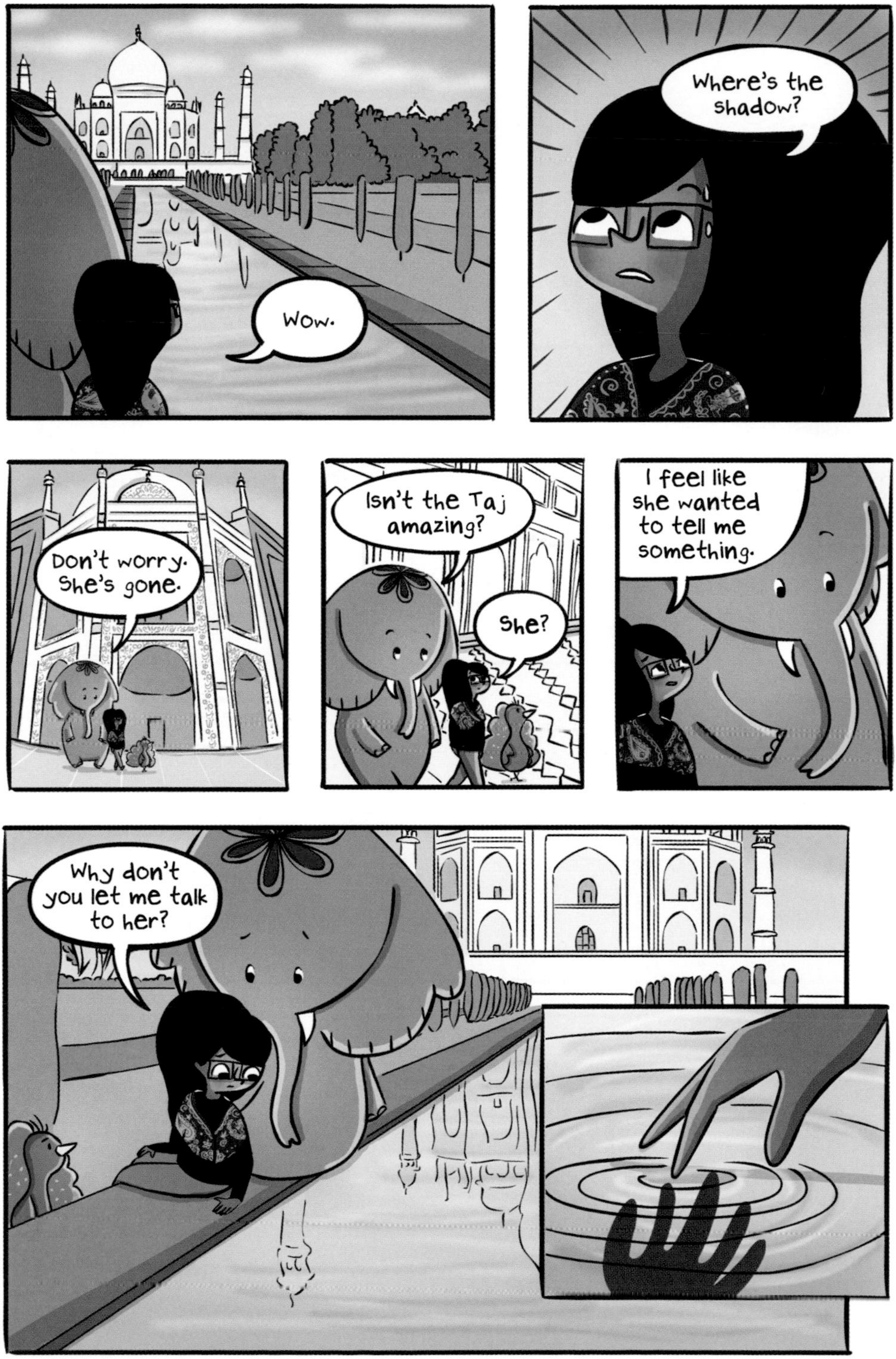
Wow.
Where's the shadow?
Don't worry. She's gone.
Isn't the Taj amazing?
She?
I feel like she wanted to tell me something.
Why don't you let me talk to her?

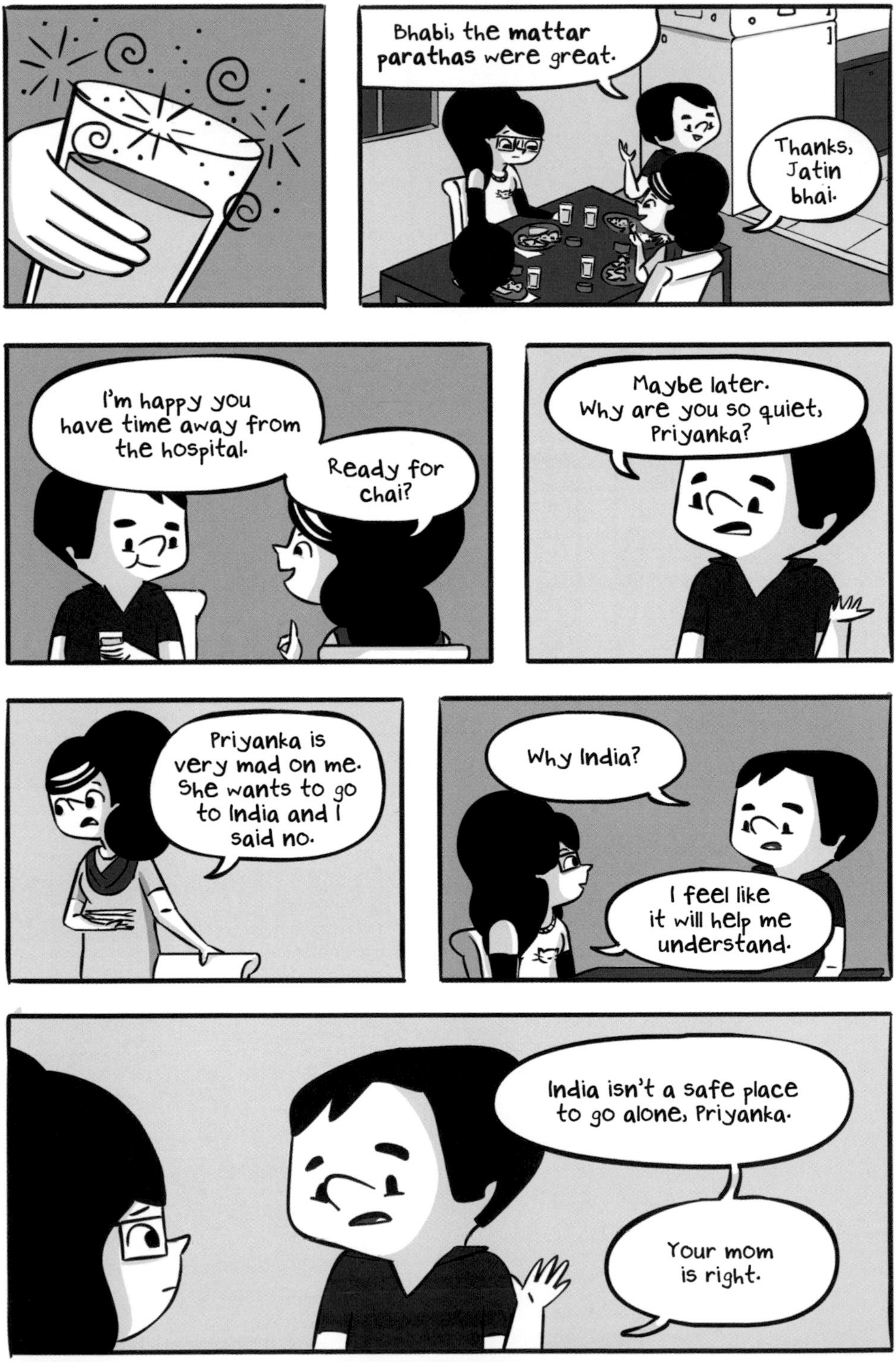
Bhabi, the mattar parathas were great.
Thanks, Jatin bhai.
I'm happy you have time away from the hospital.
Ready for chai?
Maybe later. Why are you so quiet, Priyanka?
Priyanka is very mad on me. She wants to go to India and I said no.
Why India?
I feel like it will help me understand.
India isn't a safe place to go alone, Priyanka.
Your mom is right.

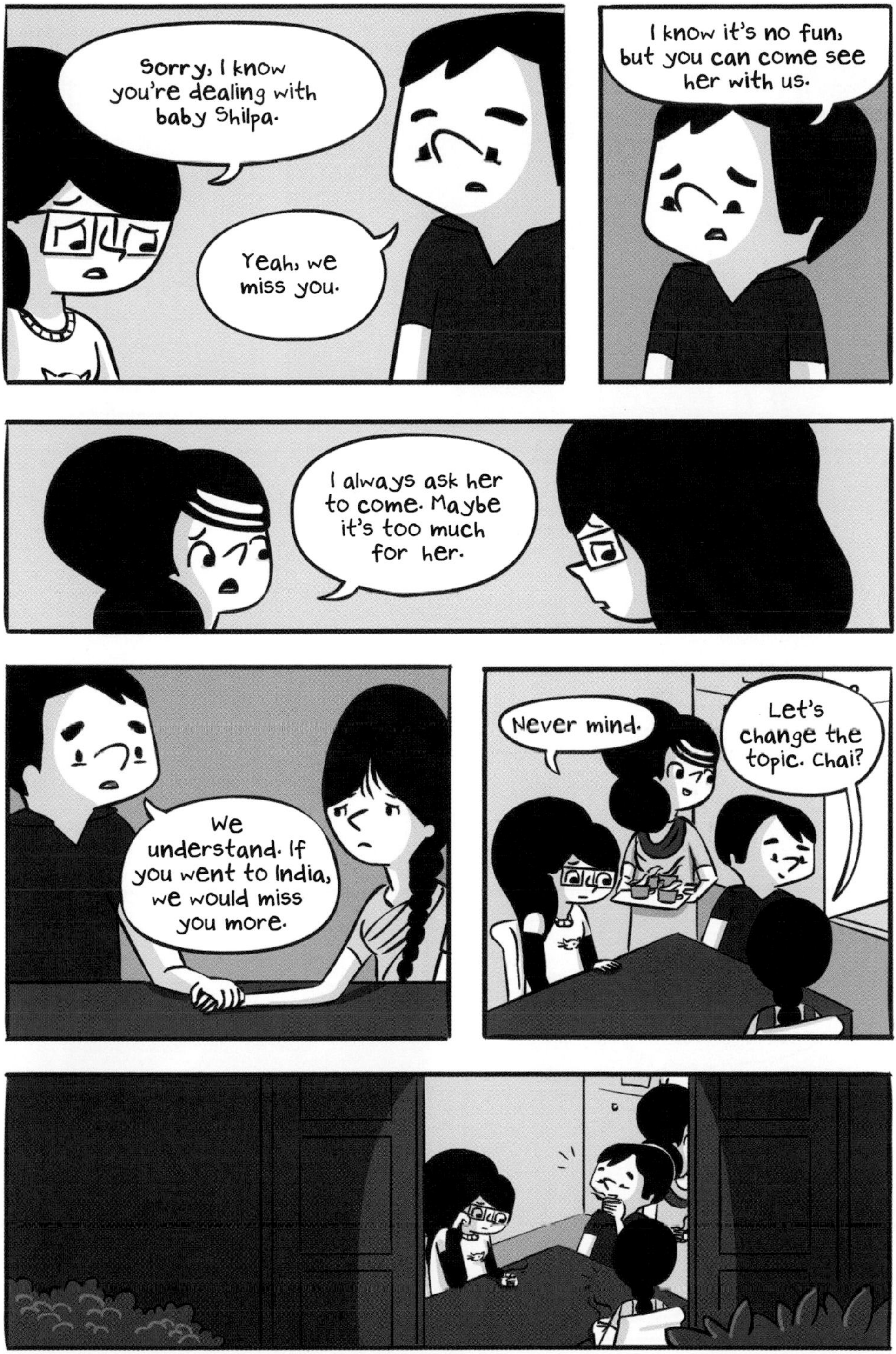
Sorry, I know you're dealing with baby Shilpa.
Yeah, we miss you.
I know it's no fun, but you can come see her with us.
I always ask her to come. Maybe it's too much for her.
We understand. If you went to India, we would miss you more.
Never mind.
Let's change the topic. Chai?

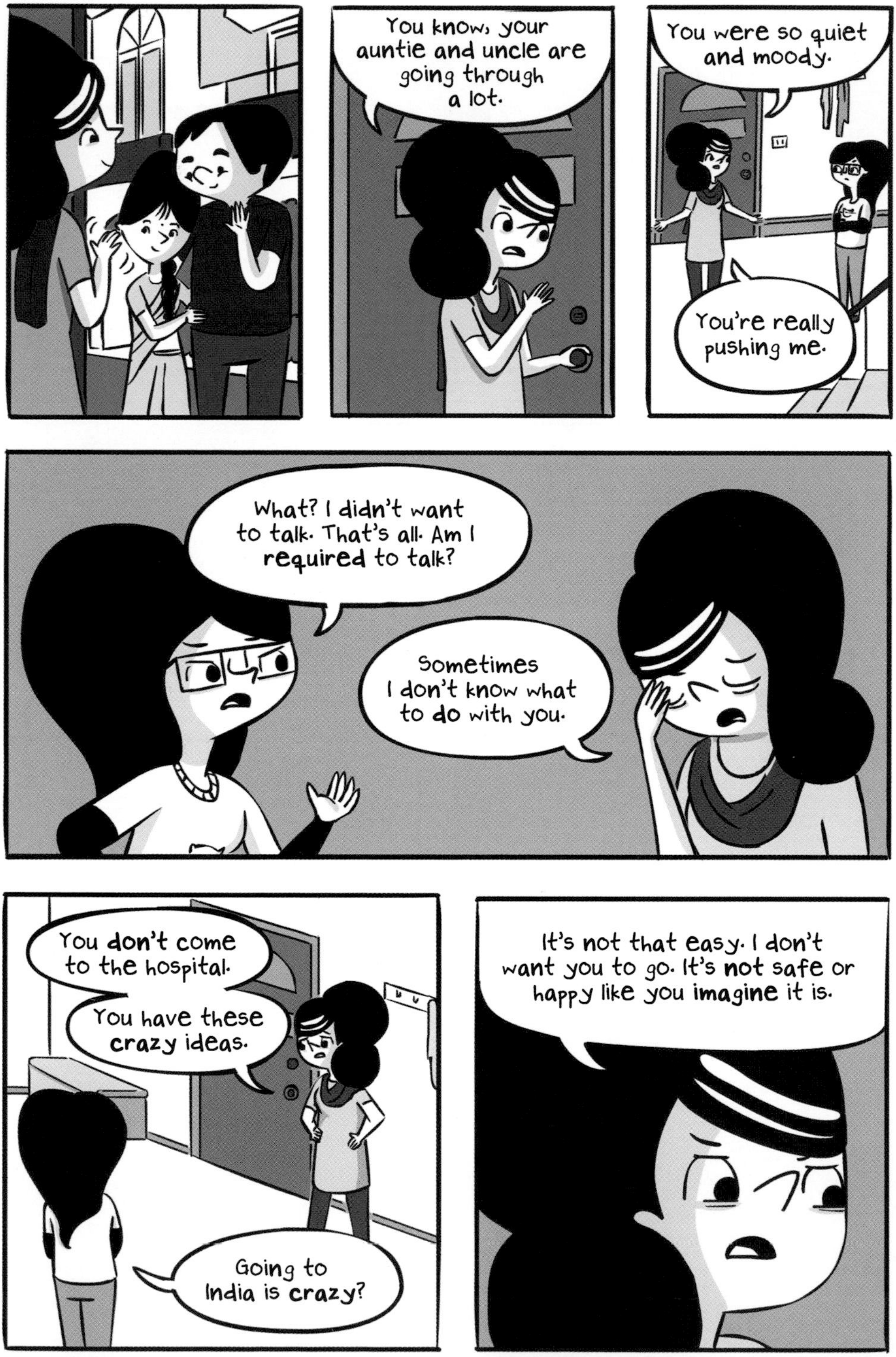

You know, your auntie and uncle are going through a lot.
You were so quiet and moody.
You're really pushing me.
What? I didn't want to talk. That's all. Am I required to talk?
Sometimes I don't know what to do with you.
You don't come to the hospital.
You have these crazy ideas.
Going to India is crazy?
It's not that easy. I don't want you to go. It's not safe or happy like you imagine it is.

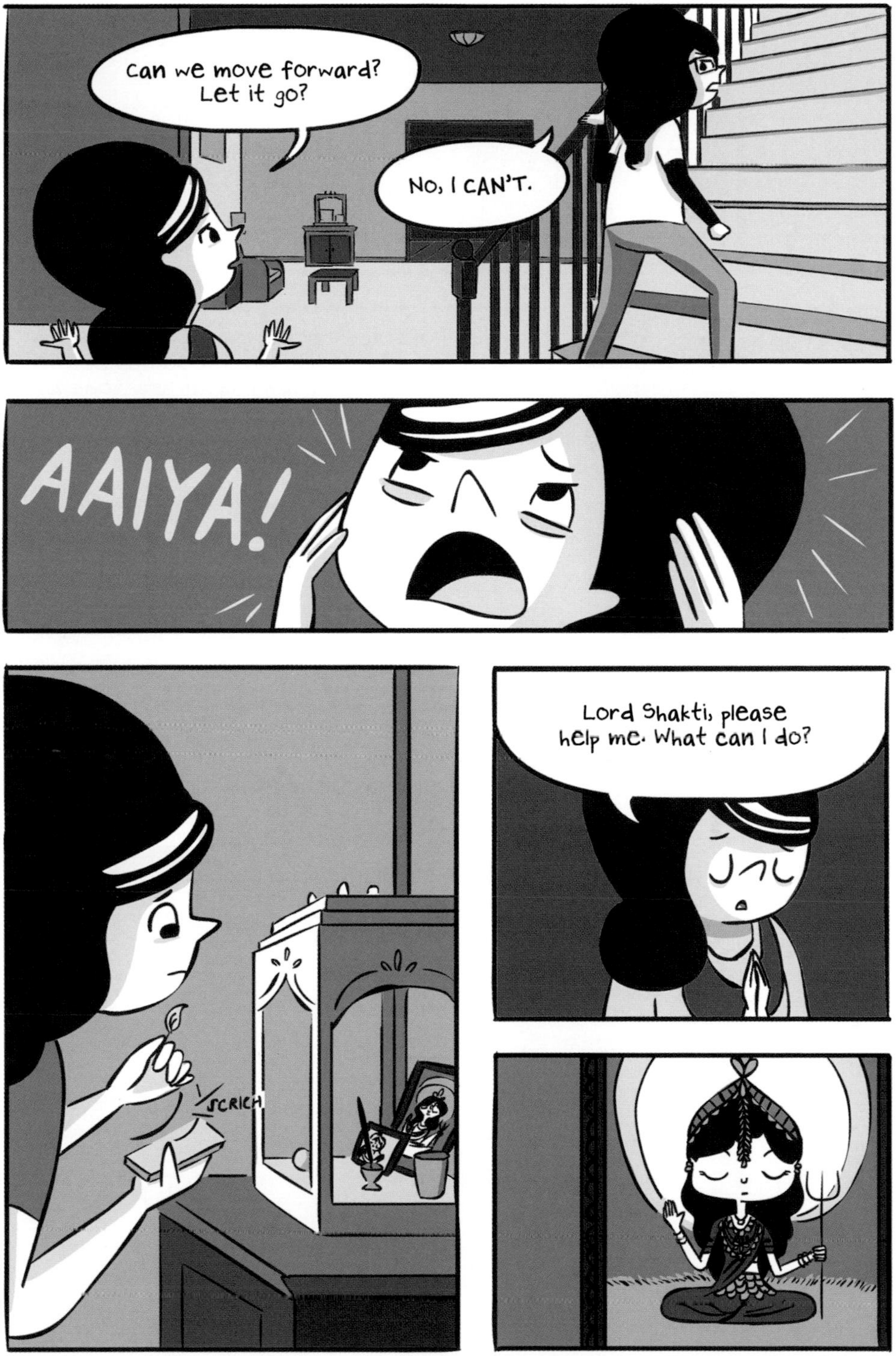
Can we move forward? Let it go?
No, I CAN'T.
AAIYA!
SCRICH
Lord Shakti, please help me. What can I do?

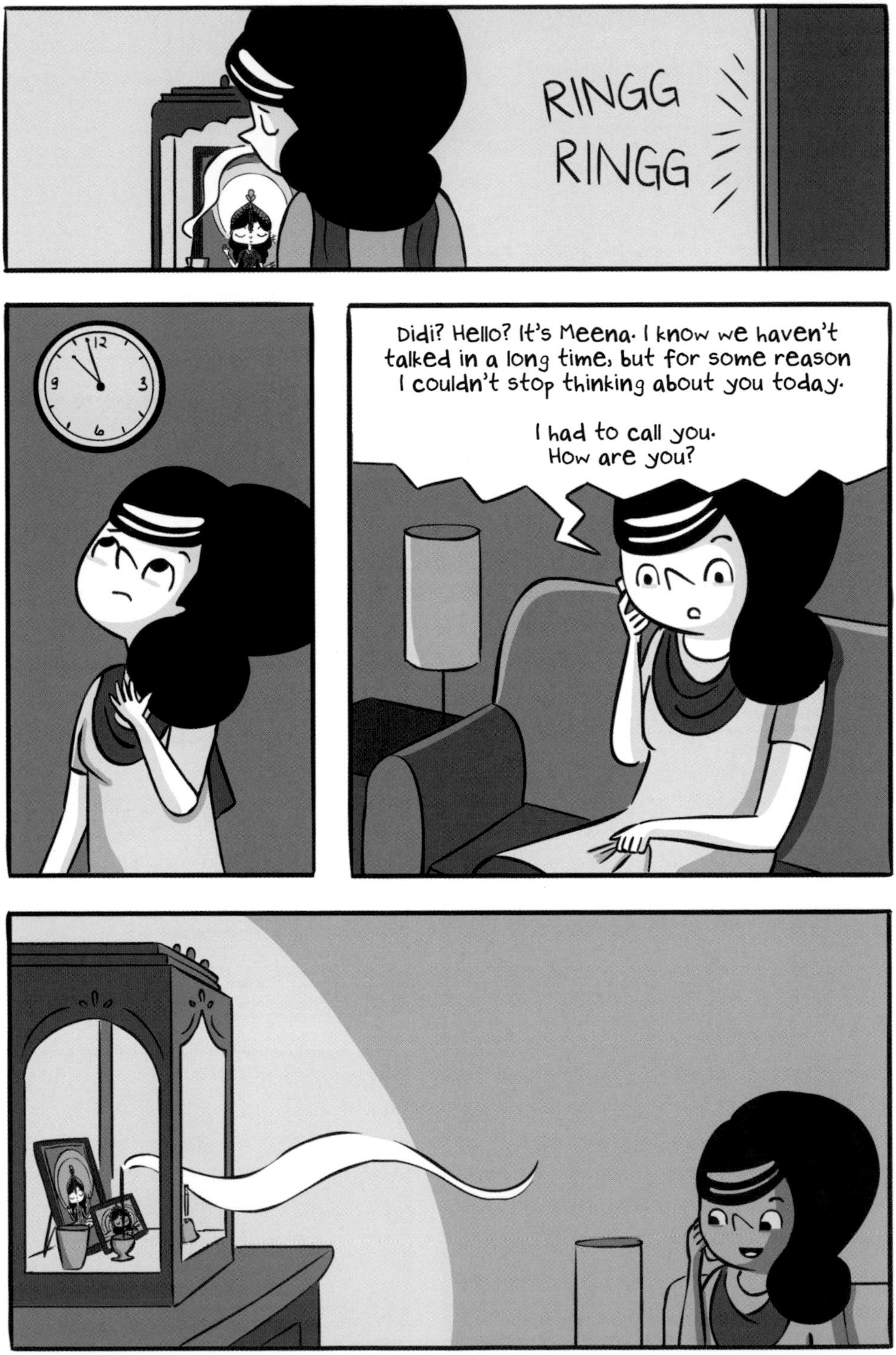
RINGG
RINGG
Didi? Hello? It's Meena. I know we haven't talked in a long time, but for some reason I couldn't stop thinking about you today.
I had to call you. How are you?

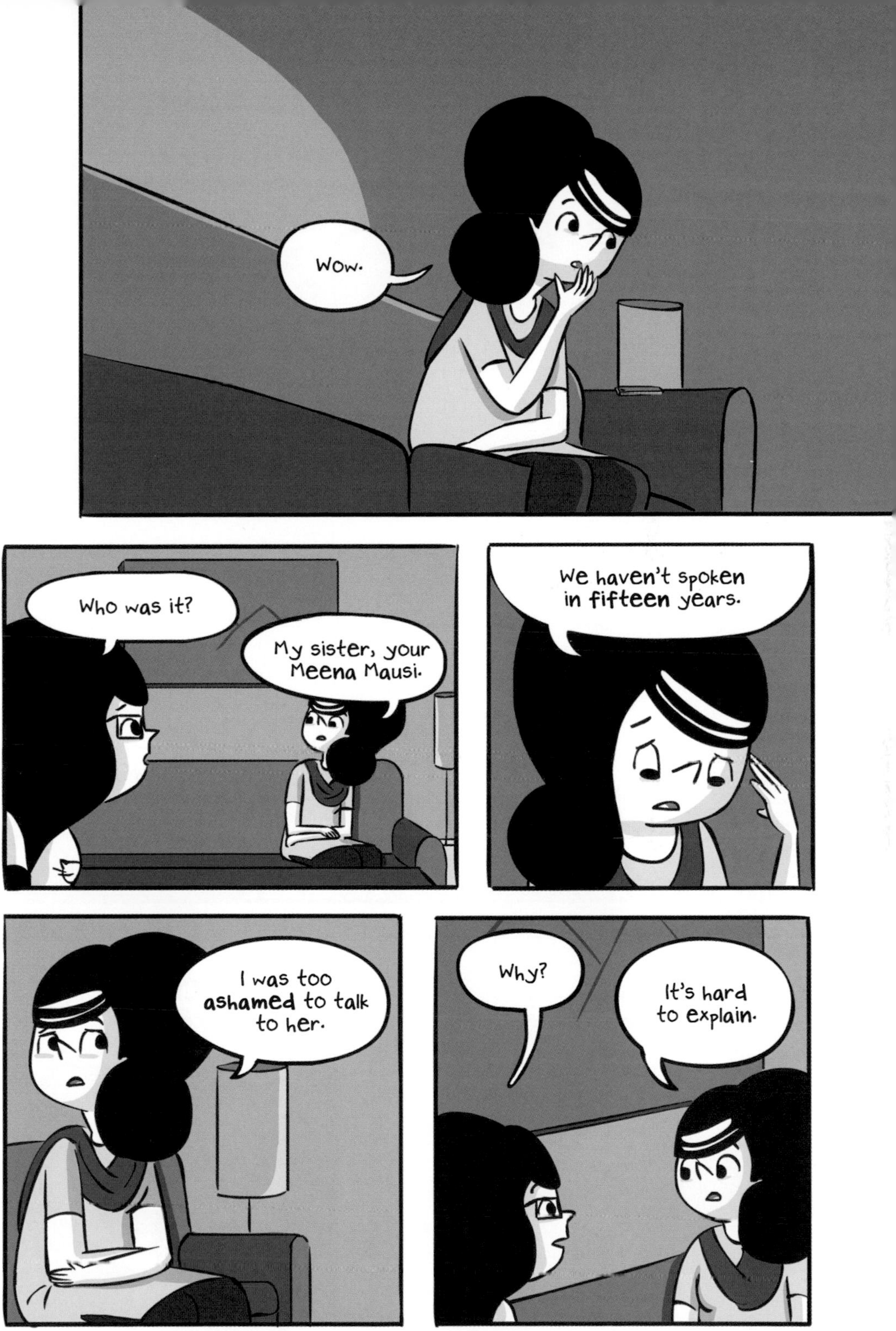
Wow.
Who was it?
My sister, your Meena Mausi.
We haven't spoken in **fifteen** years.
I was too **ashamed** to talk to her.
Why?
It's hard to explain.

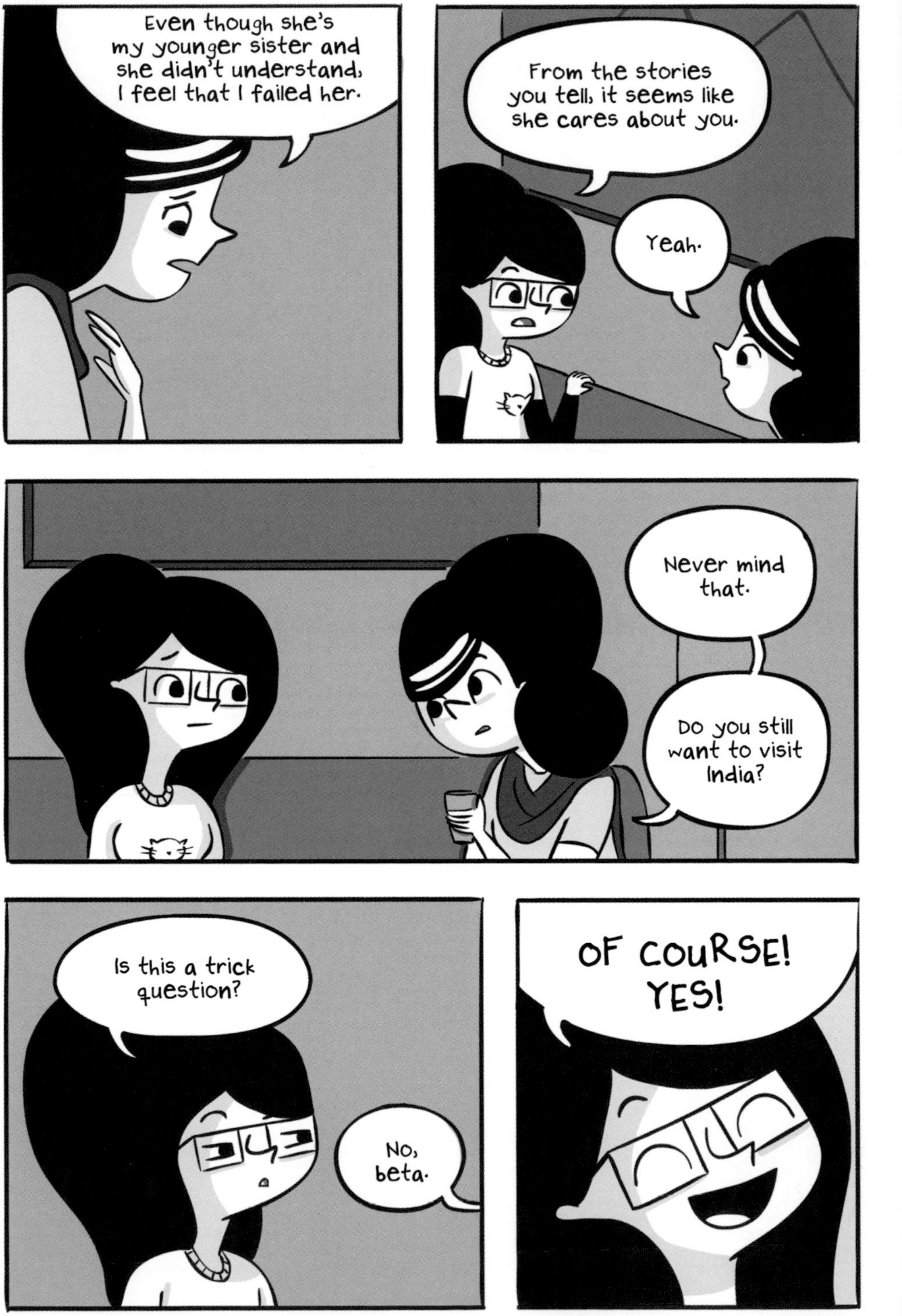
Even though she's my younger sister and she didn't understand, I feel that I failed her.
From the stories you tell, it seems like she cares about you.
Yeah.
Never mind that.
Do you still want to visit India?
Is this a trick question?
No, beta.
OF COURSE! YES!

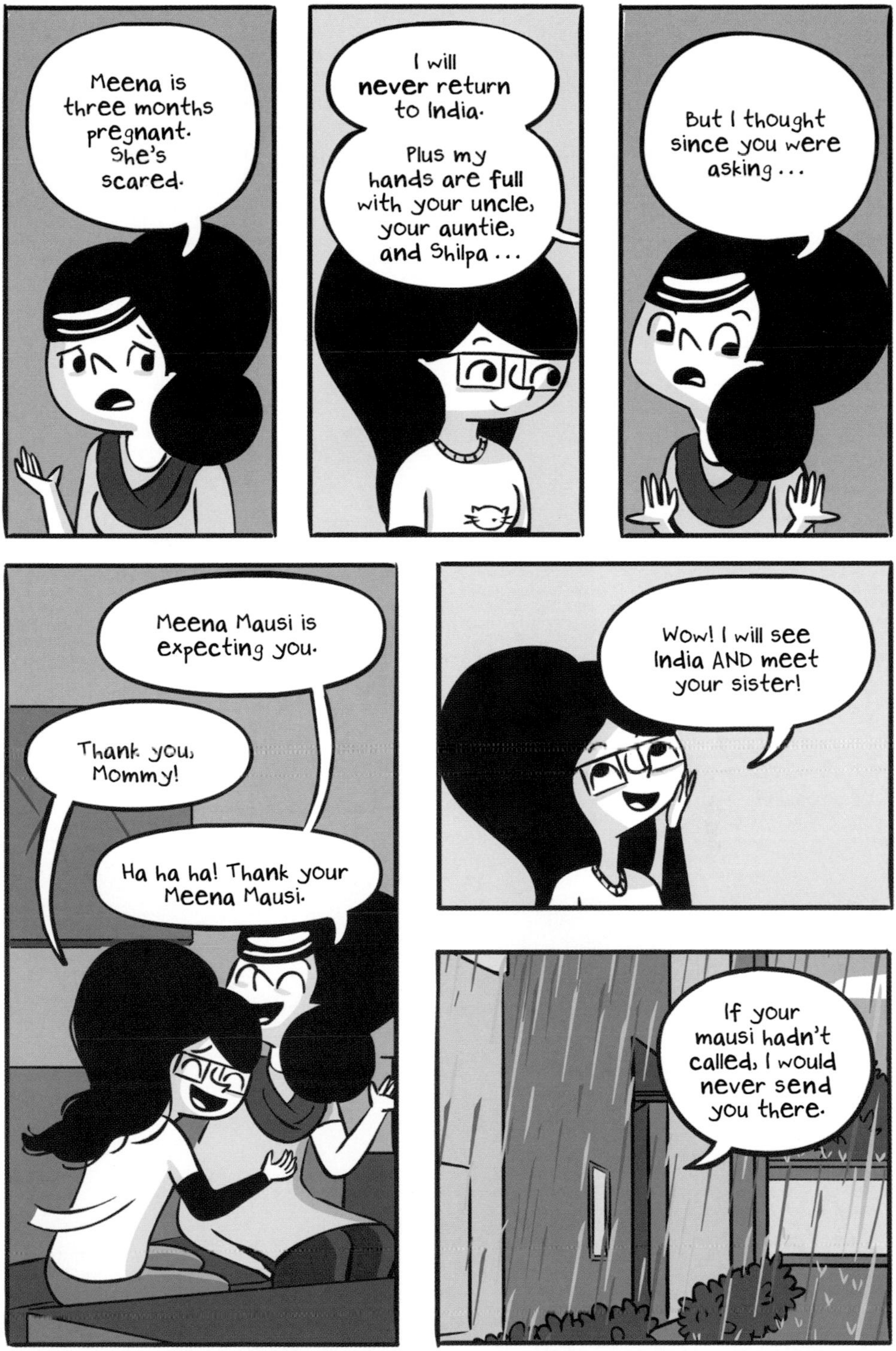
Meena is three months pregnant. She's scared.
I will **never** return to India.
Plus my hands are full with your uncle, your auntie, and Shilpa . . .
But I thought since you were asking . . .
Meena Mausi is expecting you.
Thank you, Mommy!
Ha ha ha! Thank your Meena Mausi.
Wow! I will see India AND meet your sister!
If your mausi hadn't called, I would never send you there.

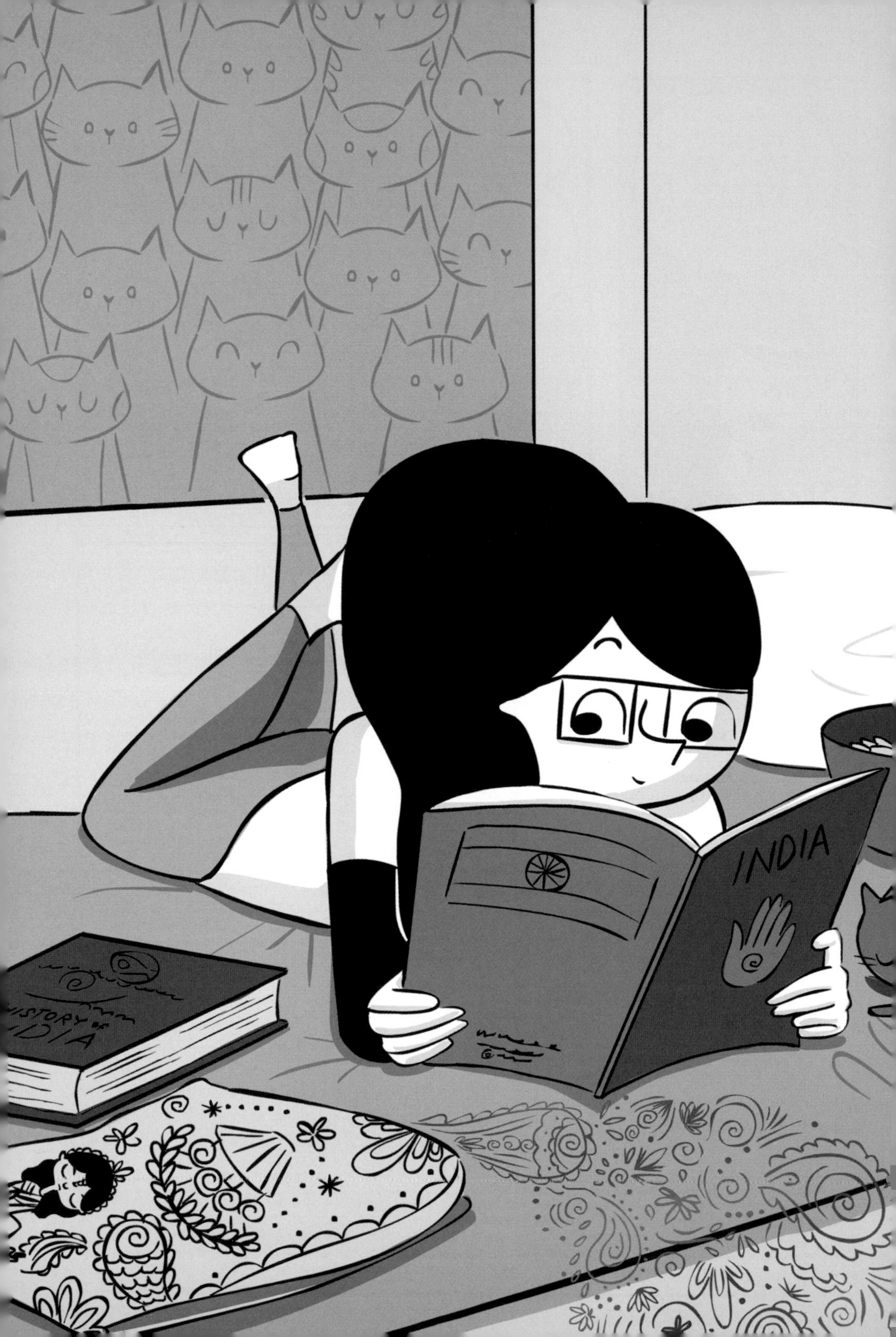
INDIA

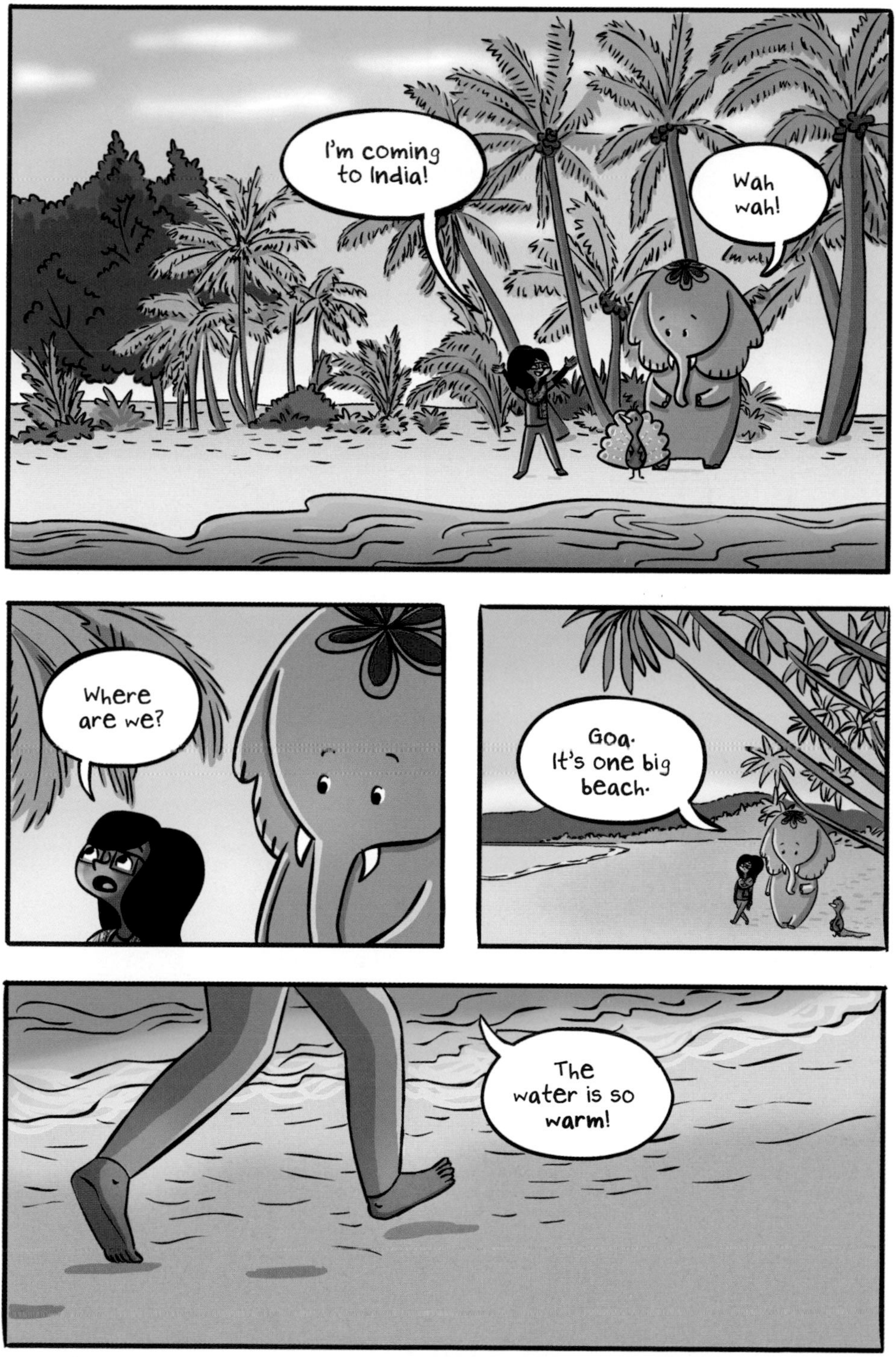
I'm coming to India!
Wah wah!
Where are we?
Goa. It's one big beach.
The water is so warm!

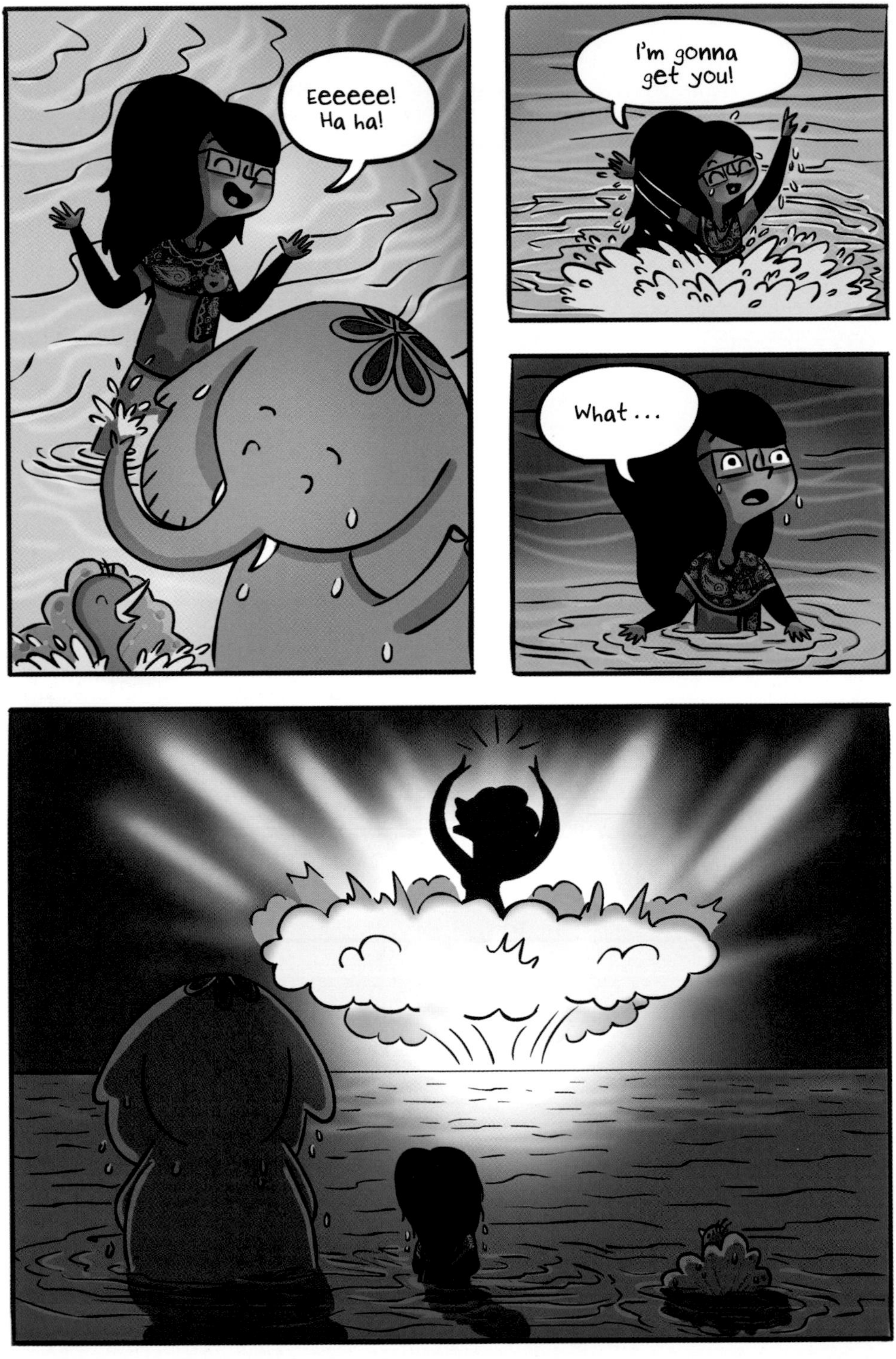
Eeeeee!
Ha ha!
I'm gonna get you!
What...

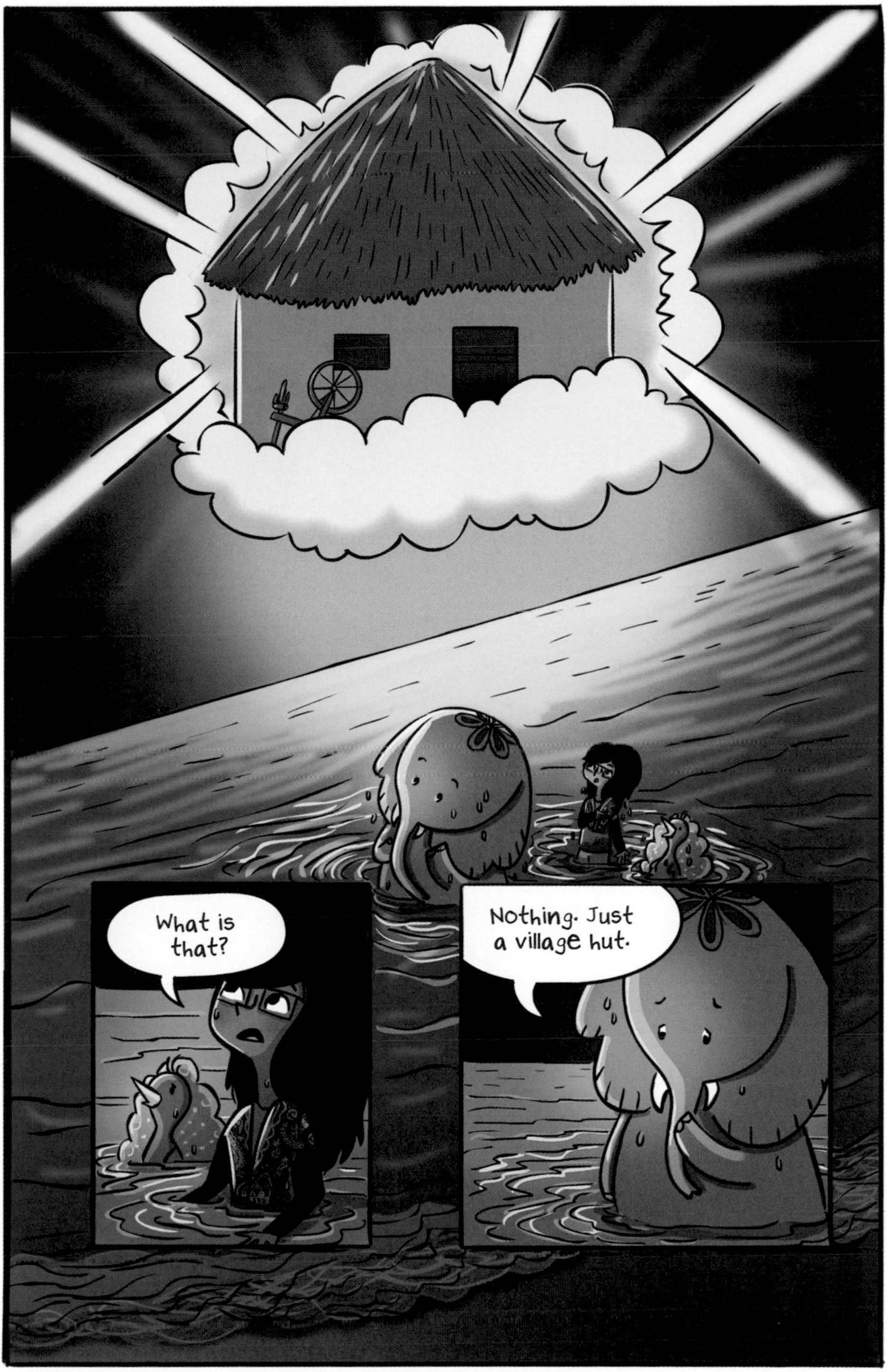
What is that?
Nothing. Just a village hut.

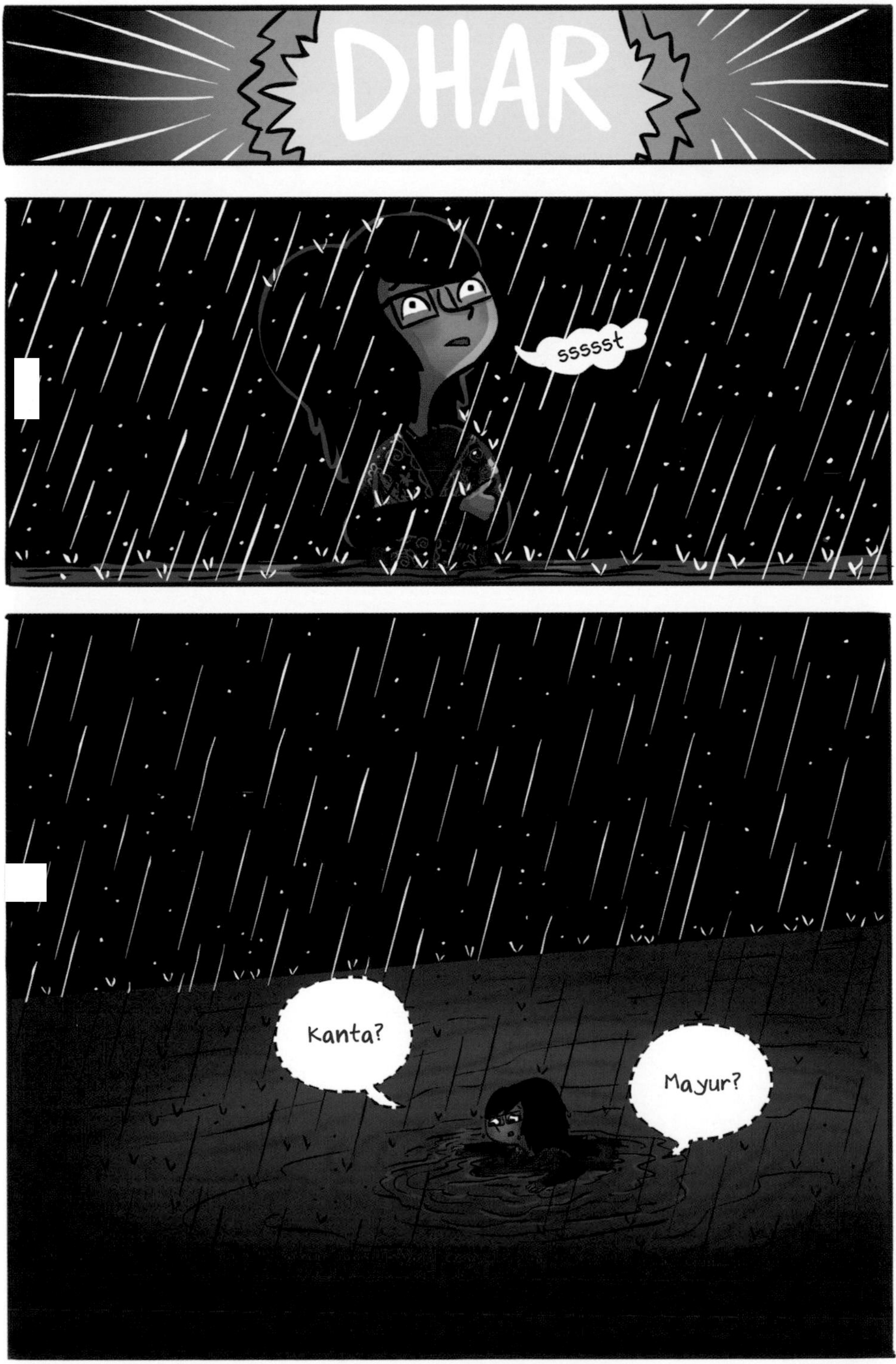
DHAR
ssssst
Kanta?
Mayur?

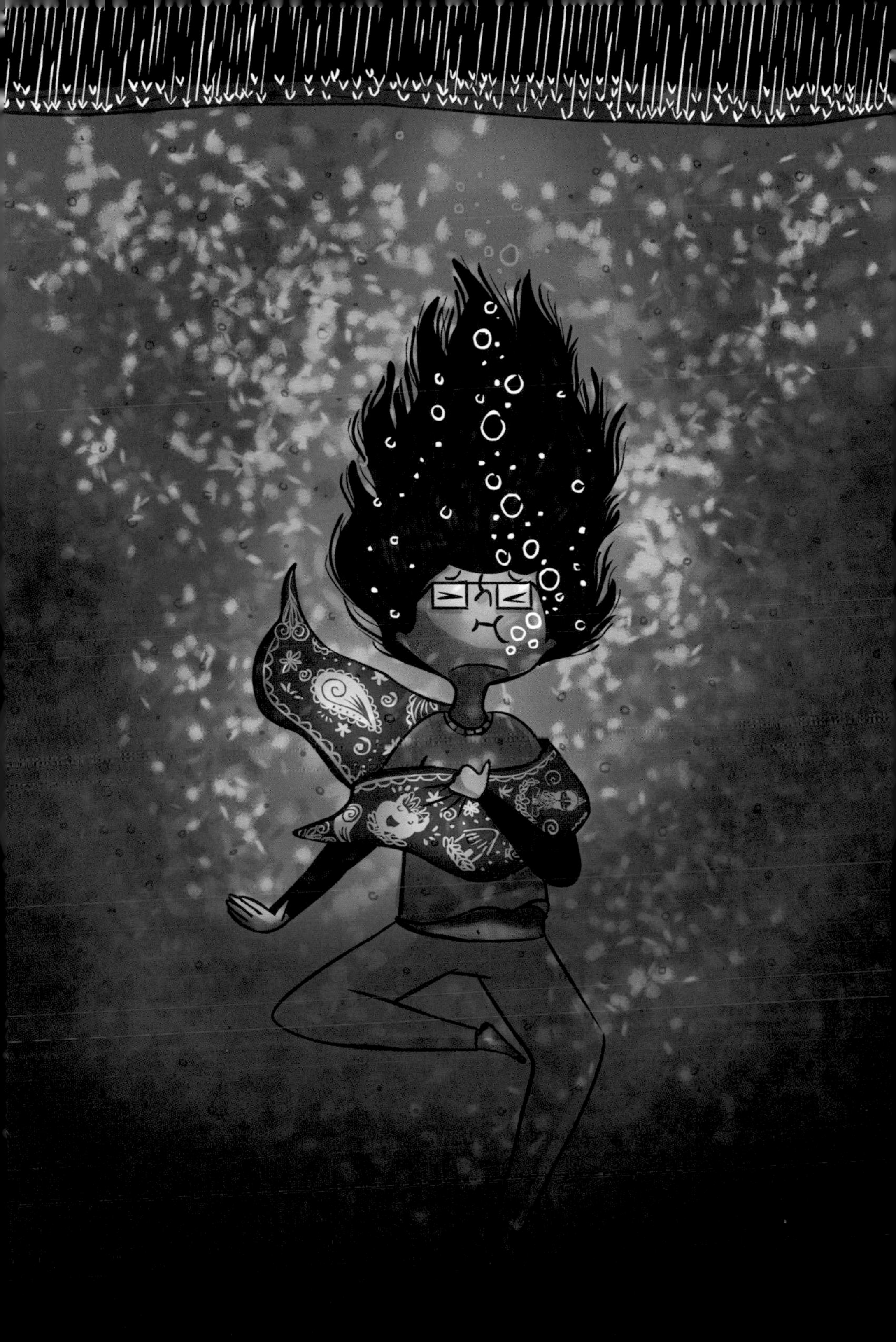

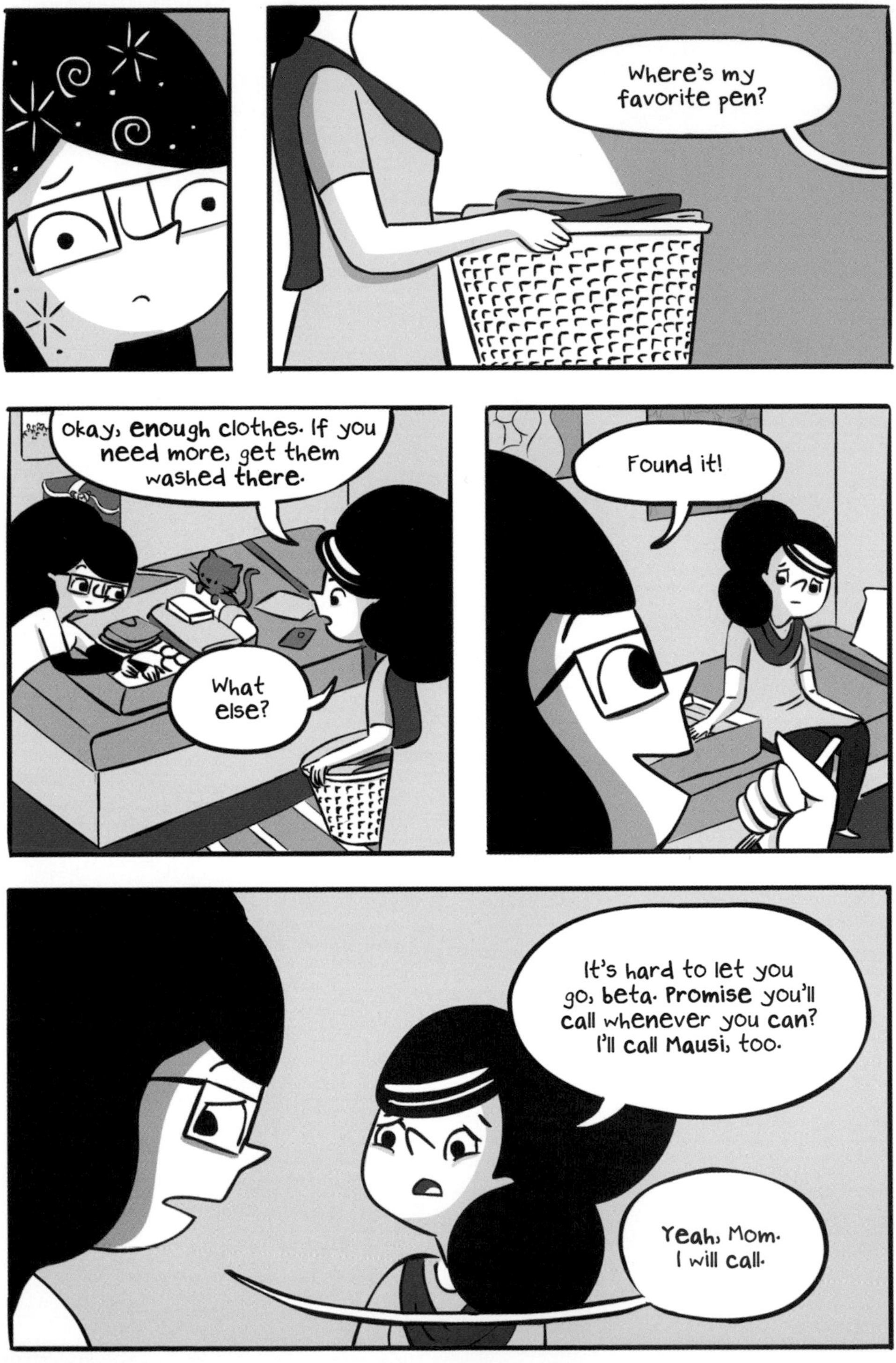
Where's my favorite pen?
Okay, enough clothes. If you need more, get them washed there.
What else?
Found it!
It's hard to let you go, beta. Promise you'll call whenever you can? I'll call Mausi, too.
Yeah, Mom. I will call.

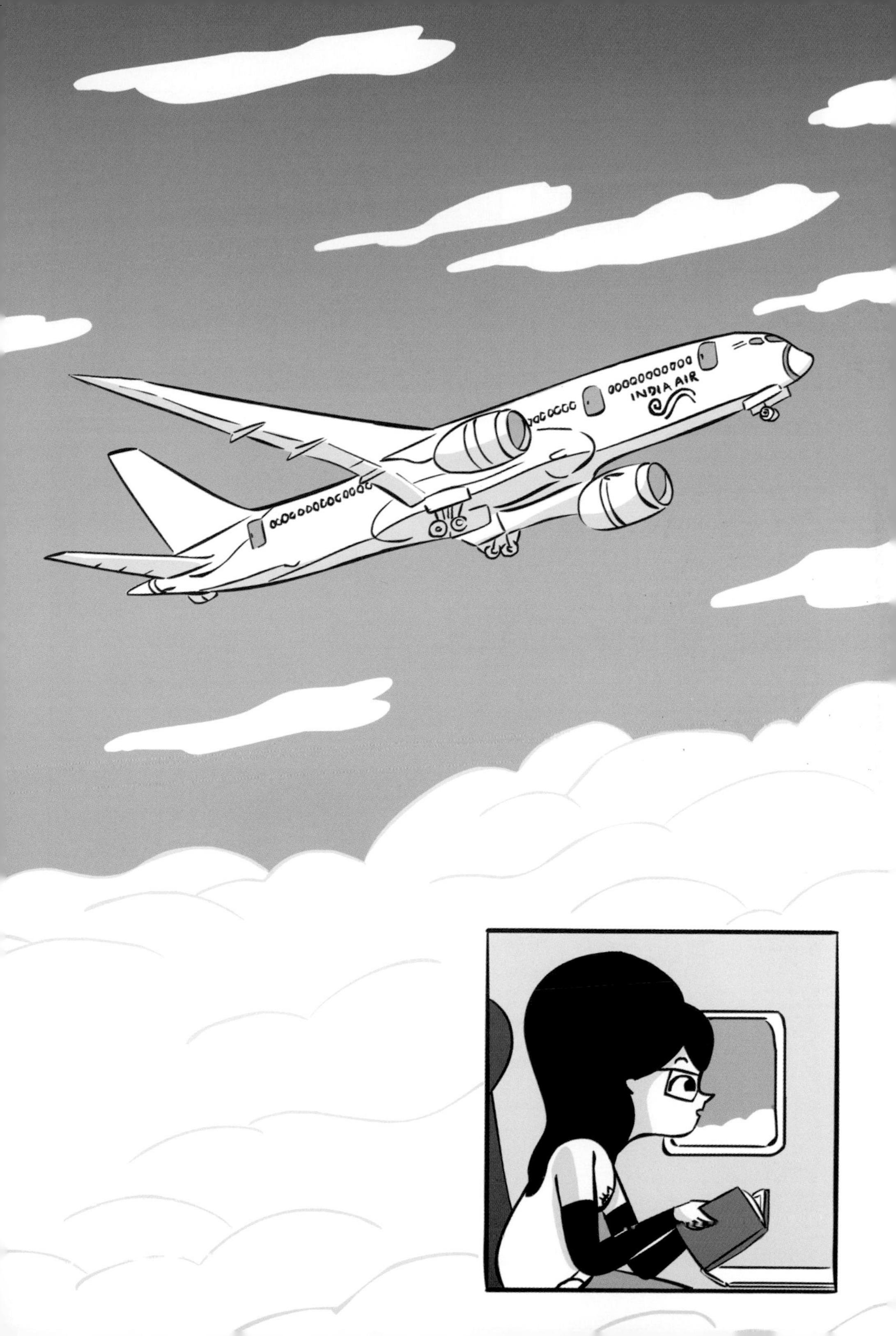
INDIA AIR

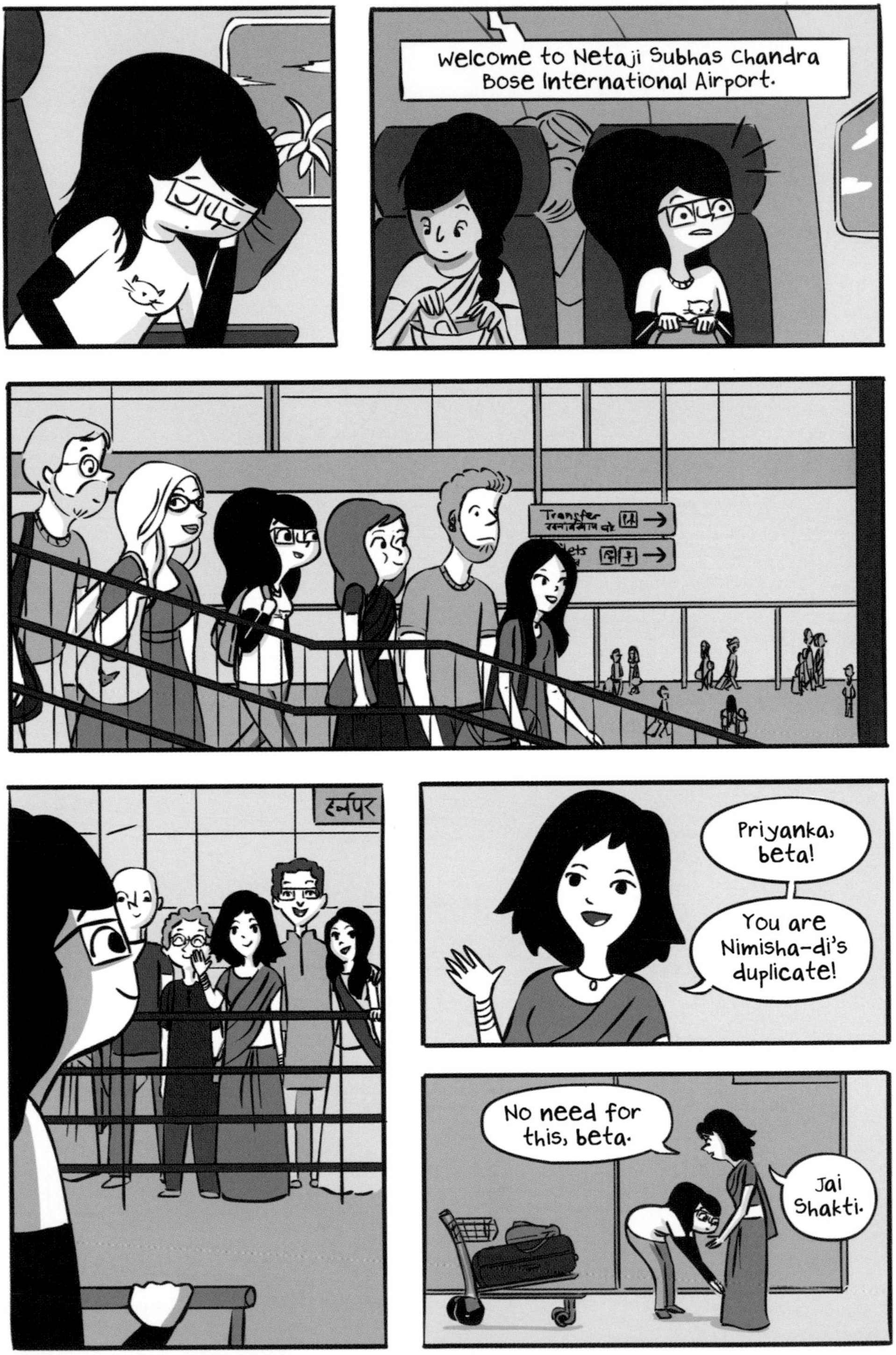
Welcome to Netaji Subhas Chandra Bose International Airport.
Transfer
Priyanka, beta!
You are Nimisha-di's duplicate!
No need for this, beta.
Jai Shakti.

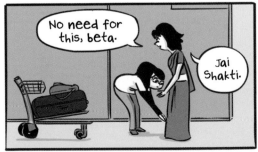

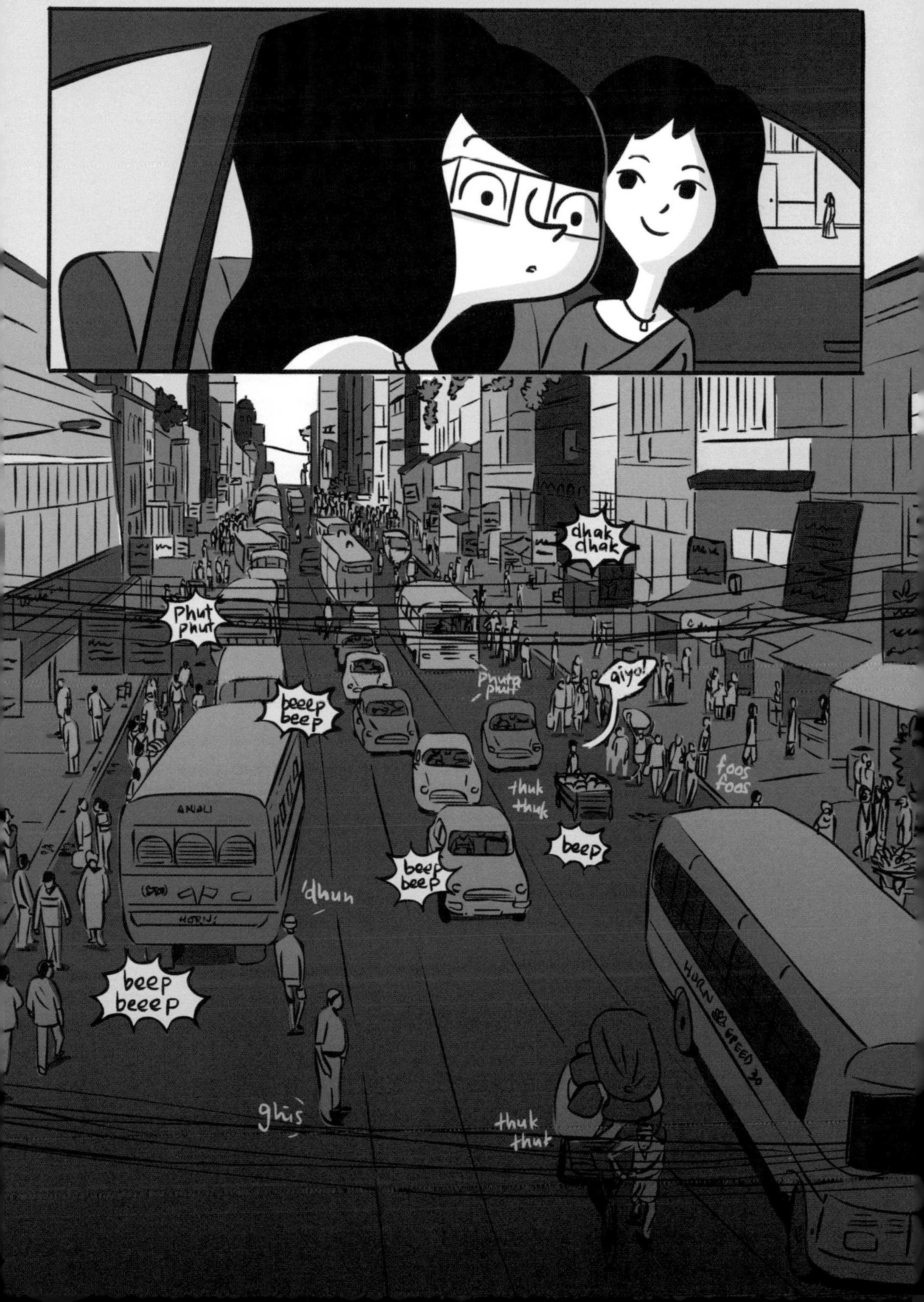
dhak dhak
phut phut
aiyo!
beeep beep
thuk thuk
foos foos
beep
beep beep
beep beeep
HORN SPEED 30

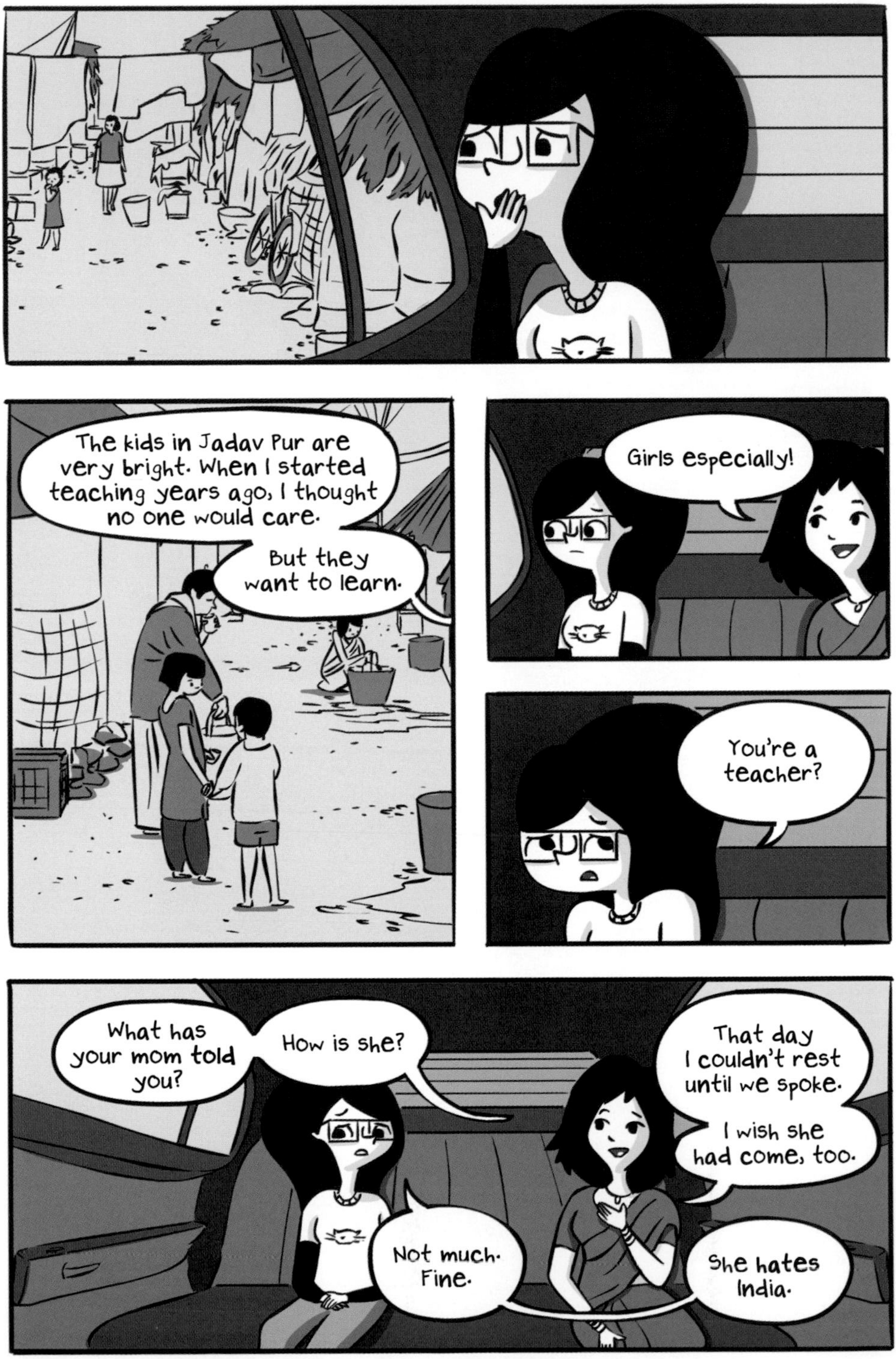
The kids in Jadav Pur are very bright. When I started teaching years ago, I thought no one would care.
But they want to learn.
Girls especially!
You're a teacher?
What has your mom told you?
How is she?
Not much. Fine.
That day I couldn't rest until we spoke.
I wish she had come, too.
She hates India.

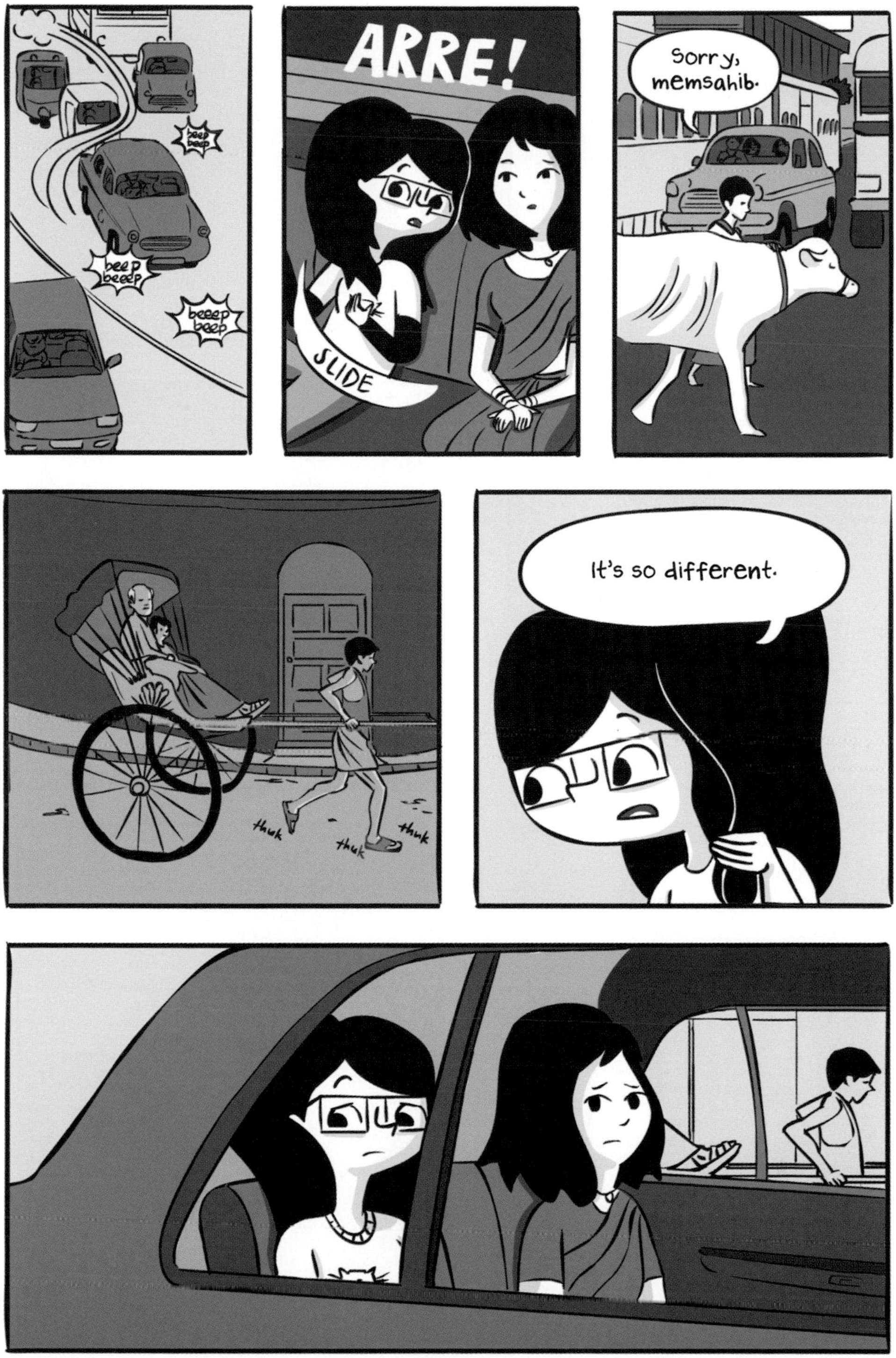
beep beep
beep beeep
beeep beep
ARRE!
SLIDE
Sorry, memsahib.
It's so different.
thuk
thuk
thuk

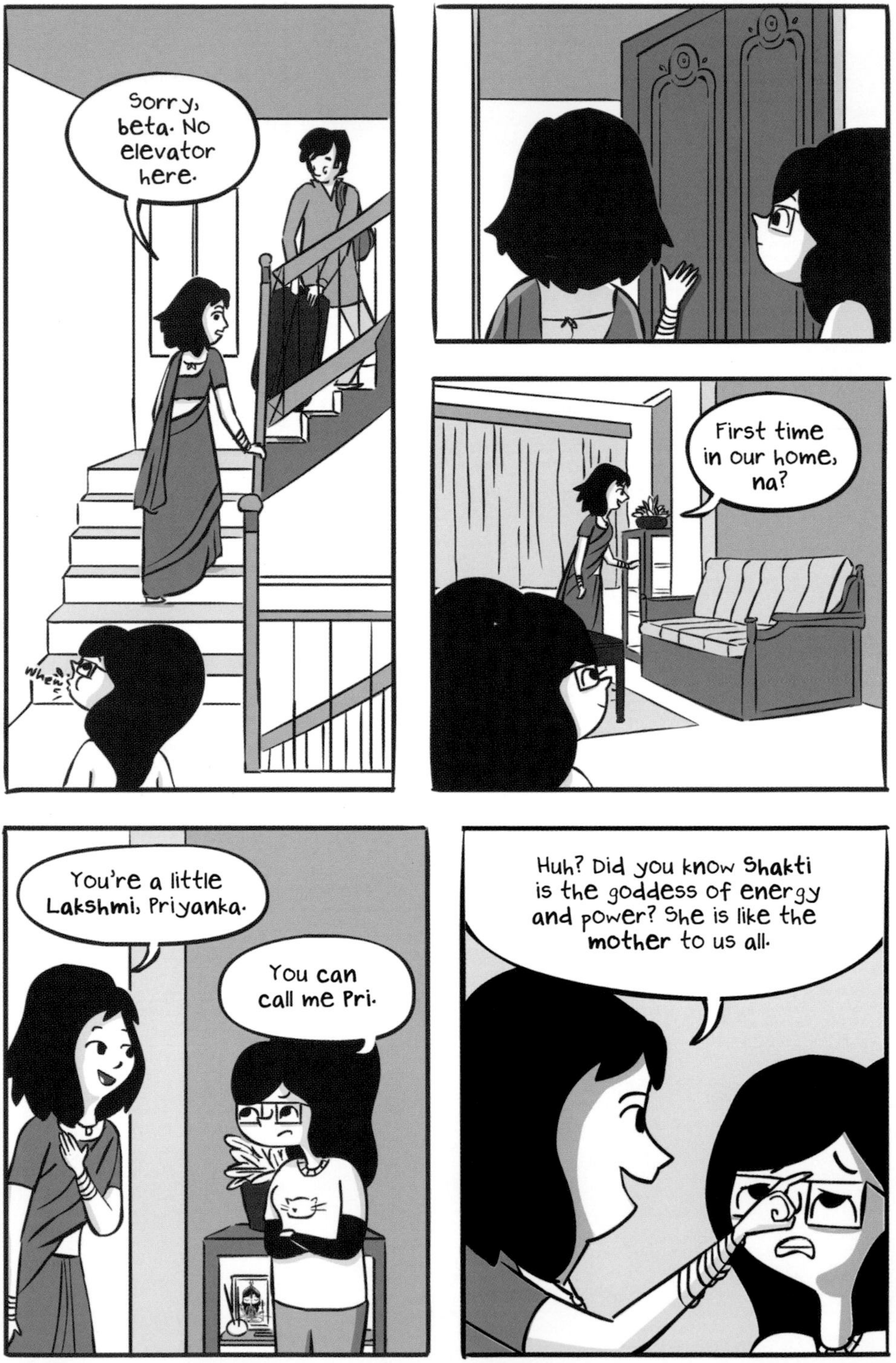
Sorry, beta. No elevator here.
Whew
First time in our home, na?
You're a little Lakshmi, Priyanka.
You can call me Pri.
Huh? Did you know Shakti is the goddess of energy and power? She is like the mother to us all.

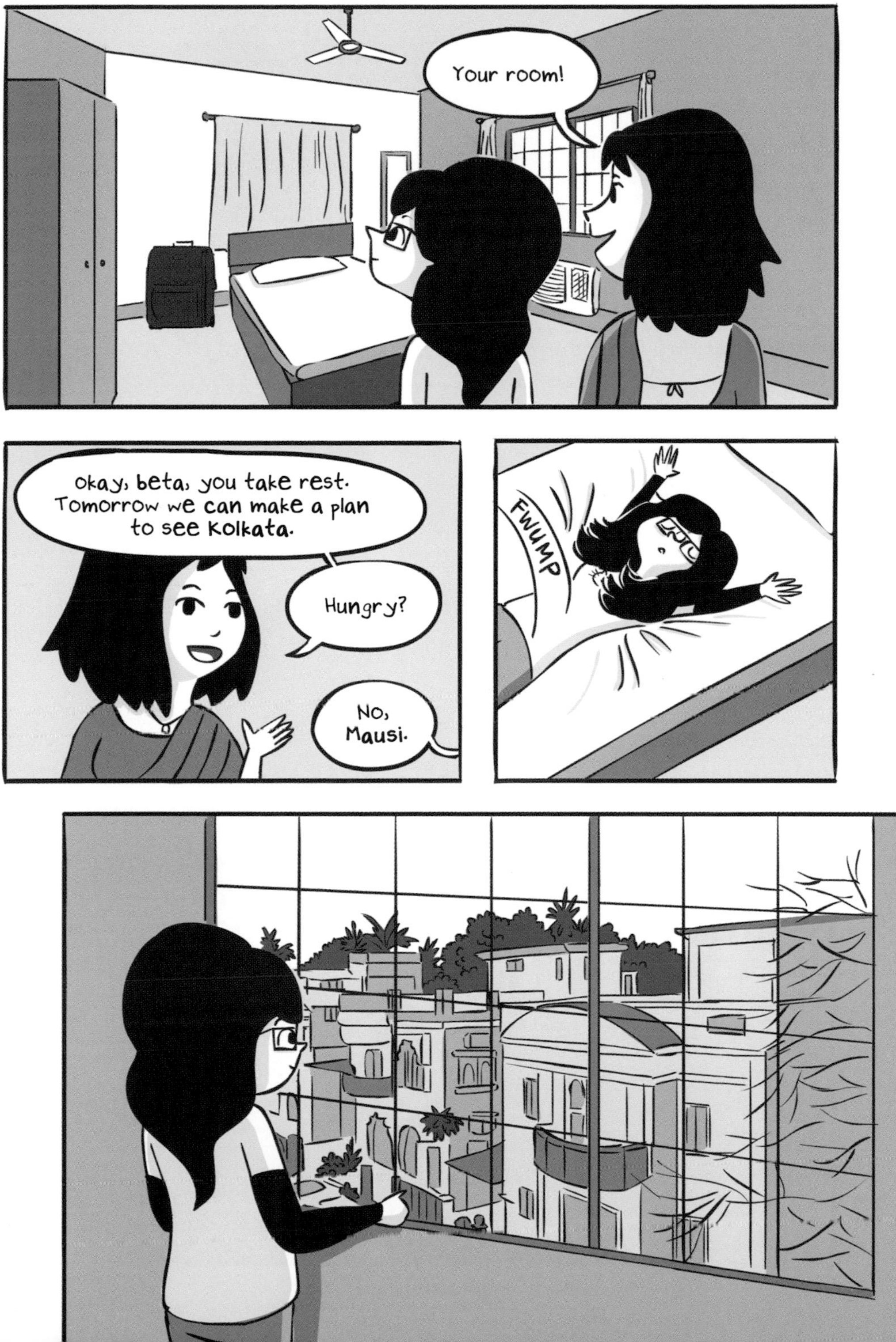
Your room!
Okay, beta, you take rest. Tomorrow we can make a plan to see Kolkata.
Hungry?
No, Mausi.
FWUMP

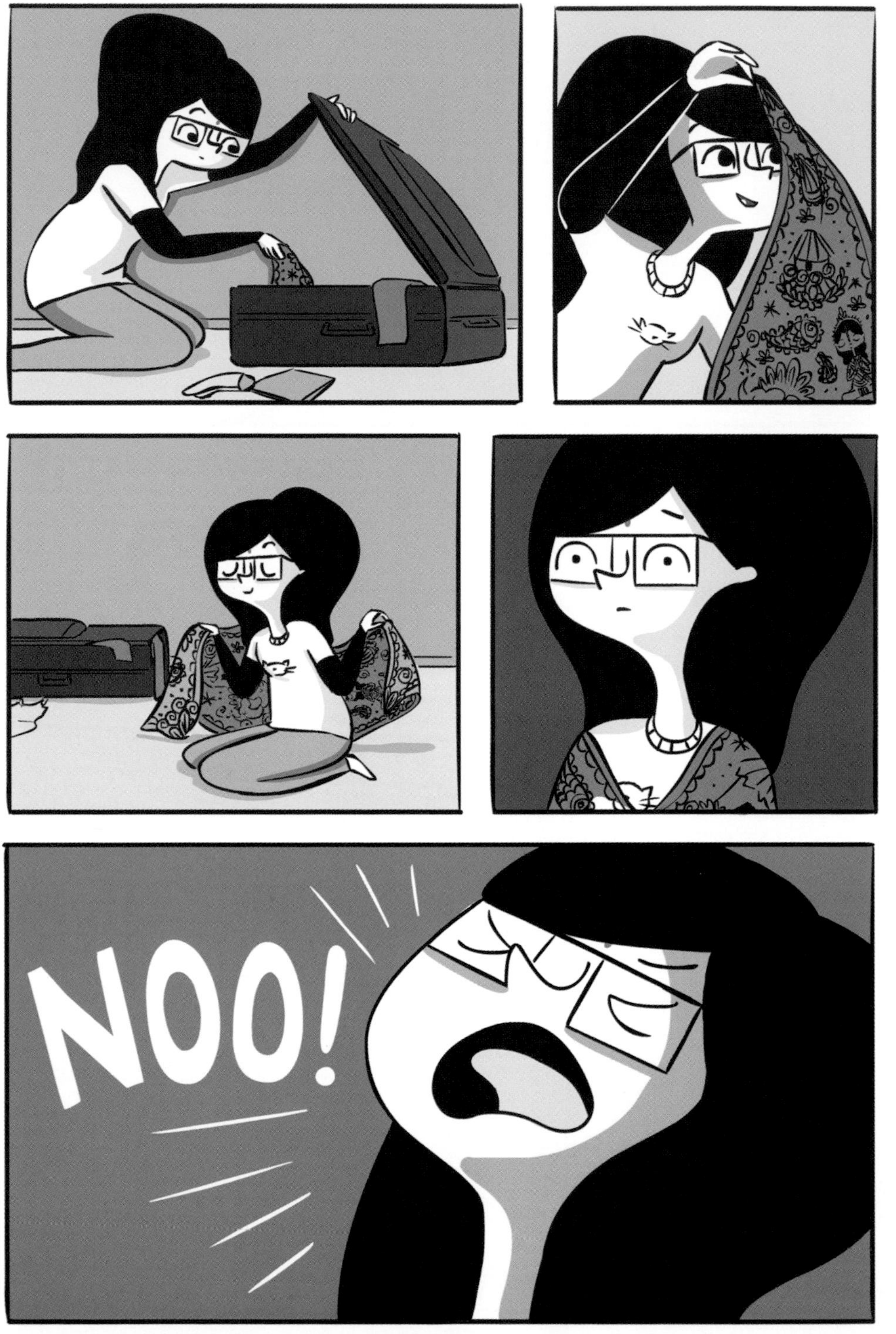
NOO!

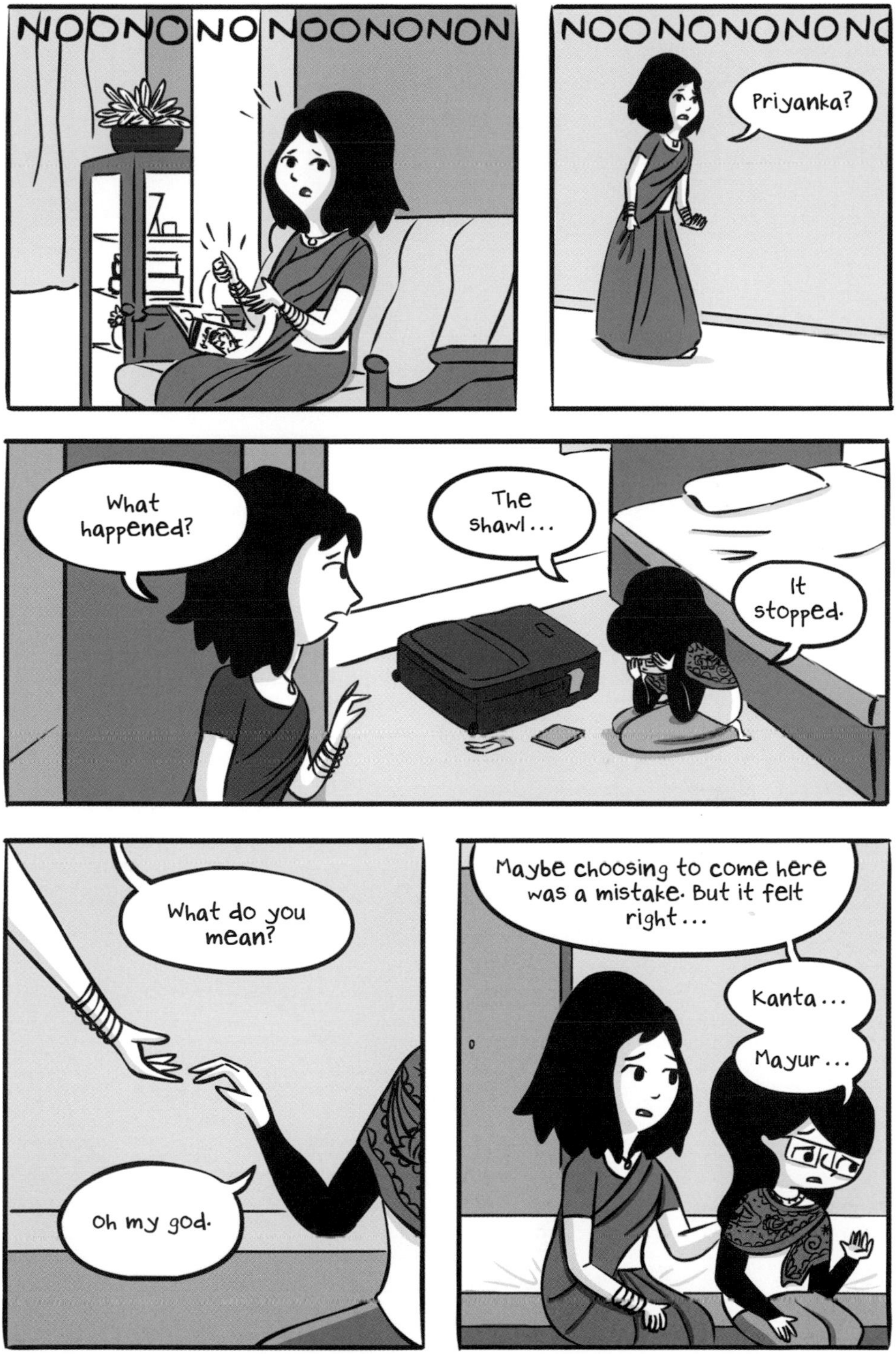
NOONONO NOONONONON
NOONONONONO
Priyanka?
What happened?
The shawl...
It stopped.
What do you mean?
Oh my god.
Maybe choosing to come here was a mistake. But it felt right...
Kanta...
Mayur...

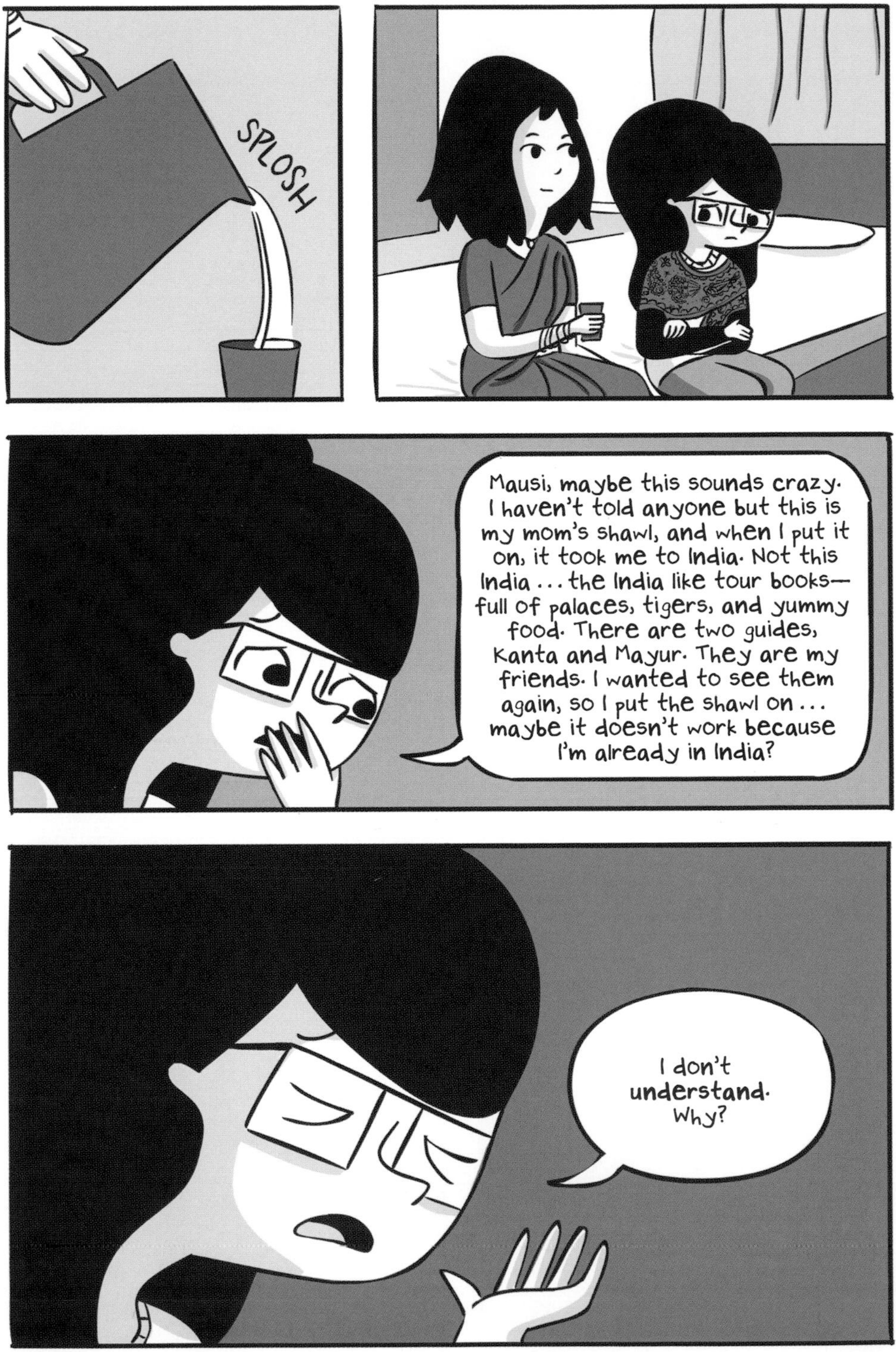
SPLOSH
Mausi, maybe this sounds crazy. I haven't told anyone but this is my mom's shawl, and when I put it on, it took me to India. Not this India . . . the India like tour books— full of palaces, tigers, and yummy food. There are two guides, Kanta and Mayur. They are my friends. I wanted to see them again, so I put the shawl on . . . maybe it doesn't work because I'm already in India?
I don't understand. Why?

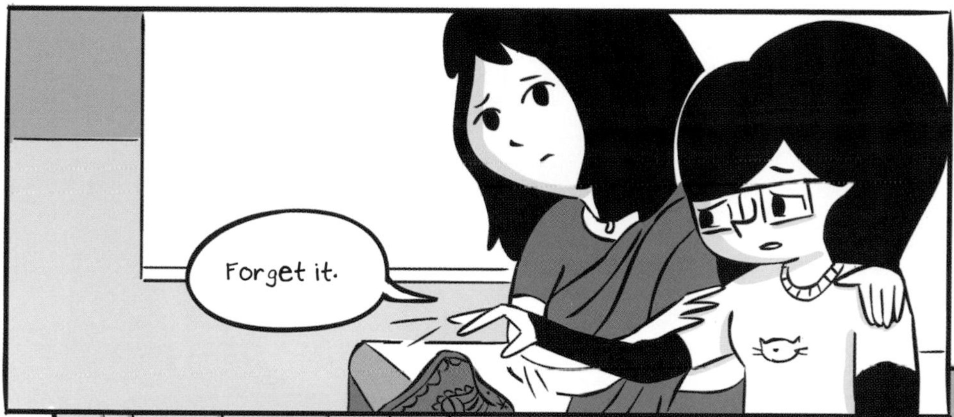
Forget it.

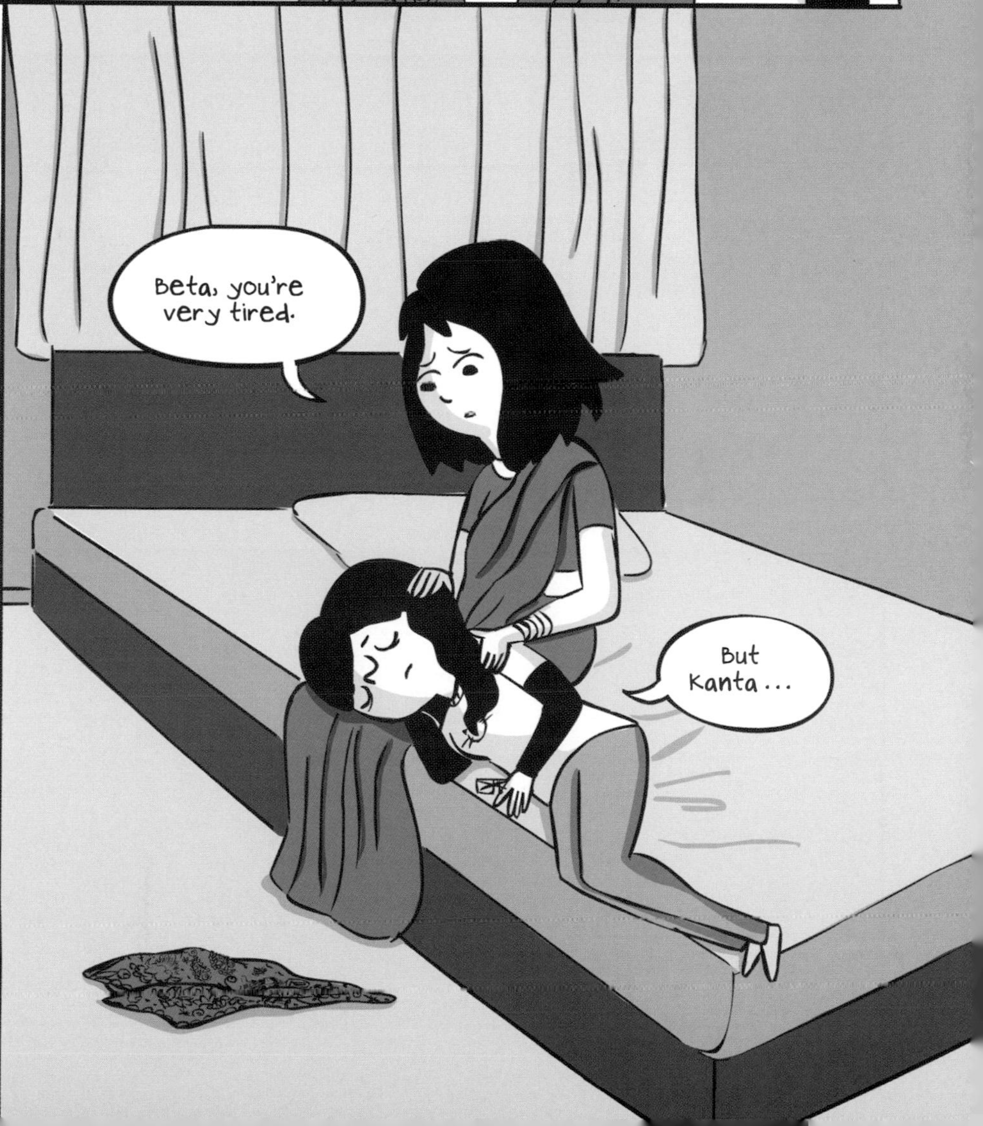
Beta, you're very tired.
But Kanta . . .

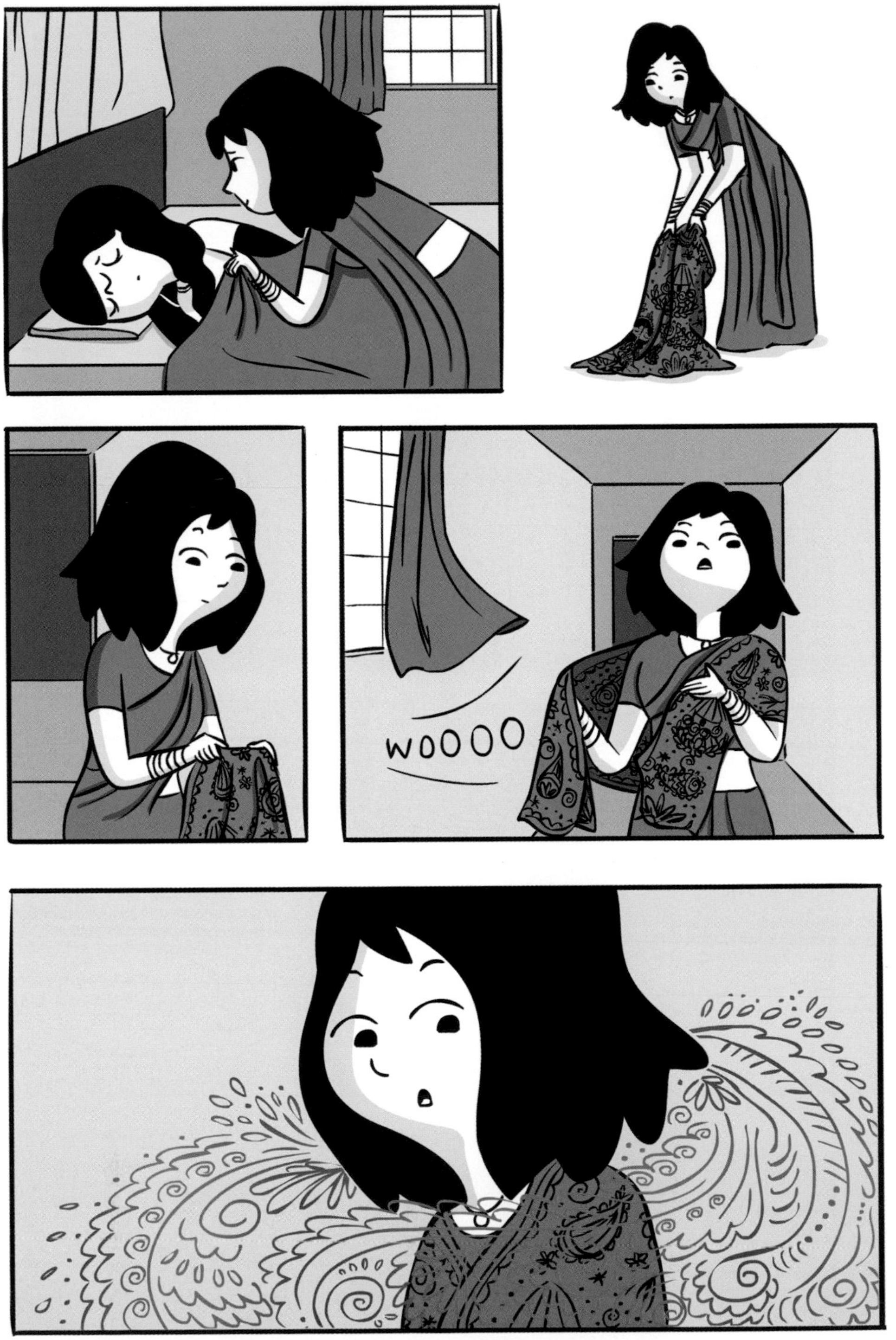
WOOOO

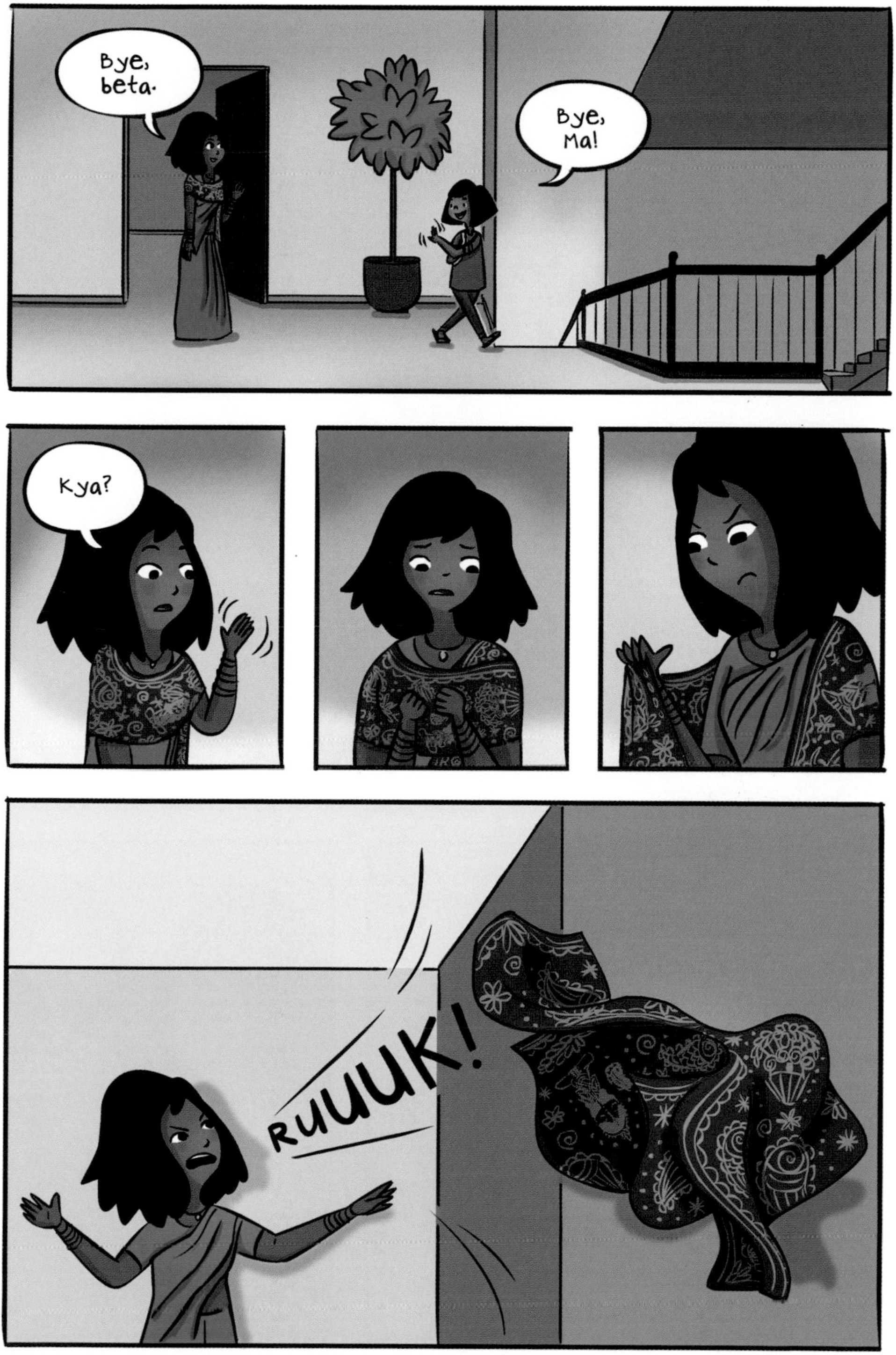

Bye, beta.
Bye, Ma!
Kya?
RUUUK!

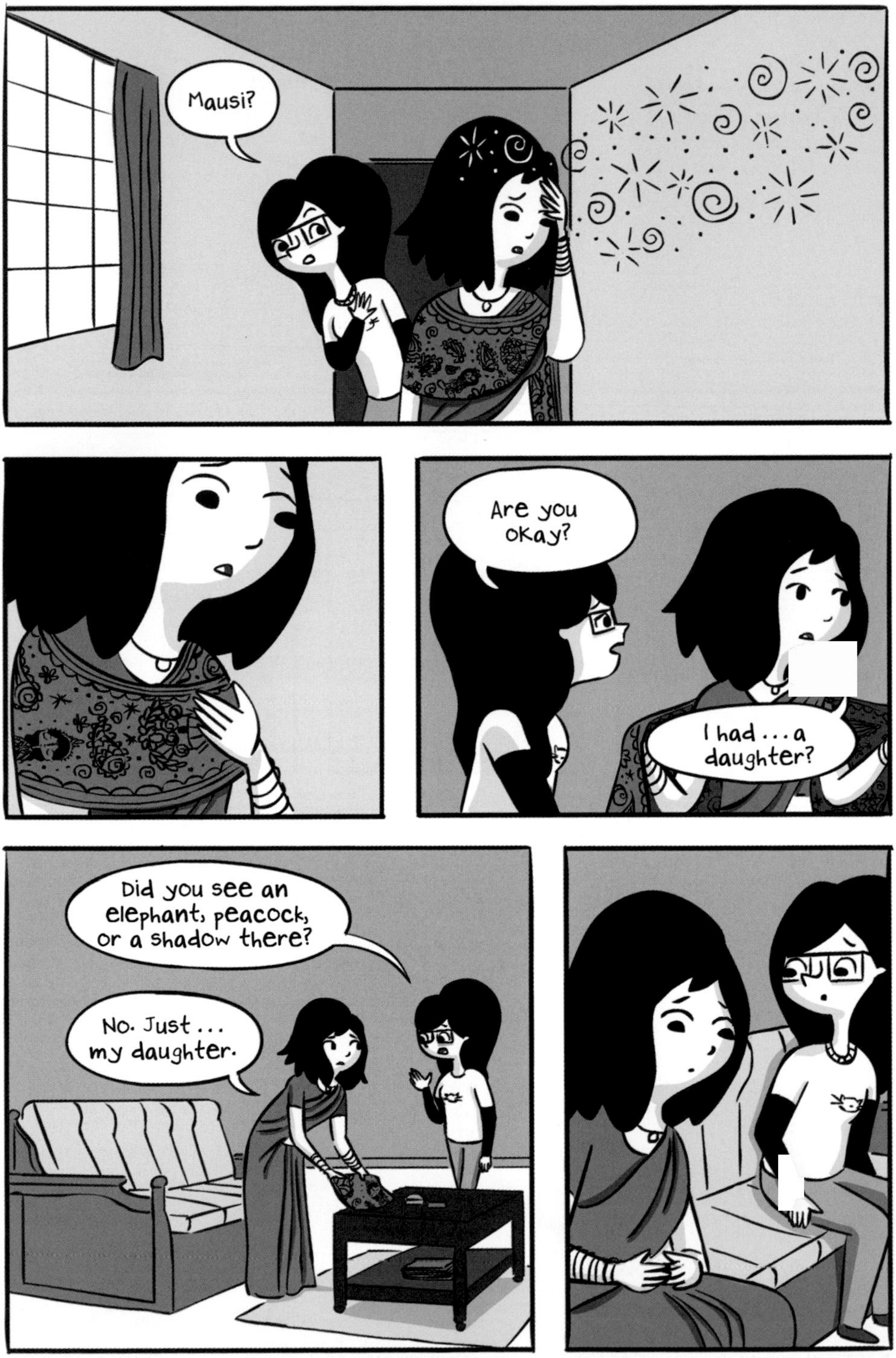
Mausi?
Are you okay?
I had . . . a daughter?
Did you see an elephant, peacock, or a shadow there?
No. Just . . . my daughter.

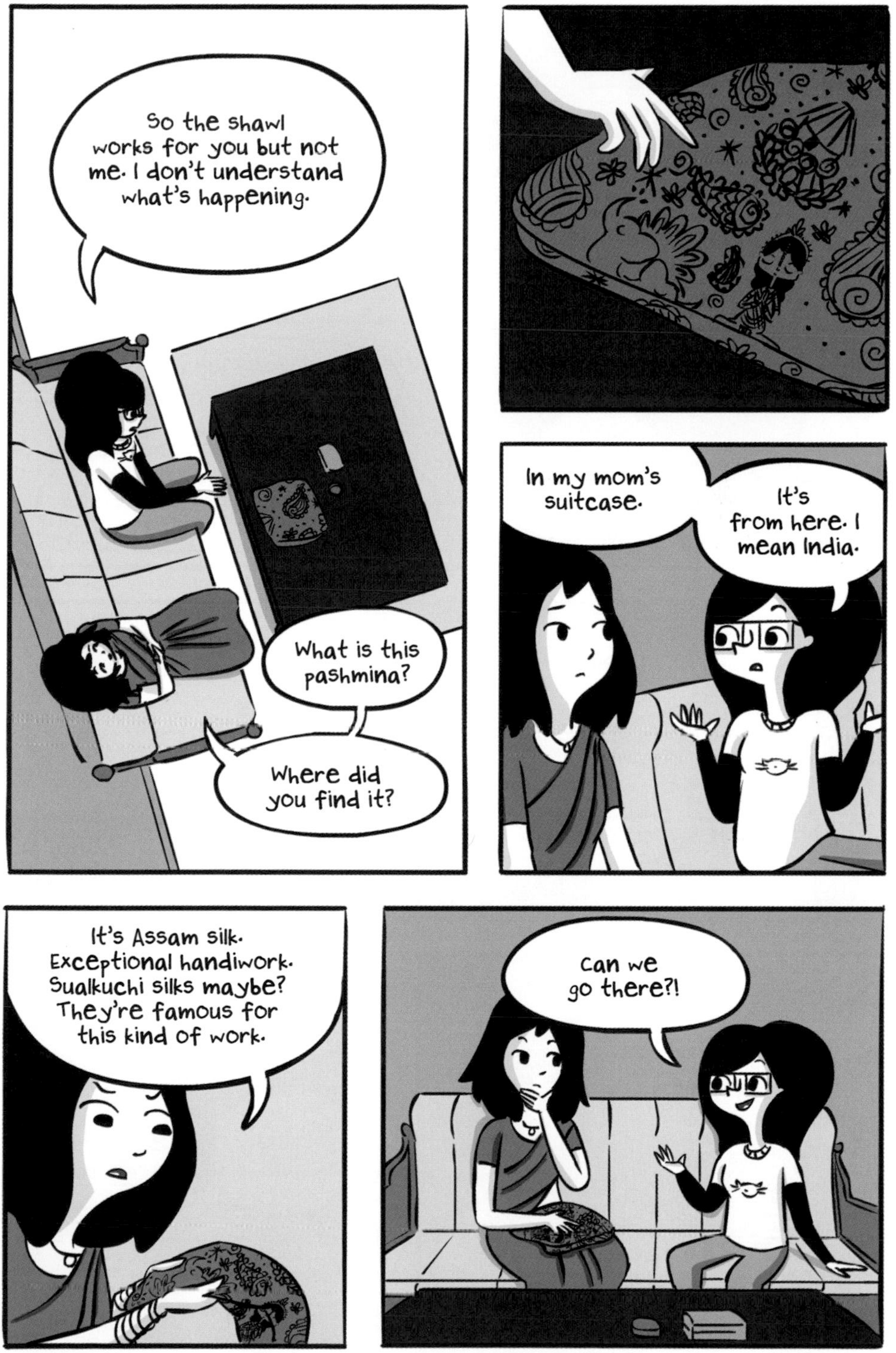
So the shawl works for you but not me. I don't understand what's happening.
What is this pashmina?
Where did you find it?
In my mom's suitcase.
It's from here. I mean India.
It's Assam silk. Exceptional handiwork. Sualkuchi silks maybe? They're famous for this kind of work.
Can we go there?!

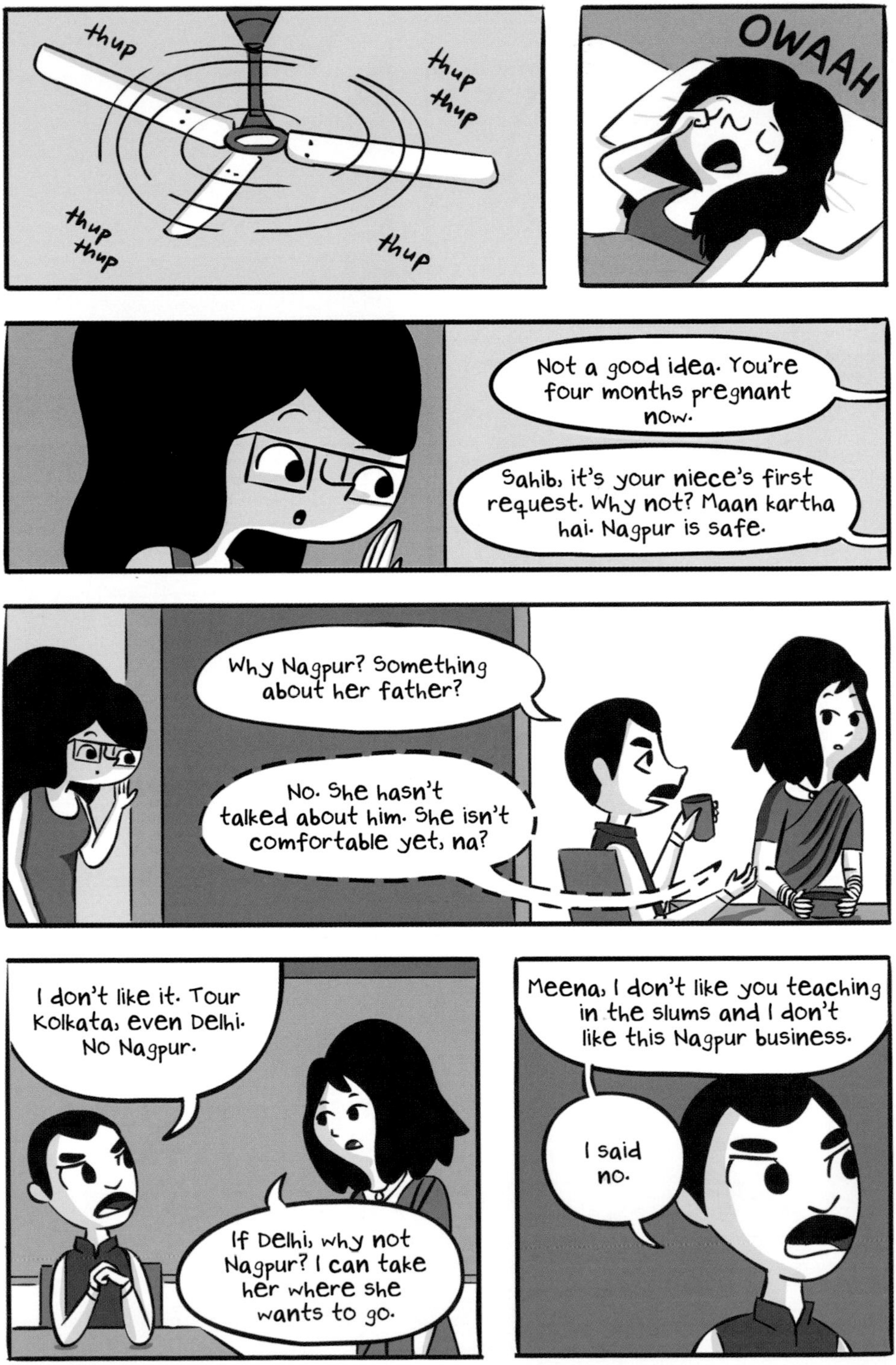
thup
thup thup
thup thup
thup
OWAAH
Not a good idea. You're four months pregnant now.
Sahib, it's your niece's first request. Why not? Maan kartha hai. Nagpur is safe.
Why Nagpur? Something about her father?
No. She hasn't talked about him. She isn't comfortable yet, na?
I don't like it. Tour Kolkata, even Delhi. No Nagpur.
If Delhi, why not Nagpur? I can take her where she wants to go.
Meena, I don't like you teaching in the slums and I don't like this Nagpur business.
I said no.

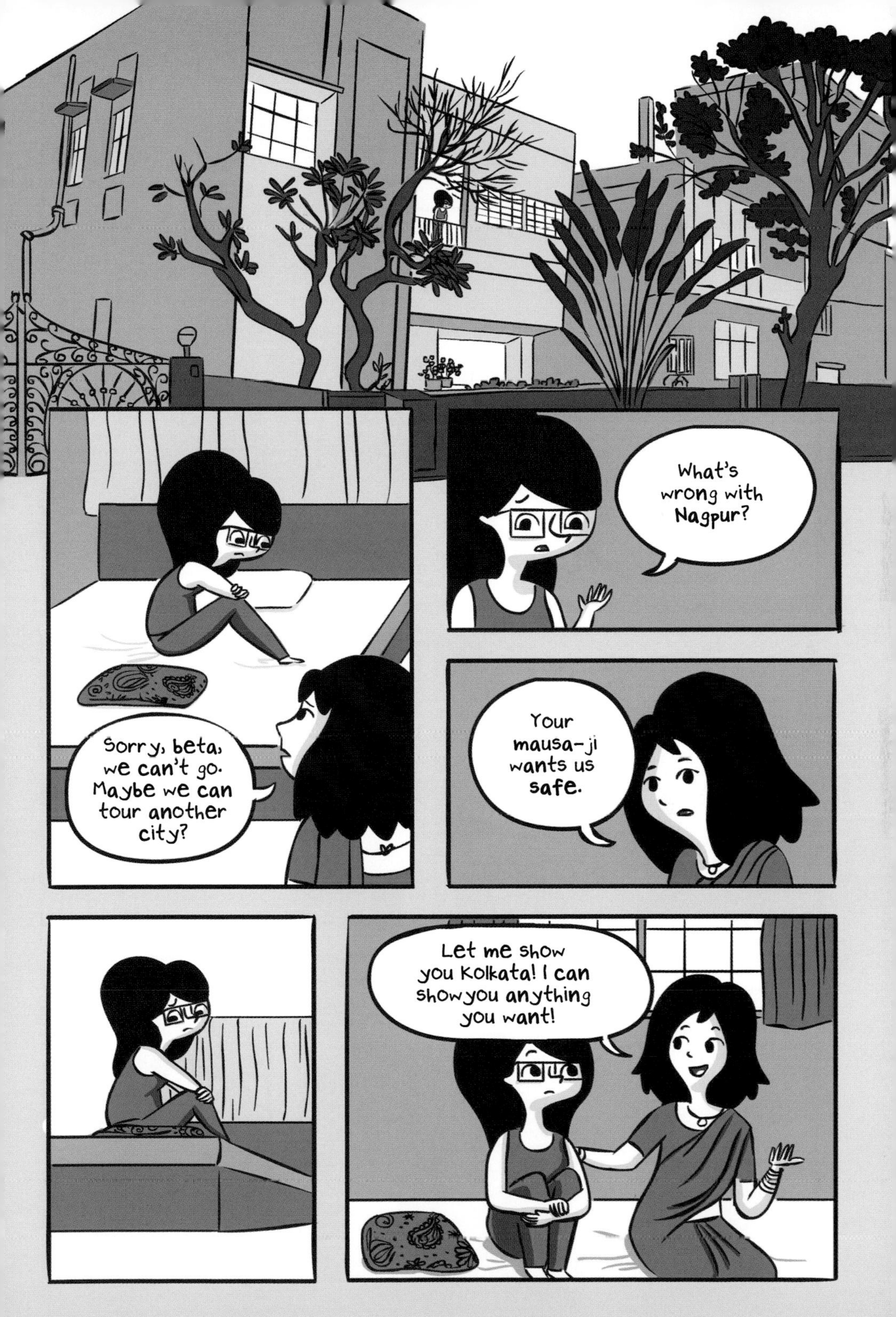
Sorry, beta, we can't go. Maybe we can tour another city?
What's wrong with Nagpur?
Your mausa-ji wants us safe.
Let me show you Kolkata! I can show you anything you want!

Yahan thik hain. Thank you.

thuk thuk

thuk

New market has everything.

Good for gifts, too.

Bangles, bhabi?

NRI-price saris!

NEERA'S SAREES

VISHAL'S fashion trends

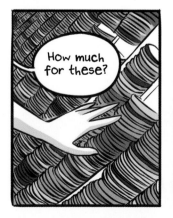

How much for these?

So pretty!

Garam-garam jelabi is the best!

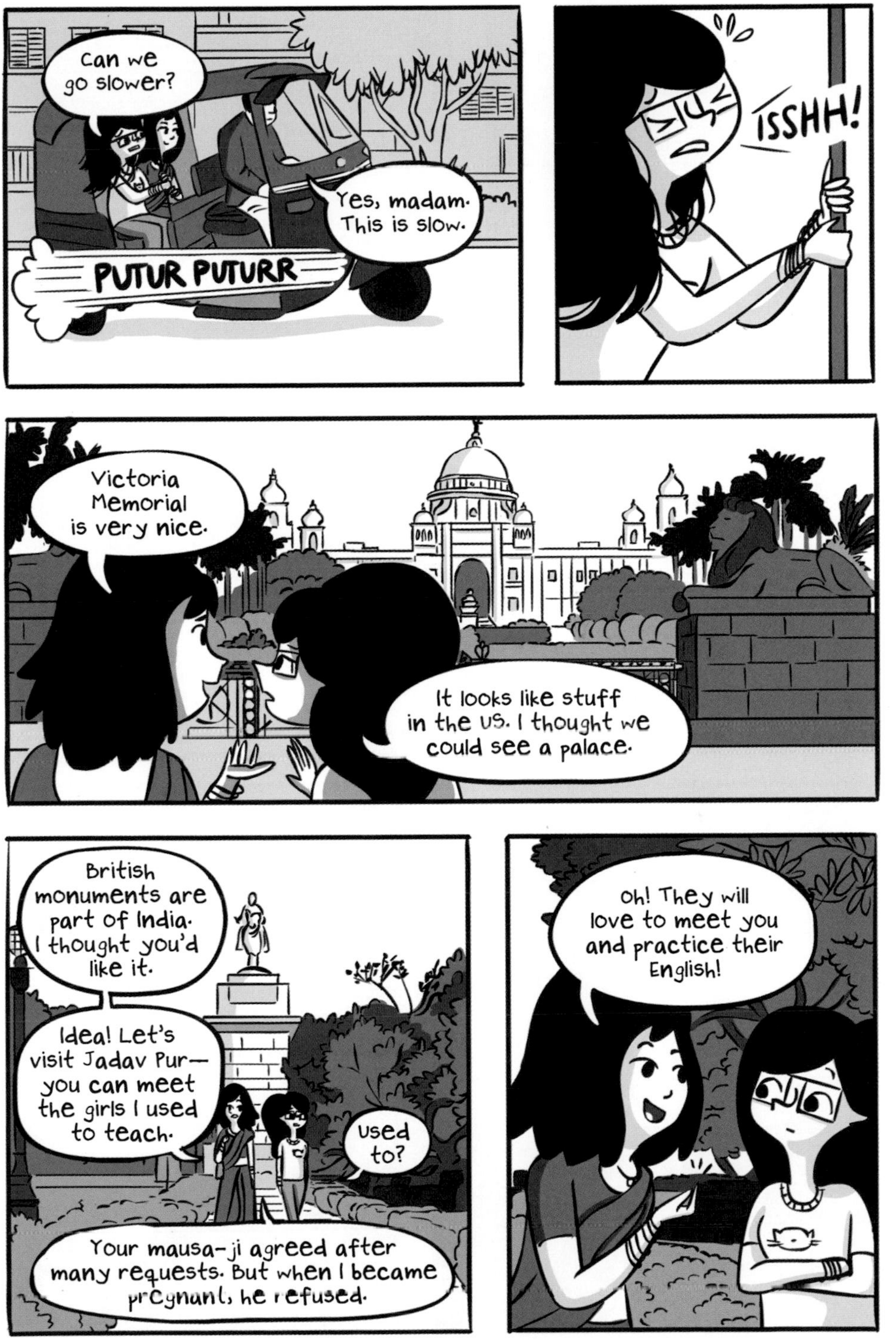
Can we go slower?
Yes, madam. This is slow.
PUTUR PUTURR
ISSHH!
Victoria Memorial is very nice.
It looks like stuff in the US. I thought we could see a palace.
British monuments are part of India. I thought you'd like it.
Idea! Let's visit Jadav Pur— you can meet the girls I used to teach.
Used to?
Your mausa-ji agreed after many requests. But when I became pregnant, he refused.
Oh! They will love to meet you and practice their English!

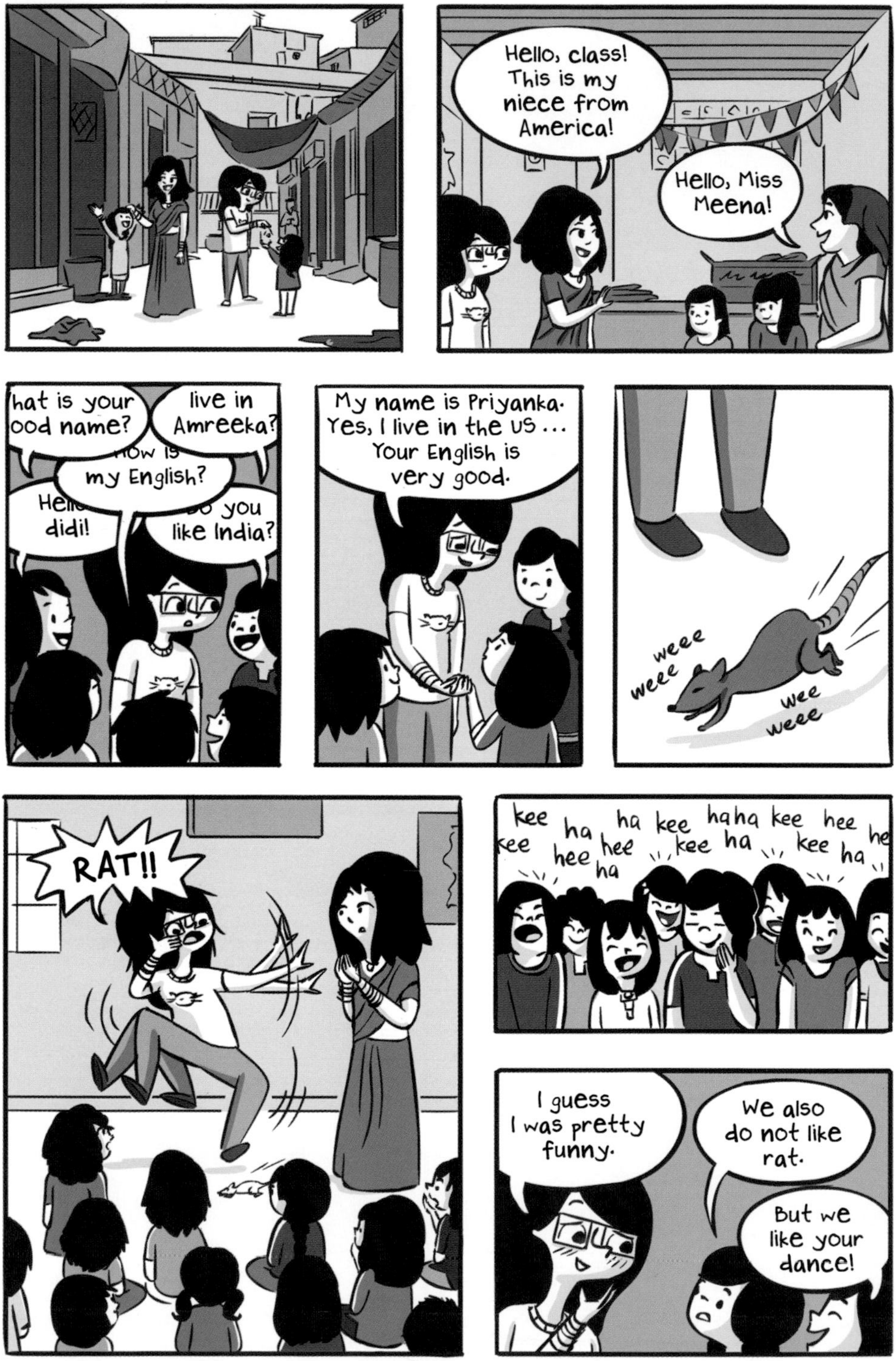
Hello, class! This is my niece from America!
Hello, Miss Meena!
hat is your ood name?
live in Amreeka?
my English?
didi!
like India?
My name is Priyanka. Yes, I live in the US ... Your English is very good.
weee weee
wee weee
RAT!!
kee ha ha kee haha kee hee
kee hee hee ha kee ha kee ha
I guess I was pretty funny.
We also do not like rat.
But we like your dance!

A leaf plate!

Oh my god, this dosa is so good.

Oops.

I've never been anywhere like that. It was so sad.

Sad? Why? They are learning and that will change their lives, Priyanka.

Do not look at the dirt. Look at the people.

But I can't help feeling sad for the girls. My mom told me about the poverty... but it's another thing to see it.

But they are being educated. That is what matters.

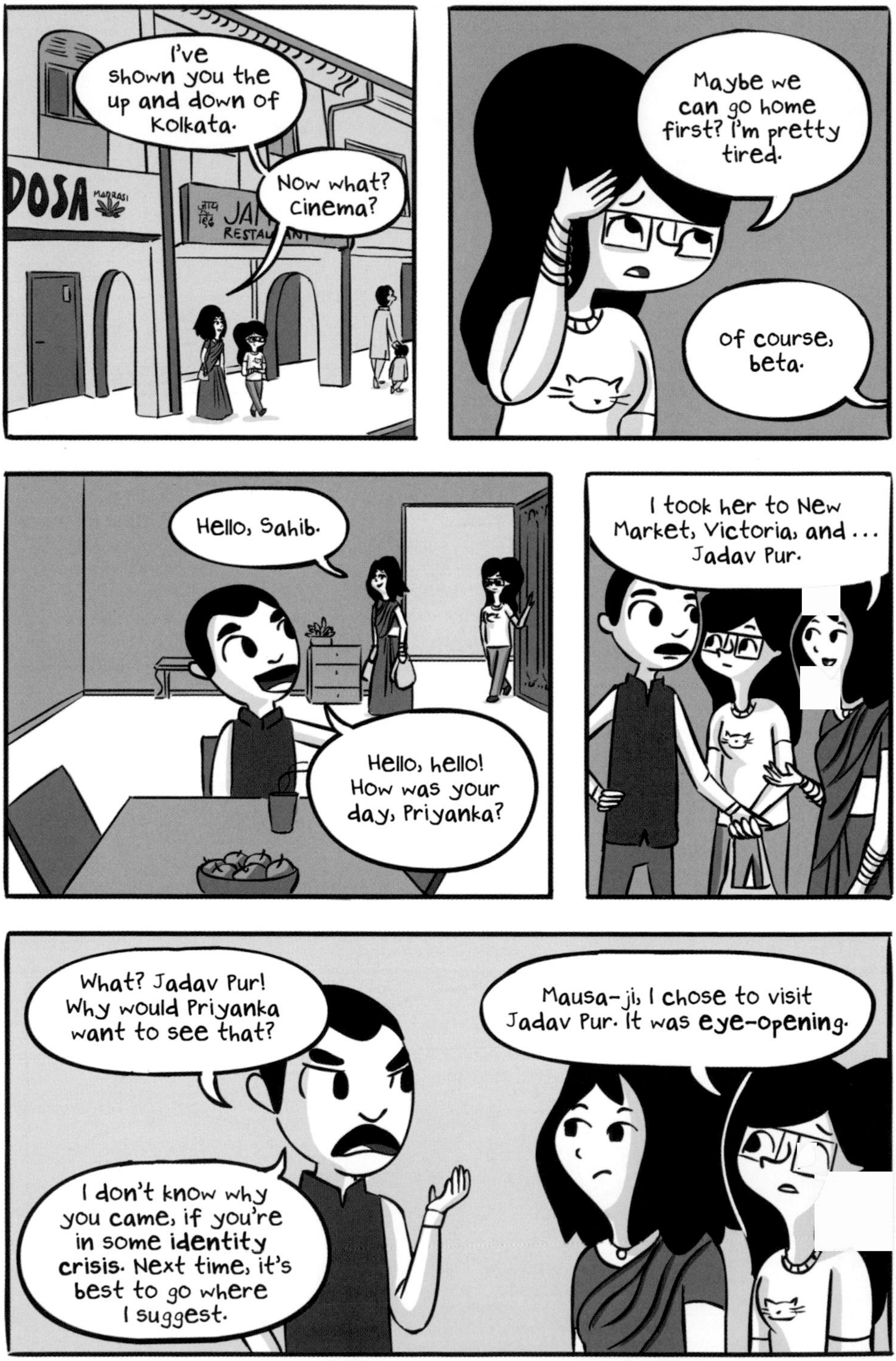
I've shown you the up and down of Kolkata.
Now what? Cinema?
DOSA MADRASI
JAM RESTAURANT
Maybe we can go home first? I'm pretty tired.
Of course, beta.
Hello, Sahib.
Hello, hello! How was your day, Priyanka?
I took her to New Market, Victoria, and . . . Jadav Pur.
What? Jadav Pur! Why would Priyanka want to see that?
I don't know why you came, if you're in some identity crisis. Next time, it's best to go where I suggest.
Mausa-ji, I chose to visit Jadav Pur. It was eye-opening.

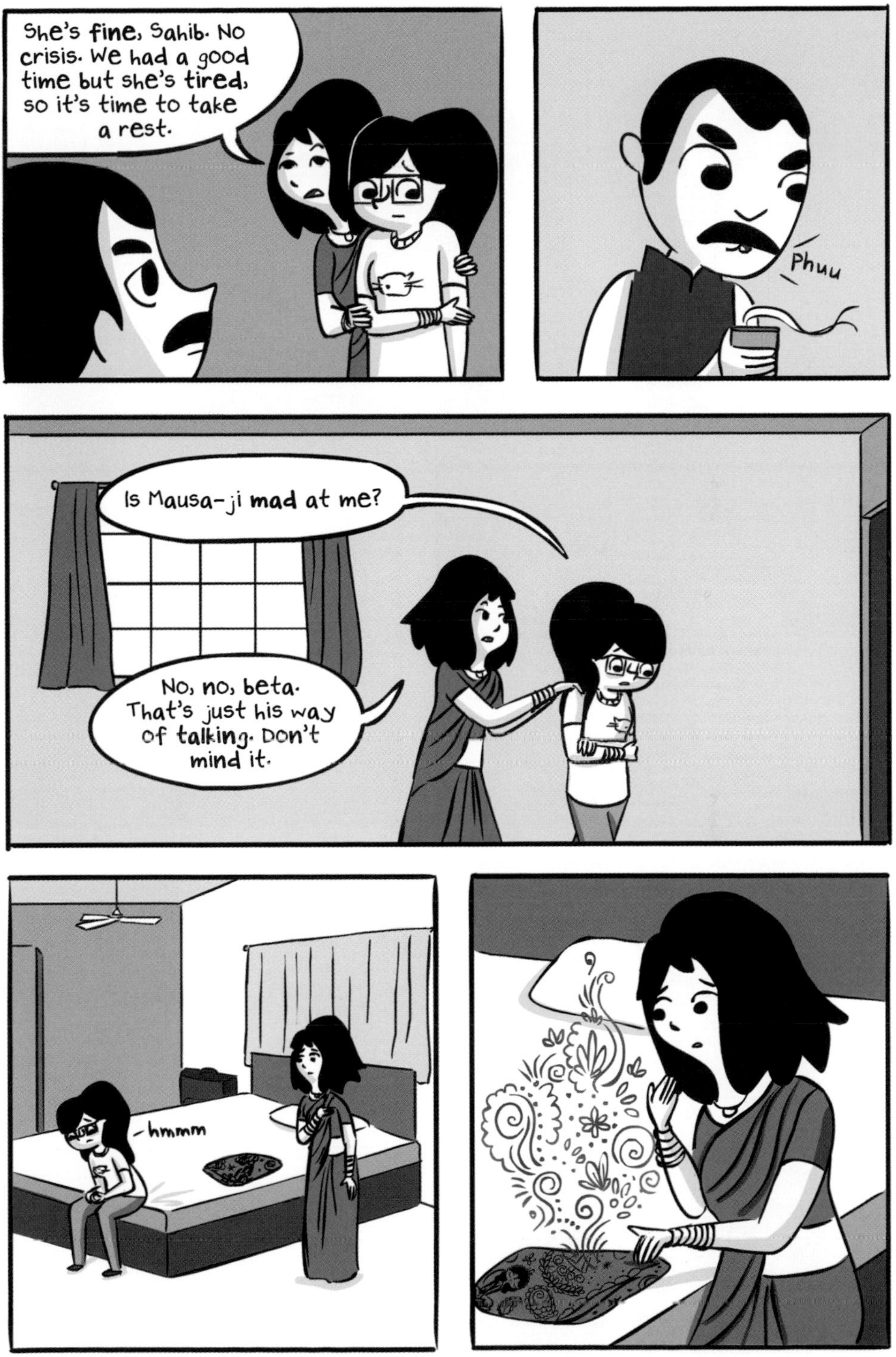
She's fine, Sahib. No crisis. We had a good time but she's tired, so it's time to take a rest.
Phuu
Is Mausa-ji mad at me?
No, no, beta. That's just his way of talking. Don't mind it.
-hmmm

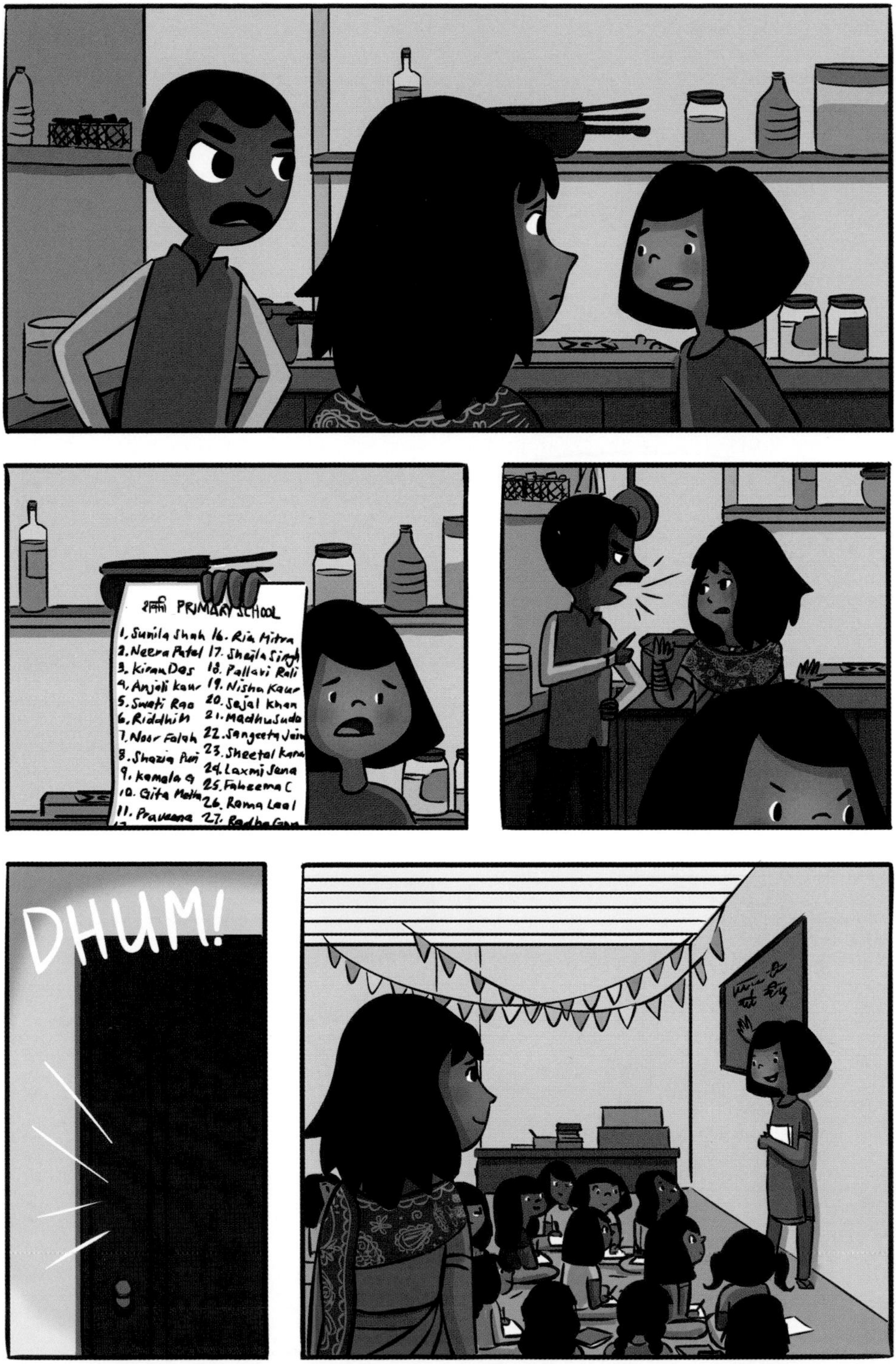
शक्ति PRIMARY SCHOOL
1. Sunila Shah
2. Neera Patel
3. Kiran Das
4. Anjali kaur
5. Swati Rao
6. Riddhi M
7. Noor Falah
8. Shazia Puri
9. kamala G
10. Gita Metha
11. Praveena
16. Ria Mitra
17. Sheila Singh
18. Pallavi Rali
19. Nisha Kaur
20. Sejal Khan
21. MadhuSuda
22. Sangeeta Jai
23. Sheetal Kana
24. Laxmi Sena
25. Faheema C
26. Rama Laal
DHUM!

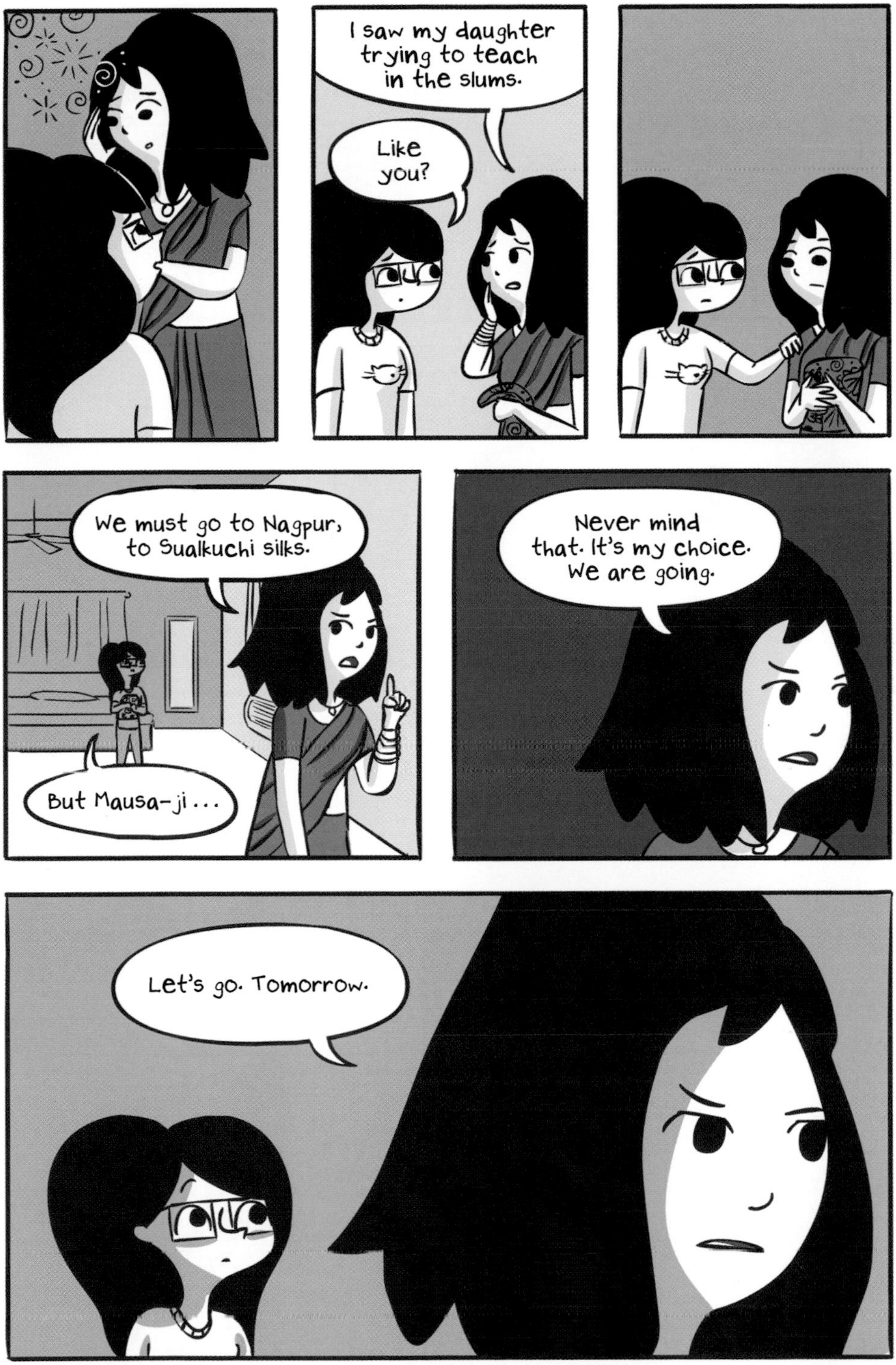
I saw my daughter trying to teach in the slums.
Like you?
We must go to Nagpur, to Sualkuchi silks.
But Mausa-ji . . .
Never mind that. It's my choice. We are going.
Let's go. Tomorrow.

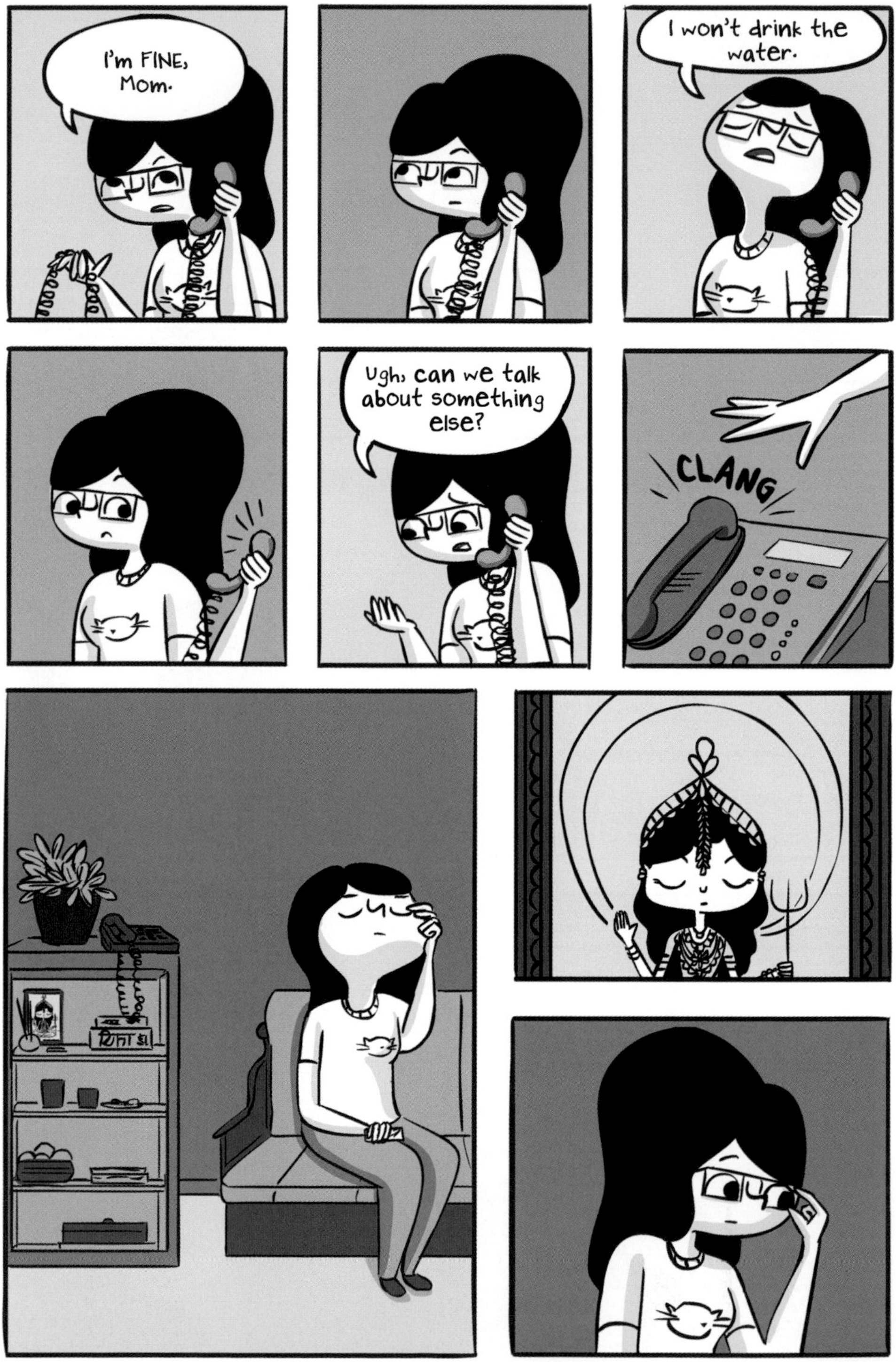
I'm FINE, Mom.
I won't drink the water.
Ugh, can we talk about something else?
CLANG

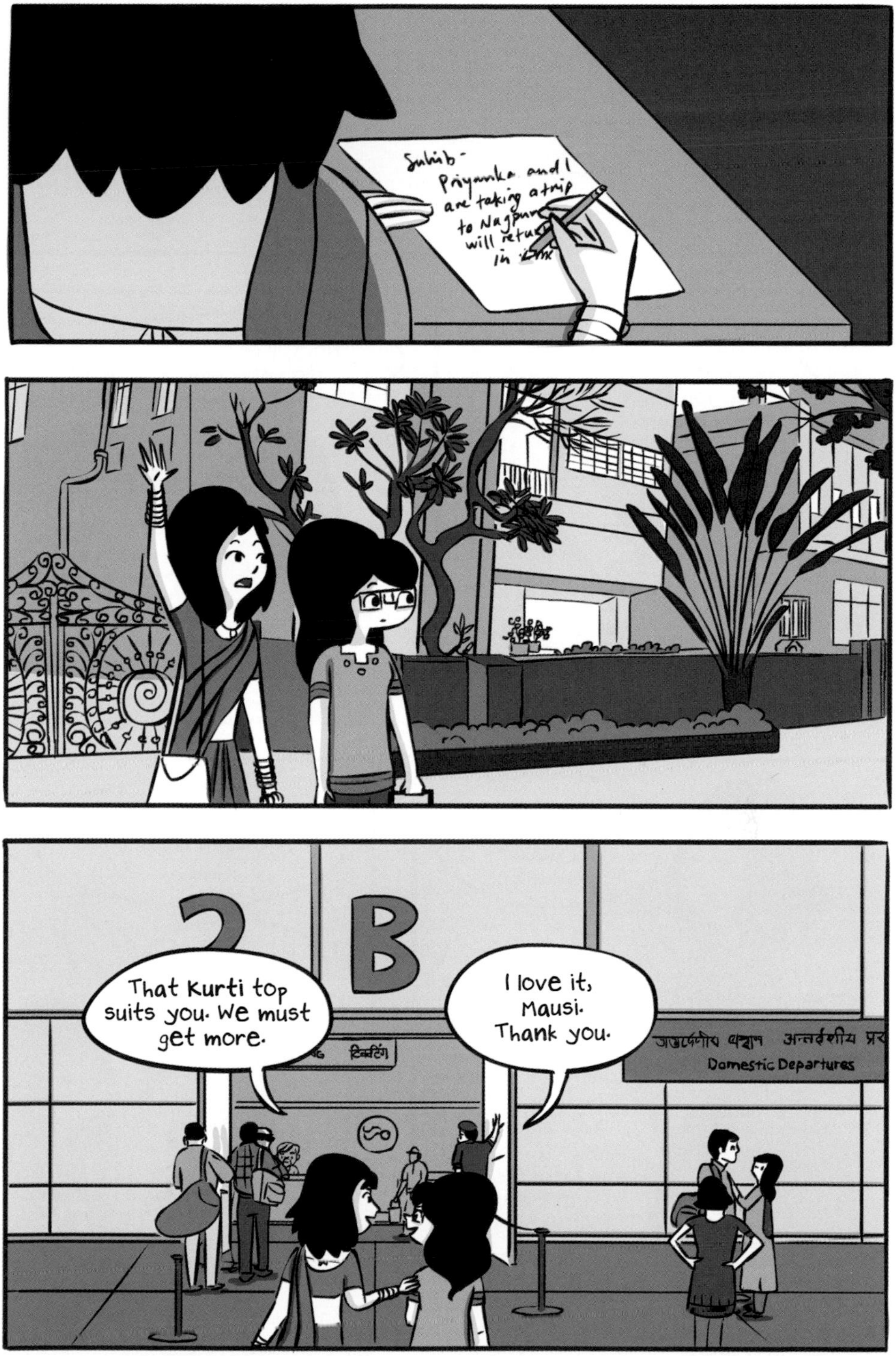
Priyanka and I
are taking a trip
2B
That Kurti top suits you. We must get more.
I love it, Mausi. Thank you.
Domestic Departures

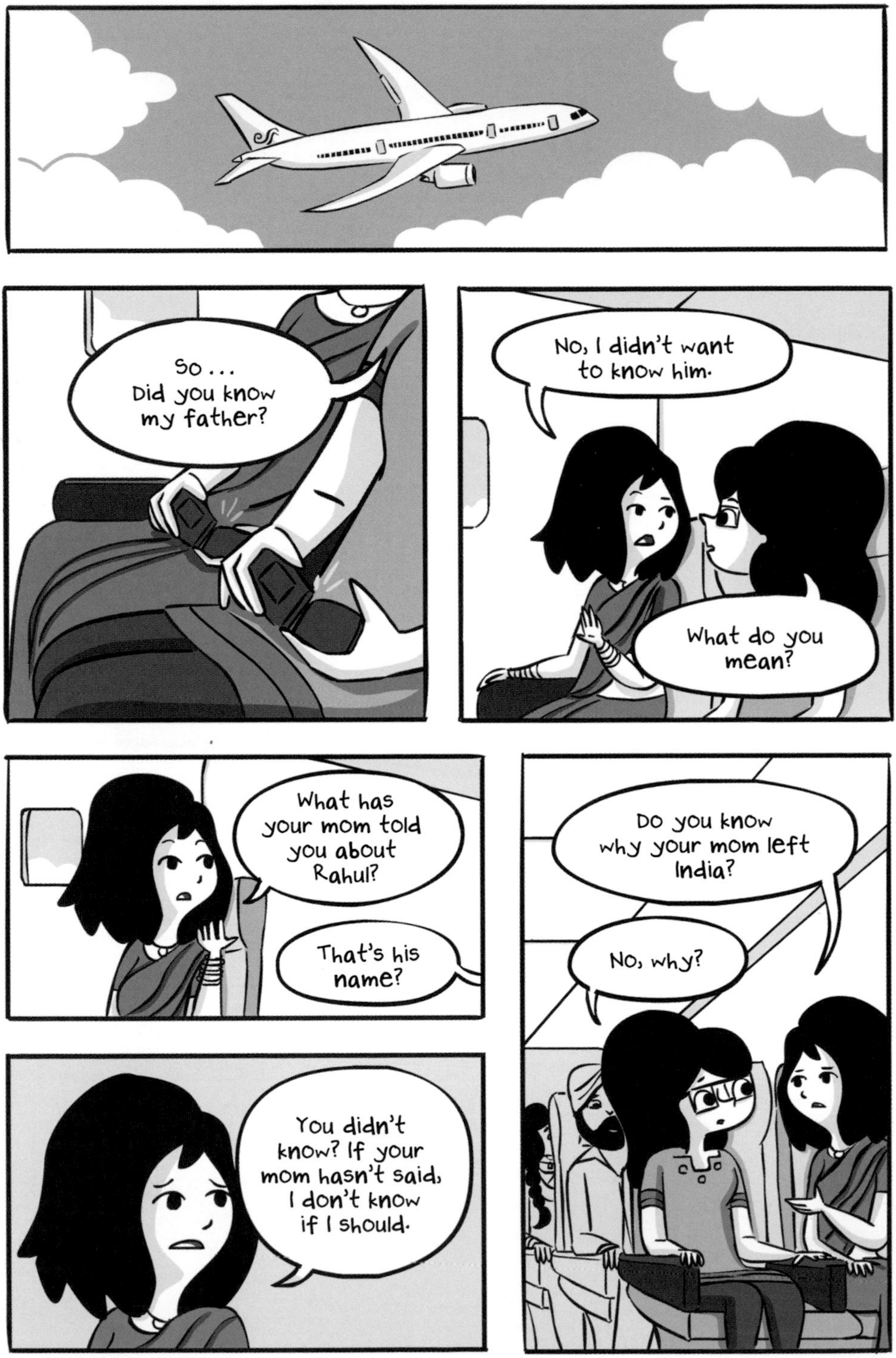
So . . .
Did you know my father?
No, I didn't want to know him.
What do you mean?
What has your mom told you about Rahul?
That's his name?
You didn't know? If your mom hasn't said, I don't know if I should.
Do you know why your mom left India?
No, why?

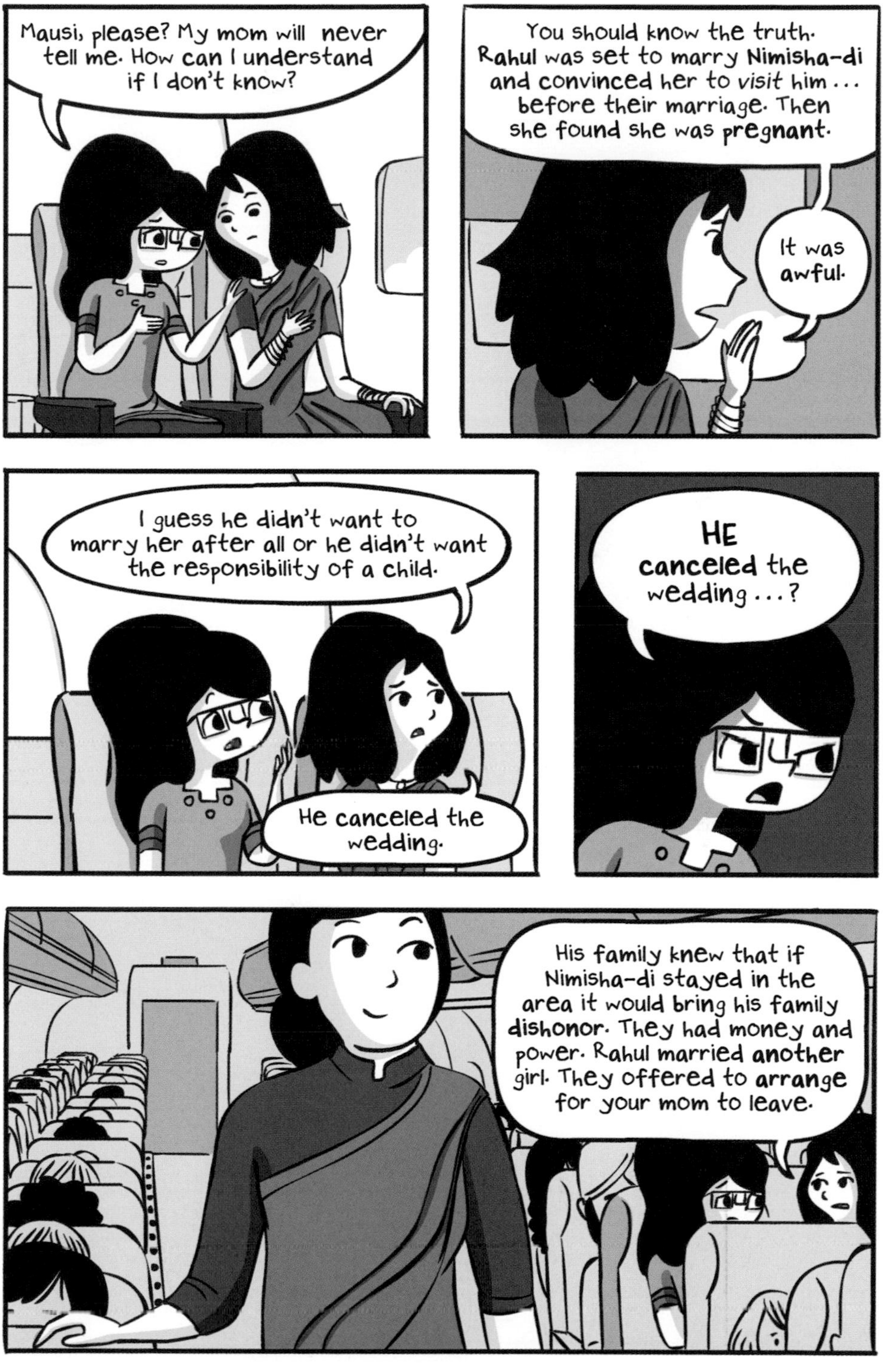
Mausi, please? My mom will never tell me. How can I understand if I don't know?
You should know the truth. Rahul was set to marry Nimisha-di and convinced her to visit him . . . before their marriage. Then she found she was pregnant.
It was awful.
I guess he didn't want to marry her after all or he didn't want the responsibility of a child.
He canceled the wedding.
HE canceled the wedding . . . ?
His family knew that if Nimisha-di stayed in the area it would bring his family dishonor. They had money and power. Rahul married another girl. They offered to arrange for your mom to leave.

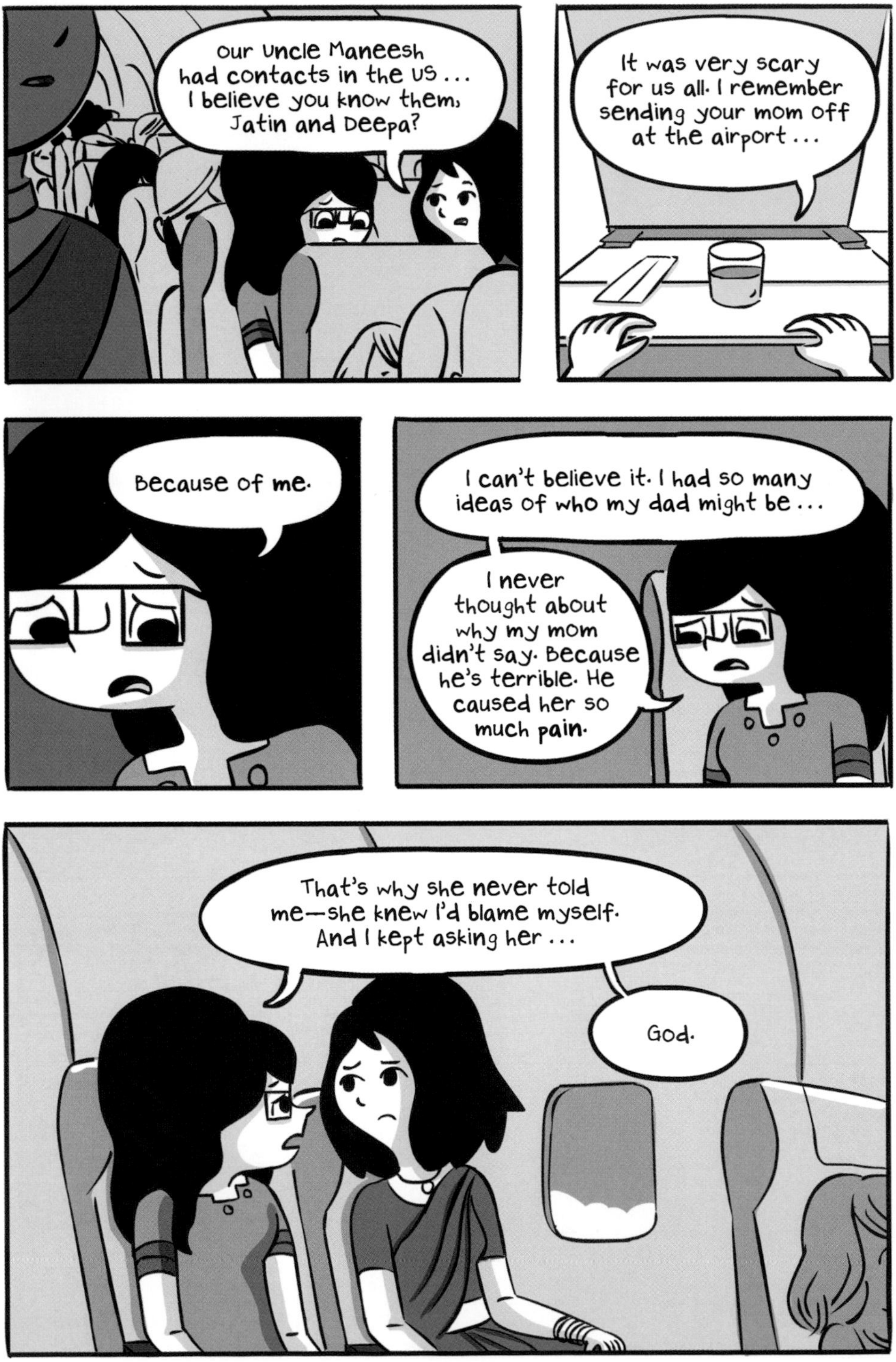
Our Uncle Maneesh had contacts in the US . . . I believe you know them, Jatin and Deepa?
It was very scary for us all. I remember sending your mom off at the airport . . .
Because of me.
I can't believe it. I had so many ideas of who my dad might be . . .
I never thought about why my mom didn't say. Because he's terrible. He caused her so much pain.
That's why she never told me—she knew I'd blame myself. And I kept asking her . . .
God.

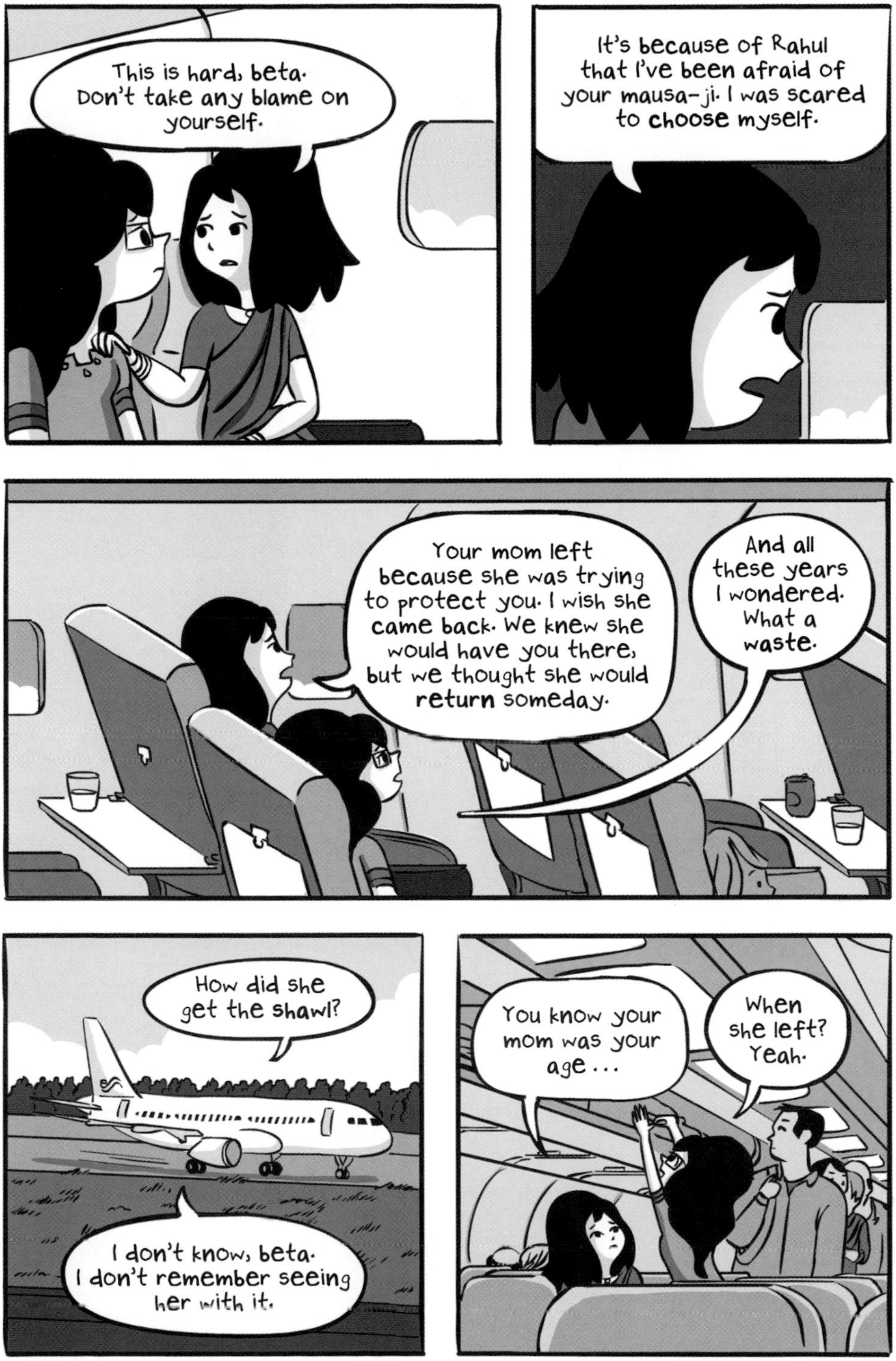
This is hard, beta. Don't take any blame on yourself.
It's because of Rahul that I've been afraid of your mausa-ji. I was scared to choose myself.
Your mom left because she was trying to protect you. I wish she came back. We knew she would have you there, but we thought she would return someday.
And all these years I wondered. What a waste.
How did she get the shawl?
I don't know, beta. I don't remember seeing her with it.
You know your mom was your age . . .
When she left? Yeah.

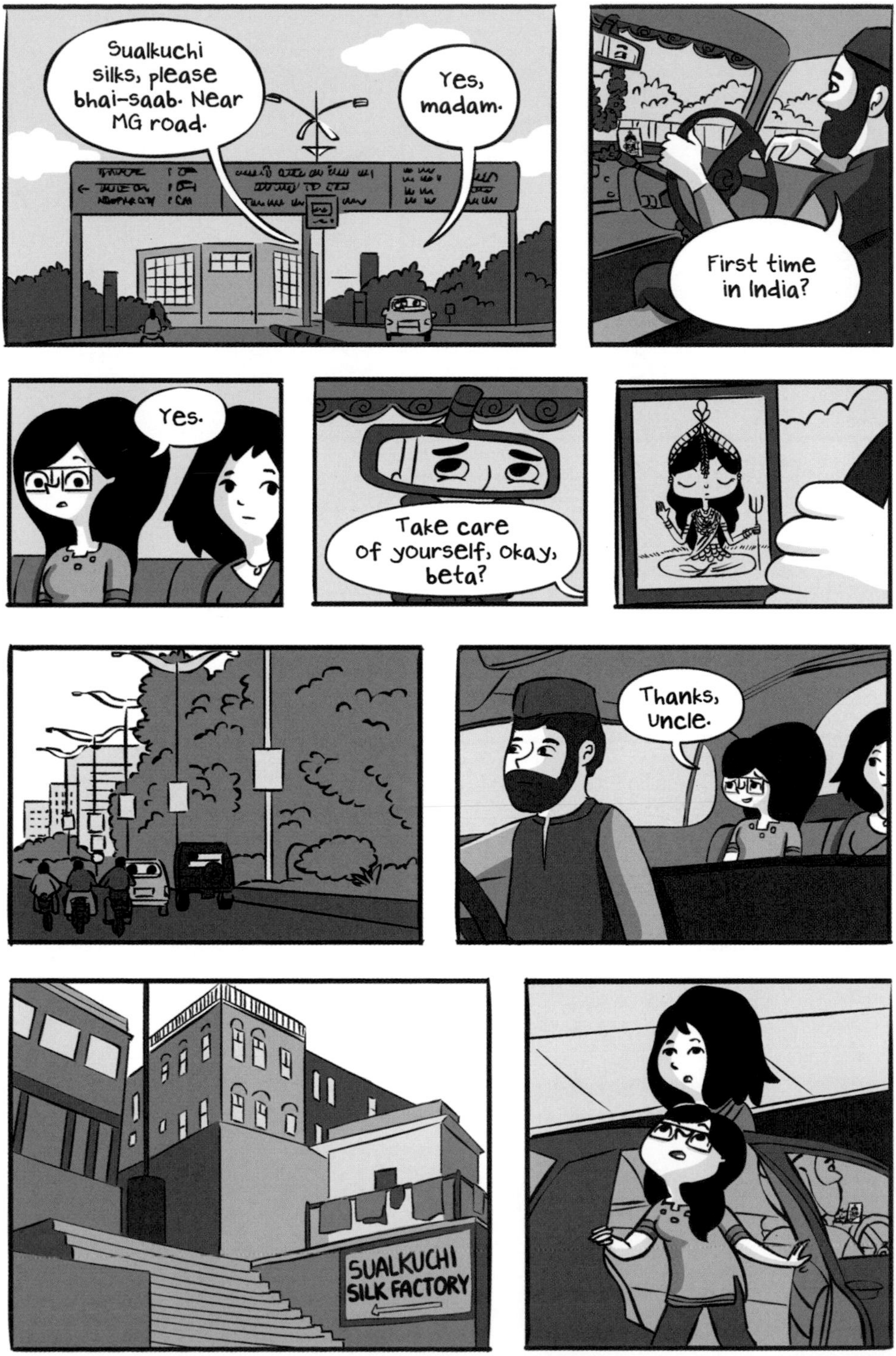
Sualkuchi silks, please bhai-saab. Near MG road.
Yes, madam.
First time in India?
Yes.
Take care of yourself, okay, beta?
Thanks, uncle.
SUALKUCHI SILK FACTORY

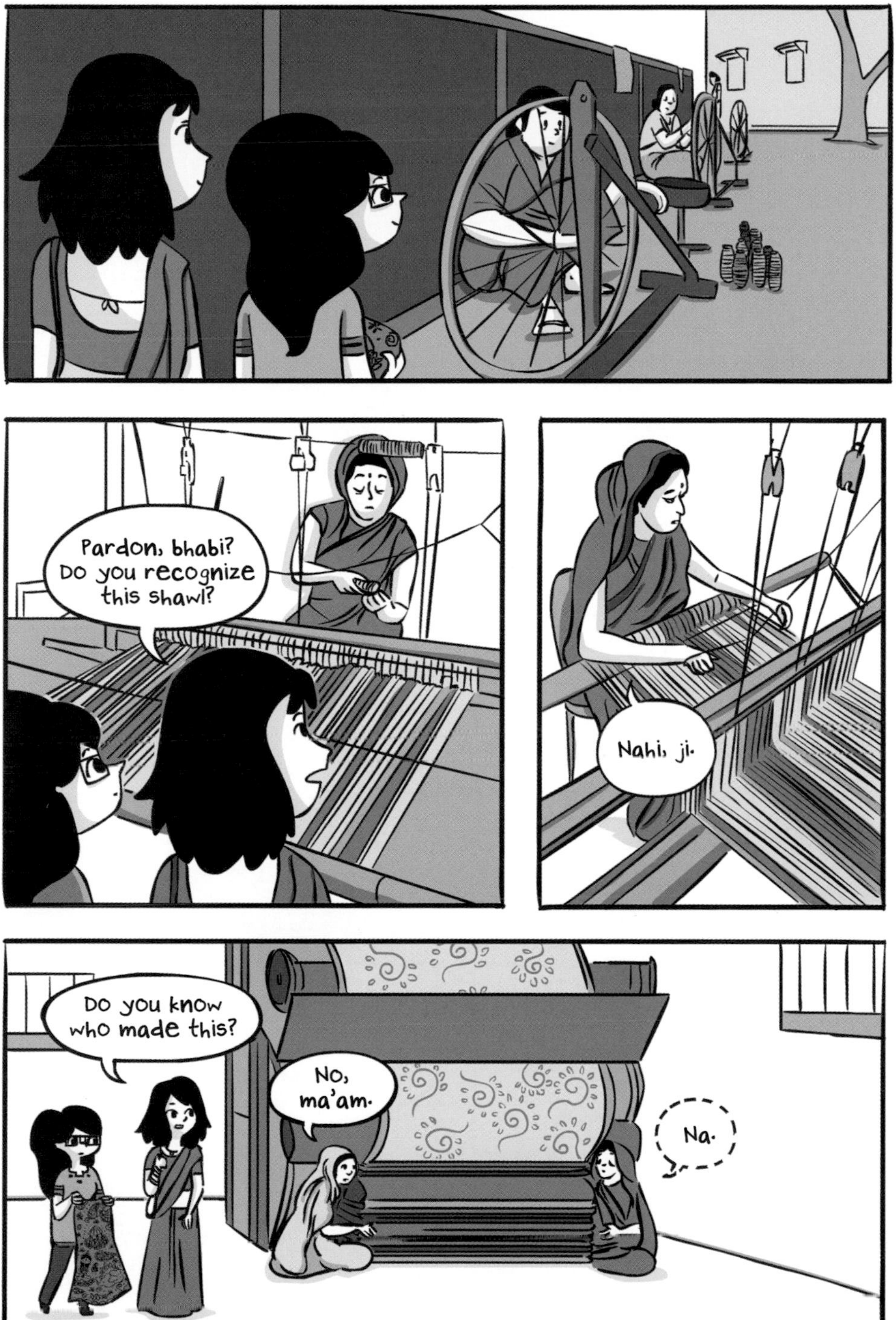
Pardon, bhabi? Do you recognize this shawl?
Nahi, ji.
Do you know who made this?
No, ma'am.
Na.

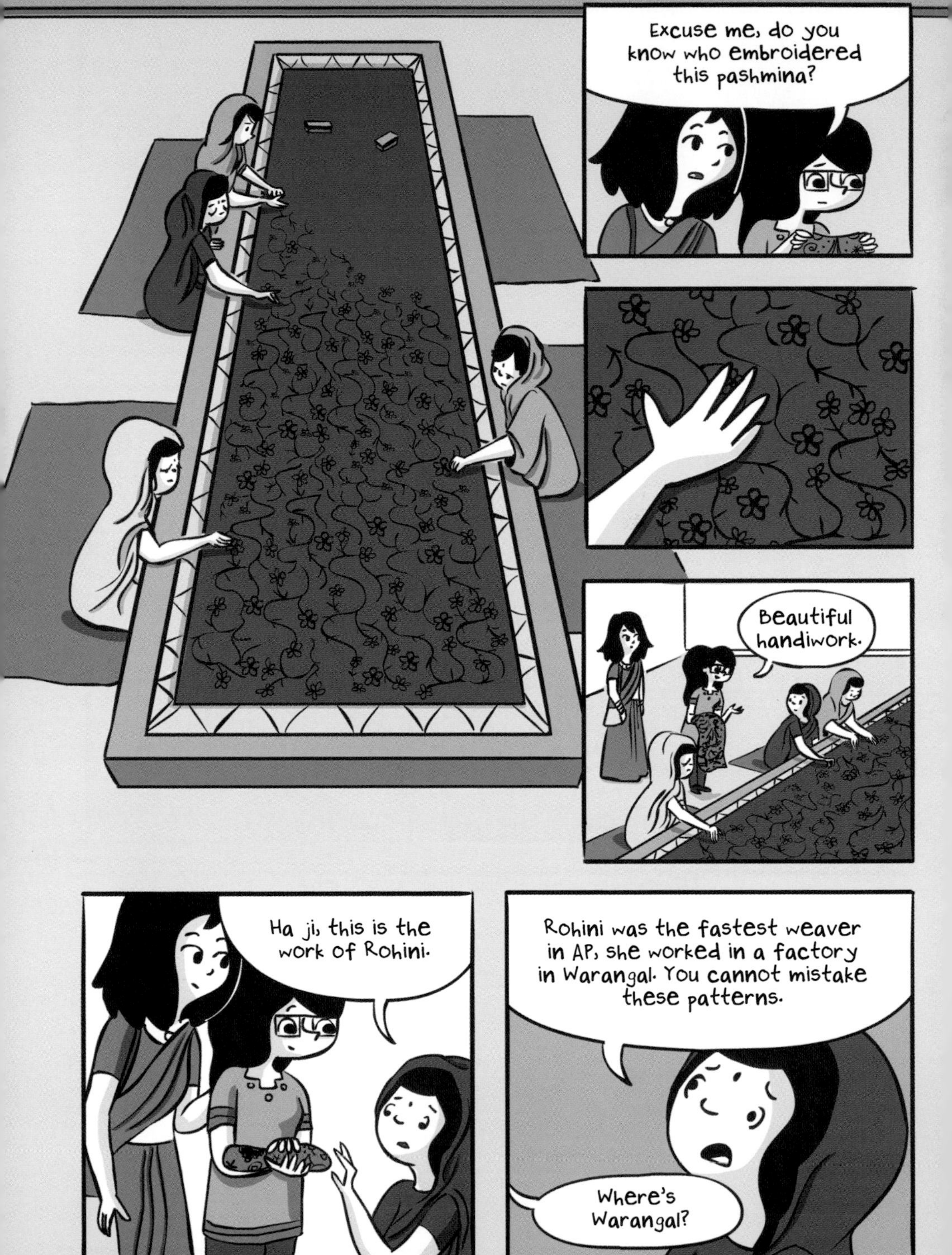
Excuse me, do you know who embroidered this pashmina?
Beautiful handiwork.
Ha ji, this is the work of Rohini.
Rohini was the fastest weaver in AP, she worked in a factory in Warangal. You cannot mistake these patterns.
Where's Warangal?

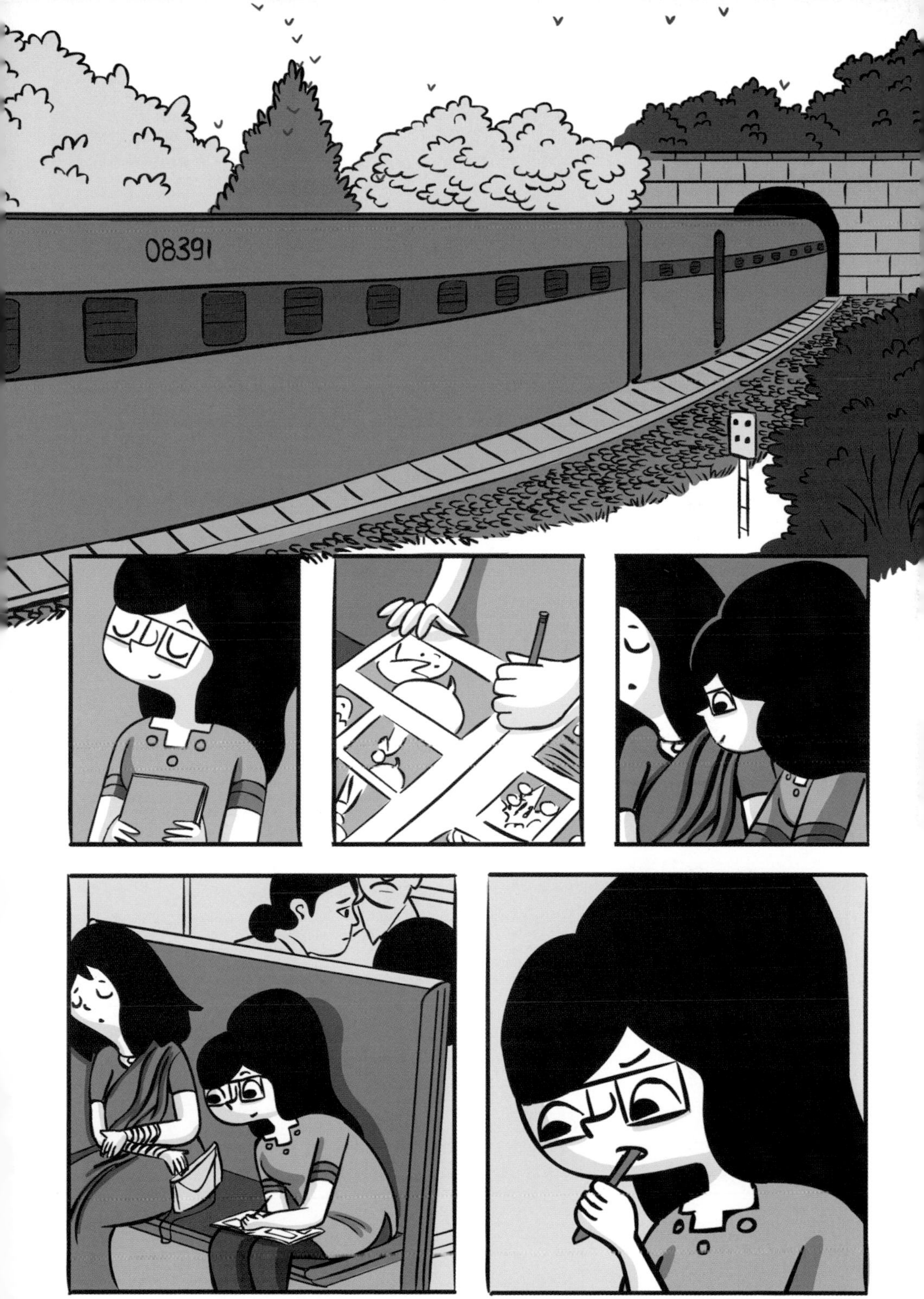
08391

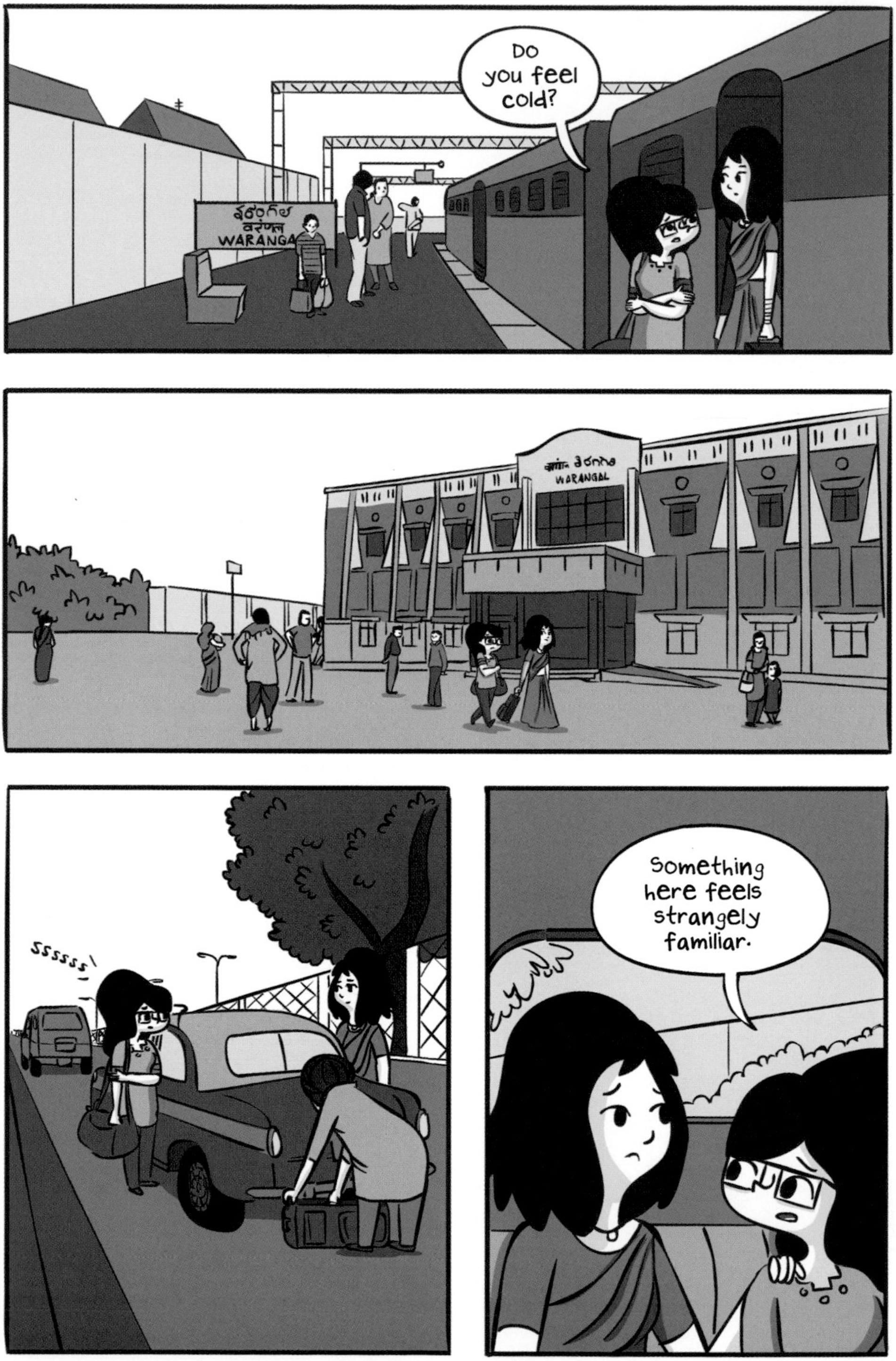
Do you feel cold?
WARANGA
WARANGAL
ssssss!
Something here feels strangely familiar.

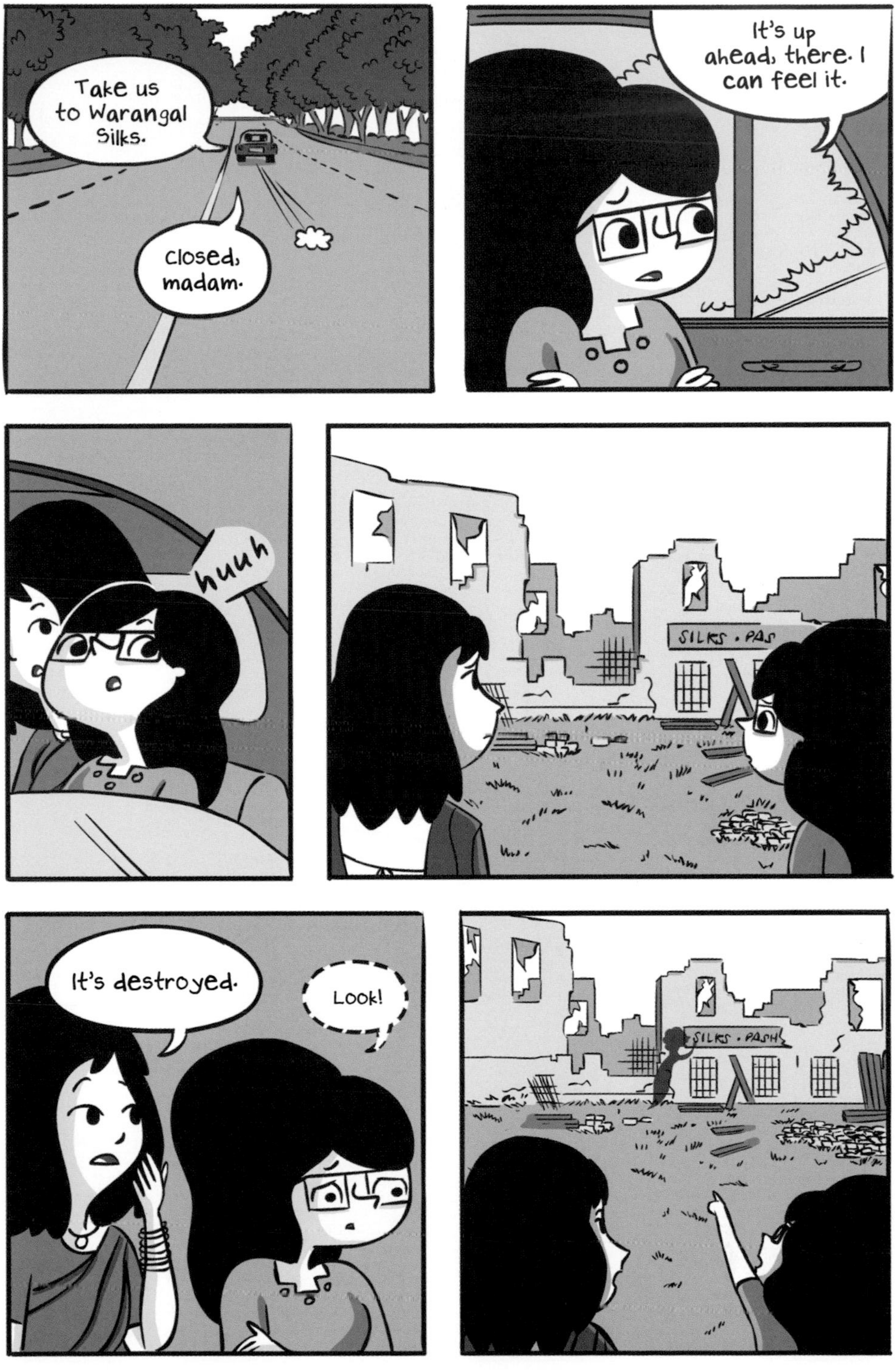

Take us to Warangal Silks.
Closed, madam.
It's up ahead, there. I can feel it.
huuh
SILKS • PAS
It's destroyed.
Look!
SILKS • PASH

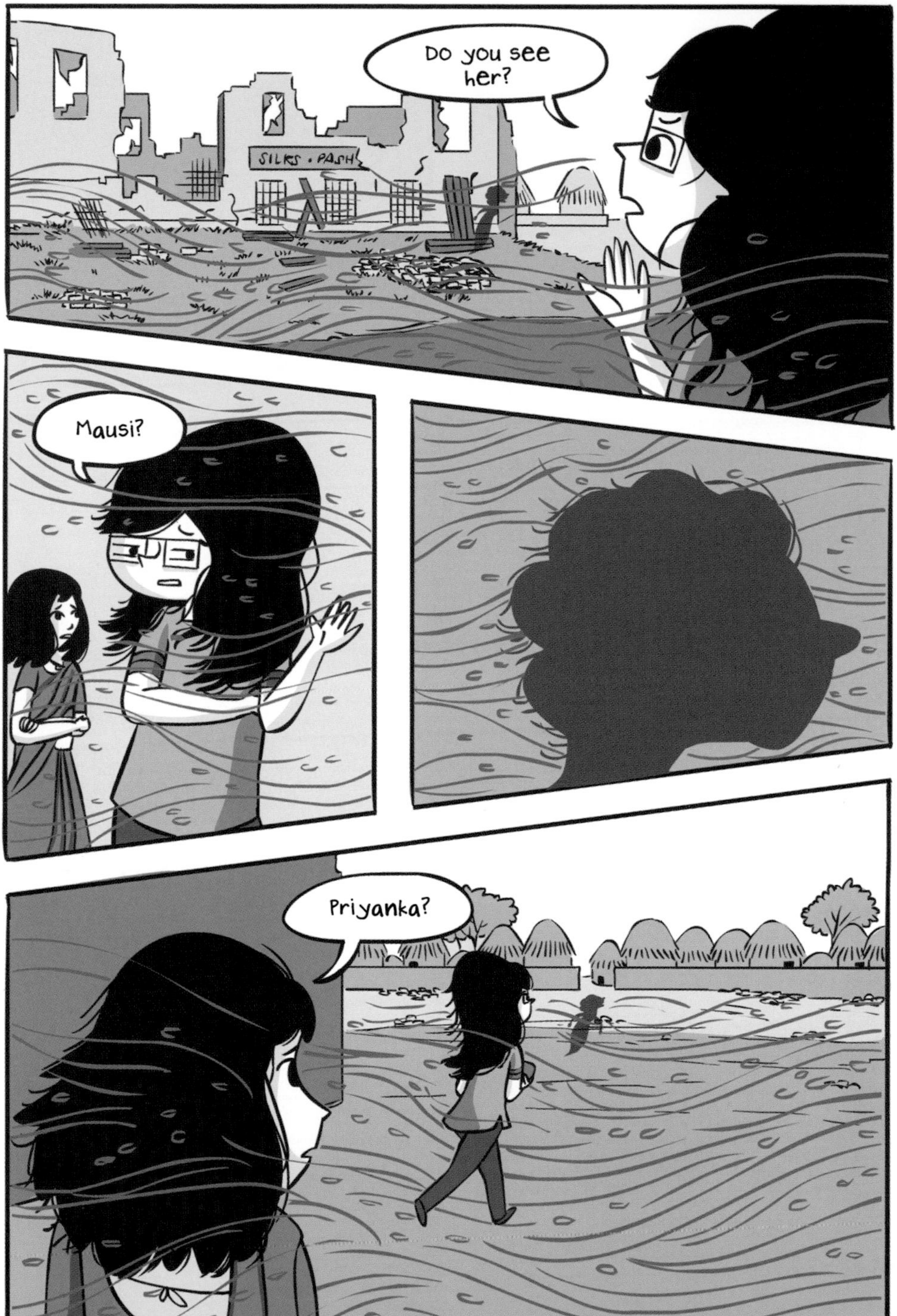
Do you see her?
SILKS • PASH
Mausi?
Priyanka?

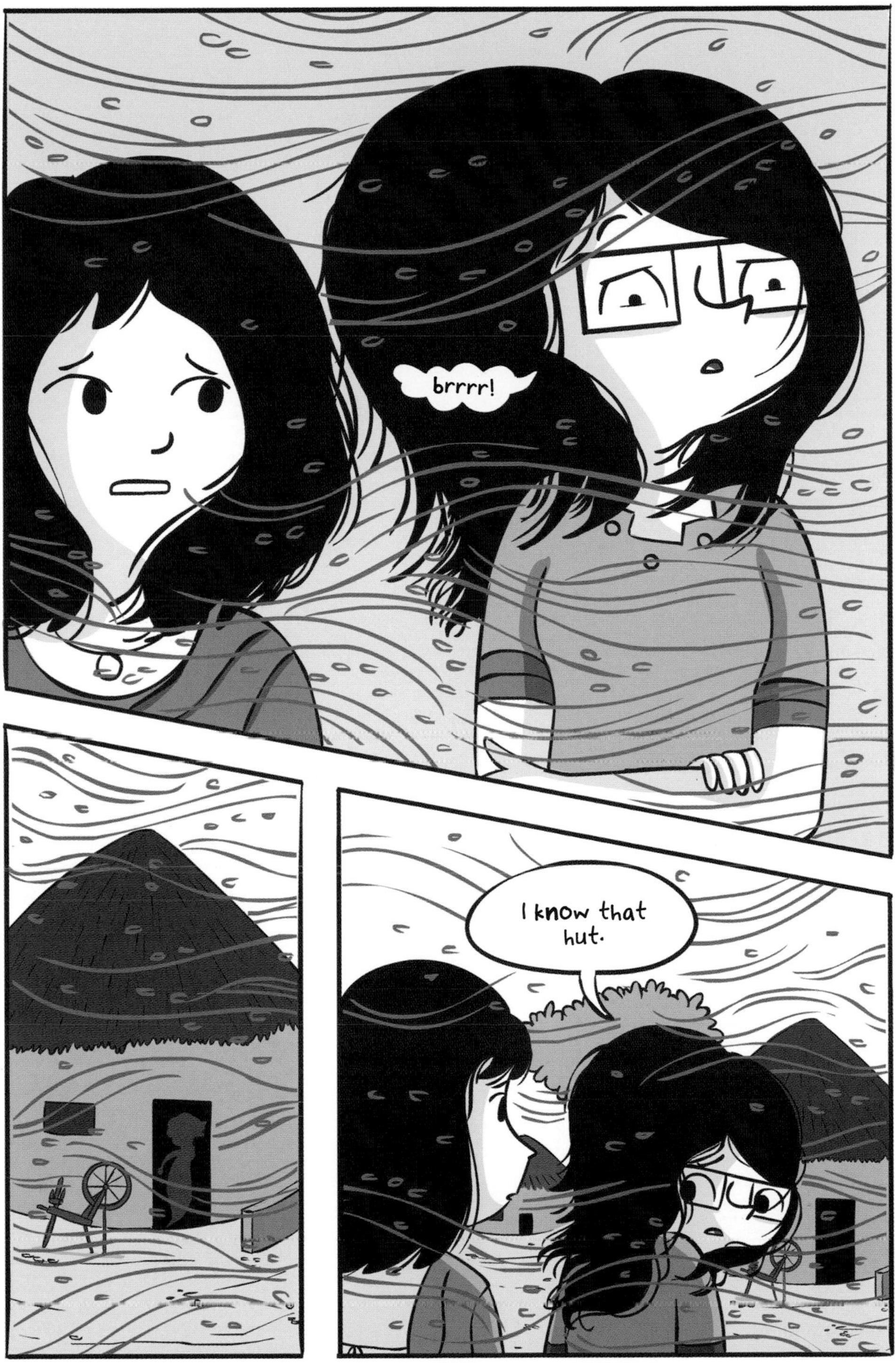
brrrr!
I know that hut.

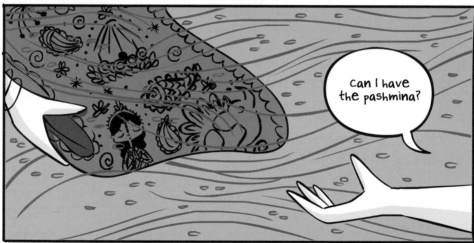

Can I have the pashmina?

Wait out here.

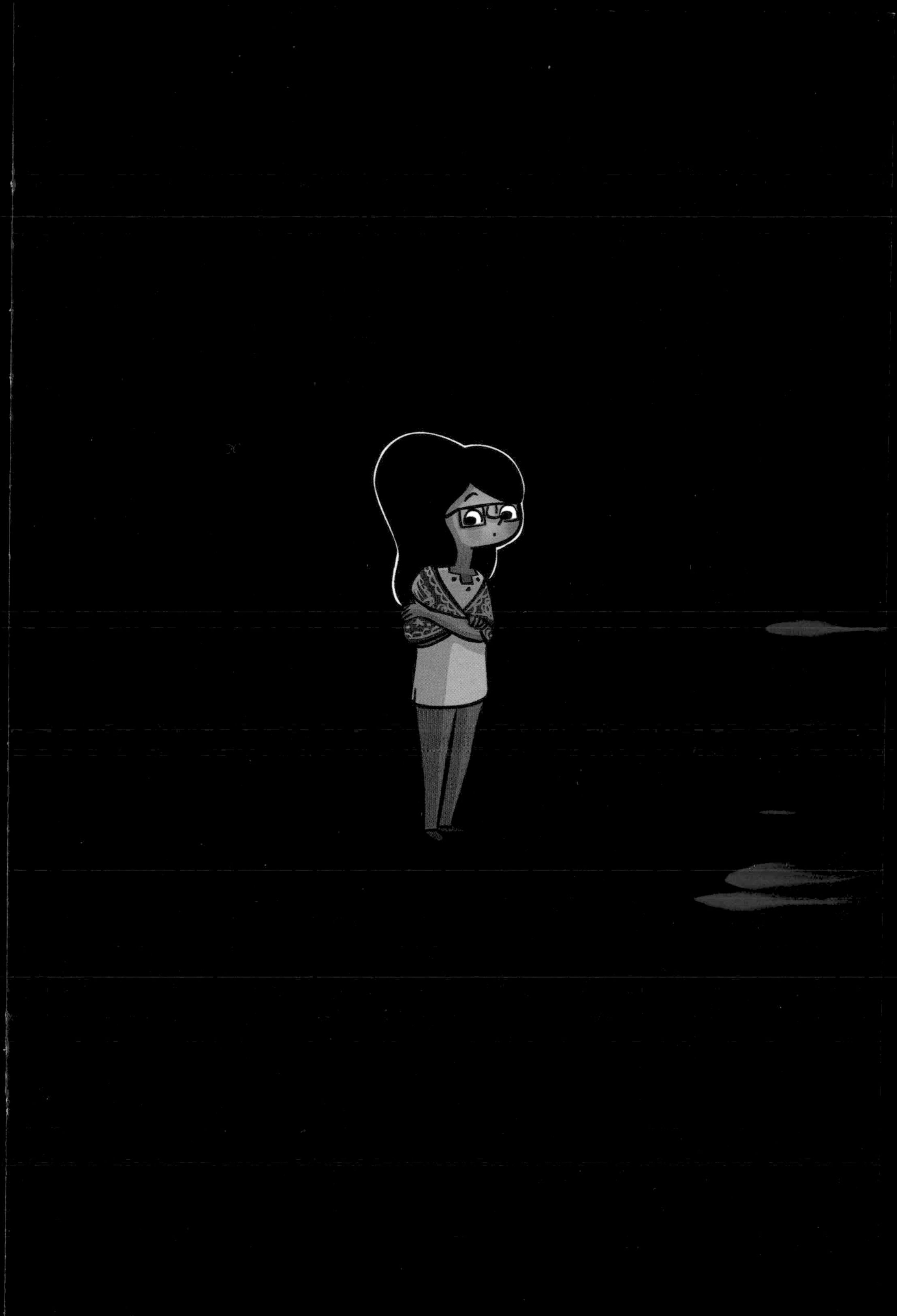

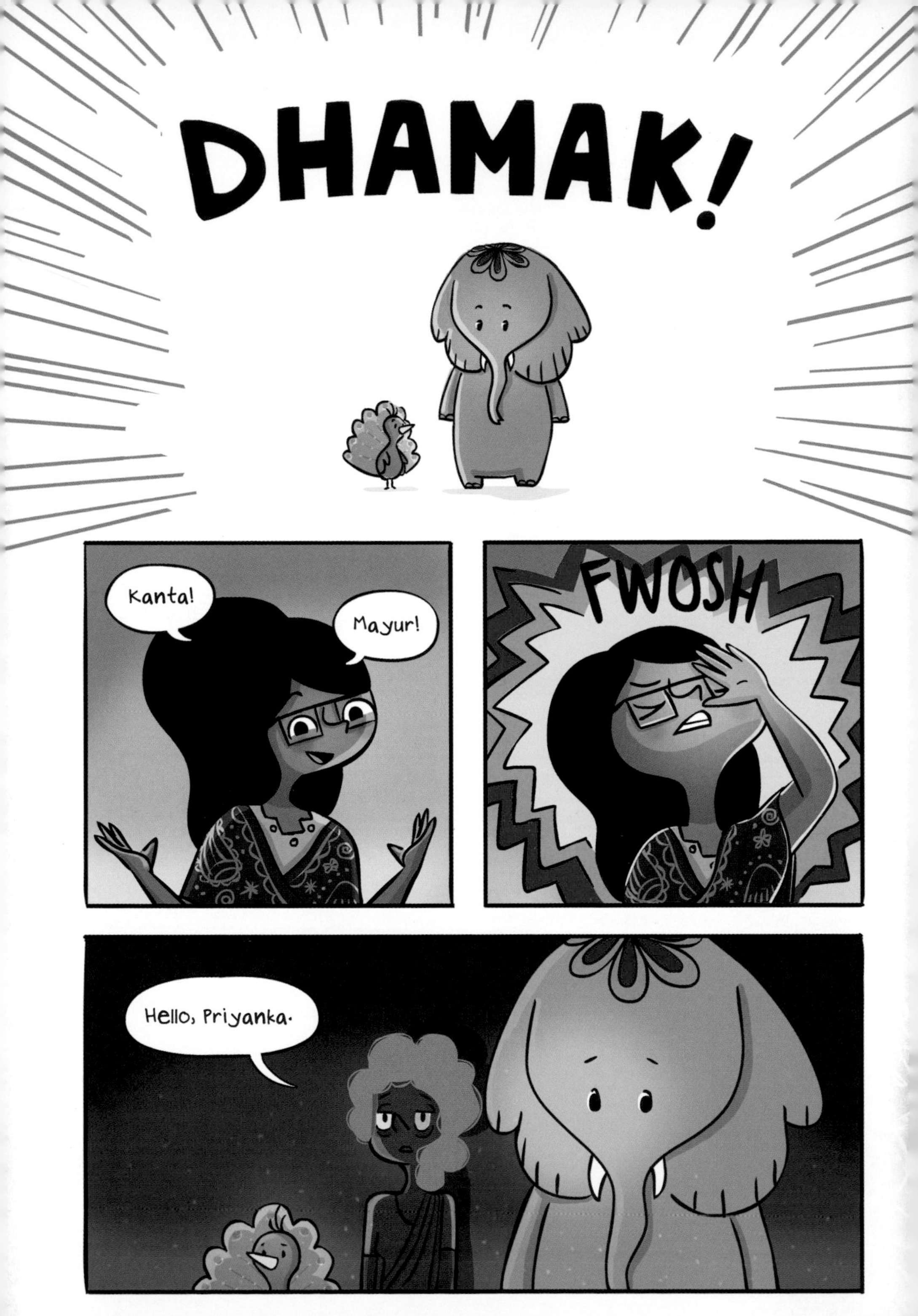
DHAMAK!
Kanta!
Mayur!
FWOSH
Hello, Priyanka.

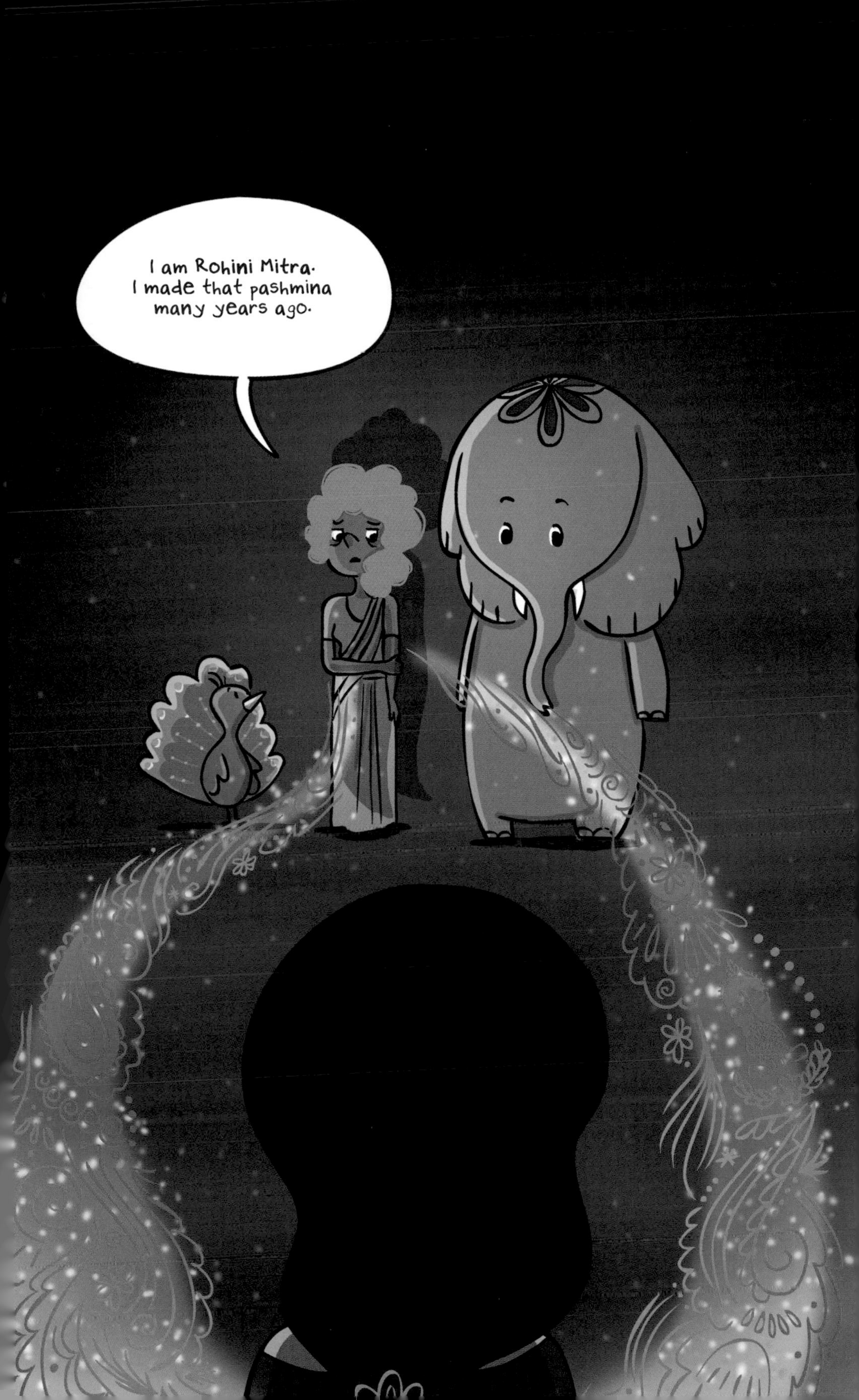
I am Rohini Mitra. I made that pashmina many years ago.

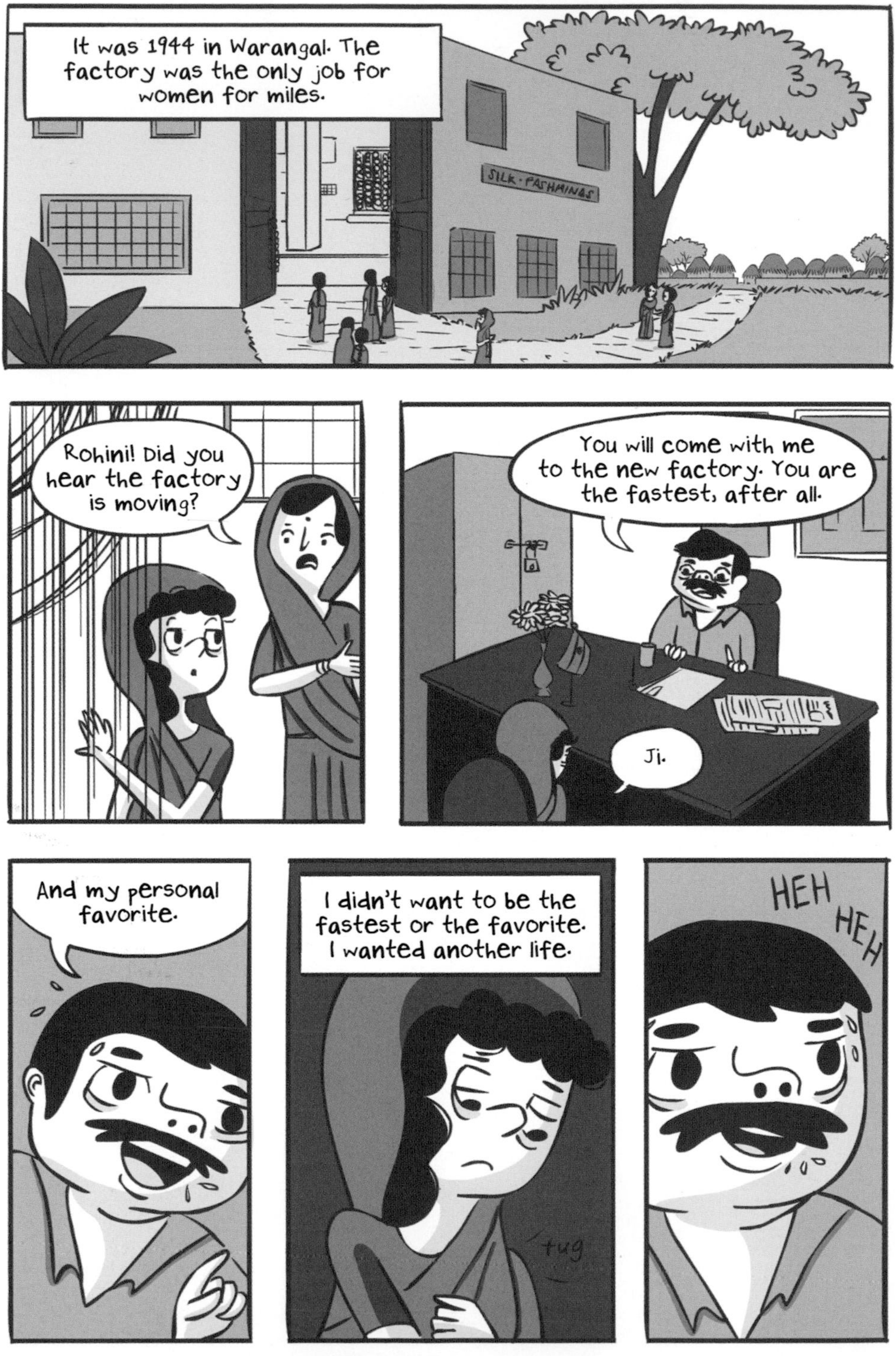
It was 1944 in Warangal. The factory was the only job for women for miles.
SILK · PASHMINAS
Rohini! Did you hear the factory is moving?
You will come with me to the new factory. You are the fastest, after all.
Ji.
And my personal favorite.
I didn't want to be the fastest or the favorite. I wanted another life.
tug
HEH HEH

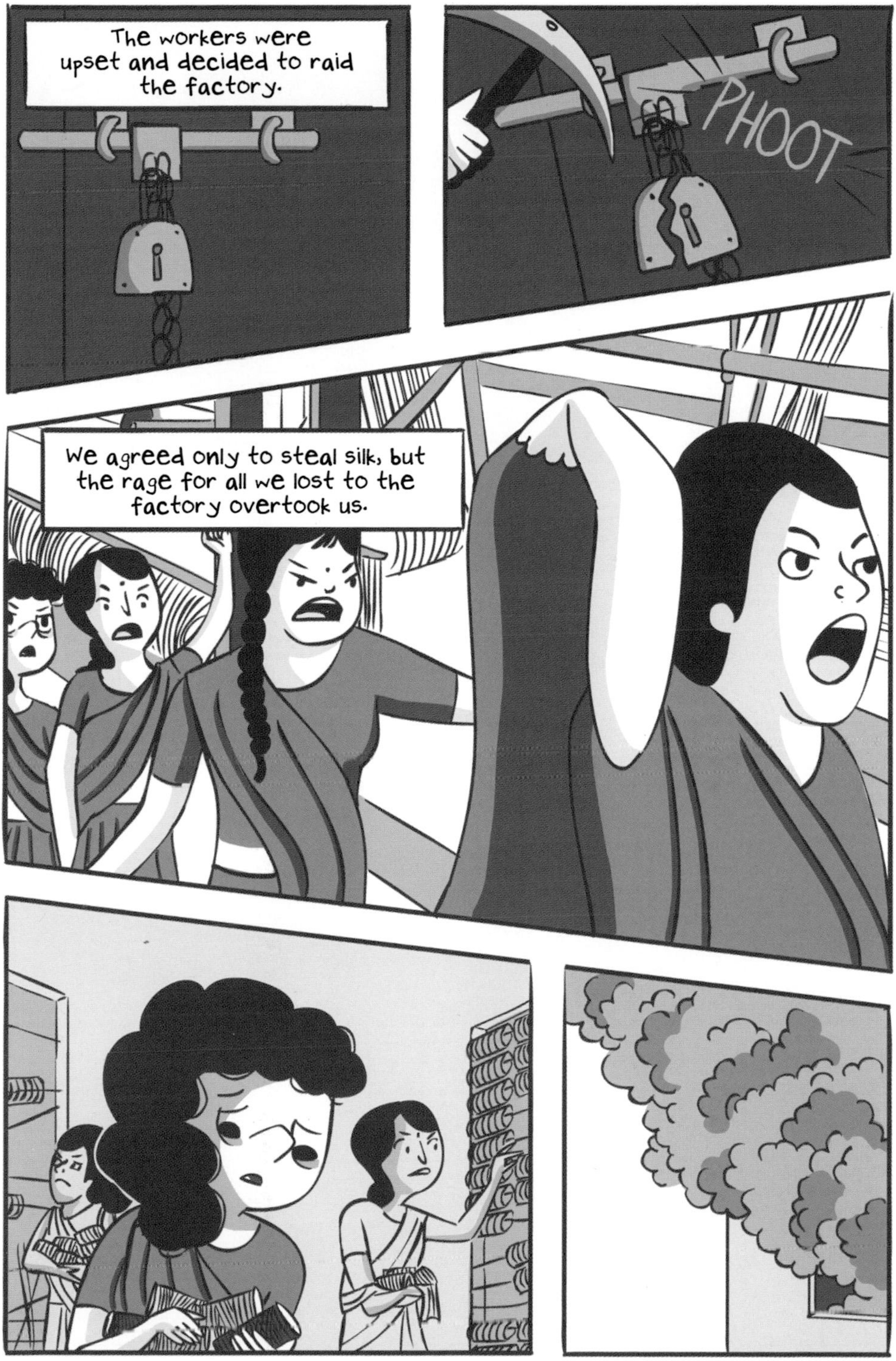
The workers were upset and decided to raid the factory.
PHOOT
We agreed only to steal silk, but the rage for all we lost to the factory overtook us.

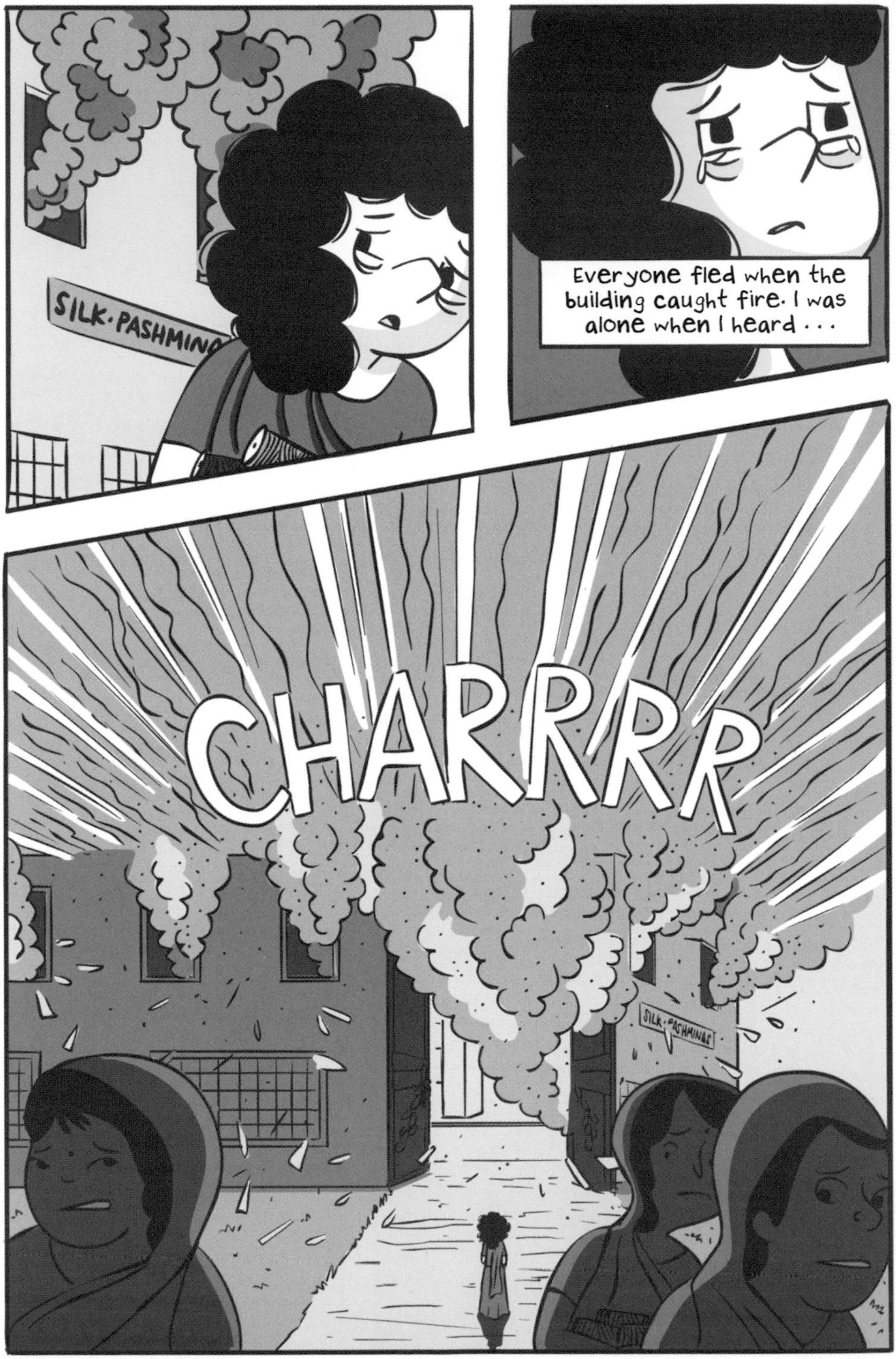
SILK·PASHMINA
Everyone fled when the building caught fire. I was alone when I heard . . .
CHARRRR
SILK·PASHMINAS

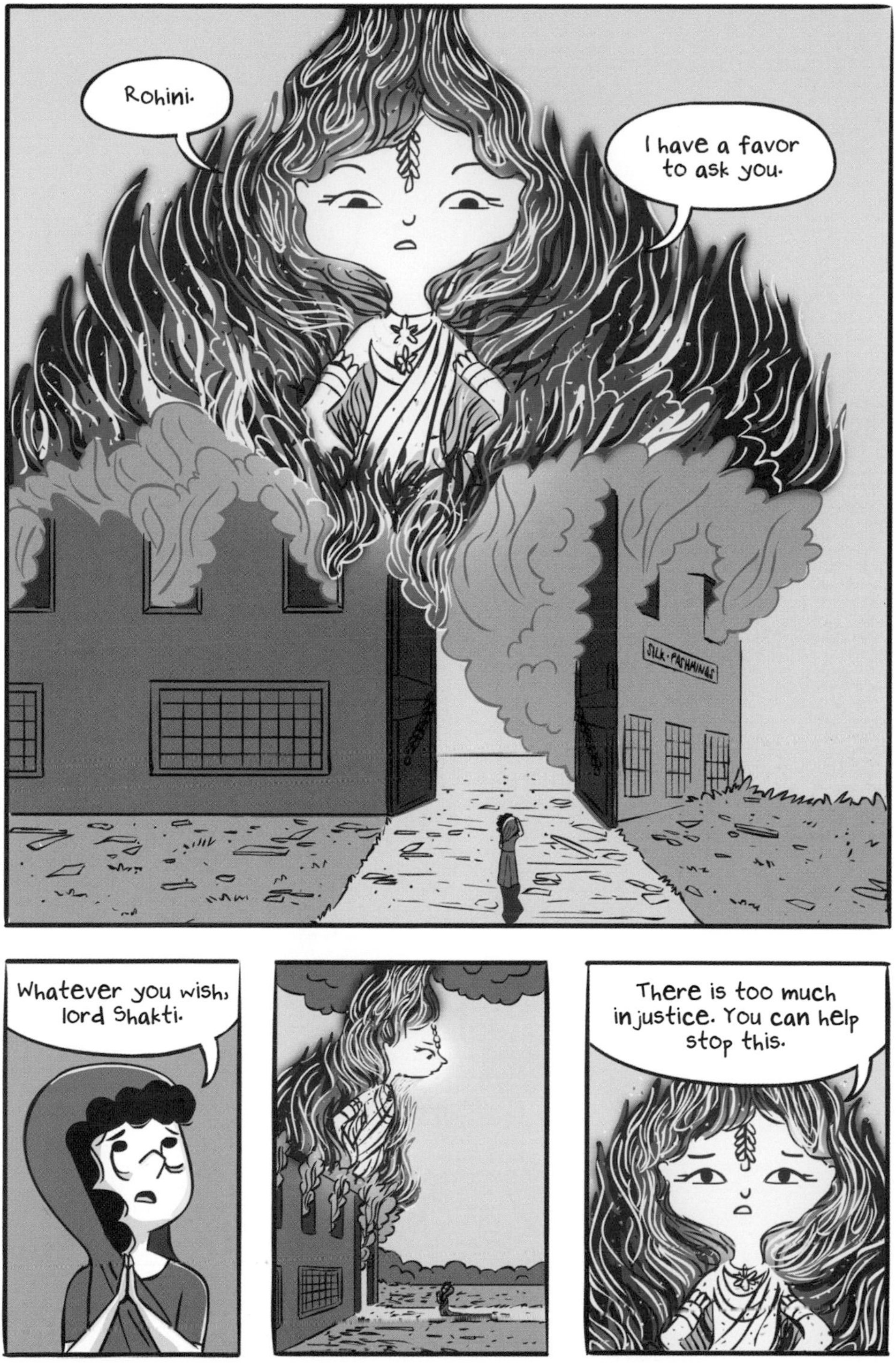
Rohini.
I have a favor to ask you.
SILK PASHMINAS
Whatever you wish, lord Shakti.
There is too much injustice. You can help stop this.

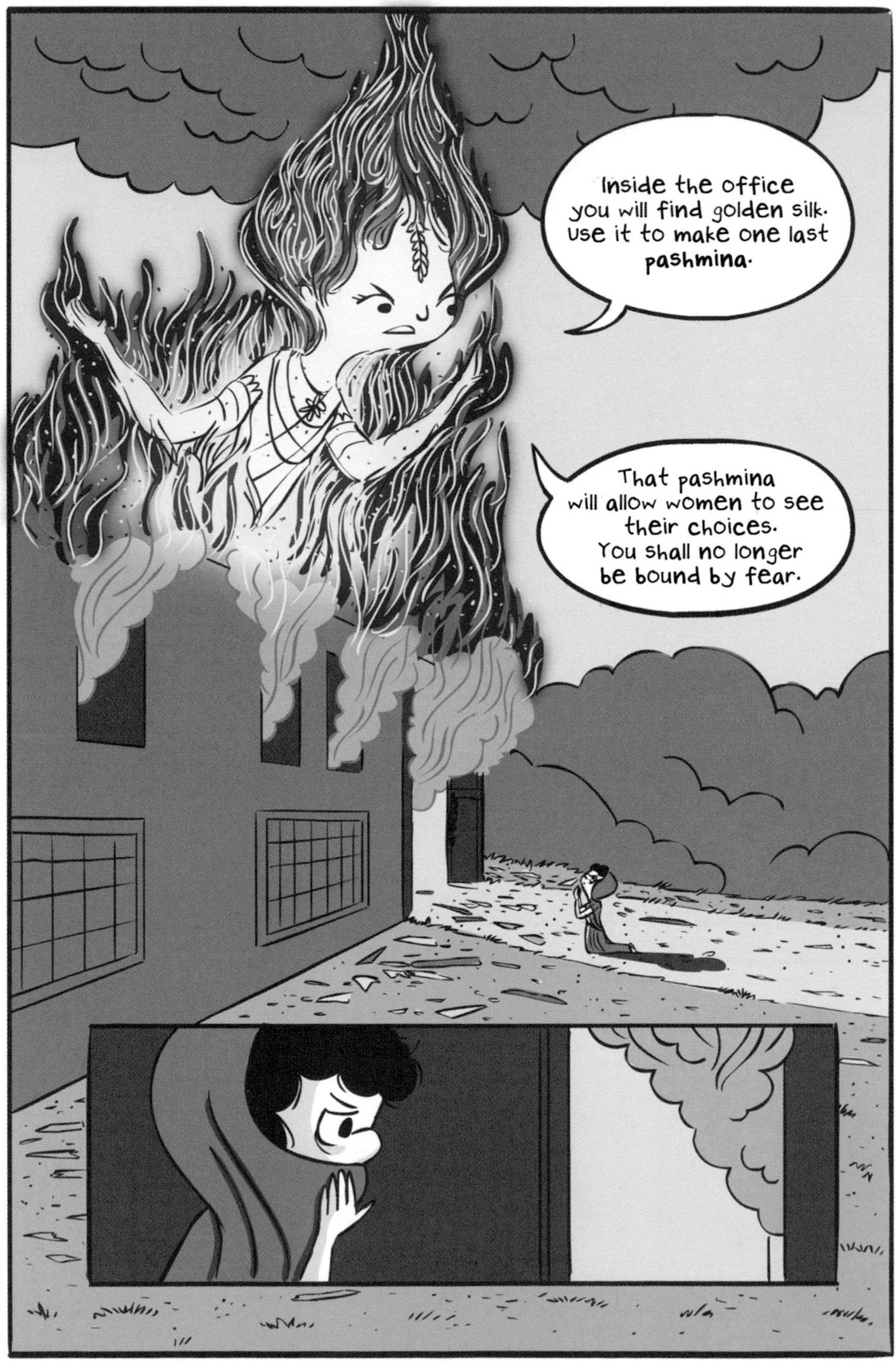
Inside the office you will find golden silk. Use it to make one last pashmina.
That pashmina will allow women to see their choices. You shall no longer be bound by fear.

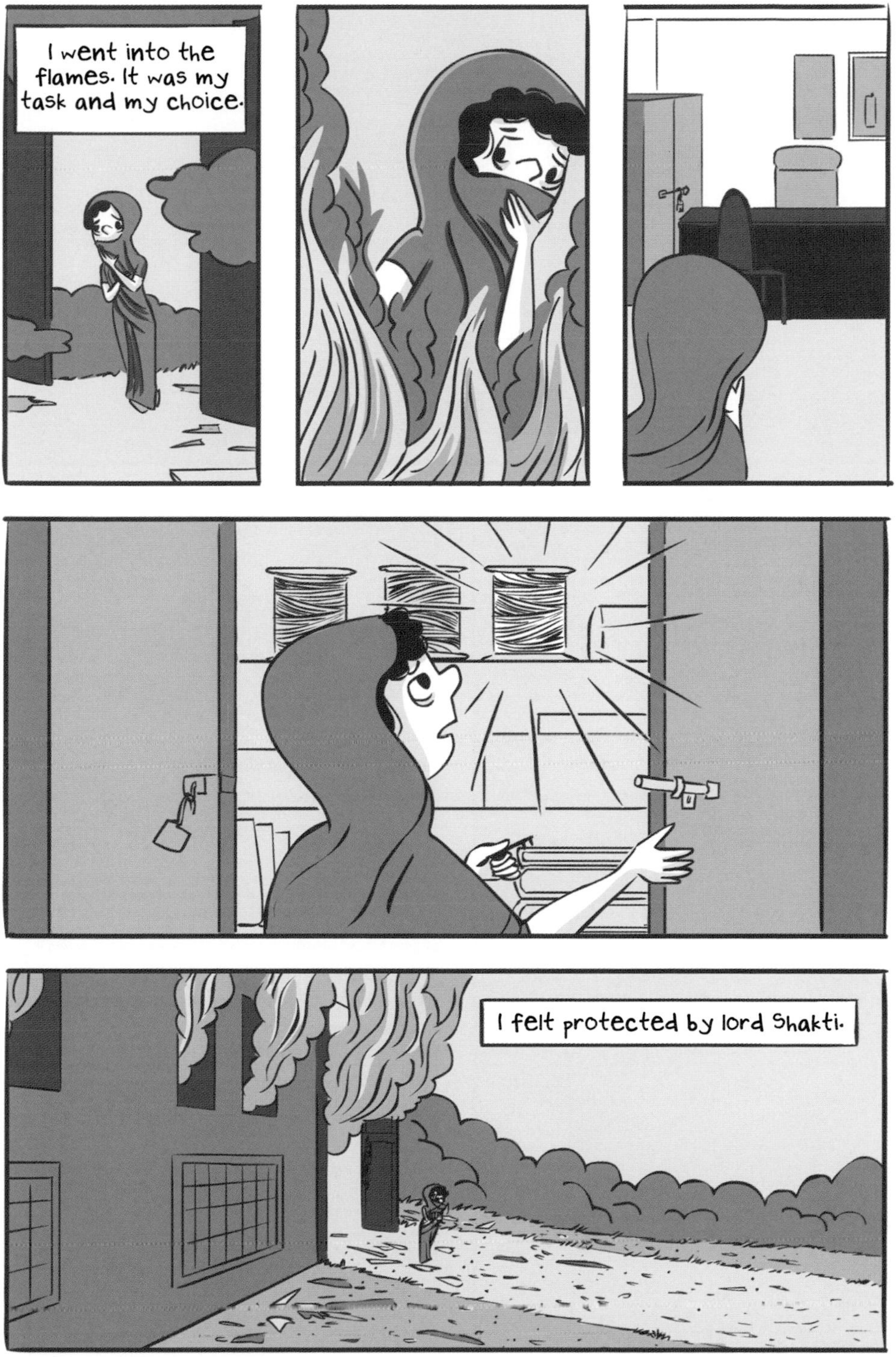
I went into the flames. It was my task and my choice.
I felt protected by lord Shakti.

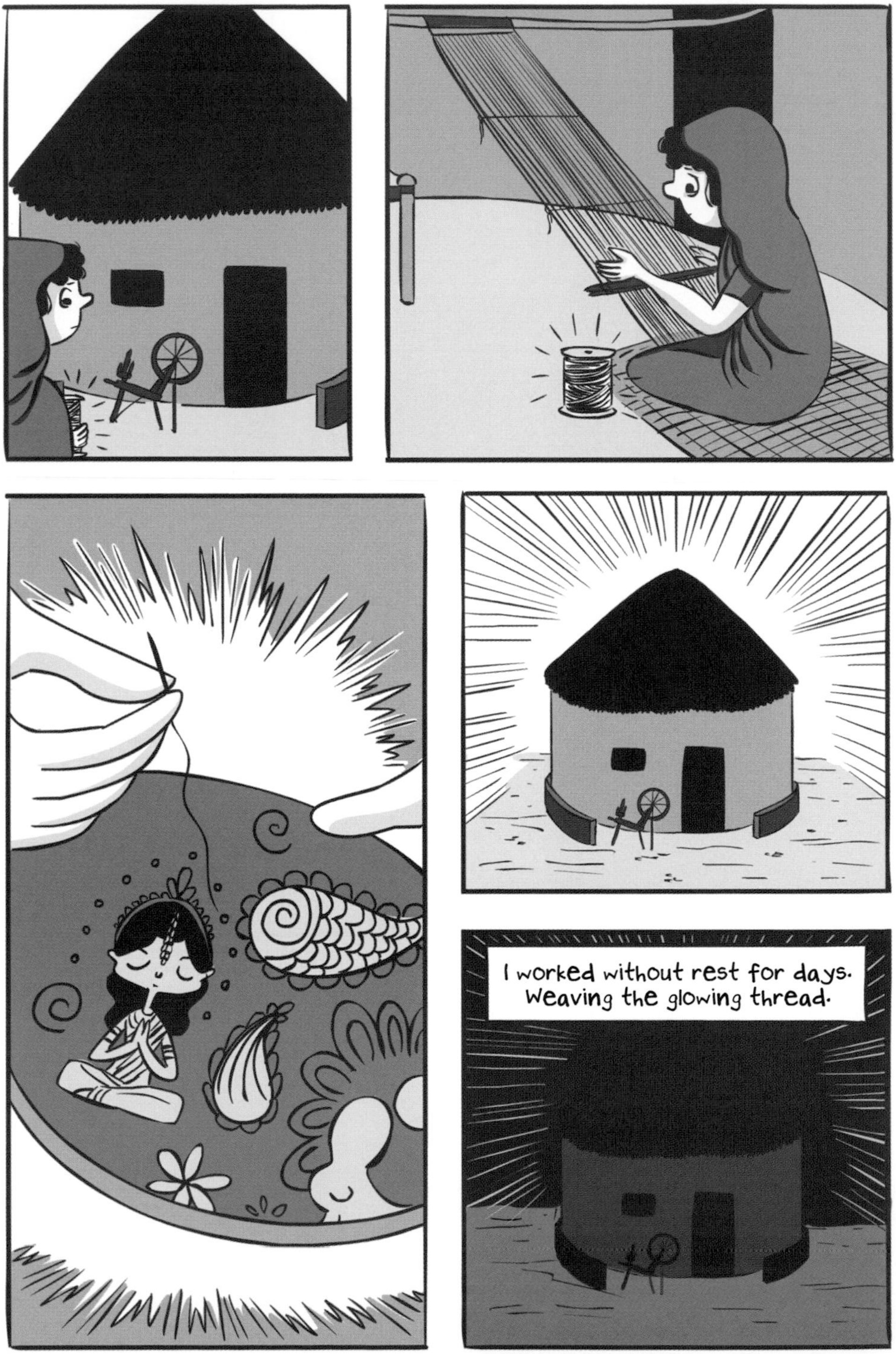
I worked without rest for days. Weaving the glowing thread.

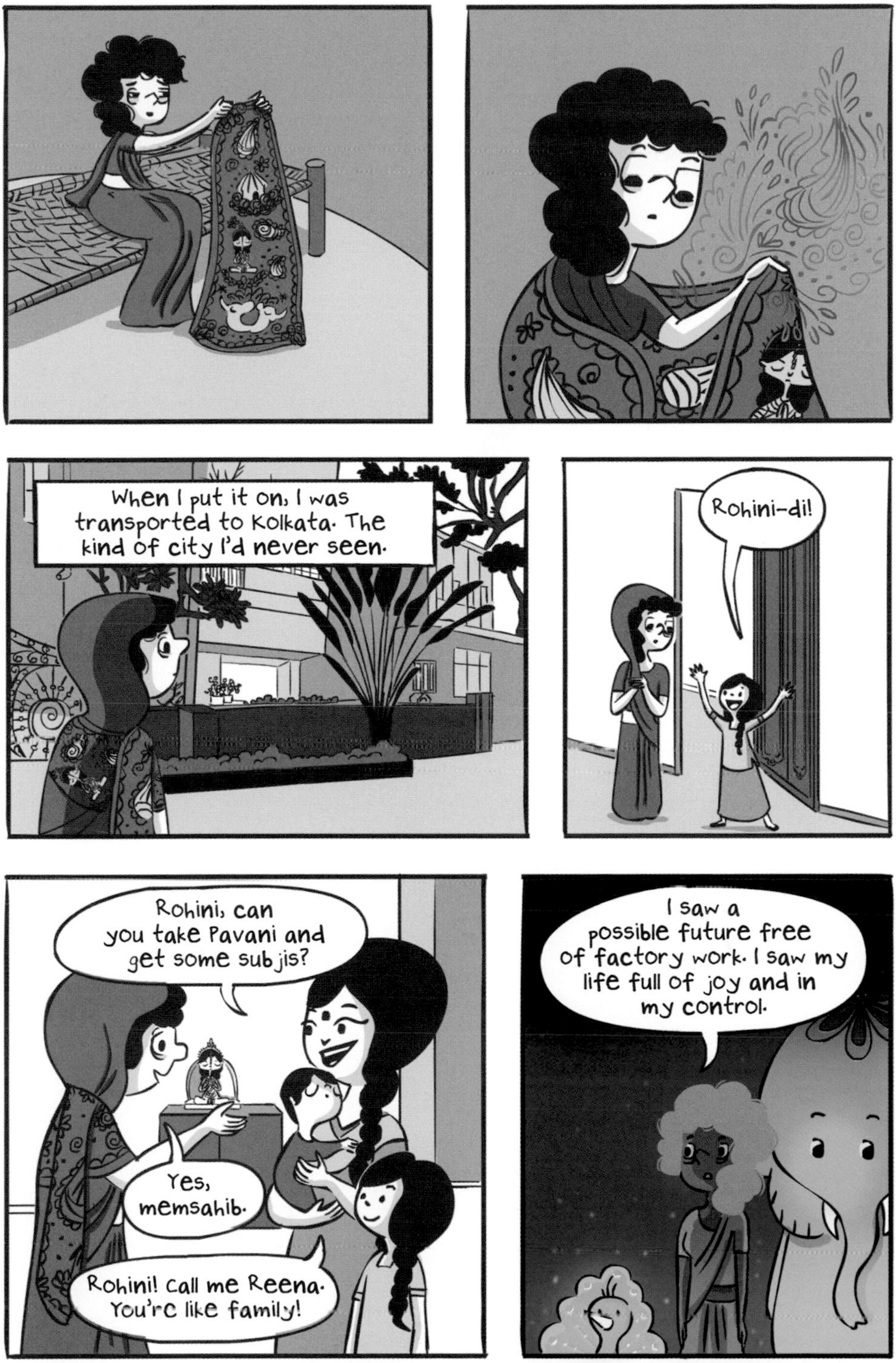
When I put it on, I was transported to Kolkata. The kind of city I'd never seen.
Rohini-di!
Rohini, can you take Pavani and get some subjis?
Yes, memsahib.
Rohini! Call me Reena. You're like family!
I saw a possible future free of factory work. I saw my life full of joy and in my control.

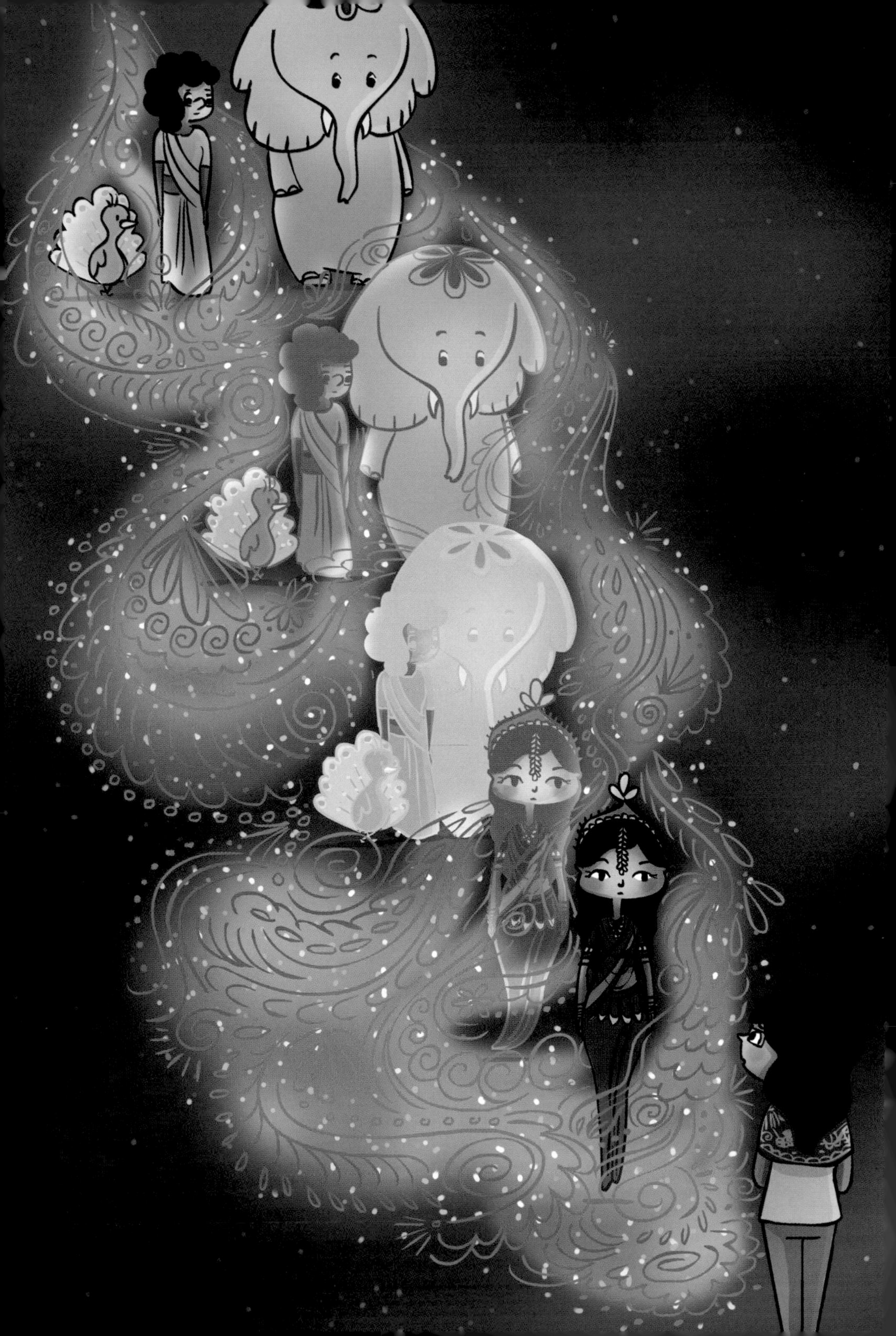

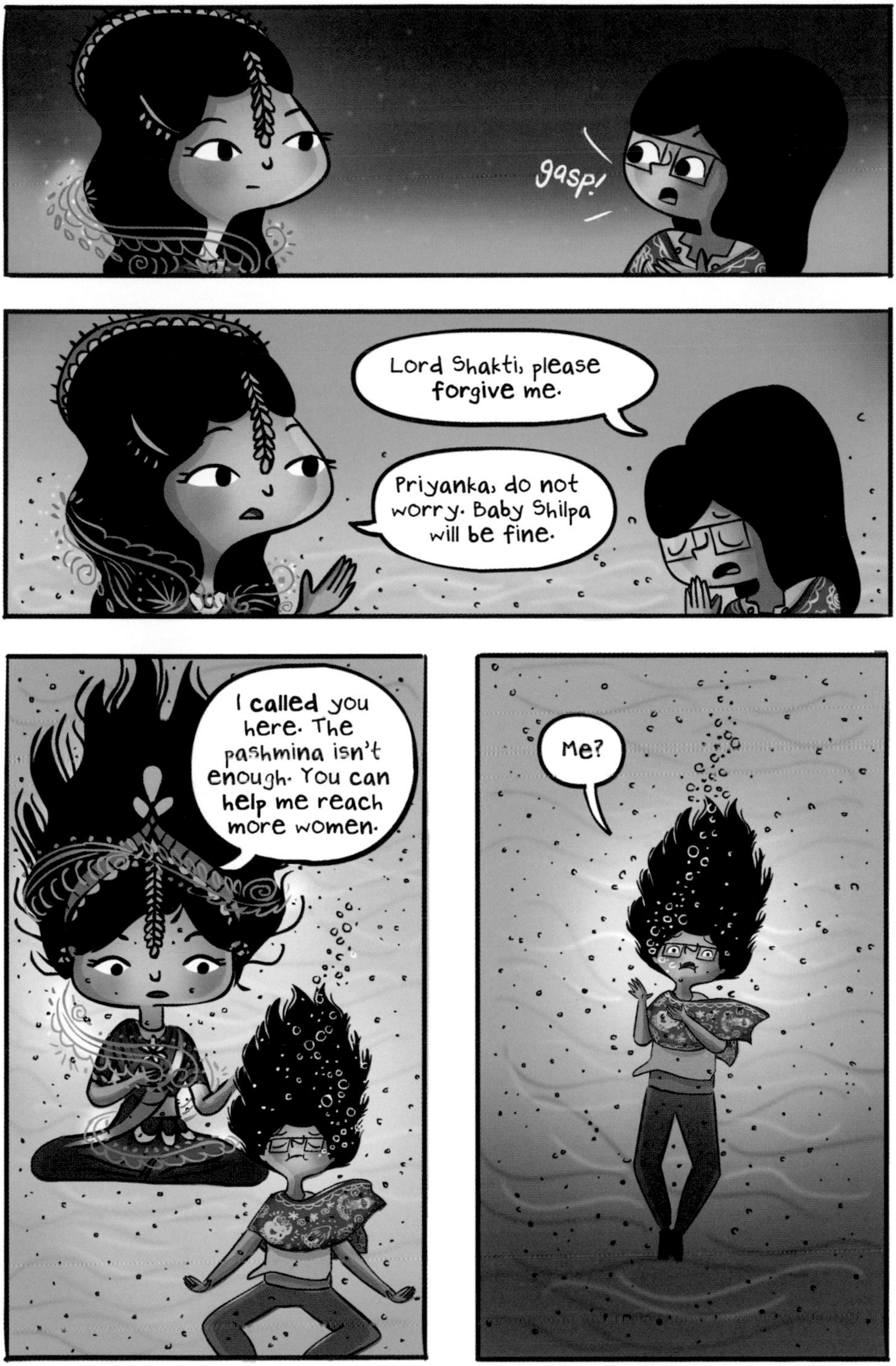
gasp!
Lord Shakti, please forgive me.
Priyanka, do not worry. Baby Shilpa will be fine.
I called you here. The pashmina isn't enough. You can help me reach more women.
Me?

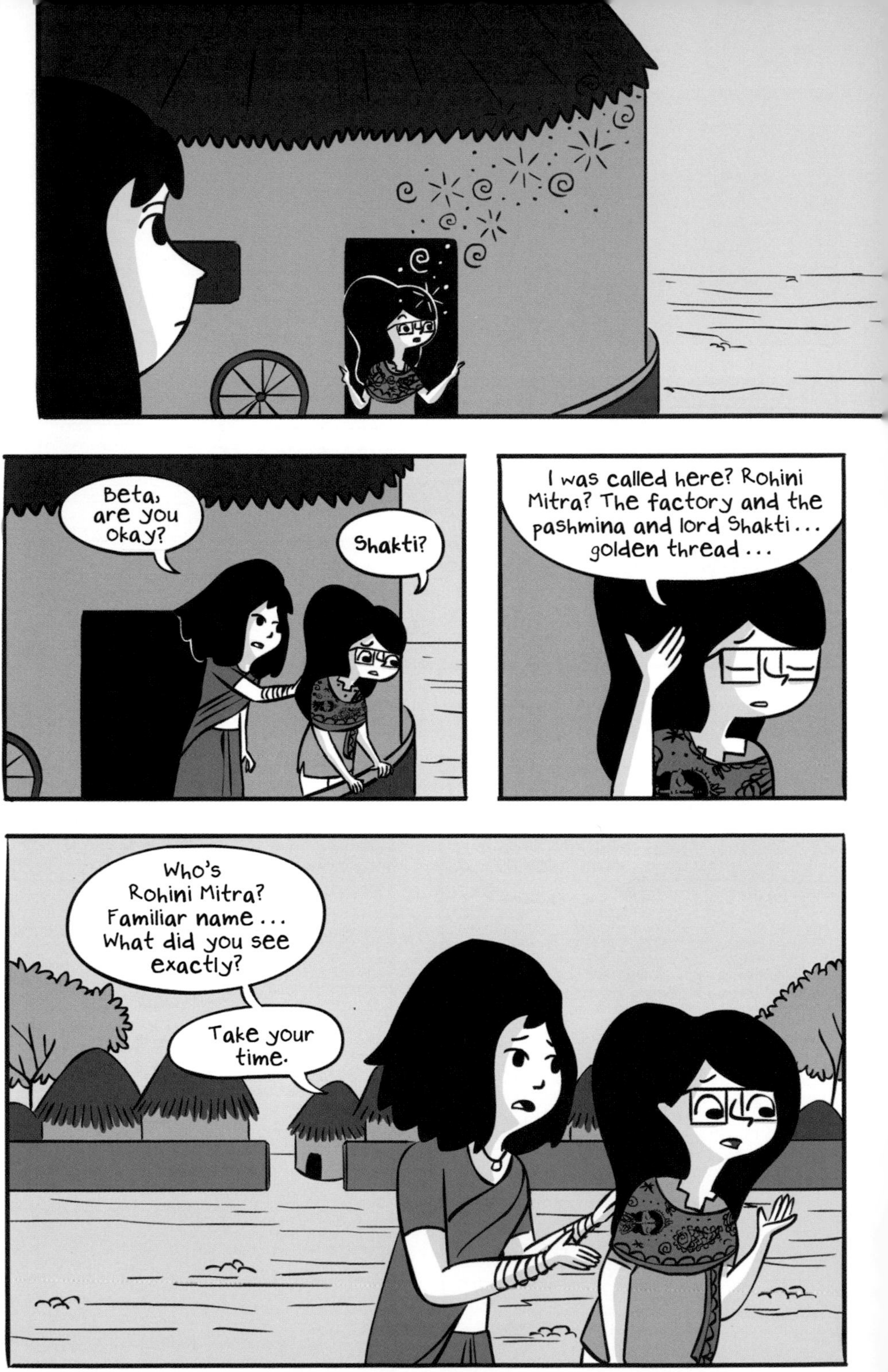
Beta, are you okay?
Shakti?
I was called here? Rohini Mitra? The factory and the pashmina and lord Shakti . . . golden thread . . .
Who's Rohini Mitra? Familiar name . . . What did you see exactly?
Take your time.

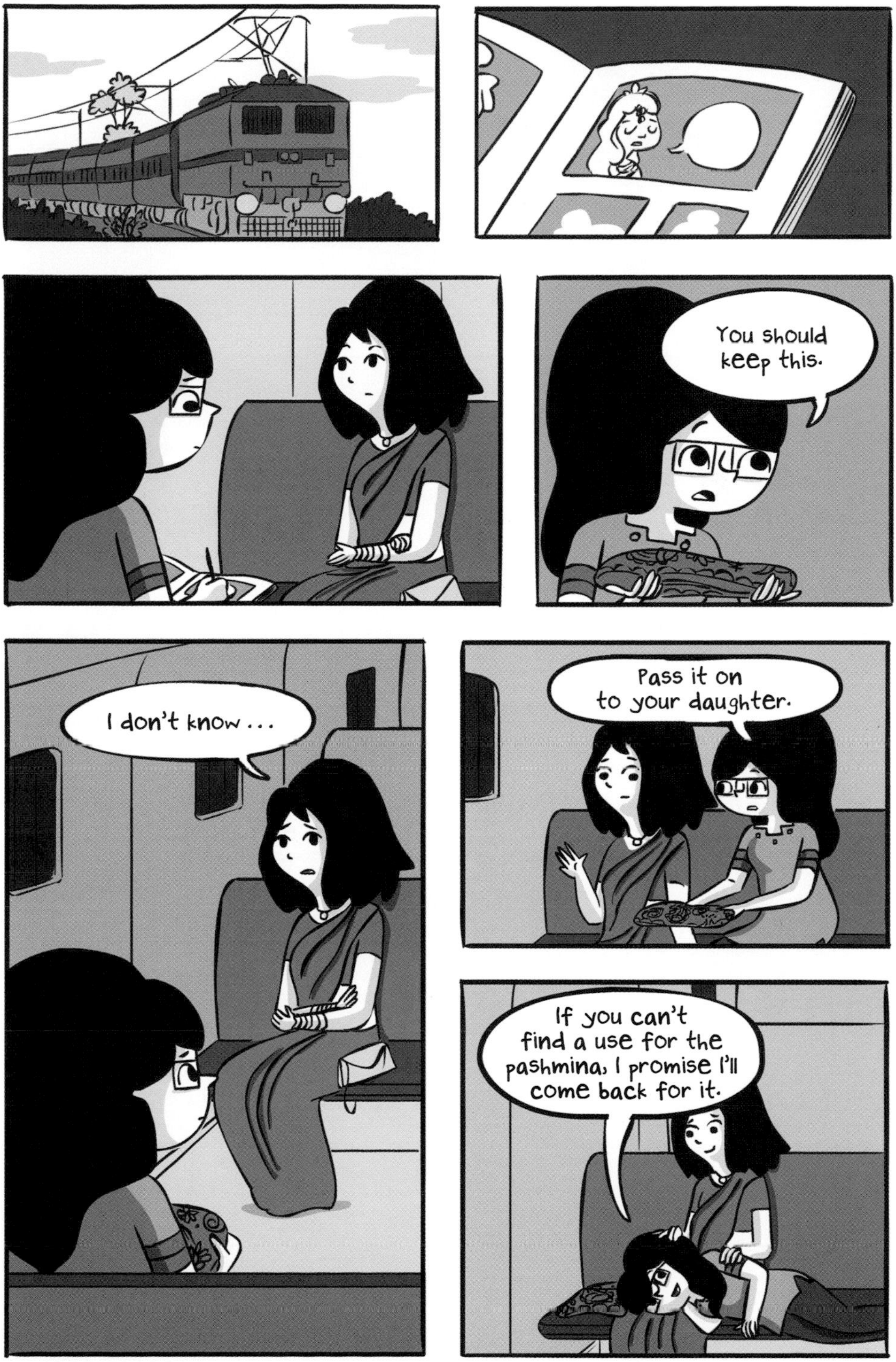
You should keep this.
I don't know . . .
Pass it on to your daughter.
If you can't find a use for the pashmina, I promise I'll come back for it.

International Departures

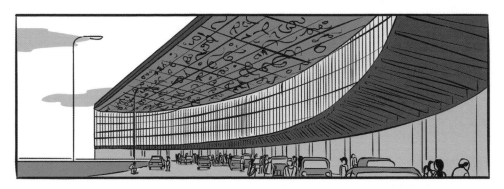

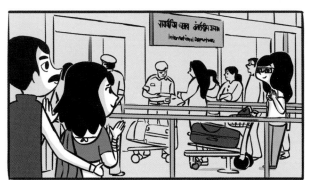

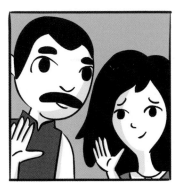

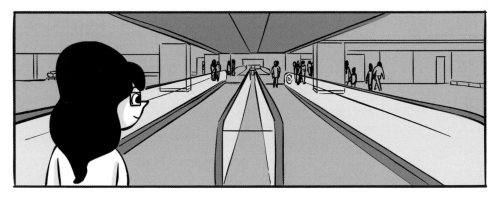

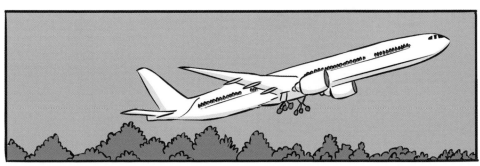

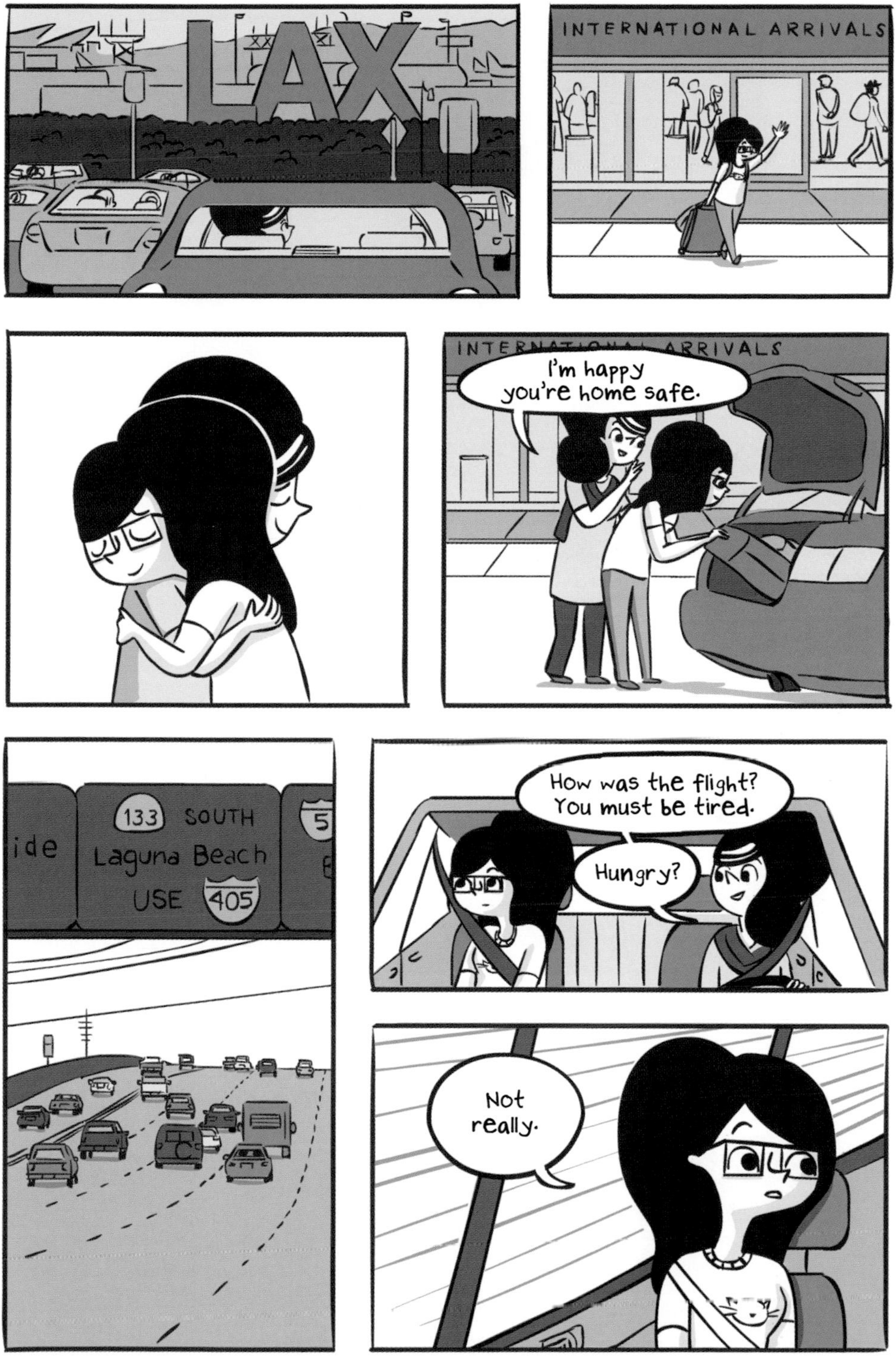
LAX
INTERNATIONAL ARRIVALS
INTERNATIONAL ARRIVALS
I'm happy you're home safe.
133 SOUTH
Laguna Beach
USE 405
ide
How was the flight? You must be tired.
Hungry?
Not really.

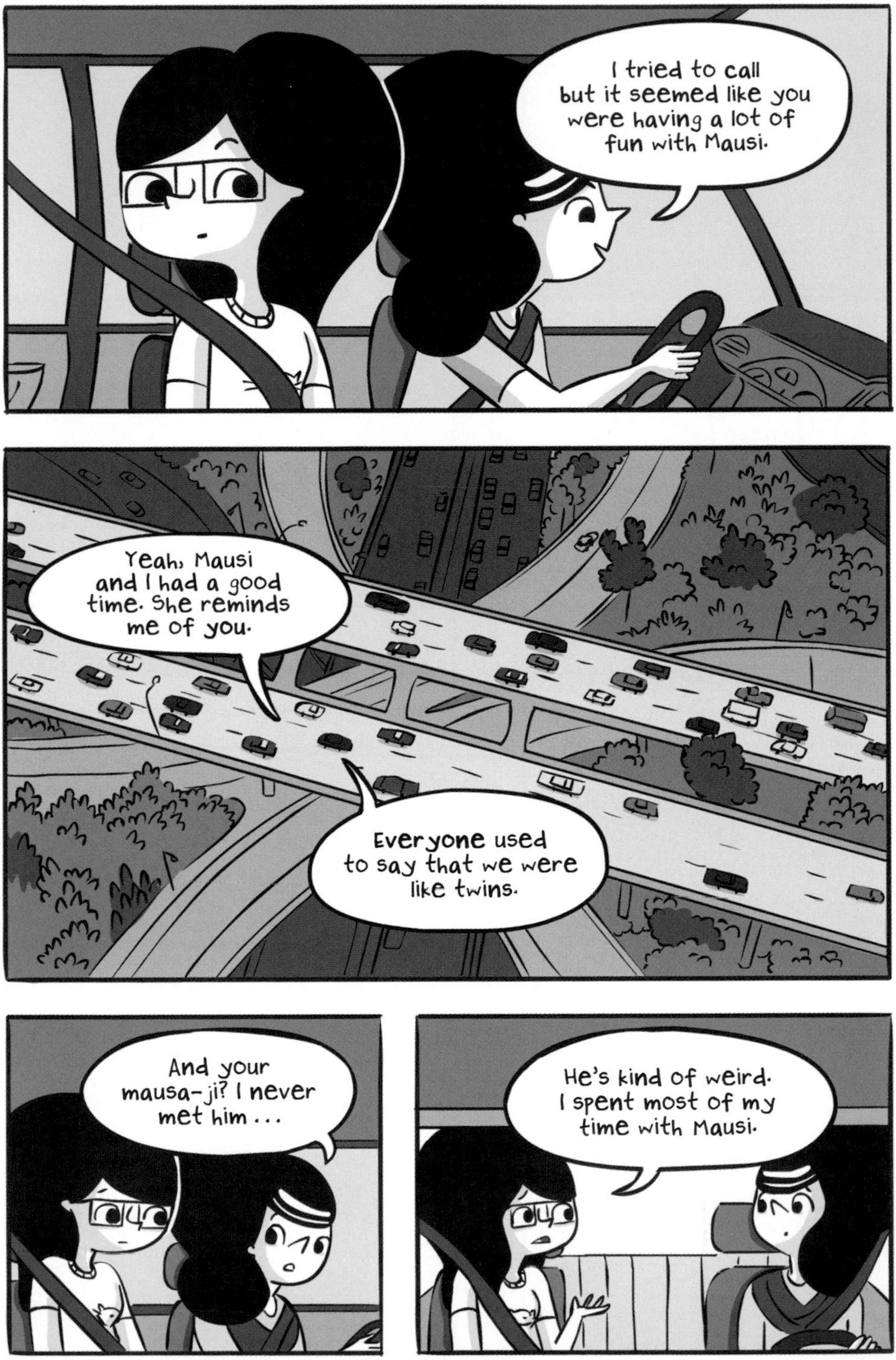
I tried to call but it seemed like you were having a lot of fun with Mausi.
Yeah, Mausi and I had a good time. She reminds me of you.
Everyone used to say that we were like twins.
And your mausa-ji? I never met him . . .
He's kind of weird. I spent most of my time with Mausi.

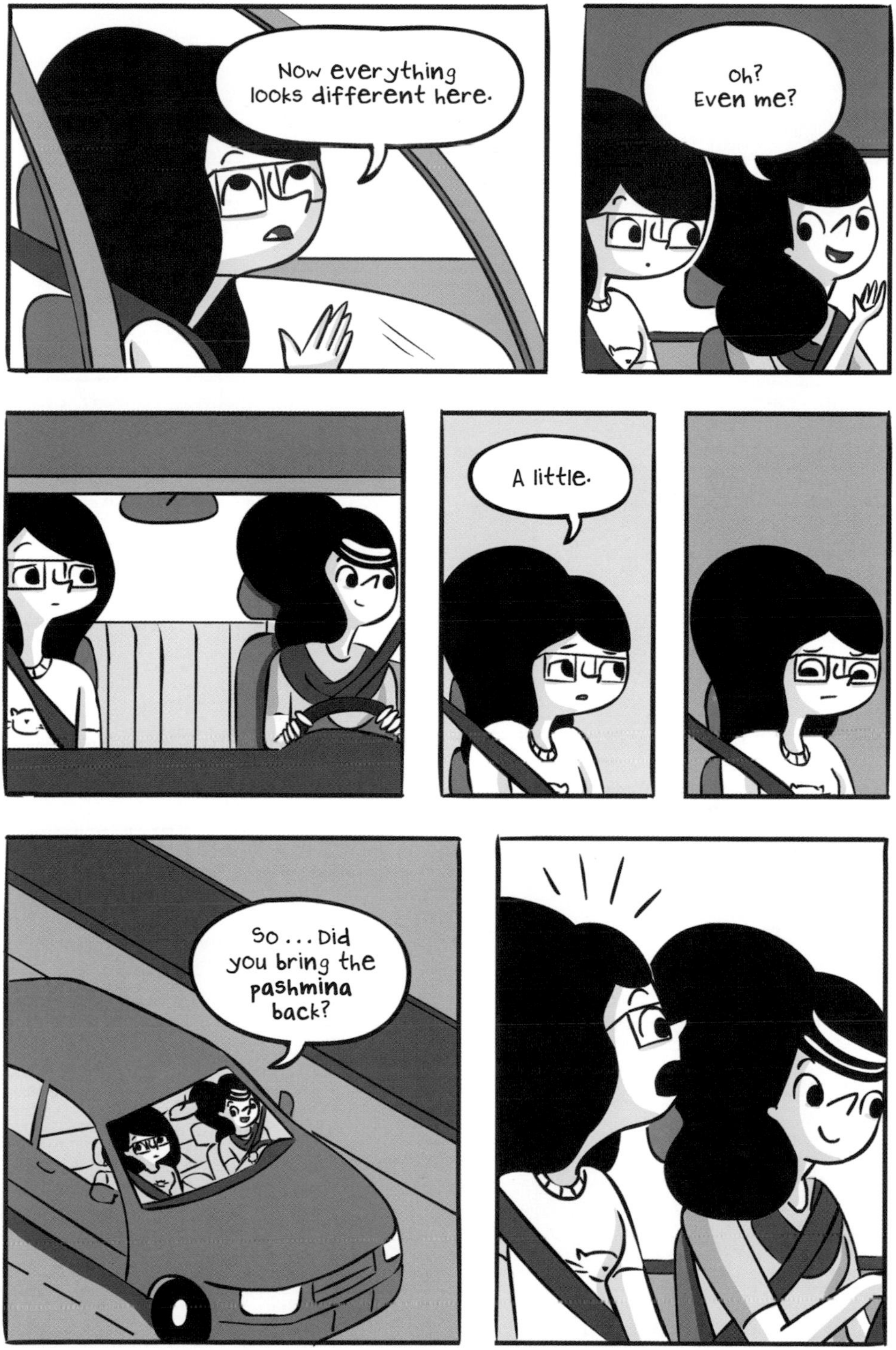
Now everything looks different here.
Oh? Even me?
A little.
So . . . Did you bring the pashmina back?

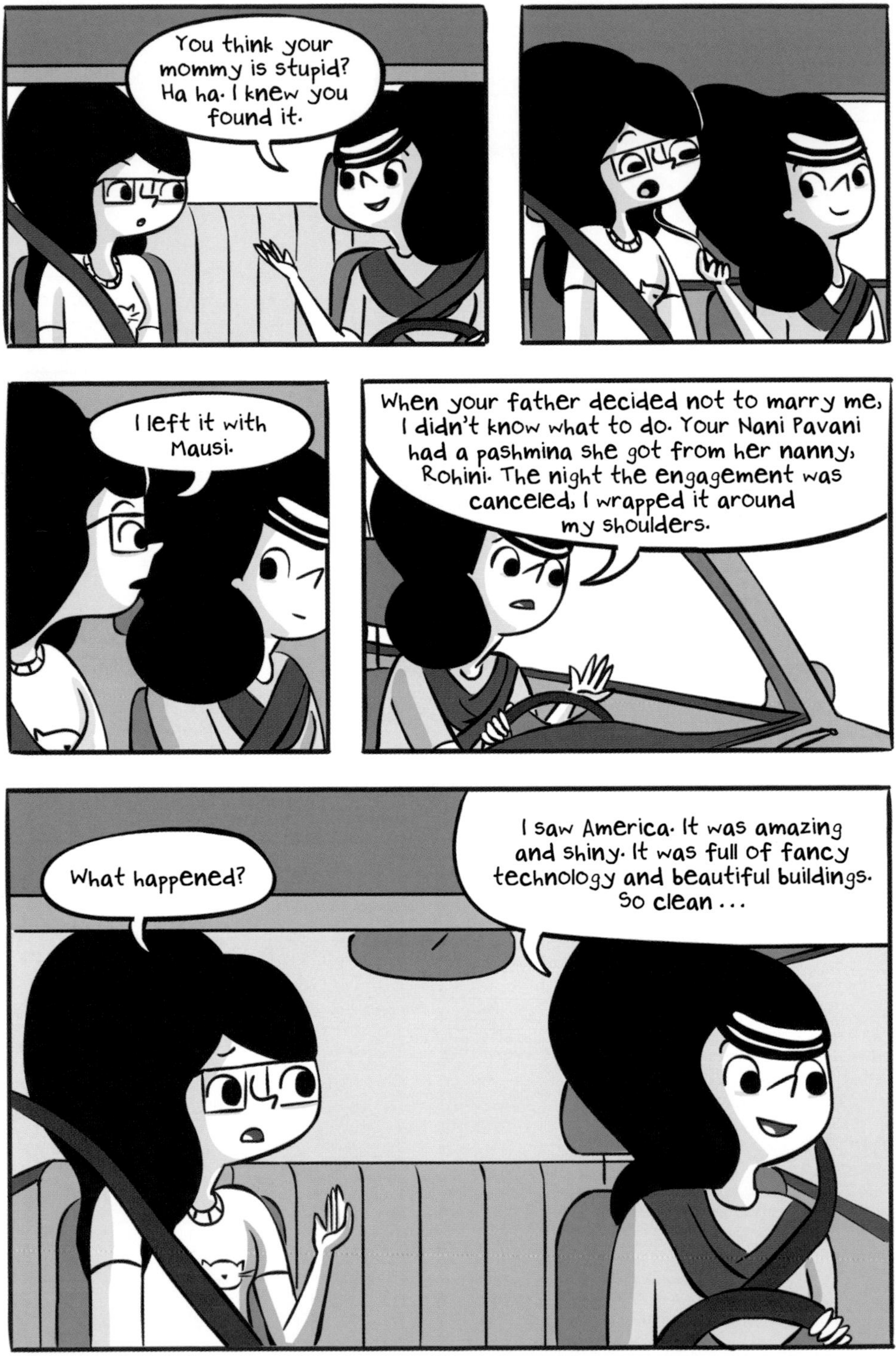
You think your mommy is stupid? Ha ha. I knew you found it.
I left it with Mausi.
When your father decided not to marry me, I didn't know what to do. Your Nani Pavani had a pashmina she got from her nanny, Rohini. The night the engagement was canceled, I wrapped it around my shoulders.
What happened?
I saw America. It was amazing and shiny. It was full of fancy technology and beautiful buildings. So clean . . .

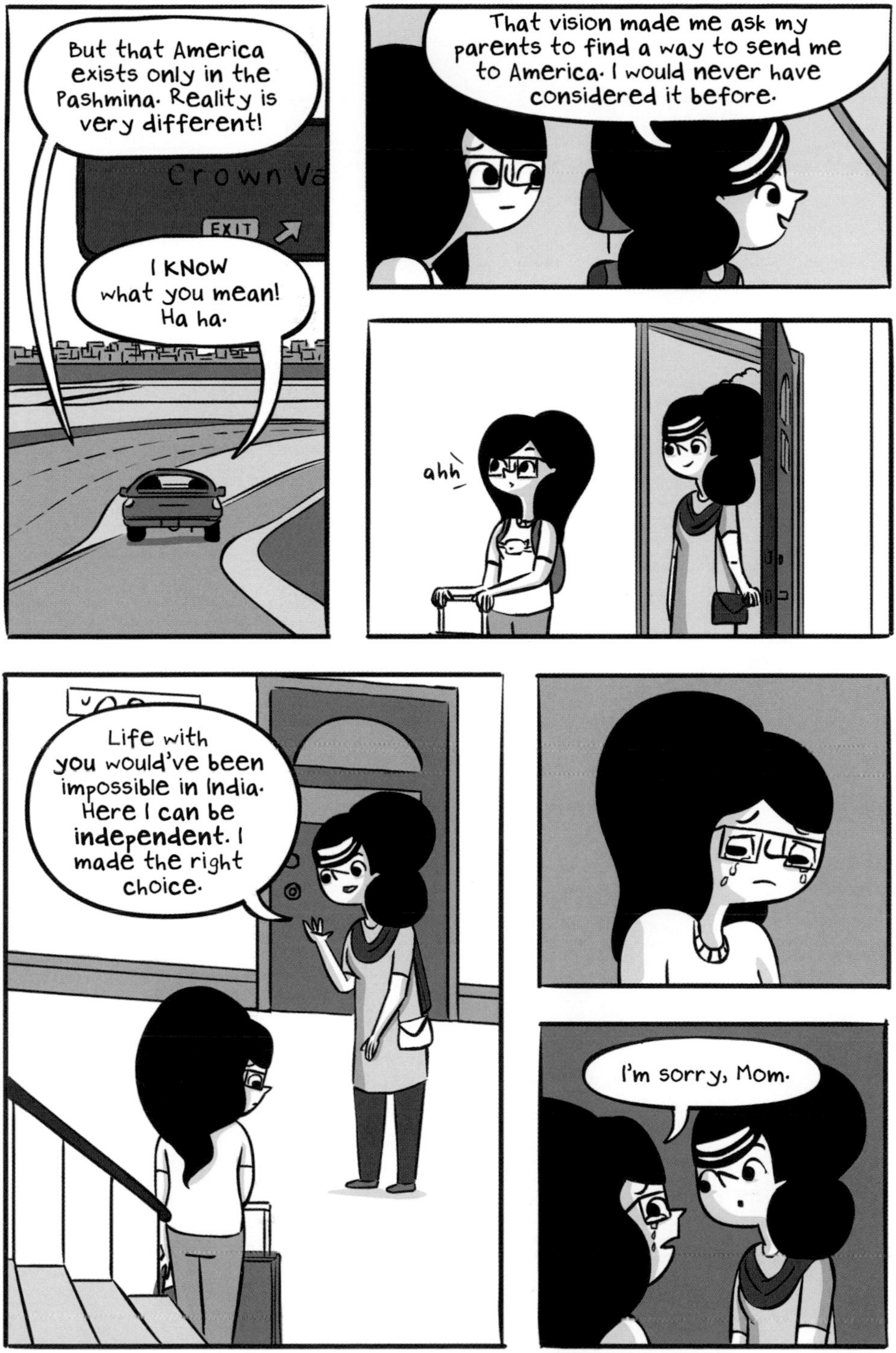
But that America exists only in the Pashmina. Reality is very different!
Crown Va
EXIT
I KNOW what you mean! Ha ha.
That vision made me ask my parents to find a way to send me to America. I would never have considered it before.
ahh
Life with you would've been impossible in India. Here I can be independent. I made the right choice.
I'm sorry, Mom.

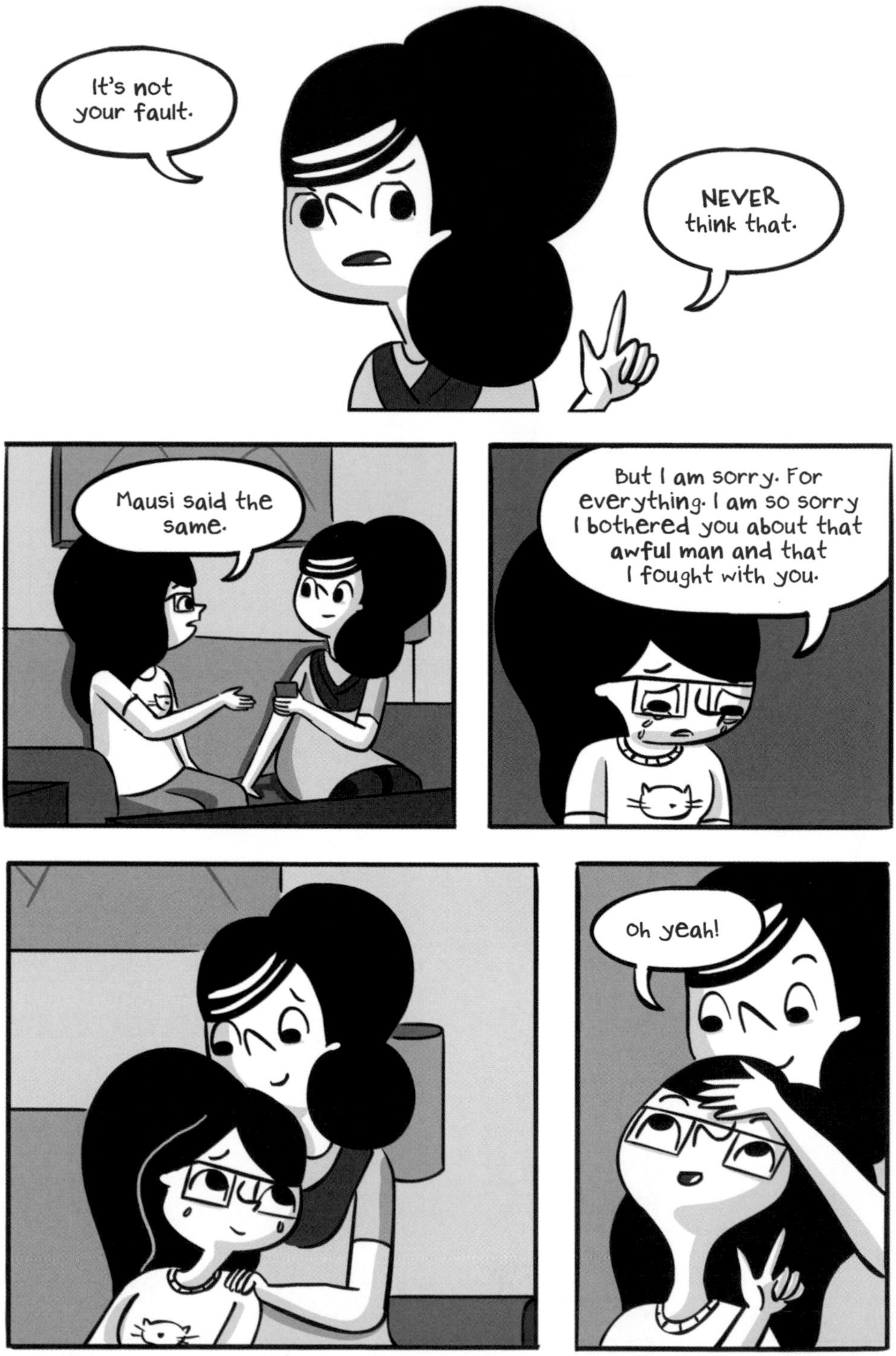
It's not your fault.
NEVER think that.
Mausi said the same.
But I am sorry. For everything. I am so sorry I bothered you about that awful man and that I fought with you.
Oh yeah!

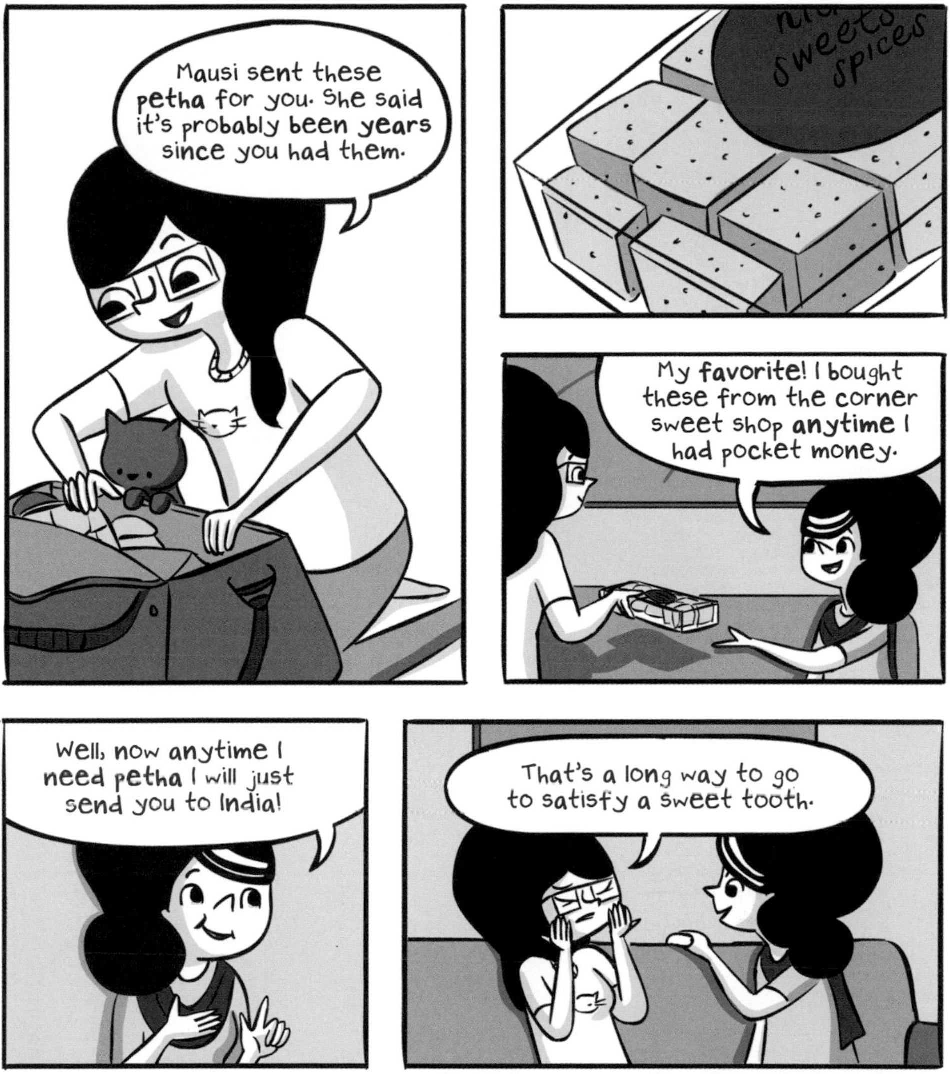
Mausi sent these petha for you. She said it's probably been years since you had them.
sweets spices
My favorite! I bought these from the corner sweet shop anytime I had pocket money.
Well, now anytime I need petha I will just send you to India!
That's a long way to go to satisfy a sweet tooth.
Not for me. That's why I have you!
PLAYA LN
RANCHO I
I do want to go back and meet the baby . . .

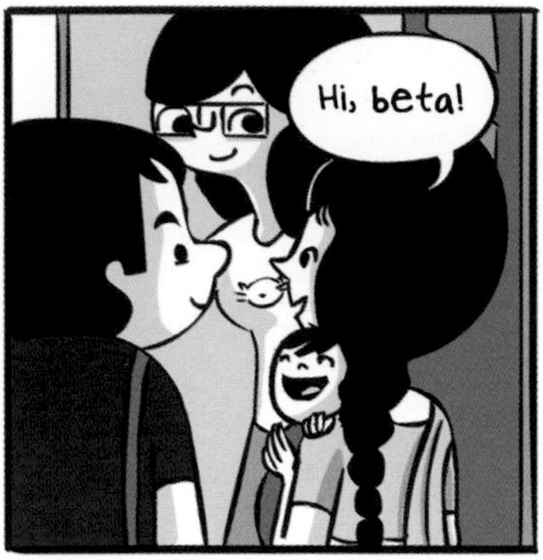
Hi, beta!

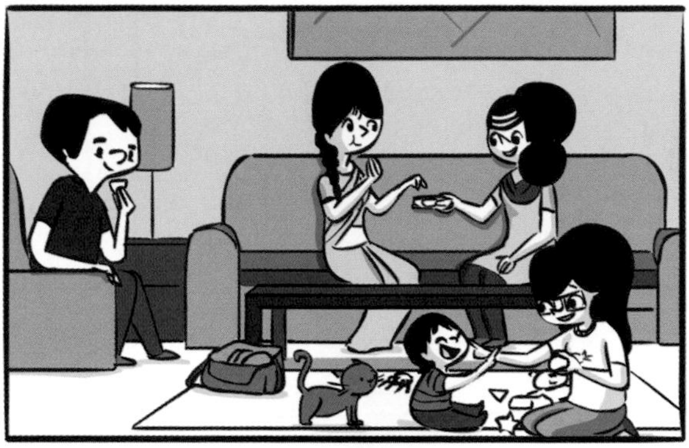

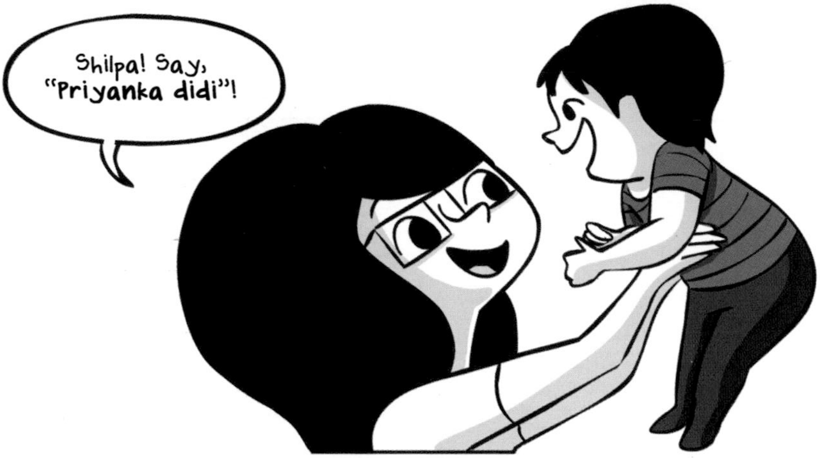
Shilpa! Say, "Priyanka didi"!

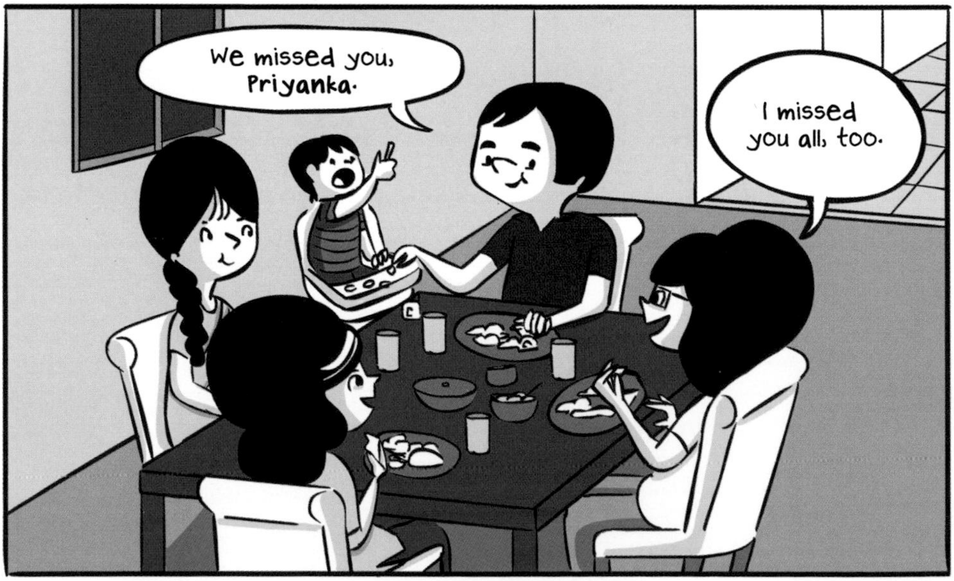
We missed you, Priyanka.
I missed you all, too.

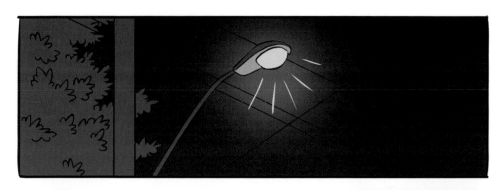

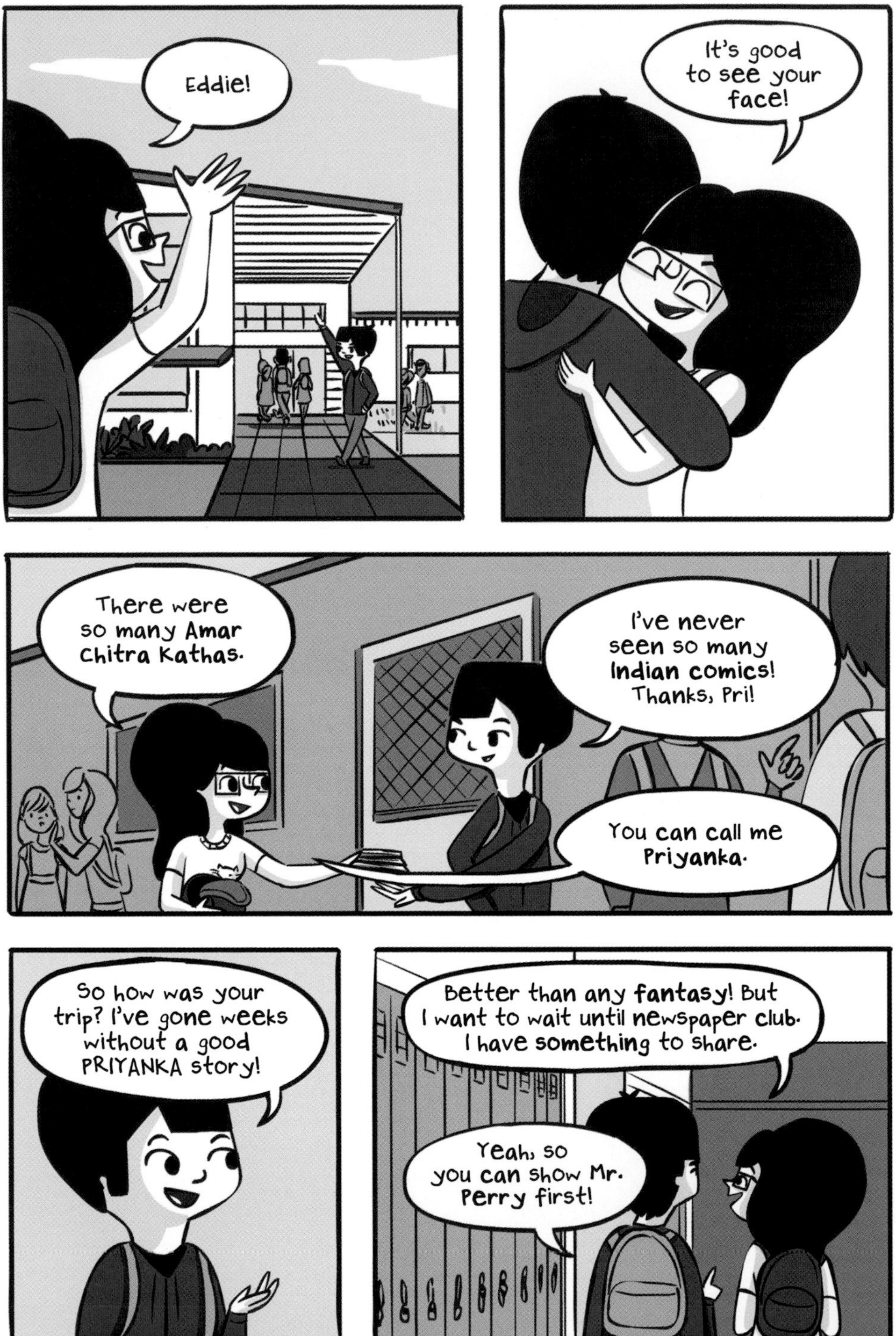
Eddie!
It's good to see your face!
There were so many Amar Chitra Kathas.
I've never seen so many Indian comics! Thanks, Pri!
You can call me Priyanka.
So how was your trip? I've gone weeks without a good PRIYANKA story!
Better than any fantasy! But I want to wait until newspaper club. I have something to share.
Yeah, so you can show Mr. Perry first!

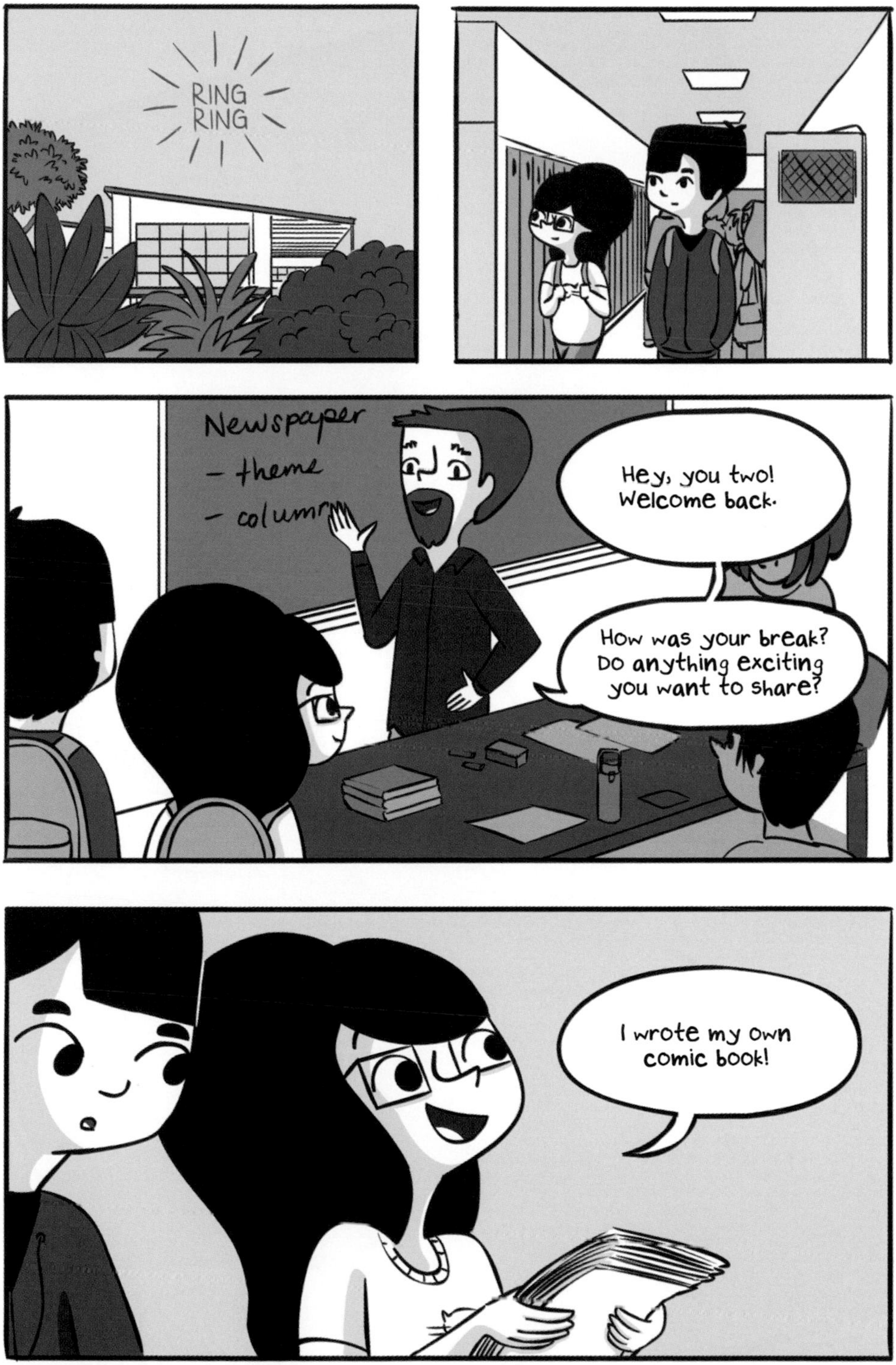
RING
RING
Newspaper
- theme
- column
Hey, you two! Welcome back.
How was your break? Do anything exciting you want to share?
I wrote my own comic book!

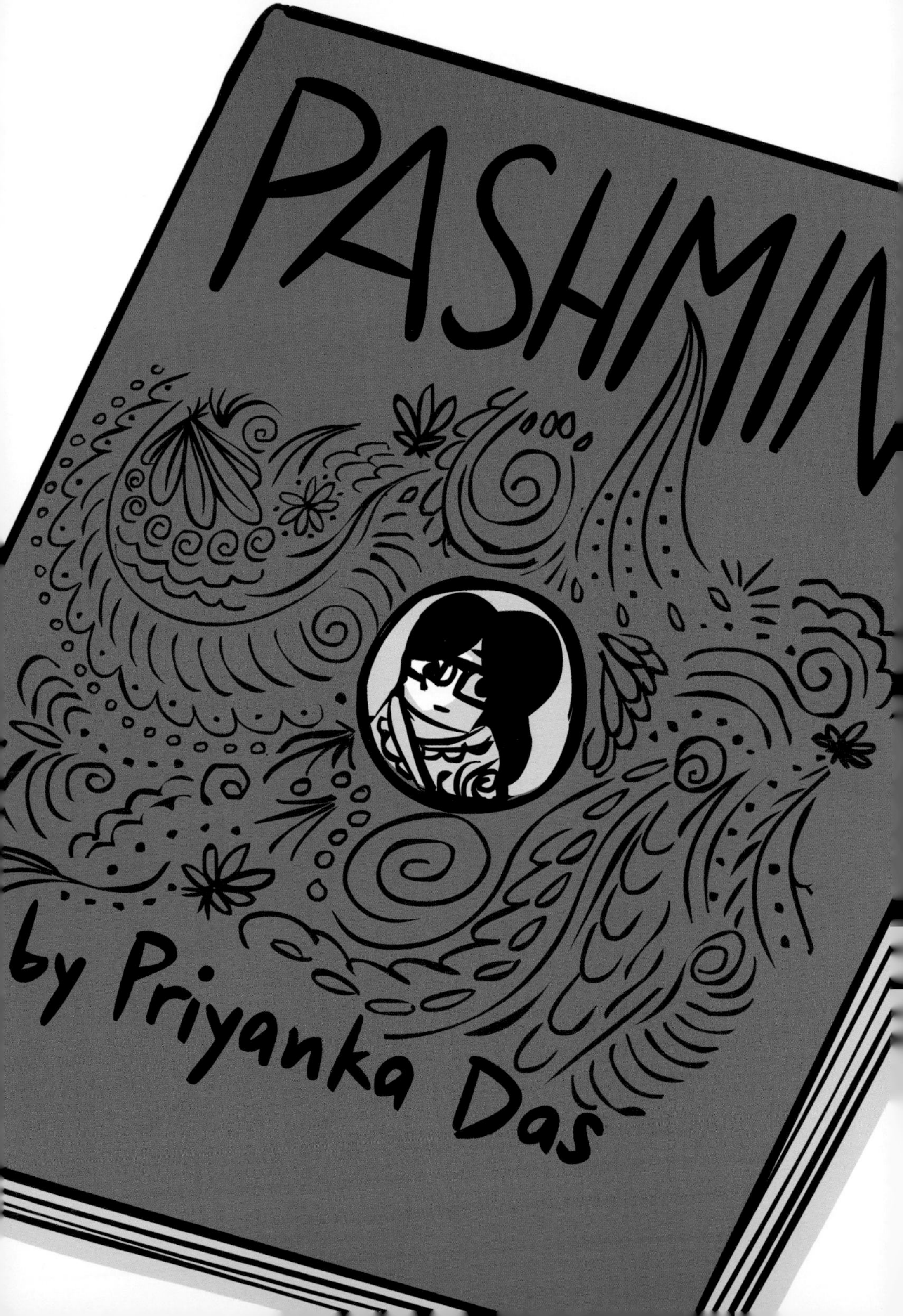
PASHMIN
by Priyanka Das

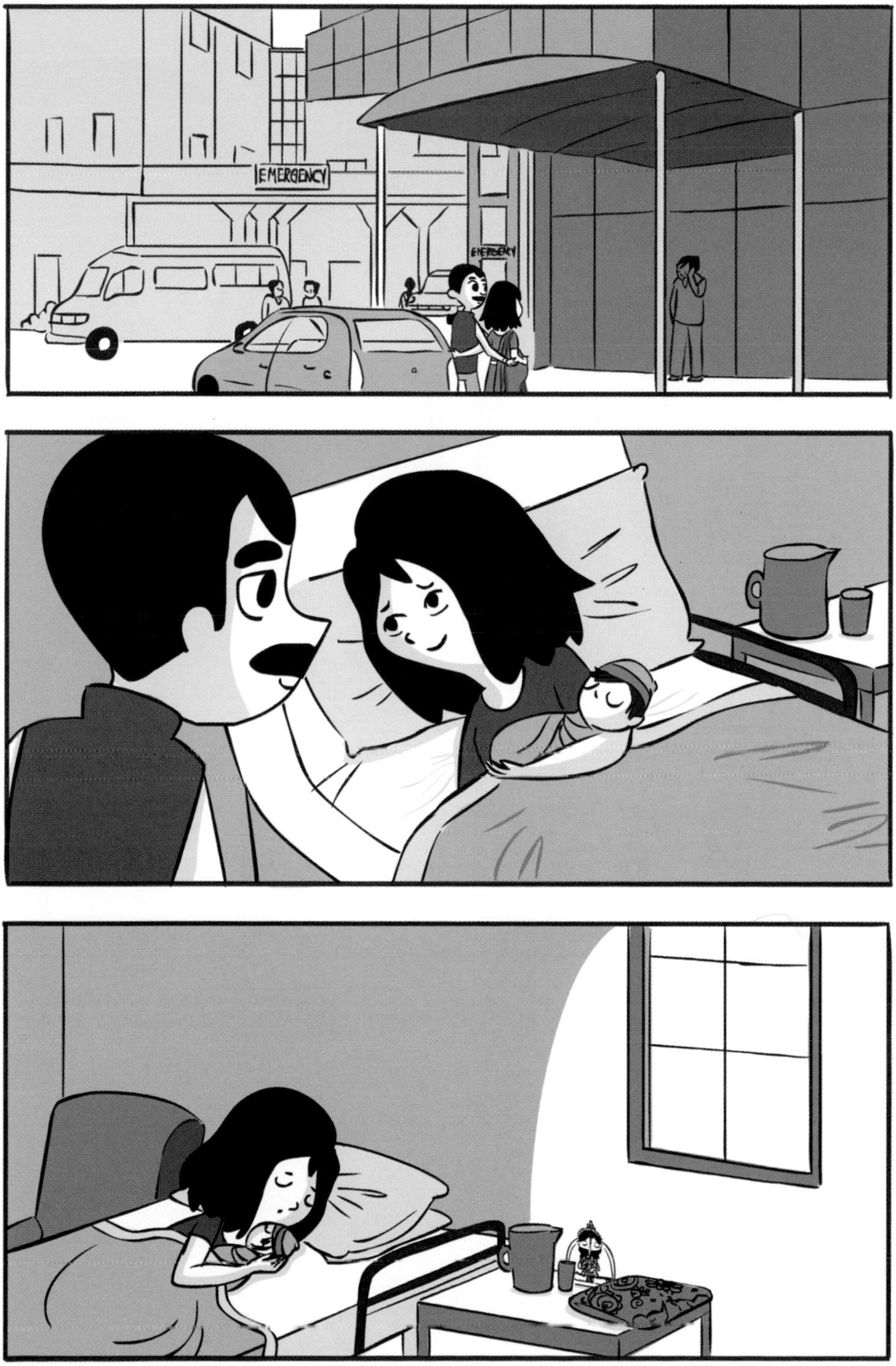
EMERGENCY
EMERGENCY

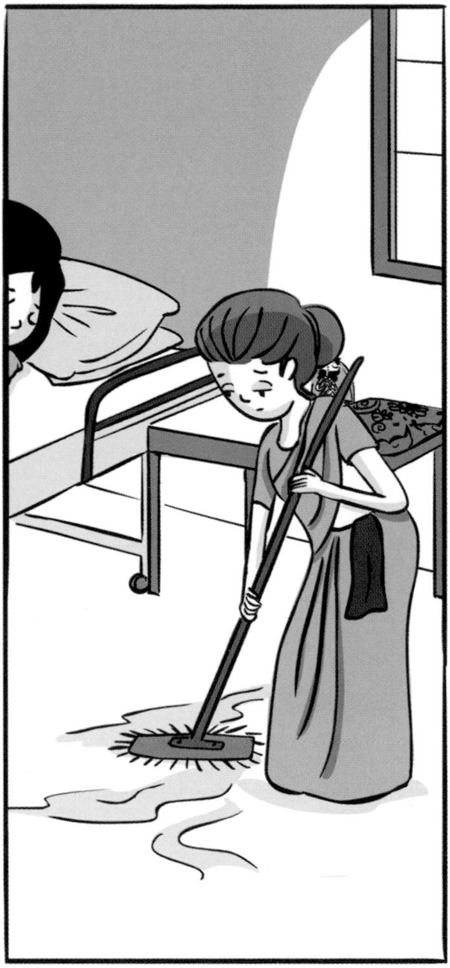
wipe
wipe
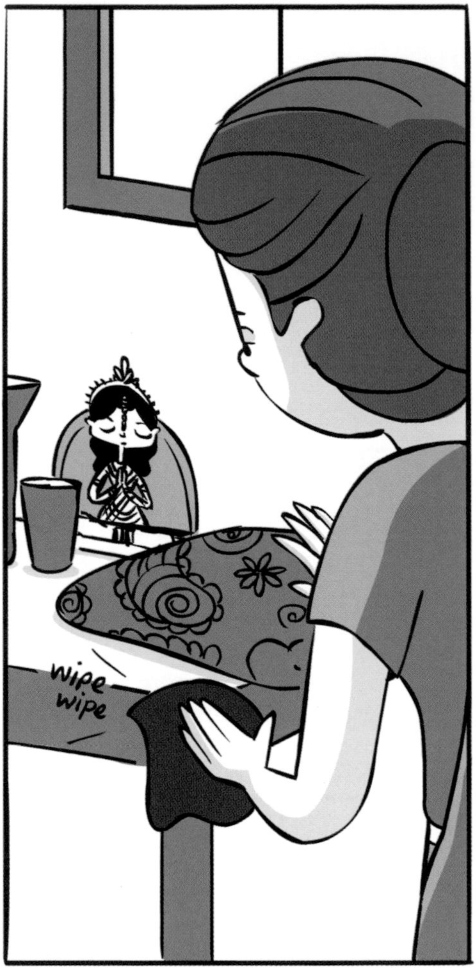
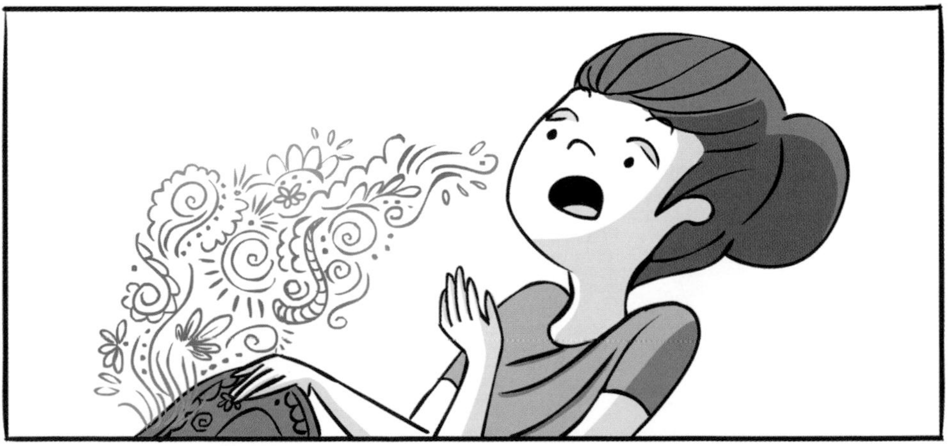

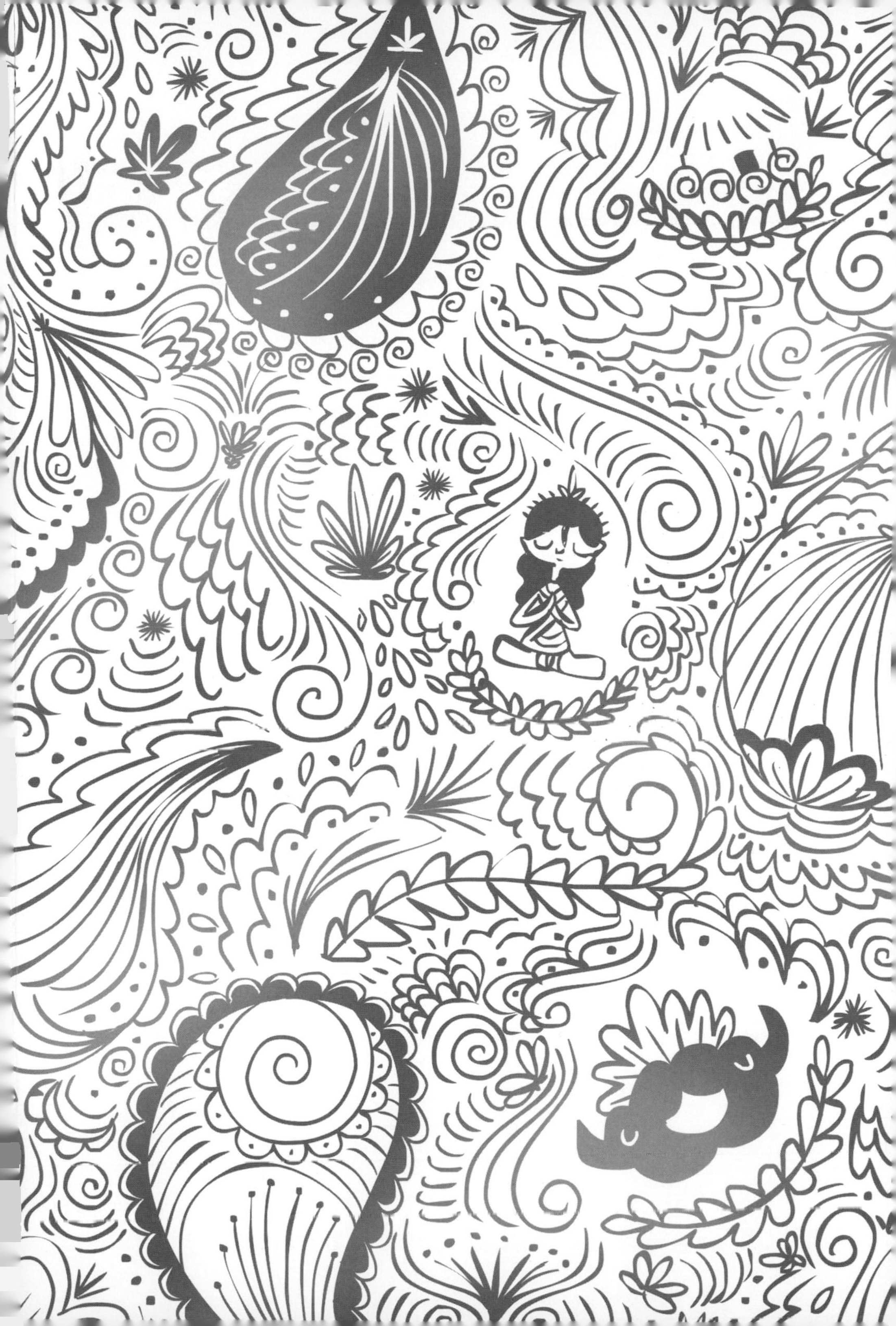

Glossary

Note: Indian children are taught to address elders as Auntie or Uncle as a form of respect. From taxi drivers to parents' friends, we refer to all Indian elders as Uncle or Auntie.

Beta: Son or daughter, often adults will address children who aren't blood related with this term as a sign of endearment

Bhabi: Sister-in-law, also symbolic term used to address friend's wife

Didi: Sister, often shortened to "di"

Diwali: The festival of lights, celebrated by lighting candles and fireworks to chase away the dark and invite light into your home for the new year—arguably one of the best holidays ever

Dosa: A large, savory Indian crepe best enjoyed with heaps of coconut chutney

Garam: Warm

Holi: Festival celebrating the arrival of spring, celebrators will play and throw colored powder and colored water on each other, accompanied by singing and dancing

Ja: Go

Ji: A gender-neutral honorific suffix, similar to the Japanese "-san"

Kya: What

Laddu/Sandesh/Jelabi/Halwa/Petha: Various Indian sweets

Mausa: Uncle, formally your mother's brother-in-law

Mausi: Auntie, formally your mother's sister

Memsahib: Madam

Mithai: Sweets

NRI: Non-resident Indian

Sabji: Vegetable

Sahib: Mister, some women address their husbands as Sahib as a sign of respect

Salwar: Indian women's dress

Samosa: A delicious triangular pastry filled with potatoes and spices

Acknowledgments

To Mark Siegel, for taking a chance on a new voice and guiding me through each phase with kindness and support. To say I couldn't have done it without you is undeniably true.

To my agent, Judy Hansen, for being my career guide and fierce advocate. Thank you for always believing that I'm worth more than the first offer.

To my mom, who taught me how to read and then allowed me to do so everywhere, including the dinner table. We both know *Pashmina* is truly about making peace with our white hair.

To my hubbahubba, Nick, it's due to your steadfast support that I became an artist and made this book. You are the reason my dreams have come true.

To my friend editors Lyla Warren and Rhode Montijo, your feedback and loving eye helped me in the crucial development phase. Your friendship and willingness to discuss story ad nauseam are wonderful gifts.

To Bernie, my sweet mother-in-law, your unreserved faith in me helps when I'm doubtful. Your help with Leela was paramount to completing this book.

To Nickole Caimol, who assisted with tone pages and prepared all the files for printing. You are my sounding board, wise beyond your years, and I am eager to see what you create next.

To my friends: Many of you appear in the backgrounds of this book. Some of your names are hidden in marquees and lists. Others, I trolled your Facebook photos and drew you, so thank you for unknowingly being my models.

Pashmina was not made alone, I relied heavily on my team of friends. To Roberto Chicas, Sunila Rao, Faheema Chaudhury, Angela Grammatas, Lefteris Grammatas, Teresa Huang, Sean Leo, Rebecca Saylor, Maneesh Yadav, Sheetal Jain, Anushka Ratnayake, Praveena Gummadam, Raina Telgemeier, Travis Kotzebue, Evan Hamilton, Christina Yunker, Anita Coulter, Tyler Null, and Catherine Kung, thank you for your unwavering support and granting me the right to bend your ear about this book. And to those unnamed supporters, I thank you, too—especially for forgiving my post-book forgetfulness.

For every person that's shared my work, sent me a note, purchased a card or print over the years, thank you many times over. Your support allows me to keep making art.

First Second

Copyright © 2017 by Nidhi Chanani
Published by First Second
First Second is an imprint of Roaring Brook Press,
a division of Holtzbrinck Publishing Holdings Limited Partnership
120 Broadway, New York, NY 10271
All rights reserved

Library of Congress Control Number: 2016961589

Paperback ISBN: 978-1-62672-087-9
Hardcover ISBN: 978-1-62672-088-6

Our books may be purchased in bulk for promotional, educational, or business use.
Please contact your local bookseller or the Macmillan Corporate and Premium Sales Department
at (800) 221-7945 ext. 5442 or by e-mail at MacmillanSpecialMarkets@macmillan.com.

FIRST
EDITION

First edition 2017
Book design by Andrew Arnold
Printed in China by RR Donnelley Asia Printing Solutions Ltd.,
Dongguan City, Guangdong Province

Inked digitally in Flash, colored with Flash and
Photoshop on a Wacom Cintiq.

Paperback: 7 9 10 8
Hardcover: 5 7 9 10 8 6 4